Julia Fitzgerald was born in North Wales and attended school in Yorkshire. She has two children and her interests include history, health and medicine (especially new discoveries), cats (she has three), mythology and Astrology.

'Oh Vincent, Vincent,' she wept. 'Why did it have to be like this? Why were we parted so cruelly?' To be so helpless, so vulnerable and alone. And in a land where everything was different from her childhood, religion, morals, customs, beliefs. It was as if she had stepped through a secret door, where everything she had once known was reversed. But there was no going back. She could not find that door again, to step back into the land she had once known so well. Vincent was there, she could see him in her mind: tall, strong, his emerald eyes glinting like jewels, his mouth curved in a smile, his charisma no less pale because she held only a mind-image of him. Catching the image she held it, was almost in his embrace when the picture clouded and vanished. He was gone. Grief and pain overwhelmed her. Without him she was soft, vulnerable flesh. She had no power, no strength, no motivation. To die would be a blessed relief. Dropping into the pit of tears, she did not trouble to swim . . .

Other Troubadour Spectaculars:

Julia Fitzgerald

Royal Slave

A Troubadour Spectacular

Futura Publications Limited
A Troubadour Book

A Troubadour Book

First published in Great Britain by
Futura Publications Limited in 1978

ISBN 0 7088 1405 0

Printed in Canada

Futura Publications Limited
110 Warner Road
Camberwell, London SE5

FOR SUE WASHINGTON

CHAPTER ONE

1776

The tension between the three people in the silent room was almost audible. To the terrified girl standing defiantly before her father it seemed as if her heart were beating in unison with the inexorable voice of the clock on the mantelpiece, ticking away the last minutes of her freedom.

John Morbilly's face was crimson, and his black brows quivered so violently that they seemed about to leap from his forehead. 'Four weeks,' he said with controlled fury, 'I have been away from home for only four weeks, but return to find my daughter throwing herself like a cheap trollop at the first available man.'

The neat, grey-gowned woman standing quietly beside the tense girl coloured faintly at his words. 'It was only by chance that I discovered they were meeting, sir,' she interposed, 'but I knew you would wish me to make enquiries. In my opinion there can be no doubt of the man's intentions. He has courted heiresses before.'

'That is a lie! He loves me. Charles loves me. Meet him! Look at him! Judge him for yourself. He cares nothing for my money.' Cassia Morbilly came to life with all the spirit and temper she had inherited from her father. Her face, which had been pale with panic and despair, was now nearly as crimson as his, her fists were clenched, and her eyes flashed as she turned to her governess. 'You didn't have the courage to say it to my face, did you? Oh no! You sneaked after me, watching, waiting to crawl to my father and tell him all your jealous eyes had seen. Yes, jealous! You've never loved, you'll never be loved. Why, I believe you wouldn't know a real man if you saw one!'

Camilla Blanchard's face was a study in cold malice as she said, 'My dear Cassia, you are a spiteful and ill-mannered little girl.'

7

'And you will go to your room this moment,' roared John Morbilly. 'Until you can control your tongue and mend your ways, you will stay there.'

'I will not!' stormed Cassia. 'Neither you nor any person living can keep me prisoner or stop me seeing the man I love. The man I intend to marry, despite my money, despite your lies.' She flung out this ultimatum with a courage she did not feel. Her stern father with his explosive rages and the contemptuous Miss Blanchard were a formidable couple. She knew that they both could and would prevent her meeting her lover, Charles Billings, again, but pride forbade her to admit it. And so she flung out her challenge, hands still clenched, blue eyes sparkling with anger.

'Go to your room, miss. At once, I say!' bellowed John Morbilly, advancing on her with such menace that she nearly turned and fled. It took all her self-control to spin quietly on her heel and walk out through the door as though she had not a care in the world.

In the drawing-room, governess and master looked at one another.

'Miss Blanchard, I apologize for my daughter's rudeness. Believe me when I say that she will bitterly rue this day.'

'Sir,' Miss Blanchard permitted herself a small, deprecating smile, 'sir, I fear that I must accept some blame for this situation.' She looked at him carefully. 'You see, I suspected nothing until that day when I found them in the park together. To tell you the truth, I was completely hoodwinked by her apparent desire to study nature. Foolish and careless of me – but I would never have imagined her capable of such duplicity. She was always adequately chaperoned when she left the house, and the work she produced after such expeditions – analyses and sketches of trees, leaves and so on – was first rate.'

But John Morbilly was scarcely listening. As he strode impatiently up and down the room, slamming his right hand into his left palm and wishing that it were Charles Billings's head, he was thinking back to his own youth, and the girl he had married when she was sixteen. Maureena O'Claire. She had been of Irish peasant stock, no name, no family, and certainly no dowry. He had seen her acting on the Dublin stage, and fallen wildly, irrevocably in love with her. Even now he could not forget her gilded-red hair, porcelain skin, and hydrangea-blue eyes, for Cassia was her mother's replica. Maureena O'Claire had allowed the shy, but eager John Morbilly to woo her. She had taken his generous gifts and let him propose to her. She had even allowed the deception to go as far as the actual ceremony and the wedding night, but she had never loved him. She had wanted his money and his name. Pregnant almost immediately, she had grown more and more restless as her condition advanced. She had started to drink, and not all John's remonstrations would stop her. She threw tantrums and smashed precious ornaments that her husband treasured. The servants despised her for her tempers and one after the other resigned their posts. It was only because she was having his child that John Morbilly tolerated her outrages. When Cassia was born, her mother refused to feed her. She cared more for regaining her health and her figure than she did for the infant. John had had to hire a wet nurse, and his discontent with his wife gained a new dimension. Any woman who was robust and yet would not feed her own baby he considered unworthy to be a mother. His ill-starred passion for Maureena died at last, leaving in its place only an impatient revulsion. She saw it, and with belated regret, accused him of unfeeling behaviour towards her.

'If I appear cool, it is your fault,' he had said, his mouth compressed. 'Look to your own behaviour before you accuse me.'

'How can I be warm when you are so cold?'

'It is your coldness that creates mine,' he had said, his eyes hard and black.

'So it is a stalemate.' Maureena had tossed back her glossy red-gilt hair. 'You do not love me.'

Icily, cruelly, and with infinite relish, John Morbilly had

9

replied: 'I do not think that I ever did. If I said that I had felt infatuation, it would be flattering you.'

Maureena had drawn back as if stung, her red lips pressed tightly together to contain her tears. She had stood up, back straight, head high. When she walked out of John Morbilly's life, as she did that day, without thought of the baby daughter she had left, he knew a great relief, a feeling of release, almost of joy. No more scenes, no more tantrums and hysteria. Cassia had her wet nurse, a good, solid woman who had lost her own baby and who was touchingly grateful for her place in the household. When the child was old enough, he would hire a governess. He had money. He was a successful dealer in Chinoiserie. Cassia would lack nothing; he would ensure that she never felt the need of a mother.

'Mr Morbilly, sir!' Miss Blanchard's voice cut into his memories. Patiently he turned to listen to her, but he found it difficult to wrench his thoughts from the past and the beautiful, voluptuous Maureena whose daughter and double was now disturbing the serenity of his life.

'Sir, I would like to suggest that Miss Cassia be sent away from London. While she is here, we run the constant danger of her escaping our vigilance and slipping out to meet this man . . .'

'Yes. Yes you are right.' John Morbilly looked at her thoughtfully. 'My sister – I do not see why she should not visit my sister. She is not a woman to be deceived easily; she has married off two of her own daughters very respectably. Yes, a long stay with my sister would do Cassia more good than we can . . . That is the answer . . .' He smiled, but it was a mirthless grimace, for he was thinking of his daughter safely tucked away in Morbilly, the town where his family had lived for centuries. A stay at Penwellyn, his sister's home, would be just what a wilful, capricious creature like Cassia needed. He rocked back and forth on his toes, and relief flooded through him as he envisaged the peace of his home without Maureena's daughter to remind him continually of the red-headed beauty he had loved and lost. His sister would discipline her, just as she had always disciplined him when they were children.

'A marvellous idea, sir.' Miss Blanchard nodded. 'I have distant cousins in Truro. It would be an excellent time to visit them –'

John Morbilly flung up his bushy, dark head. 'You will not be accompanying my daughter, Miss Blanchard. You have admitted that you neglected her. There can be no question of my continuing to employ you.'

Miss Blanchard's eyes flashed momentary hatred before she bowed her head, tight-lipped with pride and dismay. Had she looked up, she would have seen her employer's mouth curling with distaste. He was thinking what despicable creatures women were. How they tantalised and deceived and betrayed men, then thought that they could trample all over them. Well, no woman would ever do so again to him. He was no fool, nor ever had been.

Miss Blanchard's head remained bowed. Dreading that she might start to plead, he hurriedly left the drawing-room, striding out soundlessly across the Turkish carpet. Closing the door gently behind him, he retreated to the safe confines of his beloved library, where he locked the door. Safe. Alone. In peace. Sinking down in the luxuriant velvet armchair by the hearth, he picked up the tome on Oriental Porcelain which he was reading, and turned to the page where his bookmark lay.

Cassia had gone straight to her room where she proceeded, in a venomous rage, to destroy as many of her possessions as she could lay her hands on. She took the nature manuscript, on which she had been working for some months now, and when she found that it was too strong to be torn, she hacked at it with her scissors. Then she smashed a pair of porcelain cherubs which stood on either side of her walnut pier-table, and ground her heel into the glass which covered an old painting depicting the meeting of Henry VIII and Francis I at the Field of the Cloth of Gold. She knew full well that these were priceless *objets d'art*, but, at this moment, anticipating the fact that she might never see the man she loved again, she wished passionately to demolish everything that reminded her of John Morbilly. At the age of sixteen, in Charles's arms, she had sought what she had never received from her father: approbation, acceptance of herself as a woman, love . . . Now, when she had for the first time in her life discovered that these existed, they were to be snatched from her.

Taking up a Meissen figurine, she flung it across her bedroom so that it smashed into a dozen slivers against the wall. Then, panting, she looked round for something else on which to vent her fury. Seeing a Venetian glass bouquet of roses, gilly-flowers and lilac, she dashed this into the hearth, jumping back hastily when fragments of glass exploded. One of the fragments cut her hand, and she sucked at the wound. It was the pain that at last released all her pent-up grief and she fell on to her bed with its sumptuous sapphire brocade hangings, tears drowning her face and trickling down her neck to make a pool between her breasts.

All this, this panoply, these riches, were what obsessed her father. If she had been a Meissen figurine, delicate, ethereal, but lacking in emotion, he would have cherished her as he did the beautiful ornaments which crammed their home, and in a way in which he could not love a flesh and blood creature with needs and longings. But now that she had Charles, she knew what love was, what it meant, and she swore that she would never give him up.

At last the storm of weeping subsided and she sat up, brushing away her tears. Her lids were swollen and stiff, her nose hot. She knew that she must look terrible, her face bleached from weeping. She knew also that tears repelled her father more than anything else. When tears threatened, he would leave a room, coldly, without a backward glance. As a child, if she had fallen, he would never so much as ask how she was. He would disappear into his study, and not appear until the accident was repaired, the weeping finished. One of her governesses had called him an unnatural father, and then she had left. Others had not been so bold, but few had stayed overlong under the chill of his disapproving expression. Miss Blanchard had lasted an incredible two years, for, to that cold woman, insensitivity was strength.

Cassia felt drained of feeling now, and lay back against the pillows. She would find a way of getting round her father. And she must of course get word to Charles that their secret was discovered. He would be waiting for her in the park at this very moment, thinking that she had let him down. Oh, Charles, Charles, she thought, yearning for him, remembering the strength and warmth of his arms around her, the loving in his eyes, the touch of his lips. Charles was all the kindness she had ever dreamed of; he had made sense out of the chaos of her life. She cared not that he had no money, that his family was of ordinary stock. What had money ever done to make her happy? Cassia thought defiantly that she would give up all her inheritance in return for happiness with Charles.

Tossing back her long auburn hair, she surveyed the room. Such ostentation, such display. Even her bed was authentic Tudor, a full-tester, lavish with hangings and beautifully-carved headboard. Yes, she knew that it was beautiful, but she had wept too many times with that headboard looking down at her coldly. It had never been a comfort. The Turkey carpet was ankle-high, the walls were covered in blue and ivory silk, a pattern of cabbage roses intertwined with Chinese dragons, Chinoiserie being very much in vogue now. She knew of girls who would envy her her room, but if they had a father who did not love them, would they change places so willingly? Sometimes, she woke at night from a dream in which she was lying on a sandy shore, ice cold, shuddering, and she was calling, over and over, 'Papa! Papa! Please help me!' But although she knew that he was nearby, he would not answer, or come to her.

Many times when she was miserable, she had longed for her mother. She knew little about Maureena but she could imagine how different her life would have been with a mother to comfort her, to hold her in her arms and wipe away her tears. Instead, her father had even forbidden the mention of Maureena's name. Whenever little Cassia had questioned him as to her whereabouts, he had grown scarlet and his thick brows had begun to twitch. Then she knew that his anger would erupt within a few seconds and it would be better if she were far away. There had been a cook who had been more often drunk than sober. She, in one indiscreet moment, had told Cassia a few harsh truths about her Irish actress mother who had hated domesticity, and who had walked out when Cassia was a baby. Soon after that, the woman had been sacked for her drunkenness.

Years ago, Cassia had met her Aunt Julitta. She barely remembered that occasion, but she did recall how her father had seemed to shrink in his sister's presence. To his daughter's astonishment, he had become submissive, one could almost have said obsequious.

So she was trapped, like the butterflies caught for eternity in the fossil paperweights on her father's desk. Caught in a snare that was none of her doing, and ignorant as to how she could escape, she was the perfect prey for the first fortune-hunter who chanced to come along. . . .

'Oh Charles, what am I going to do? How shall I see you again?' She could ask little Bessie, her maid, to take him a message. Bessie had frequently done so before, thinking it a lark, and being happy to see her mistress enlivened.

'Yes, why not?' Cassia got up, smoothed back her untidy hair, and fetched quill and parchment out of her writing case.

'*Dearest,*' she wrote, telling her lover of the discovery of their secret and that she would not be able to see him until she had won round her father. '*Please, Charles, have patience. I know that I can talk him round. But it will take time. I will let you know what happens, via Bessie. Oh, beloved one, how I miss you and long for your kisses. Dear heart, think of that time when we shall be together again. Do not forget me.*'

When Bessie brought up her supper that evening, she slipped her the note, now securely sealed. Bessie grinned and winked, but they did not exchange a word, for it was safer that way. If her father found out that Bessie was a willing collaborator, he would dismiss her immediately. Miss Blanchard would be sent up with her meals. How that woman made her flesh crawl!

Afterwards, Cassia prepared herself for the meeting with her father. She bathed her face and put on a clean gown of white fringed silk patterned with rosettes and supported by panniers at the hips. She brushed her hair until it gleamed and bound it with a pink ribbon bow. Round her neck was the *rivière* of priceless, perfectly-matched pearls that had been her sixteenth birthday gift from her father. She was ready, waiting with her plan of campaign, when she heard the front door slam and her father's imperious footfalls ringing down the steps and out on to the pavement.

He had gone out. At this time of night he would be going to his club, Almack's, to gamble, and that meant that he would not be back until very late. She sank on to the bed and wept again, her shoulders drooping.

When morning came, she was wan, and rings encircled her eyes. She knew that she must not approach her father too early. She must wait until he had read his paper and drunk two cups of coffee. Only then was it safe to speak to him. Dressing once more in the silk gown and the pearls, she went down to the sunny breakfast room.

When she saw her father's face her courage ebbed. He could have been a stranger, a cold and angry alien in the street. John Morbilly looked up from his paper, his expression stony.

'I do not think that I gave you permission to leave your room.' He folded the paper neatly, precisely, as he always did, laying it exactly two inches to the left of his plate. Then he stood up, and they faced one another, father and daughter. The air in the breakfast room seemed to fall a few degrees. Clouds obscured the sun. Cassia shivered and then squared her shoulders defiantly.

'I wished to speak to you, Papa,' she said, only the tightening of her voice betraying her fear. Her hand rose unconsciously to touch the pearls at her neck. Her father's eyes followed the movement, and, for a second, his eyes glowed as they fell on the pearls, then they became black and icy once more as they rose to her face.

'We have nothing to discuss. You have betrayed me, and you will never receive the benevolence of my trust again. If you think that you can stay here, under my roof, after what you have done . . .'

'Stay here?' she interrupted sharply. 'What do you mean? This is my home . . .' She had gone very white. Her eyes were dazzlingly blue. John Morbilly had only worshipped beauty in a woman once before in his life, and he had no intention of ever doing so again.

'You have not been told?' His wide nostrils flared, his teeth gritted together. 'Where is that damned creature . . . ?' Reaching for the tasselled bellrope by the hearth, he jerked it roughly. When Maude scuttled into the room, and bobbed her curtsey, eyes wide, he barked: 'Where is Miss Blanchard? Tell her to come to me immediately.'

'Yes, sir!' Maude bobbed again, and scuttled out, to return moments later with the report that Miss Blanchard's room was empty, her clothes and all her personal belongings gone. 'Sir, Cook said that she 'eard Miss Blanchard bangin' and scratchin' about her room last night, and that she – Miss Blanchard, that is – went outta the back door wi' 'er valise. Late it was, Cook said.' Maude sucked in her lower lip, terrified at the thought that the master's anger might fall on her for bringing him this news. Stuttering, she added: 'C-Cook, she s-said she thought you *knew*, sir!'

John Morbilly had gone very pale. His hands twitched at his sides, his big thumbs catching Maude's attention. She thought of them pressing against her windpipe and she swallowed, feeling faint. When the master dismissed her, she almost fell out of the room, leaning against the wall outside and taking in deep, gusty breaths of air. That poor child, to have a pa like that, God 'elp 'er!

The discovery of Miss Blanchard's perfidy put John Morbilly beyond the reach of all blandishments. Cassia could have stormed and wept, smiled and dimpled, nothing she could have said or done would have altered his decision. Peremptorily, he told her that she was going to stay with her Aunt Julitta at Penwellyn, and that she could anticipate a long absence from London.

'I have no wish to see you again for some time,' he said, his voice devoid of emotion. 'You have brought me unbearable grief and pain by your treachery. I cannot countenance such deceit under my roof. You will live with your aunt, and you will do as she says. She represents me; she has my absolute authority to do as she wishes with you. I have nothing further to add.' He turned his back on Cassia, who opened her mouth to riposte, then closed it again.

Instead, she said, 'When shall I leave?'

'I have already written to your aunt. She has long wished to have you stay with her. Now that her daughters have left home, she is quite alone. Provided that you do as she says, you will be allowed some freedom, but you will not be allowed out unchaperoned at *any* time.' He smiled, that cold rictus which made her stomach churn. 'Bessie will travel with you.'

She managed to keep the sudden light out of her eyes. Bessie to go with her! Then her father knew nothing of the note-carrying . . . She wanted to sing, to laugh, to dance.

Dismissed, she went up to her room to pack. Tucked in the base of the silver statuette of Spring which stood on her bedside cabinet was Charles's reply to her note. He told her that he would not fail her, that she was his, and that nothing was going to keep him from her.

'*Dearest heart,*' he wrote, '*I love you too – never doubt that. I long to hold you and to kiss your beautiful eyes.*'

Rereading that line, she knew a surge of joy. Charles would not let her down. Hastily scribbling another message for him, she told him of her banishment to Penwellyn, Morbilly, Cornwall. She might not, after all, be able to see him in London now, but could he not come to Morbilly and visit her there in secret until her father's anger cooled?

His reply was all that she had hoped. How could she have doubted that he would come to Morbilly? Of course he would see her there. He said he missed her. He said he loved her, as he had never loved before.

Folding the letter into as tiny a square as possible, she tucked it along with the others into the hollow base of the statuette. Charles, her own dear love, would be with her soon. He would have a plan for them; she need fear for nothing.

Subdued and pale, the picture of the penitent, subservient daughter, Cassia said goodbye to John Morbilly, who barely looked up from the tome on Oriental Porcelain which was opened on his knee. His teeth were gritted, his jaw clenched. He made it plain that he could not wait for her to leave, and his back was turned to her before she left his study. Outside, the carriage waited, and soon Cassia and Bessie were sitting inside, rugs over their knees, mouths compressed so that they would not giggle and give the game away to Patch, the driver, who would surely report to the master.

The two girls were anticipating a journey of five days, or possibly more if all did not go smoothly. Julitta Morbilly had written a long, detailed letter regarding the Cornish roads, or rather the lack of them, the inclement weather, and the shortage of turnpikes: '*Fortunately it is now early summer, and so the weather, one hopes, will be drier. However, when it rains, as it is wont to do much of the time, the cart tracks become swamps, and holes are thus concealed by mud so that one's horse can stumble and break a leg.*' She then informed them that there was a fairly new turnpike from Grampound to Falmouth, passing through Truro, and that it would be wiser to use this, even if it took them a few miles out of their way. They must diverge at Penryn, however, and head straight down the coast to Morbilly, which lay between Marazion and Helston.

Patch, and Jem, the postillion, would be accompanying them, but there was also a hired outrider armed with a blunderbuss and two pistols to guard them. These three men had been warned not to leave Miss Cassia Morbilly alone for one moment, except when she was in her rooms at the inns where they must pause on the journey. If Cassia had not been able to slip that message to Charles and receive his reply, she would have been chastened indeed by now. For it had become obvious to her that she would be little more than a prisoner on the journey, that she would be closely guarded all the way to the door of Penwellyn, and that, from then on, her aunt would be her gaoler.

The swaying, jolting movement of the carriage became unbearable after the first day. To climb back into it after their first night's rest took an act of courage. Cassia had travelled before, but rarely on journeys lasting longer than a few hours, and always with a halt of some length before turning back. Now, they were victims of the appalling conditions of the main thoroughfares of England, which, in every case, were nothing more than rutted quagmires. They passed an upturned coach, heard the explosion of a pistol, and looked out to see, to their dismay, that a fine chestnut mare had been shot because both her forelegs were broken after a fall into a ditch. The young woman who had been riding in the coach was standing with her hands over her face, screaming repeatedly. The sound of her screams followed them down the road.

Further on they came upon a farm waggon that had lost a wheel, and found that the track was awash with vegetables and smashed eggs. They reached the Wiltshire border, crossed into Dorset, and, by the time they alighted, they found it difficult to maintain a steady walk.

'People will think I have been drinking!' Cassia gasped, putting out a hand to right herself as she and Bessie walked across the courtyard of the inn, closely followed by Patch, Jem, and the hired outrider, who had barely done more than grunt the odd word since they set out from Orchard Square.

'Me, too, miss! Coo, I'll not arf be glad when we gets ter Morbilly.' Bessie grinned, staggering, and looked up gratefully at Jem when he offered her his arm.

The innkeeper was a huge man, well over six feet, and

his face was big, too, and broad, so that his eyes looked oddly small and shifty. Cassia did not like the look of him. He was impatient to be paid, and unwilling to exert himself by way of exchange. Also, as she soon found out, he had an unpleasant habit of spitting on the floor. True, he did avert his face, but even so Cassia found this an unnerving habit. The food was passable; coney pie swimming in succulent juices, and fruit tarts with thick yellow cream to follow. The men, who sat apart from Miss Cassia and her maid, watched them all the while they dined, as poachers watch the hare that will be their supper. For John Morbilly had offered a generous extra payment to each of them if the young lady was delivered safely.

When the innkeeper himself brought a platter of cheeses to their table, Cassia pursed her lips. She could not stop thinking of his nasty habit. His nails were black, too, and his hands grimed. Declining the cheeses, she sipped at her mulled wine and looked about her, pretending that she was unaware of the attentive scrutiny of Patch, Jem and the hired man.

It would have been a pleasant enough parlour if it had been clean. But the whole inn wore an air of neglect, and although the sheets were fresh (for she had investigated these) their bedrooms were stuffy and one could not help but think of the previous occupants . . . But she told herself she must think of all this as a stepping-stone, nothing more. What was a little discomfort when it would lead to her sweetheart's arms? She could bear far worse than this when she knew that there was such a marvellous reward at the end of it.

She pondered for a moment on what would have happened had she been forced to stay in London. Her father might have kept her confined to her room for weeks. He would have been well within his rights to do so. Erring children could be locked up, and beaten for their rebelliousness. It happened all the time. She might have been shut away for weeks, months, to subjugate her spirit, and although she did not envisage a day when her spirit could be broken, she knew that her life would have been exceedingly unpleasant. But now, because of her Aunt Julitta, in Morbilly, she would be able to see the man she loved again. The thought made her hands tremble, and pink sprang into her cheeks. Had they noticed? She glanced up slyly. No, the innkeeper was refilling their mugs and their attention was on their ale. She imagined what would happen if she suddenly jumped up and tried to run out of the parlour of the inn – the men's shocked faces, their mugs of ale spilling over as they crashed after her, the clumsy struggles, her cries for help . . . No, she would never get away with it.

When they went to bed shortly afterwards, Bessie settled herself in a truckle bed at the foot of her mistress's, and the three men shared one room next door. Each night, as Cassia and her maid retired, Patch had turned the key in their door and incarcerated them until morning. It was very humiliating – especially when she or Bessie had a call of nature and were forced to use the cracked washbasin which stood on a warped wooden stand in the corner or one of the other and varied containers left for this purpose. At one inn it was a bucket. At another, a jug stood beneath the bed.

'Well, miss, I reckons we've seen everythin' now.' Bessie giggled, waving aloft the jug.

Cassia clapped her hands together. 'Imagine what Miss Blanchard would have made of that, Bessie!' she laughed.

'She'd 'ave fainted right away, she would! Jugged 'are, anyone?' Bessie marched round the room, waving the jug, then put a finger to her mouth. 'Ooh, mustn't let them men 'ear us 'aving a good time! Tain't allowed. Smilin' and laughin' is frowned on, ain't it, miss?'

Cassia nodded, making a rude gesture towards the dividing wall between them and the men. In normal circumstances, the three servants would have had to sleep in the stables like the other coachmen, on lumpy straw pallets, but because her father had ordered them to watch her at all times, they were treated to rooms and comfortable beds. It was infuriating. Only her longing to see Charles again kept her from screaming out loud at the mortification. Patch, with his sour face, and Jem who jumped if you looked at him, and as for that monosyllabic outrider: she would be delighted to see the back of the three of them.

Just wait until they reached Penwellyn! she told herself. Then she would show them that she did not mean to be treated in this contemptuous fashion for one moment longer than necessary.

Penwellyn was charming. Pretty white stucco, and surrounded by bluebell woods ... If Cassia had not been brought here in such circumstances, she would have been entranced. The house was built in the Palladian style, but on a scale which did not alarm the eye with too colossal and imposing a frontage. She had truly not known what to expect, for she had not dared question her father about their destination, and he had never willingly spoken of Morbilly to her. The town where he had grown up, and where his family had lived for centuries, numbering Elizabethan adventurers and seamen amongst their ranks, was nothing more than a name to his daughter. He had left Morbilly early in life eager for London and its promise of riches and, from that time on, with an unwavering resoluteness, he had thought of nothing but making money.

She thought of him as she gazed at the bone-white façade of Penwellyn, and, then, after that, she did not think of him again. With the same resoluteness that he had applied to accruing his fortune, she put him from her mind. It was the best thing she had ever done.

Servants came out of the door of Penwellyn at sound of their carriage. They were busy in no time, leading the horses round to the stables, followed by Patch, Jem and the outrider. Cassia, wishing to assess the enemy forces, examined the servants intently, but they looked exactly like the menials one would find in London, except that their clothes were fashioned in the country style, shapeless and rough-textured. The men wore low-heeled, heavy buckled shoes and their hose were wrinkled and mud-splashed. Their shirts flapped at the neck and were rolled up to the elbows, their breeches baggy and shiny-seated, their hair hedge-wild. The small, plump woman who came puffing to greet them, her cheeks maroon with the effort of hurrying, was not, as Cassia first thought, her aunt, but Mrs Rowse, the housekeeper. Dipping a curtsey, the woman introduced herself and welcomed her to Penwellyn.

'Ye be much welcome, mistress. Do be makin' yoursel' et 'ome. Your aunt she be out ridin' on Helston Down, but she'll net be long.'

Cassia smiled, deciding that she liked the woman. When she introduced Bessie, Mrs Rowse nodded to her, saying that their rooms were ready and would Mistress Cassia be wishing her maid to sleep with her, on a truckle bed, or in the next room?

Cassia thought quickly. What if her aunt were like her brother and fond of locking doors on spirited young girls? If Bessie were locked in with her, she could not carry notes to Charles. On the other hand, Bessie's company would be more than welcome if she were to be locked in for hours at a time. But had she any intention of misbehaving and thus alienating her aunt? No, not if that could be avoided. Cool reflection had told her that sweetness and charm bred better rewards than hostility.

'Bessie will have the room next to mine, if there is such a room prepared, Mrs Rowse?' She smiled winningly, and saw the housekeeper succumb.

Within seconds, they were in the hall of Penwellyn, looking round at the glossy oak panelling, lovingly polished for decades until one could see the reflections of all who stood before it. There were massive portraits on the walls, illustrious and dare-devil ancestors in Tudor and Stuart garb, their eyes looking out to distant horizons, and each one exhibiting, with what seemed to be an insouciant pride, the Morbilly nose with its strong, straight bridge and flaring nostrils. There was a young girl with a sad face and pro-tuberant eyes. Perhaps it was because of the tight, starched cartwheel ruff she was wearing. It would have made mobility

23

impossible, thought Cassia as she leaned forward to look more closely at the picture.

'That's Julitta Elizabeth Morbilly,' Mrs Rowse offered. 'She's one of the most 'llustrious ancestors of your'n mistress, or so your aunt says. Attendant on King James's wife she wa' – favoured o' Queen Anne o' Denmark, died young, though, very sad. Came 'ere to Penwellyn to die, she ded.'

Cassia dipped her head by way of response. Lady-in-waiting to the dumpy Danish Queen, and at Daft Jamie's court: she must have been strong-stomached.

But Mrs Rowse was hovering at the foot of the carved oak staircase, eager to escort them to the upper rooms. There would be time for exploring the house later. Cassia followed the housekeeper upstairs while Bessie plodded behind them, her eyes wide in awe. Their baggage was left in the hall for one of the men to bring up.

Along a carpeted corridor, glass-windowed, with exquisite views of the gardens and the moors beyond, past some half dozen doors, and then Mrs Rowse was showing Bessie into her room and taking Cassia to hers beside it. Cassia stepped into the past as she crossed the threshold of her room. Furnished in the Stuart style, complete with full-tester bed splendidly carved and hung with rich yellowish-green and gold tapestries, the room was bathed in deep-gold light from the late sun. Her heart lifted. It was a friendly room – welcoming. It seemed to say: You are home now. Another portrait of Julitta Elizabeth hung over the cabinet in one corner, and when Cassia looked enquiringly at Mrs Rowse the woman nodded and said, 'Yes, this 'ere's 'er room, mistress. Just as she hed it when she was alive. Net one theng been changed.'

Cassia wanted to laugh for joy. To find out all about one's ancestry in this way, when one had never even guessed . . . and to be able to live in such a beautiful, welcoming house was like discovering that one belonged to a large family after being an only child for years. Her thoughts returned to Charles. She had almost forgotten him. And her aunt – she knew nothing as yet of *her*, except that she was supposed to be a disciplinarian and know how to handle young ladies.

The joy went out of her. She sank on to the bed, her eyes dimming, for there was a new feeling now inside her, and it did not presage happiness.

CHAPTER TWO

It was dusk before Julitta Morbilly returned. Cassia heard the horse's hoofs ringing on the cobbled terrace and looked out of her bedroom window. One of the grooms was taking the reins, and her aunt was dismounting with the graceful, flowing movement of a much younger woman.

Aunt Julitta stood on the cobbles for a few moments, looking round her, then she glanced up at Cassia's window. Her niece stepped hastily back into the room. She had no wish to be seen peering inquisitively through the curtains. The woman she had watched dismounting was tall and slender, but an aura of power emanated from her. She wore a neat riding habit of tan worsted, tan leather boots and a black velvet tricorne trimmed with braid. She now removed her hat, to hold it in her right hand as she surveyed her home. Her hair was not dressed with pomatum and powder, nor did she wear a wig. It was thick and black, as were her brows, and only a black ribbon bow prevented the lively tresses from springing free and wild about her shoulders. The same colouring as her father's, Cassia thought with dismay. She, with her auburn hair and blue eyes, looked nothing like a Morbilly. She could not help feeling that it would have made her way easier here if she had resembled her aunt's family.

Cassia heard the front door bang shut, and she rose hastily from the bed where she had slumped despondently. Pushing back her hair and refastening her blue velvet ribbon, she glanced in the mirror to ensure that her polonaise gown was neat. She had worn it to give herself confidence, for she loved its blue silken rosebuds and the striped taffeta underskirt which exactly matched the colour of her eyes. Despite this, her hands trembled slightly as she straightened one of the shoulder bows and then ran lightly down the staircase to greet her aunt.

Julitta Catherine Morbilly was certainly a tall woman, and her severely-cut riding habit made Cassia feel over-dressed, although she knew that in a London drawing-room she would have been simply robed.

Aunt and niece faced one another, blue eyes looking into eyes the colour of dying wallflowers, a dense, velvety brown. Long black lashes fringed the brown eyes, and a perfect skin, tanned by the sun for forty-four years, framed the Morbilly nose and a wide, uncurving mouth.

'Aunt Julitta, I am so pleased to see you again after all this time,' Cassia began, wondering if she ought to kiss her aunt, but as no move was made by the older woman, she did not dare approach her first. 'It is so kind of you to let me come here, I . . .'

Her aunt flung back her head, and, to her astonishment, let out a peal of laughter. 'I *let* you come here, child? I had little choice! You were foisted on me! "Send her to the Cornish harridan, she will sort her out," that is what your papa thought, I have no doubt. Did he not say as much to ye?' Aunt Julitta slapped her thigh with the riding crop, her shoulders twitching.

'I – oh no, nothing like that, Aunt Julitta!' Cassia opened her eyes wide in the innocent expression that usually served to reassure those to whom she was speaking.

'Well, child, what did he say, then?' barked her aunt, slapping her thigh again.

'He – he really said very little. Aunt, He – he he never does say very much. He told you why he sent me here?'

'Indeed he did! I have no time for fools, my child, and I vow that your papa always was, and still is, a fool. Even as a boy he was the same.'

Cassia must have looked surprised, for her aunt contin-ued, 'If there was a judgement to be made, or a path to be chosen, your papa would invariably select the wrong one. It was like a curse laid upon him – as if he felt compelled to err. But come into the solar, my dear, and we will talk there. It's more comfortable.'

Cassia followed her aunt into a spacious room that was

a suntrap during the day. Capacious and well-upholstered chairs with rigid, carved backs stood in each corner, and there was a luxuriant blue and white Turkey carpet on the floor. Glossy wooden benches ran along three of the walls, and a window seat crammed with voluminous tapestry cushions looked towards the sun.

A servant brought in tea and saffron cake and Cassia sipped the hot, fragrant liquid with pleasure. Her aunt was by no means a harridan, and this house was beautiful. The cake, too, was delicious, and Cassia said so.

Her aunt looked pleased. 'It's from a Cornish recipe, of course, made with yeast, half a teaspoon of saffron, and one pound of butter. Currants and a half a pound of peel go in it, too. But let us not be distracted from our discussion. We were discussing your unfortunate papa. Yes, unfortunate, for even at his birth, he caused a great tragedy. His arrival killed our mama, did ye ever hear of it?' Cassia shook her head. 'Well, our father never forgave him – for he was devoted to our mother, and he did not live for many years after that. Without Clarissa, he was like a ship without its rigging adrift in the Bay of Biscay . . .' Julitta sniffed, loudly. 'I raised your papa, with the nurse's help at first of course, and, I might add, with his hindrance. Have another slab of cake, m'dear, we dine late here.'

Cassia took the proferred cake, and thanked her aunt. 'I – I knew nothing of this, Aunt Julitta. You must think me stupid, but Papa never breathed a word about his childhood, and he is not a man to be questioned.'

'Ah, well I know, well I know! Always tantrums and rages as a boy, and, if he was shown up, or it was obvious that he had made a fool of himself yet again, he would grow scarlet – in the face and the back of his neck – and then he would attack whoever was careless enough to be within striking distance. Naturally, this meant that one could not leave precious ornaments on view, for he would shatter these, too. I had everything packed away, and the house at one time looked bleak as a prison.' She chuckled and sniffed again even louder, filled her mouth with more cake and

sipped tea through the mass. How she did it without choking, Cassia did not know.

'I have never seen him exert physical violence, Aunt
Julitta. He has a terrible temper, of course, as you say.' She
was thinking ashamedly of her own attack on her bedroom
ornaments. If such behaviour meant that she was taking
after her father, then she would never smash anything again.

'Men are children. Petulant and spoiled. Born like
that, and only a miracle drums it out of 'em. I did m'best,
but it wasn't enough.' Julitta shook her head from side
to side, then took another noisy sup of tea and put the
fragile porcelain cup down so heavily that Cassia feared
it would smash. 'They never grow up, nor have reason
to,' her aunt continued. 'Women treat 'em like babies
and pamper 'em. Men are swine, m'dear, but women are
fools for letting 'em be.' Julitta finished her fourth slab
of cake and leaned back, velvet eyes bright, knees crossed
in a most unladylike fashion. 'Ah, I see that you do not
agree, but you will one day. You are young now, and it
is right that you are hopeful and see things brightly. Wait
till y'are my age.'

Cassia wanted to ask if her uncle were still alive, or if it
was his treatment of her that made Julitta so caustic about
men, but she could not envisage any man getting the better
of her aunt. It was at this point that, to her niece's amazement, Julitta stood up and began to unhook her skirt.

'Ah, that's better!' she exclaimed, flinging the heavy skirt
over a chair. 'Only wear it to keep the locals quiet. Grousy
lot, scared of God. Cannot say why.' She stood before her
niece in riding jacket and comfortable breeches, slapping
her stomach. 'Much more sensible to wear these, d'you not
agree?'

'If you like them, yes, Aunt.' Cassia's first surprise over,
she thought: What a good idea. Skirts hampered one's freedom, the huge hoops and panniers necessitating a slow,
sideways movement through doorways and narrow pas-
sages – and they were so heavy. Beneath the layers of pet-
ticoats and underskirts, there was the cumbersome

arrangement of two convex cages, one on either side of the hips, which were secured by a tie round the waist. These, which were called panniers, were thankfully not as wide as they once had been, but were still a chore to wear. Their sole objective was to make the waist appear as minute as possible.

A servant entered discreetly and withdrew, carrying the tray. Aunt Julitta slapped her knee unexpectedly, making Cassia jump. 'Well, I should imagine that ye'll want to see round the house, child. We've time before we eat.'

Cassia followed her aunt out into the hall and up the stairs, wondering at her high-mettled mood. Where was the dour, ferocious woman her father had led her to believe would act as gaoler, keeping her under close surveillance at Penwellyn?

The upper rooms led off one wide, airy corridor at the rear of the house. The night wind was rising as they made their way from room to room, and the corridor was like a glass oblong suspended by the buffeting motion so that one could imagine it was lacking proper foundations beneath it. It was an eerie experience, and Cassia did not know whether or not she liked it. Each bedroom, from her aunt's, which was hung in moss-green, beige, and lemon, to the master bedroom, which glowed in apricots, golds and ivory, was spruce and spotless. She was shown the chamber where Robert Persimmon Morbilly, one of Drake's aides, had died; and, next to this, the bedroom where Julitta and John were born, and where Cassia's grandmother had died. What was Clarissa like? she wanted to know, but was afraid of opening old wounds. However, her aunt proved eager to talk, and, without any prompting, she told Cassia of the woman who had died giving birth to John, her second child.

'She was twenty, pretty, light-boned, but most important of all, she was a Jolith of Dorsetshire. She was proud but sweet, and my father had only to see her once to know that he must wed her. I remember little of her, for I was three when she died, but my nurses made sure that I never forgot. Her favourite colour was china blue, and her favourite perfume was jasmine. She had one elder brother, and she grew up at the ancestral home of the Joliths, Cumborne Hall near Lyme Regis. She loved dancing, and music and riding to the hunt – and she loved the sea, for her family had been seafarers of one mode or another for four hundred years, just like ours. It is only recently that a Morbilly has chosen to make his fortune by trade . . .' Aunt Julitta's mouth curled.

'You mean my father?'

'I do, child. No coward ever set out to sea, and your papa is – no, let us not spoil the day with recriminations.' Her aunt forced a smile, taking Cassia's fingers in hers. 'Come, there's the gong. Dinner is waiting.'

The wind moaned round them as they made for the stairs. It sighed, paused, then sighed again, all the harder, as if wishing to stop them, to catch their attention, to tell them something urgent. Cassia almost imagined that she could feel it pushing against her back, trying to make her turn round. She did not relish having to go back along the corridor to her room when it was dark.

Supper was a feast. A chine of mutton, chicken broth heavy with tasty vegetables, asparagus in thick yellow cream, roast beef brown at the edges and poppy-pink in the centre, and a massive apple, apricot and sugar tart on which was ladled a good four inches of thick clotted cream. Cassia had not enjoyed a meal so much in her life; it was succulent, beautifully cooked and nothing like the dried-out, over-salted food her father's cook produced with nause-ating regularity. Her aunt knew how to enjoy her food, too, and the amount she consumed would have weighted two people to their chairs. Cassia, between mouthfuls, watched in awe as her relative chewed her way through generous helpings of everything on the board, finishing off with three slices of pie and a jug full of cream. Then, to her niece's even greater astonishment, a silver salver was brought in, on which lay a long-stemmed clay pipe and a tinder box. Within a few minutes, Cassia was treated to the sight of her aunt puffing at a pipe.

31

She managed not to smile, nor to look amazed, but it was an effort. Comfortably full, she leaned back too, and let the food relax her. It was an entirely new experience.

She woke in the night to the sound of the rain sputtering angrily against her window. A storm had begun and the wind was goading the rain into eerie sounds. Fingertips tapped on the pane, urgently demanding entry; tap tap tap, they went, until Cassia sprang out of bed and ran to the window, flinging wide the curtains. There were no spirit hands to be seen, only a shroud of rain and trees genuflecting in the wind. The sea was not far away, and she imagined what it would be like to be out in it now, in a frail vessel, flung and tossed, terrified of being drowned. Yet her ancestors, Robert Persimmon for one, had spent their whole lives on the waves, and when they had grown too infirm to venture there again, they had died of heartbreak, suffocated by four walls that had become a prison, or so her aunt had told her.

Next morning she ran down eagerly to breakfast, and only when she had finished it did she realize that an evening, a night and a morning had passed without her having thought of Charles, or missed him. Now that she had remembered him, she felt guilty and ashamed. How could she have forgotten him like that, even for a short time? Soon, he would be here with her, and, with good fortune, Bessie would be able to pass their notes to one another without Aunt Julitta discovering. Then they would be able to arrange a meeting . . .

'. . . Printemps, she's a fine, steady mare and not likely to throw you – unless you're foolish enough to stab her sides with your heels.'

Cassia heard her aunt's voice and realized that Julitta had been talking for some time and that she had not been paying attention. She tried to look bright and interested, and her aunt went on: 'I'll ride Satan. You'll never be allowed to mount him, m'dear, he's got a black nature – the very devil to ride. Do not ever be tempted to take him out, promise me that, will you not?' Cassia nodded. 'Stay with Printemps or Clare, or maybe Sylvine – but none other.' Cassia nodding again, they turned round the side of Penwellyn and walked towards the stables.

'My daughter Melody rode Satan once – she was thrown at Morbilly Porth, flung right into the water in her new riding habit. I've never seen a gal so choleric!' Aunt Julitta laughed heartily.

'And was she hurt?'

'Hurt? Melody? She's made of steel, child. A real Morbilly. Never seen her so much as scratched for all her exploits.'

'She is married now, I suppose.' Cassia looked round the light, airy stables and patted the nearest two horses on their sleek noses.

'This three years. And not a grandchild in sight for me yet –' Julitta sighed heartrendingly. 'I keep on telling 'em what a difference a grandchild would mean to me, but these young ones, they take not a dash of notice.'

'What of your other daughters?' Cassia patted an auburn nose, and read a brass name plate at the head of one stall which said, *Printemps*.

'Huh!' Julitta snorted. 'A fine pair. Disappointment to me. Elizabeth's abroad with a schoolfriend's family, in Venice, and Alicia is unhappily married. Sleeping in different rooms! Huh!' Julitta stomped through the stables, shoulders twitching, wrenched a fistful of hay out of a latticed arrangement on one wall and offered it to the black horse in the end stall. As she had guessed, Cassia saw the name *Satan* on the brass plate by this horse's head. Satan's eyes were wild and glittering, and when he saw a stranger approaching, he stamped and blew threateningly through his nostrils.

'Take no notice, child. All show unless you're on his back and then God help ye if he don't like you!' said Julitta. Nonetheless, Cassia stepped back a pace or two.

A groom was lifting down the harnesses and leading out Printemps for Cassia to ride. Julitta herself led out Satan, and then the two horses were saddled up, Cassia watching this procedure with interest. When it was time for her to mount, the groom gave her a leg up, grinning like a split apple. Before she knew it, she was gently cantering after her aunt who at first galloped off at a frantic pace, circled two or three times, then rejoined her niece.

'Get him tired and the battle's half won!' she called out to Cassia who was watching her aunt's performance with admiration. Black stallion and black-haired mistress made a handsome couple. Julitta sat like a young girl, back straight, head high, and the horse was a beauty. 'Arab blood, as well as Irish,' her aunt had said. 'Valuable horse. Envied hereabouts.'

The neat gardens of Penwellyn were giving way to moors, furze and bracken. Scatterings of granite rocks lay everywhere, just as if some giant hand had been playing bowls and left his playthings where they had rolled. Amongst the bracken, patches of purple glowed. These, her aunt told her, were the flowers of the sea pea.

'Handy little genus. Times of starvation in the past have seen the locals flocking down here in droves to gather its seeds. Can't say they're very pleasant, but better than naught, eh?'

The flowers were now growing more profuse as they neared the sea. Sea poppies, erect and brilliantly hued, wild daffodils, cowslips, mallow, flourishing like jewels amongst the dun bracken. Cassia was strongly conscious of a lightening of spirit as the sea came into view. How blue the sky was, sapphire, and so clear, and the scent of the sea was intoxicating. For sixteen years, Cassia had never been to the sea, nor smelt its heady odour, nor seen the sky cutting into the blue of the waters beneath. She had not lived.

As they came to the edge of the moor, halting their mounts so that they could look down over the cliff, Cassia felt something coming alive inside her. It was like a second spirit, a power, a memory she had not known she possessed. The sea, the beautiful, wide, stretching sea was beckoning to her, its waves were breaking inside her, telling her that she was a Morbilly, a Cornishwoman born and bred, asking why had she lingered so long a time before coming here?

She allowed the sensation to take her over; she gave herself to it. What seemed hours later, she heard her aunt laughing gently.

'So ye are a Morbilly, aye, and a Jolith, too, despite that wild Irish colouring.'

'I – I cannot explain how I feel,' Cassia shook her head. 'It is just as if I have always been here, always known this. Oh, how strange it is . . .'

'Not strange at all, child. Have you not heard of race memory? We Morbillys have it stronger than any I know. What makes generation after generation cleave to the same life? It is more than copying, I vow. If 'twere copying, there'd be some who'd hate what they were doing, and give it up, not being suited to it. But we Morbillys have never backed out of aught we've begun.' She grinned, adding, 'Well, excepting one, that is, and 'tis almost as if he never counted.'

Cassia knew that she spoke of her father. She agreed with what her aunt was saying. Whatever devil had leapt on to John Morbilly's back, he was burdened by it for his lifetime, and it had excommunicated him from his family and indeed from life. How could he have known this marvel existed and yet turned his back on it?

Satan was growing impatient and stamping his hoofs as if to say, 'Cease prattling, women.' Aunt Julitta jerked his reins, calling out, 'I'll give him his head for a space, you enjoy the scenery – go down to the cove if you like. I'll join you there later.'

Cassia smiled, waving, watching horse and mistress gallop off at a rattling speed, then she took in two or three deep gulps of air, and slowly led Printemps along the edge of the cliff, looking for a way down to the cove.

She found a level path and guided the horse carefully down. The cliff behind now formed a shield against which the sound of the breakers echoed. It was one of the strangest sounds Cassia had ever heard. She dismounted, standing on the shingle, to listen, while her horse cropped a tuft of grass nearby. It seemed as if the sea were not only in front of her, but also behind her. Closing her eyes, she imagined herself actually amidst the waves, being lulled by their gently rocking movement. She was calmed, pacified by the feeling. The sea had the same message for her as Penwellyn: Welcome home.

'You look as if ye've seen the light, child!' Her aunt's voice jolted her from her reverie, the clatter of flying stones announcing Satan's reckless journey down into the cove. 'Did Poseidon himself come out to chat to ye?'

Cassia laughed. 'Something like that, Aunt. Yes, perhaps he did – I don't think I could feel more surprised if that really had happened. Oh, this cove is beautiful – beautiful, and the way the sea seems to surround one is marvellous!'

'This was your grandfather's favourite place. Brought your grandmother here to propose to her – gave her a bunch of sea convolvulus, scarlet pimpernel, and seapeas, and said if she'd accept those in place of the orchids she was accustomed to – her papa cultivated orchids, y'see – then he'd love her until he died and even beyond.'

'And she accepted of course?' Cassia's eyes shone.

'Like a shot from a musket. Said orchids were fine to wear for balls and festive occasions, but you couldn't wear 'em day in, day out. That was her way of saying yes. Anyway, they were wed soon after. And like as not, they're still together where they've gone.' Julitta's voice sounded gruff, and she turned her head away for a few moments. 'The locals call this the Marriage Cove. Good idea, eh? There's an old legend dating back centuries that if you stand here, you'll find the one you're to wed. Came true for your grandparents, anyway. And by the look on your face, I'd say Poseidon's claimed you for his bride already.'

Cassia laughed, blushing, but the words stayed in her mind. Something had happened to her in the cove, but what exactly it was she could not pinpoint. Perhaps she would never know. With some things it was better just to accept, to be aware, without analysing why.

The ride back to Penwellyn was uneventful. After their horses had been led away by the grooms, Julitta took her niece round the gardens. It was too early for the roses to be in bloom, but the bluebells were spread out like rich Turkey carpets, and there were crocuses buttercup-yellow and mauve. 'Planted 'em m'self,' Aunt Julitta told Cassia, 'prefer the natural look to anything too cultivated.' Purple irises banked a ha-ha, which, Cassia was told, had been fashioned to keep the moorland ponies from straying into the gardens. Ferns of emerald and lime-green spread out like fans round a lily pond where silvered fish darted about, luxuriating in the sunshine. The heady scents of orange and maroon wallflowers filled the air, and, far at the bottom of the lawns, apple, pear, and plum trees stood sentinel. To their right, a row of blossom trees led down to a spinney.

'Marvellous hidey hole for children to play in, but alas, there aren't any little Morbillys now.'

Having trailed her fingers in the lily pond and watched the fishes dashing to left and right as her shadow fell across them, Cassia followed her aunt down to the orchards.

'Fruit trees have stood here for longer than anyone can say. My great grandfather replanted some which had died – for they have a fairly short life compared with other trees – and I myself shall do the same when the time comes. It is rewarding to plant a tree, y'know. Like making oneself immortal.' Julitta chuckled.

'I have always loved trees with pink and white blossom,' said Cassia, looking down the path leading to the spinney. 'Orchard Park, near my home in London, was full of them. I made some sketches, which I was going to paint . . .' She stopped, remembering what had become of her nature manuscript and those sketches. Cut to shreds in anger . . . how far away that anger, that frustration, now seemed.

'Painting, eh? Can't say I've ever been drawn to that pastime. But if you've a mind to do me a painting of Penwellyn, I'd be more than grateful.' Julitta shot her niece a winsome glance, and a wave of affection rose in Cassia's heart. 'Herbs and recipes are what I enjoy dabblin' in,' Julitta continued. 'Not much to see in the herb garden at this time of year, just greenery now, the flowers come later, but ye can smell 'em.'

'I do not think that I have ever seen a herb growing, let alone smelled one – our cook at home did not use such additions,' Cassia confessed.

'Not use herbs? Christmas tidings, what a criminal thing! There's a herb to cure every ailment, y'know, as well as to flavour each type of food. Thyme, sage, borage – comfrey especially is an excellent healer –'mint, of course, you'll surely know of that? And so many more. Have you yourself never used 'em in cooking?'

'Aunt, I have never even cooked,' Cassia said. 'I was not allowed near the kitchens at home. Papa said such an occupation was unfitting for ladies, that it was servants' work, and the cook was such a grim body anyway, that I never dared encroach on her territory.'

Her aunt had stopped walking, and was standing surveying her niece, hands on hips, her omnipresent riding crop tucked in her jacket pocket.

'Never cooked? Not cooked? *Ever*? Lord above, m'gal, but someone's been denying you a whole heap of enjoyment. Not seen a plum cake, rich and fruity, just coming out of the oven, nor eaten a honey cake made by your own hands? Have you never even made stickjaw toffee?'

Cassia shook her head.

'Well, we've a lot to make up for and the sooner we start the better. I'll add cooking to my list of occupations to keep you young and vigorous. Yes, riding in the mornings, chatter in the afternoons – you'll soon be meeting the local gentry for they're all agog to meet my niece – and dining, walking and backgammon in the evenings. And 'twixt times, cooking and herbwifery. Yes, we'll soon make an expert of ye, m'dear!' Julitta patted her niece's shoulder affectionately.

'Mum, mum,' Bessie's voice interrupted them. They turned to see the little maid who was hurrying towards them down the path. Bobbing a curtsey, Bessie said, 'Mum, there's a message for you – a gennelman waiting ter see yer.'

'I wonder who that is.' Julitta strode up the path to the house, shoulders back, skirts swinging. Bessie turned to her mistress.

'Miss, Miss, he's 'ere! 'E's 'ere!'

For a moment, Cassia failed to realize whom she meant, then she flushed bright pink. 'He is? How did he contact you? Oh, tell me quickly!'

'That gennelman who's just arrived ter see yer aunt – 'e slipped me this note.' Bessie held out a folded note, securely sealed with sealing wax. ' 'E winked when 'e gave it me, and said "Secret lover, eh? Min' I don't tell yer mistress about it!" ' Bessie giggled. 'Yer see 'e thinks it's a note from me beau. Ain't it a scream?'

Hastily Cassia broke open the seals, and read the letter, her heart banging wildly against her ribs.

'*Beloved*,' she read, '*I am staying at the Three Feathers, and shall remain here until I hear from you. Dearest heart, I have missed you – life has seemed grey and miserable without you. I could not bear to think of not seeing you again, my darling Cassia. Tell me that you have not forgotten me, that you will meet me soon. Soon, dear heart! You cannot imagine how I yearn for your caresses.*

'*Your devoted, ever loving Charles.*'

'Ooh, miss, are you all right? Yer've gone all white!' Bessie gasped. ''Tain't bad news is it?'

'Oh – no, no, it's beautiful news, Bessie, a beautiful letter! I feel so excited. He's here, he's really here! He still loves me.' Cassia pressed the letter to her breast and whirled round and round joyfully. She told herself that this was the most wonderful day of her entire life. Everything had gone so well, right from the beginning, and now Charles had written her a beautiful letter, and he was staying at the Three Feathers, only a few miles away. They could be in

39

one another's arms within a few hours, kissing, holding each other . . . planning to elope.

She had never been so happy.

CHAPTER THREE

'Oh, and I want some blue velvet ribbon as well, please, Bessie, and if you see any blue thread, too, that would be ideal.' Cassia handed her maid the necessary money, smiling conspiratorially at her. Bessie's trip to Morbilly market was also going to encompass a visit to the Three Feathers to give Charles a letter.

'I doubt if you'll get blue velvet anywhere round here,' Aunt Julitta said, looking up from her bread-making, her sinewy arms coated with flour and a patch of the same on her tanned cheek. 'If you must have such fine furbelows you'll have to send to Truro. Oliver goes there for me every few months or so.'

Oliver was Julitta's coachman, a red-faced, rust-haired Cornishman with the broadest chest Cassia had ever seen, and a smile and an accent to match. Sometimes, Cassia could not understand what he was saying, then he would bellow with laughter and not attempt to translate for her. He seemed to enjoy mystifying the young lady from London, as he called her. 'You must learn the language hereabouts,' her aunt had said when she complained ruefully.

'But I thought markets had everything,' Cassia now said, frowning, thinking of Covent Garden and the other flourishing London markets, with their extensive wares, places where one could purchase rare fruits in mid-winter, tropical produce all year round, orchids at a moment's notice, materials from everywhere in the world. 'Don't the market folk come here from miles around to sell their produce?'

'They do indeed, m'dear. But what would a fisherman's wife want with velvet ribbon? 'Twould be like decking a duckling in silks. The gentry send out like I do, or travel for what they want.'

Bessie bobbed her curtsey and set off, having informed Oliver that she wished to walk, the day being fair. The drizzle which had dampened spirits as well as the ground had now cleared up, Cassia seeing this as an omen of good fortune. The sea mists, which came almost as far as Penwellyn in bad weather, had now receded, leaving everything drenched for a time in a clammy veil. Even these, chilly and intrusive as they were, Cassia had relished, thinking of her long-ago ancestors having to deal with such inclement conditions at sea.

The next three hours dragged for Cassia. She helped her aunt to knead the bread and set it to rise on the vast iron stove, then she measured out poppy seeds with which to scatter the loaves before they went into the oven. She was becoming quite proficient at making bread, and the previous day she had made buns and a cake which delighted her aunt with their light, tasty texture. Soon, she was to learn the secret of making Cornish clotted cream, which the locals called 'clouted' cream and which was quite the most delicious thing Cassia had ever tasted. And there was the recipe for Cornish cinnamon rhubarb to eat with cold meats, which she would also master this week. Her aunt was wasting no time in instructing her in the culinary arts.

When Bessie finally returned, her cheeks pink, her basket laden, Cassia almost pounced on her. 'Did you get them?' she cried, looking pointedly at her maid, who grinned and said, 'Yes, miss, I did indeed.' Then the basket was being unpacked, and there was the length of plain blue ribbon (not velvet), with thread to match, a packet of needles, some pins, and a scarf for Aunt Julitta (a surprise gift which she received with gruff delight). Then came the items she had ordered, linen to be made into cushions for the summer house, coloured thread to embroider the cushions, and one pound of Mulligan's candy which was made by the Irishman of that name who sold sweets and candy at the market. This was Aunt Julitta's secret weakness, and she consumed it in huge quantities, usually late at night. Cassia had discovered her doing just this at about twelve one night when she had been unable to sleep and had gone in search of hot milk. Her aunt had been sitting at the kitchen table, her cheeks bulging with Mulligan's candy. 'Good for m'chest,' she had mumbled, as if there were some great crime in eating sweets. Cassia had laughed, flinging her arms round her aunt's neck and hugging her, to Julitta's immense pleasure. They had then finished the remainder of the candy together.

There was something else in the basket, something very important, hidden under the cloth of the base. The reply from Charles. Cassia managed to remove it and tuck it into her sleeve without anyone except Bessie noticing, then she excused herself, running up to her room, locking the door, and taking out the letter with trembling fingers.

'Bessie says that you know the cove which the locals call the Marriage Cove. Dearest love, I cannot think of a better place for us to meet. I shall be there at eleven o'clock on Tuesday. Sweetest Heart I long to see you again.

Your Charles.'

Sighing with joy, Cassia reread the letter. Only two days to go before they met, and yet how would she get through that time? She wanted to be in his arms now, this second, enjoying his kisses, hearing his voice telling her that he cherished her above all else on earth . . . How could she survive until eleven of the clock on Tuesday? Surely she would explode with impatience before then.

Tuesday dawned, and Aunt Julitta was deep in preparations for her visitors that same afternoon. Mr and Mrs Briscoe of PolMaen House were calling to view her niece and everything had to be organized down to the last detail. Julitta had not entertained for such a reason since her youngest daughter had gone abroad, and she was not only exhilarated but nervous as a young bride showing off her home for the first time. A huge saffron cake had been baked, with minted honey buns, one of her own recipes, and cold beef would be served with the cinnamon rhubarb which Cassia herself had made.

And so Cassia was able to announce that she would go for a ride on Printemps alone, without fear of her aunt joining her. 'Enjoy y'self, child,' was Julitta's kindly response as she watched her young niece walking down the hall in skirt and riding jacket.

Seagulls dipped and circled high above in the blue, their double-noted cry echoing Cassia's joy. She saddled up Printemps herself as she had been taught, then headed for the place where Charles awaited her. This time she did not notice the clumps of flowers jewelling the bracken, nor did she look up to watch the wheeling gulls who seemed to sense her excitement. Her whole body rigid with antici-pation, she rode straight for the Marriage Cove.

It seemed years since she had seen Charles's face, yet it was barely two months. How she had endured these past weeks she did not know. But now they were over, and she would be with him in a few moments. Her skin tingled deliciously at the prospect of his kisses.

At first she could not see him, and her spirits slumped. Then he stepped out from behind the rock where he had been sitting, and she was pulling Printemps to a hasty halt, jumping down and running across the shingle into his arms.

'Cassia, my angel, my dove!' he crushed her against him, kissing her cheeks and forehead and then her lips, and it seemed to her that the waves were flowing inside her head, backwards, forwards, until she was dizzy and Charles had to support her or she would have fallen. She could not speak, no sound would come, and they sank down together on a patch of marshgrass which was rough against her back, but she barely noticed it.

'Darling, how I've missed you! Never leave me again like that – if we part again, I shall die. I shall have nothing to live for if you go, sweetheart!' whispered Charles against her hair, which had come loose and was now spread out around her, glittering golden-red in the sunlight. 'These past weeks have been agony, I have barely eaten or slept. I tried to imagine life without you, and I could not. I would welcome death if you left me!'

Cassia found her voice, but her throat was dry. 'Charles, darling, do not speak of death. Are we not together now?

44

Oh, how I have missed you too. The hours have seemed like months, and each one lay on me like a weight.'

She pulled away a little to look at him properly, adoringly. Charles Billings was extraordinarily handsome by any standards. Tall, slender, his skin was bronzed by the sun and his hair had been bleached gold at the tips. His blue eyes crinkled. 'Am I as you remembered me, dearest? I have not changed, I assure you, darling. I am still your loving devoted Charles.' He pulled her to him again, kissing her face and neck, then lower, and she gasped, colour rushing into her cheeks.

'Oh Charles, if only we could be together now, all the time, day and night! When can it be, when, oh when?' Her voice tailed off as a surge of feeling engulfed her. She burned inside, yet she was cold, so cold that her skin sang with the iciness. Everywhere, she was chilled, except where her lover's lips and hands were touching her, and now his fingers were reaching inside her jacket, pushing aside its lapels, palming her breasts. In Orchard Park, they had done little more than exchange fervent looks and steal kisses behind the screen of bushes. Now, his palms were pressing against her nipples, and the sensation this evoked in her was like nothing she had ever known before. She could feel her control snapping. Gasping, she thrust away his hands, but he groaned as if in pain.

'Darling, don't stop me, please, I beg of you! I need you, oh how I need you, my sweet! Do not torture me like this . . .'

Instantly, she felt cruel, looking at his crestfallen expression, seeing the pain in his eyes at her rejection. Where was the harm? No one would know. Why should she resist? Were they not to be married soon? This was Charles, her adored, faithful Charles, who loved her enough to follow her down to Morbilly, who would never ever let her down . . .

'Please, beloved,' he said again, pleadingly, and she relaxed, helping him to remove her jacket and letting him unlace her bodice so that her breasts could be pulled free, the sun beating down on them. 'God, what beautiful breasts you have,' he groaned, cupping them in his hands, and

45

laying his head against them, his tongue snaking out across her nipples, so that she thought she would faint with the ecstasy. He caressed her breasts again with his tongue, pushing himself against her, climbing on top of her so that she was pinned to the ground. She felt a hardness crushing her thighs, and, realizing what this was, heat surged through her, rushing up to her neck and face. Her mouth opened in a faint sound of amazement. This was what she had been created for, this was love, this she had been waiting for all her life . . . It was so natural, so familiar, as if she had been through it all before, in this very same place. Gasping, throwing back her head, she strained against him.

He pushed up her skirts, then his hands were on her thighs, and he was exclaiming at their softness. She felt his fingers brushing at the auburn triangle between her legs and electric shocks seared her body, making her jerk against him. He laughed softly, pushing her legs apart, and she moaned, 'Love me, darling, love me now, *now*!' Cradling him with her knees, she felt him reach down to guide himself inside her. His breath was flame against her cheeks, he was panting, moving against her, and she was up high, flying with the gulls, crying in ecstasy with them, sun and breeze rippling on her skin . . .

Then suddenly he had stopped, he was stumbling to his feet, dragging his breeches together and she thought she heard a muffled curse beneath his breath. Startled, she opened her eyes, to see his furious face. What had happened? She could not believe it – expecting so much, and then, nothing . . .

Then she too heard the voices. Cornishmen returning from their fishing. They were rounding the point and coming in sight of the cove at this very minute, and they were singing heartily. Shocked, Cassia pulled down her skirts and dragged her bodice together over her breasts, trying to affect a ladylike posture, back averted to the approaching fishermen. Charles too stood with his back to the sea, as if examining an outcrop of flowers thrusting from the cliff behind them.

Only when the fishing boats had gone round the point, out of sight, did Charles turn to face Cassia. She did not look as if she had been unduly shaken by the interruption, but her eyes were glittering, and he still wanted very much to make love to her.

'I have to go, darling – Aunt Julitta is expecting guests, and she will be anxious if I do not return soon. She knows I am not a very adept horsewoman as yet, and –' Cassia rose, smiling, holding out her hands.

'Go? But you have barely been here a moment – I thought, I hoped – well, Cassia, sweet love, do you not love me after all?'

Cassia's face softened. 'Darling, how can you doubt that I love you? But we must not make my aunt suspicious, must we? She has been so kind to me – and, as I said, her friends are coming this afternoon. This is very important to her, you see. She wants to show me off.' Cassia made an apologetic little *moue*.

'Visitors? But have you not had sufficient time to entertain all Cornwall in these past few weeks?'

'In fact, dearest, that is true, but – oh, let us not argue! You are here, now, and so am I, and I shall be meeting you again soon, shall I not, Charles, darling? Tomorrow morning?' Cassia opened her blue eyes wide, looking up into Charles's face pleadingly. She really had no doubt that he would say yes.

Fighting down the desire to insist that he make love to her now, Charles grinned boyishly. He had never looked more handsome, tanned, with his light brown hair ruffled by the sea breeze, his blue eyes brilliant in the sunlight.

'Sweetheart, how could you doubt that I would be here? Have I not travelled all the way down here just for your sake?' he said, squeezing her hands in his and looking deep into her eyes. 'Tomorrow, the same time, here? How I shall look forward to that, darling. I shall dream of you tonight, and I shall be up at dawnbreak to prepare.'

'So shall I, darling!' Cassia leaned against him for a few moments, drinking in the scent of his tanned skin and well-cut linen jacket. He was so smart, so lovable, her Charles. She wanted to be his bride more than anything else in the world.

Taking hold of her horse's reins, Cassia turned towards the slope which led up onto the moors. She turned to wave, Charles waving back, his smile broad. He blew her kisses, and she returned them, memorizing the sight of him, spruce and smart in cream linen jacket and breeches, the sea a sparkling sapphire blue behind him, white clouds scudding, gulls dipping. Her lover. And tomorrow, the mere anticipation of which made her thrill, he would meet her here and they would make love . . .

It was more than the combined effects of sun and air that made her cheeks rosy as she mounted Printemps and cantered across the moors to Penwellyn. She was discovering so much, an excitement that she had not realized existed. Her lover's arms were the key to physical delights that she wanted to taste as soon as possible. Today was just the beginning. As she recalled the way Charles had kissed her breasts, she could feel again his tongue on her nipples and they stood out against her bodice, almost painfully. She was acutely conscious, too, of the heat between her thighs, and the cure for this. Charles's strong tanned hands on her body, the memory of his naked hardness against her, and the tangle of soft golden curls surrounding it, she remembered with a shudder of delight. Tensing, an electric sensation coursed through her, from breasts to thighs, little waves of the same feeling filling her head, so that she became dizzy and almost let the reins drop. Leaning forward, she let the feeling control her, gripping her like invisible hands, wave after wave of ecstasy. Later, when she analysed it, the nearest sensation to which she could compare it was brushing against nettles, that same stinging, but accompanied by bliss, not pain.

She let Printemps find her own way home, which she was quite capable of doing fortunately, for her rider was in no fit state to guide her. One of the grooms took the reins as Cassia dismounted at Penwellyn, and he glanced up at her flushed face but said nothing. She hardly noticed him. She saw no one as she hastened upstairs to change. She was hot and sticky and airborne seeds clung to her hair and clothes. Stepping out of her skirt and jacket, she flung them over a chair, to dip her arms into the bowl of water which Bessie had brought her.

' 'Ad a nice gallop, miss?' Bessie giggled, and Cassia shot her an admonitory look.

'Ssh, you minx!'

'Sorry, I'm sure!' said Bessie pertly, feigning indignation.

Aunt Julitta's commanding voice rolled up the stairs, halting further conversation.

'They are here, m'dear. Pray do not keep us waiting overlong.'

When the Briscoes had gone, Cassia and her aunt spent a peaceful evening together, and it gave Cassia time to recover from her day. She and her aunt played backgammon and drank tea, then Cassia was shown sketches of her cousins at various ages. They were pretty girls, but the Morbilly nose and thick black, unruly hair somewhat marred their appearance. Alicia was the handsomest, with fine shoulders, large eyes and a minute waist. Elizabeth had smaller bones, tiny hands, and a long neck. But there was a haughty air about them both, and as for Melody, Cassia felt instinctively that she would not wish to get on the wrong side of her. Bright black eyes stared reprovingly from a classical face that resembled John Morbilly's too closely for Cassia's liking. She was glad that her cousins no longer lived at Penwellyn, for she guessed that she and her aunt would not be having as relaxed and pleasant a time together if they were here.

They went early to bed, and after breakfast at ten of the clock, Cassia set off for the cove. She felt light-headed with the dazzling sun and the stridency of the sea air. She longed to see Charles again, but she had found her thoughts occupied by her aunt. If Julitta were left on her own when Cassia eloped, she would be a very unhappy and lonely woman whose generosity and warm welcome had been cruelly rebuffed. Conscious of this, Cassia felt uneasy as well as excited as she approached the cove. Before, she had only had herself and her love to consider, and an intolerable home situation to escape from. Now, there was her warm-hearted aunt and a house which was fast becoming precious to her . . . Cassia was only just beginning to understand how difficult it would be to leave. Perhaps . . . perhaps even impossible.

Then Charles was racing towards her, and as usual she forgot everything except his presence. He crushed her to him, kissing her over and over until she was breathless.

'Sweetheart, I have not slept for thinking of you!' he murmured against her hair, his tongue darting into her ear, and then between her lips. She felt the snaking heat of it, and found herself surrendering involuntarily to his caresses. One arm was firmly round her, while his other arm was free to pull open her bodice and stroke her breasts. As his fingers slipped over her nipples, she felt the rushing sensation beginning, coursing its way down to her thighs and gathering in strength. She shuddered, and he looked at her with surprised delight. The hand which had been caressing her breasts moved down to his breeches, and she felt something hard and hot pulsing against her. Looking down, seeing what it was, she swayed against him eagerly.

Afterwards he could not have said what happened. He had not expected such a passionate response from her, but she had gripped him with her fingers, and this had so taken him by surprise that it was all over, in searing seconds of ecstatic bliss. To be followed by a cold fury . . .

'Darling – what has happened – I do not understand,' she gasped, alarmed by the way he let go of her and sank to the shingle so abruptly. Was he hurt? Had she hurt him in some way? He was red-faced, panting, he was trying to hide himself . . . 'Darling,' she repeated, 'are you all right?'

She kneeled beside her lover, stroking back his silky hair and kissing his damp forehead. She could not understand what had happened, but could see that he was not yet in a fit state to explain. She cradled him in her arms, feeling that in some obscure way she had failed him, longing for him to speak, to explain why the crescendo of sensation had turned so suddenly into aching deprivation.

CHAPTER FOUR

Bessie was standing at the door, face white, eyes dilated, when Cassia returned. The groom, too, had looked anxious, but it was not his place to speak first to his mistress's guests. The air of tension in the hallway did not dissipate as Cassia entered. Bessie opened and shut her mouth a few times, flapping her hands distractedly when she could not find the right words. At last she managed, 'It's yer aunt, miss! Ooh, it's terrible, miss! There she were all sprightly like she usually is, then all of a sudden, she went strange like – all stiff and her face began to twitch! Give me the proper 'orrors it did! Ooh, miss, she's been calling fer yer since it 'appened. She's up in 'er bed now, miss – Mrs Rowse is wiv 'er . . .'

Cassia felt cold fingers touching her. Her aunt ill! Strong, tireless Aunt Julitta ill? Rushing past Bessie, she ran up the stairs, heart pounding, acid tears stabbing behind her lids. All my fault, all my fault, I should have been here, she thought as she ran.

Julitta was propped up on two enormous white pillows, but it was her face that drew Cassia's horrified attention. Her mouth and eye, on the left side, looked as if they had been dragged down, while the right side of her face was still normal. When she saw her niece, Julitta mumbled her name, 'Cassie,' but it was barely intelligible, for she spoke through wooden lips.

'Oh God!' Cassia whispered, falling to her knees at Julitta's bedside and gripping her cold hands.

'Gently miss, she is very ill.' Cassia heard the low voice with a start of alarm, for she had not noticed anyone in the room, not even Mrs Rowse who stood wringing her hands at the foot of the bed. Looking up, she saw Doctor Hookly, her aunt's physician, whom she had met on one or two occasions. His pallor made her heart sink again, for she knew him to be an excellent physician and she thought that if there were any hope for her aunt, he would at least have smiled at her.

Julitta's hands felt like cold, fleshless bones. Cassia had not realized how thin her aunt was. But surely it was a strong slenderness – or so she had imagined. She could not bear it if her aunt were going to die when they had only just discovered each other. How could anyone leave a world in which there was so much love for them? She felt at that moment that she would do anything – anything – for Julitta, if only she would not die.

Her aunt mumbled again, something which sounded like, 'Yours, all yours. Everything. Not to them, cold bitches. To you. All yours. Penwellyn.' Then her face went so still that Cassia thought she had died, and she burst out weeping, gripping the cold hands frantically, willing the spirit to return to the deathly still flesh.

The doctor pulled her gently away, whispering to her to be quiet. 'She sleeps now. She is not dead. Leave her now.'

'She is not dead?' Cassia's eyes lit with hope.

'Come outside where we can talk, my dear.'

As they stood outside Julitta's bedroom Cassia was told that her aunt had suffered a stroke, 'But only a mild one,' Doctor Hookly assured her. 'She needs rest and peace now. She thinks a great deal of you, you know. I have known her all her life, and I have never seen her as fond of anyone as she is of you. She wants you to have the estate if she dies – you understood what she was saying?' Cassia nodded, tears filling her eyes. 'No doubt her daughters will have something to say about that, as will their husbands, but ye'll have my support when the time comes.' The doctor's kindly eyes glittered. 'I loved her myself once, you know. Still do, if it comes to that. But she chose Gerald instead, and although he did not make her happy, she will not marry again.'

Cassia stared, tears trickling down her cheeks. This tubby little man, with his florid complexion, bristly hair and twinkling eyes, could have been her uncle? 'I never knew . . .' she whispered.

'Julitta does not talk overmuch of herself and her past, as ye'll have gathered. She's hardy, and she's never been bowed by self-pity. This stroke, well, I've seen others recover from worse, and she's a strapping woman. With loving care, which I know ye will give her, she will mend. But she'll have to take life more easily. Naps in the afternoon, early to bed and late to rise. She'll have to eat less, too . . .' He gave a little chuckle. 'She always did love her food.'

Cassia brushed away her tears. Relief flooded her; she felt gratitude welling up.

'Don't worry, Doctor, I'll nurse her day and night. I'll be the most devoted nurse ever. She has made me so happy these past few months, it is the least I can do to repay her kindness. Just tell me what to do, and what medicine she must have, and I shall see it is all done exactly as you order it.'

'You're a sweet girl.' The doctor patted her cheek. 'Would have liked to have been your uncle.'

'It may not be too late, Doctor.' Cassia smiled. 'When my aunt is better, I'll see what I can do to persuade her.'

The doctor gave a bark of laughter. 'Be like persuading Satan to give rides to the local children, my dear.' Nonetheless, he went away with a secret look of pleasure on his face, leaving Cassia detailed instructions and various phials of medicine for Julitta to take during the day and at night time.

The next two days were so frantic that Cassia had no time for anyone but her aunt. She barely had a moment to wash, change, or eat the rushed snacks that Bessie brought her. Julitta continued to look drawn and, to her niece's acute anxiety, her mouth and eye stayed in the same drooping position. The doctor assured her that there was a chance partial, if not full muscle control would return. He visited frequently, bringing with him a confidence that inspired Cassia to keep calm and to look forward hopefully to the day when her aunt would be well again.

It was at the end of the second day that Bessie hissed something in her mistress's ear. 'Miss, what abaht 'im –

what'll we do? Shall I tek a note now? Like as not 'e'll be frantic wiv worry – I know I would be!'

Cassia's hand flew to her mouth. Charles! He would be sick with anxiety. They had parted in such a strained manner, despite her frantic reassurances. Desperate to put things right, she had arranged to meet him again at the cove that morning – and she had completely forgotten about it.

'Oh, Bessie, what a mess! Yes, of course you'll have to take him a note. Oh dear, how could I have forgotten about him? Poor Charles!'

'Oliver'll tek me, miss. He was goin' to tek me fer a ride anyhow. I can mek up some tale about 'aving to go into the Three Feathers: 'e's not too bright, ain't Olly. 'E won't say nuffink. 'E's a bit up 'ere, yer know.' Bessie tapped the side of her temple. In other circumstances, Cassia would have laughed.

Now she hastily scribbled a loving note full of apology, gave it to her maid, and sent her off on her carriage ride with Oliver. The hours passed so swiftly that Cassia forgot all about the note until her maid's return. Aunt Julitta had to be washed, gently, with herbal soap, and her body massaged with unguents to keep it supple and to protect it from bed sores. Her hair was brushed and tied back out of the way, Cassia dabbed orange flower water at her neck and wrists. She thought her aunt gave a semblance of a smile in response, but she could not be sure. 'Cass, Cassie,' she would mumble continually – even while her niece was in the room, but especially if Cassia were ever absent. She also repeated that she wished Cassia to inherit Penwellyn. Cassia found herself dreading that Julitta would say this in front of her daughters when they arrived.

Alicia came first, in a flurry of ruched silk and embroidered taffeta, her carriage boldly emblazoned with the Morbilly arms, her coachmen fancifully attired in splendid uniforms of red and white. Musk and ambergris billowed from Alicia Morbilly as she moved, and her hands waved to and fro as if propelled by strings. She had no warm greeting for her cousin, nor a kind word. Cassia was sniffed at as though she were some menial attempting to mingle with those too good for her, and Alicia's interview with her mother so upset Julitta that the doctor was impelled to say:

'Miss Alicia, I have known you since ye were a child, and I am warning ye there must be no shows of temperament now. Your mother is an exceedingly sick woman, and if ye snap at her like ye have been doing, I cannot allow ye to see her again until she is well.'

'Snap at her? I did not *snap* at her!' Alicia flapped her scented fan impatiently.

'Oh but ye did, Miss Alicia. She cannot speak, so 'tis no good demanding that she greet ye. I warned ye not to expect anything of her. Ye never did have a kind word to say for her when ye lived here, and she's been a deal happier since ye left!' The doctor's grey-brown hair seemed to bristle with anger.

Alicia's cold, painted face hardened. Cassia was reminded of her father's icy, forbidding expression when he was angered. Alicia rose to her feet, wide panniers swinging, her hands quivering furiously.

'I should not have come. I did not wish to. You're a nasty old man, Hookly, and you always have been. I know what you want: my mother. There's only one reason for your putting up with her spiteful, cantankerous tongue and that is to get Penwellyn and her money. I have always known it, and I shall never be persuaded otherwise.' And with that, Alicia Morbilly billowed out of the solar, followed by her shocked, pink-faced maid. Within half an hour Alicia and her entourage were leaving Penwellyn, and all was peaceful again. That was, until Elizabeth's arrival.

Cassia's first thought on meeting her cousin Elizabeth was, 'How could I have thought her pretty?' for the long neck bore a sulky face, and the small hands were stiff and unyielding. Every movement Elizabeth made seemed to announce her impatience, her wish to be gone, her disapproval of Penwellyn and all who resided there. She feels trapped, Cassia thought, after observing her for a few hours. But it was not really something at Penwellyn that fright-

56

ened her, it was something within her own self, or so Cassia finally decided. Elizabeth was breeding the very thing from which she most wished to escape.

Elizabeth kissed her mother respectfully, but without warmth. She had brought her a herb pillow decorated with silk ribbons and love-knots, which would have been a touching gift had it been bestowed with love. But there was no love in Elizabeth, nor was she capable of manufacturing it. Doctor Hookly told Cassia in private that he had never seen Elizabeth so much as touch her mother before, and he could only deduce that it was for effect. 'Julitta has tried all her life to reach Elizabeth, but she has never managed it – nor has the girl's poor husband. There is a barrier of ice round that girl, and God knows who placed it there. She is more like a Jolith than a Morbilly.'

'The Joliths are cold people, then?'

'Compared with the Morbillys they are lumps of ice. Oh, occasionally there'll be a normal one – your grandmother for example, but it is not common. Strange family, detached, self-sufficient. Maybe all right for them, but 'tis mortally unpleasant for those who love 'em, or try to.'

'So you think that my father is more of a Jolith then?'

'I suppose he is, my dear. Did your aunt not tell ye as much? No, perhaps she would not. She does not like to speak ill of her mother's family. She reveres Clarissa's memory ye know.'

Cassia looked down at her linked hands. So much seemed clearer to her now. She wished she had known this before. She hoped that she had the courage to endure Elizabeth's visit. And then she had to face the problem of how to meet Charles, who had sent an impatient, demanding note in answer to her apologetic one, and followed it up with two more plaintive letters in quick succession.

Although she yearned for the comfort of his arms, Cassia had no intention of leaving her aunt until she was much better. She knew that she could not think of eloping while the invalid was so drawn, so weak.

Five days passed, and a fifth letter arrived from Charles,

via Bessie who was now regularly visiting the Three Feathers, sometimes on foot, sometimes with Oliver. Cassia opened the letter with shaking hands.

'Cassia, beloved, I can only assume from your repeated refusals to see me that our love is over. That being so, I have no more wish to go on living. I cannot endure one day more without your love. Oh, sweetheart, if only you still loved me, how happy I would be, how truly, wonderfully happy. But as you have forgotten me, I shall go now to the cove where we spent so many happy hours together, and there fling myself into the waters to seek oblivion from this agony . . .
'Your devoted, adoring Charles.'

Cassia's face, that had been skull white, turned a deep and painful scarlet. The letter fluttered from her fingers unregarded as Bessie, terrified by the expression on her face, ran to her mistress's side.

'He says,' Cassia said slowly, 'he says he's going to kill himself.'

'Oh my gawd, miss!' shrieked Bessie, then clamped her lips together as she remembered the sleeping invalid upstairs. On a hushed note she said 'Omigawd, what're we goin' to do, miss?'

'Go to him at once, I suppose. If my aunt asks for me, you will have to make some excuse – say I am bathing, anything. Bessie, I shall have to rely on you.'

Cassia ran to her room, and hastily donned her riding clothes, fumbling with the fastenings of her skirt, while tears blinded her vision. They were tears of weariness, and they were also tears of anger. For somewhere in Cassia's innately shrewd mind a voice was whispering that Charles's letter represented an unpardonable selfishness. Her native commonsense, that five days ago would have been silenced in the name of love, was re-asserting itself, telling her that the letter was childish, melodramatic, that a truly mature man would have understood her predicament. And hard on the heels of this realization came remorse – guilt that she had forced the man she loved to follow her for hundreds of miles and then endure shameful inactivity, and fear that she was doomed forever to handle her life ineptly.

Outside she ran to the stable and saddled up Printemps. Then she headed for the cove as fast as the mare would go – urging her on, her voice whipped away by the breeze from the sea that was increasing in velocity. All the signs presaged a storm, the sky was an ugly pewter grey, the sound of the waves smacked against the cliffs like pistol shots. She urged Printemps down the slope into the cove so rapidly that the horse stumbled and only managed to regain its footing before she was flung over its head. She screamed, clinging to the reins and mane, gripping with her knees, tears of fright rolling down her face. Shouting Charles's name, she urged Printemps onto the beach, but could see nothing save the empty cove and the lashing breakers, foam-limned, while the wind tore at her hair and skirts.

Then she saw him, half sitting, half lying at the edge of the point, the calves of his legs actually in the sea; he was leaning towards the water, as if about to slip into the waves, out of sight.

'Charles! *Charles!*' she screamed, now genuinely afraid for him, and saw his head turning slowly in her direction, then he seemed to jerk as if startled, and she saw him disappear from sight. 'Oh God, oh God!' she sobbed, jumping down from Printemps's back and racing across the slippery, uneven rocks towards the point.

But he was not in the sea after all. He had fainted and rolled down a slope of rock, out of sight. He lay, white and still, the waves frothing against his body, his eyes closed. She bit back a cry. Running her hands over his body, she could find no wound, nor any sign of blood, and she whispered his name, over and over, as if hoping this would revive him. At last his eyes fluttered, then opened slowly.

'Charles, are you hurt?' she asked, kissing his cold face and cradling his head in her hands, silently asking forgiveness for her earlier anger.

'I – I – what happened, where am I?'

'You are in the cove, darling – I got your letter, remember?' Fresh tears came, and she cradled him, her head on his chest.

59

'I – was – just about to jump,' Charles said, his voice faint, his eyes still half-closed. 'I think I must have slipped on the wet rock.' He frowned, rubbing the back of his head. 'I feel dazed – I think I struck my head on something.'

Cassia had to lean close to hear his voice above the bellow of the wind. Now she said, 'But you're alive, darling, and that's all that matters!' She grasped his cold hands. 'Oh, darling, when I got your letter, I was angry with you for not understanding, but now I'm so sorry. You came all this way from London, to see me, to marry me, and then I neglected you. You must have thought I didn't love you any more, but it isn't true – I *do* love you. Oh darling, when my aunt is better –'

'You said that she was seriously ill. That she would be an invalid and you must nurse her . . .'

'Yes, but it won't be forever, dearest. When she is strong again, we will elope as planned. I promise you that with all my heart. I do, really I do, darling!' Cassia looked earnestly at her sweetheart, wondering how he could doubt her sincerity, while at the back of her mind was the thought that her aunt might be calling for her at this very moment.

'You will meet me again soon?' Charles was now sitting up, still looking very pale, and he was shivering.

'Of course.' Cassia sighed, squeezing his icy hands. 'Come now, we must go to shelter under the cliff. The rain is starting . . .' Helping Charles to his feet, they half walked, half ran to the cliff, where the rain could not find them. There, concealed beneath an overhang of rock, they clung together, kissing and sighing, promising to meet again the next day at dusk, when Aunt Julitta would be settled for the night.

'She sleeps well at night now. Doctor Hookly has given her a sleeping draught which never fails. When she is settled, I'll come at once to you. Watch for me darling . . .' Cassia whispered.

Charles crushed her to him, thinking of the following evening, of their lovemaking, of what they would do when alone together in the concealment of the dark. She felt his rising passion and clung to him.

'I'll be waiting, my dove, and I shall carry a torch so that you will see me. I usually walk round the point, when the tide is out, so that no one sees me coming here from the village, but as I don't know what time the tides are tomorrow, I can't say which way I will come.' Charles kissed her ardently on the mouth, cupping her neck with his hands and stroking the back of her head. His touch was so skilled and persuasive that she found herself wanting to stay here with him more than anything, despite the storm now raging, despite her aunt lying sick at Penwellyn, despite poor Printemps standing patiently in the rain. Despite that insistent voice of commonsense asking her if this were really the strong lover she had yearned for, whispering that he had never really meant to die at all . . .

When finally she drew away, it was with a painful ache of unfulfilled passion. They kissed again, repeated their promise to meet the next night, and then she was mounting Printemps and making her way up onto the moors, waving to Charles as she went. By the time she reached Penwellyn, she was soaked, and the grooms were waiting with blankets and oats for the horse. She ran into the house, stripped off her wet clothing, towelled herself dry and put on a plain gown to go and sit with her aunt.

Bessie had been watching over Julitta, and now rose to greet her mistress with a whispered, 'She ain't stirred, miss. Slept like a lawg. Proper lucky it were.'

Sighing with relief, Cassia moved silently to her aunt's bedside, gazing down at her. It was tragic to see such strong, alert features, and such a vibrant, generous nature crushed in this way. If she could have done anything to prevent it, then she would have tried. But at least she was here, thank God, and could be of some use. Where would Julitta have been without her? Mrs Rowse was kind and loyal, but it was Cassia for whom her aunt called constantly. It was as though the very presence of the girl helped to heal the distressed woman.

61

Cassia slept soundly that night, exhausted by anxiety and her adventure in the cove. The next morning her aunt seemed brighter, and watched her niece moving about the room with love in her eyes. As usual, Cassia washed her, massaged her body with unguents and rubbed comfrey salve into her shoulders and hips where, despite all her efforts, red pressure marks were beginning to show. Julitta's eyes filled with tears of tender gratitude, and she mumbled her thanks with clumsy lips, bringing up one hand, slowly, jerkily, to touch her niece's arm.

'Sweet Cass-ie,' she said slowly, wincing as if the words caused her anguish.

'Dearest Aunt, don't try to talk,' Cassia begged, kissing Julitta's cheek tenderly. 'I'm here, and I'm not going to leave you until you are well. You will see, you'll soon be up and about again, riding Satan and helping me to cook. Just think: very soon, Satan will be a father. You don't want to miss that, do you?'

'No, o-h, n-o-o,' Julitta sighed.

Doctor Hookly had told Cassia to talk of the future in this way, to mention all the good things that were to happen, to give her aunt a reason for getting better. To see Satan's foal, to ride Satan on the moors, were two of Julitta's main interests, so Cassia mentioned these frequently. Already, she believed her to be responding.

The day seemed to drag, especially the two hours following tea, when Julitta managed to eat some honey cake and drank three cups of tea: her first solid food since her stroke. Would the sky never darken? Cassia thought, as the sun continued burning as brightly as ever. But slowly dusk drew in and she was able to settle her aunt for the night, making sure that she was comfortable, kissing her with extra tenderness and telling her that she would soon be well again. She went to her room, washed, brushed her hair and slipped into her riding clothes which had been dried and pressed by Mrs Rowse. Then she was on Printemps's back and heading for the cove.

She felt tired, for her emotions had been well and truly

jarred during the past few days. This, she reasoned, was why she did not feel excited about seeing Charles. She was drained, emotionally and physically, that was all. When she saw him, when he held her in his arms, as he surely would, she would feel better.

As she began her descent into the cove, she noticed a ship in the distance. There were ships of all kinds in these waters, going to and from France and other destinations. This one had an unusual outline; it seemed to ride lower in the water than most, and its sails were striped red and white and blue and white, or at least she thought these were the colours. It was hard to see now that the light was fading. It was driven from her mind by the sight of torch-light bobbing into view, and Charles hurrying towards her. Dismounting, she ran into his arms, eager for his kisses, then he was pulling her to the ground and they were cling-ing together wildly. It was happening so quickly that she barely had time to consider, to think. But she was not the same girl who had been so desperate to acquiesce a few days ago.

'What's wrong?' he said as she pushed his questing hand away from her thighs.

'Oh I don't know – I'm so tired. I'll be all right in a little while, darling. Give me time. It's exhausting being a nurse,' she laughed, expecting understanding, never dreaming that what she had said represented the end for Charles. Some-thing snapped in his head. Almost snarling, he flung him-self on top of her, careless of her cries.

'Charles – no, *no!*' she screamed, but he was beyond hearing. There was now only one idea in his mind, one driving force, and that was what motivated him as he tore open her bodice and hitched up her skirts, forcing her legs open with his knees so that she gasped with pain and alarm.

'Please, no, no, Charles – *don't! Please!* Stop it – I –'

'Shut up,' he growled, crushing her beneath him, bruis-ing her back against the pebbles on the shore. 'Shut up and do as you're told. When I've finished with you, you'll be ready to follow me anywhere, oh yes! Listen!' he jabbed her

63

inner thigh with his knee, so that she went dizzy with pain. 'There's a boat just round the point and you're coming with me tonight, to France. We're eloping, d'you hear me? I've waited long enough! We're going to marry, d'you *hear*?' Roughly he shook her by the shoulders, all the frustrations and disappointments of the past months welling up in him. She burst out sobbing, striking at him with her clenched fists, now as desperate to resist him as she had been to encourage him only days before. This was not Charles, this was a monster, a vicious stranger . . . All the anger she had felt at his suicide note returned, redoubled into seething fury.

She fought him, blind with pain, as he drove his fist into her groin to stop her drawing her legs together. Wildly she struggled, but her arms were aching intolerably and her thighs throbbing from his onslaught. Oh God, she thought, this could not really be happening. It was a nightmare, yes, a nightmare and soon she would wake up. Tears of anger and fear poured down her face, her throat was raw, her back stinging from the stones thrusting into her spine. Still she resisted, crying his name, trying to hit his face, but each time he ducked skilfully. She knew that she was tiring, that she could not fight much longer, that any minute it would be over and she would be dirtied, humiliated, despoiled – that he did not care so long as he got what he wanted. Her father had been right all this time, and she had been a blind, witless fool.

She scratched at his throat, drops of blood fell on to her face. 'Bitch, you'll regret that!' he snarled, thinking of his beauty marred, of scars on his neck for the rest of his life. But even this pain was not going to stop him raping her. He had not waited, attentive, tender, loving, all these months, for her to escape him now. Not this time, no; this girl he would have.

The youngest son of a family of thirteen, Charles Billings had always been acutely aware of his being the thirteenth in the family. From the age of three or four, he could remember people making such remarks as, 'Hmm, unlucky

arrival, eh? Have to watch hisself with a bad start like that.'
Consequently, he had imbibed the idea that not only had
his birth been unplanned, and unwanted, but that he could
not avoid disaster. Being stubborn, he had resolved that he
would show all the critics what he was made of. His way
had not been easy, for his father had died when he was five,
and his mother had struggled to keep the family together,
eventually finding that her efforts were fruitless. The day
had come when the family had been split up; Charles had
been sent to his uncle, who had six children of his own.
Two years later, Charles's mother had married again, but
she had not sent for him, as she had promised she would.
He had waited, three months, six months, a year. His mother
gave birth to twins, he dreamed of being their brother, of
helping her to care for them – but his stepfather was a
jealous, possessive man who had no intention of allowing
his wife to fritter her affections on anyone except himself
and the children he gave her.

Charles, old beyond his years, had understood the weakness and fear that had prevented his mother defying his
stepfather, and in time he had been able to forgive her. But
he had never forgiven nor forgotten the fact that it was
poverty that had destroyed his childhood, torn the family
apart, cast him out to send for himself. He swore then that
no matter how long it took him he would find money and
that when that day came he would see to it that he never
felt the pinch of poverty again. Cassia was not the first
heiress he had wooed but she was the most susceptible and
the most desirable – and Charles Billings was a fastidious
man. In his own perversely selfish way he had loved Cassia,
for she represented the embodiment of a dream – a woman
who could flatter his vanity with her love, soothe his pride
with her beauty, and restore his fortunes with her inheritance.

Even now, through the raging of his passion he knew
that whatever it took to ensure that Cassia Morbilly became
his wife, he would do. Her struggles were only serving to
increase his ardour; she was exhausted now, and he sensed

that she would soon surrender. He smacked her face, once, twice, kneeling down on her thighs, tearing at her bodice to free her beautiful breasts, and then he began to unfasten his breeches, leaning towards her, his left hand tangled in her hair to prevent her from moving. He had never felt so excited, so exhilarated. He was going to have her – then they would elope and there would be no more talk of waiting, of having to nurse the old harridan. He grinned, his eyes glittering, preparing to enter her body mercilessly.

Cassia was dazed from pain and shock. She was dreadfully tired and knew that it would be over any minute, for she could not go on struggling. Her dreams were ending; she was facing reality. Once again begging him to stop, she heard him gasp, 'Shut up!' and then she closed her eyes to await her fate.

What happened next was so unexpected that she could only gasp. Charles was suddenly lifted off her, like a weightless bundle of rags, and she saw a small group of men laughing at his alarm and looking down at her with lascivious eyes.

Men – men here in the cove? Fishermen? No, they were dark-skinned! One was nearly black. They wore gaudy, ill-kempt shirts and breeches, brilliant cloths were swathed round their tangled hair. They were speaking some strange guttural tongue, and she thought she heard one or two French words but she could not be sure.

Shocked still, and weak from struggling, she watched the men bear away Charles, who, kicking and screaming, was bundled into a boat at the water's edge. Then she too was being swept up in powerful arms, and carried to the boat where she was flung, brutally, so that her bones juddered and she struck her head on one of the slats which served as seats. She lost consciousness instantly.

CHAPTER FIVE

Screaming woke her. She was dreaming, of course. That terrible nightmare was still going on. But now it was Charles's voice raised in terror; he was shrieking hysterically.

'I know about you – I know what you are! *Slavers! Pirates!* Don't think for a minute that you'll get away with this. The law knows all about you. They'll get you, oh yes they will! And you'll be hanged, you devils!'

Shocked, Cassia took in the scene. Her former lover was on his knees in the base of the boat, fists clenched, begging to be freed, while simultaneously threatening every fate that could befall their kidnappers. *Pirates. Slavers.* Realization dawned on her; she went white with shock, not that it mattered, for no one was looking at her. She had heard of the raiding sorties which took place on the Cornish coast – once, her aunt had told her, almost an entire village at St Michael's Mount had been abducted, to be sold in the slave markets on the Barbary Coast. But had not her aunt said that it was years since such a raid had taken place? Disbelief warred with what she soon could not deny. The men were vicious, now they were kicking out at Charles to quieten him. His screams died, blood oozed from the pulpy wounds on his face and neck. He became very still.

The pirates smelled foul, their clothes were bizarre, their faces gaunt bones devoid of warmth or humanity. Knives were tucked into their coloured sashes, or behind their ears. The one with the blackest skin was grinning; she could see his white teeth glinting in the glare from their torches.

The little boat dipped and rose on the waves. Cassia kept very still, dreading that the men would turn on her next. Cold numbness was creeping over her. Briefly, she thought of jumping out of the boat, but she could not swim and they were now far from land. If she protested, she was sure that they would kick her too, and she had no wish to be harmed. Fear encased her like a shroud. She could do nothing. If Charles's attack on her had been a nightmare, this now was worse, far worse. Oh how she wished she were asleep and dreaming this. Remaining as immobile as possible, she prayed they would not notice that she had recovered from the blow on her head. Listening to their guttural voices, she sensed that they were pleased. From beneath half-opened lids, she watched them. One pointed to her hair, nodding and grinning, then he poked a bony finger into her left breast so that she could not help but wince with pain. He said something, and they all roared with laughter. One adjusted his breeches, made a crude gesture, and they laughed again. Oh God, no, she thought – if they touched her! Terror blanked her mind for a few seconds. She wanted to faint so that the horror would recede, but she could not. She had to lie there, cold, terrified, filled with dread, until the little boat came to a halt, and she saw looming over them the side of a larger vessel, heard cries of greeting, the thump of a rope ladder being thrown down for them.

Roughly, she was hauled to her feet, slung over one of the pirate's shoulders and then they were making the perilous ascent into the privateer, the sky swaying above Cassia's head until they reached the deck, and there she was flung down, left to lie in a bruised heap. Stunned, sick, she heard Charles still pleading and sobbing to the men, who, as before, paid him absolutely no heed. She was too bemused to look at her surroundings, to take her bearings, beyond knowing that she was on a ship whose massive sails billowed above her. This nightmare was already more than she could stand, yet it must go on – she could not stop it. This was no civilized place where gentlemen were courteous to ladies, where women could beg help and rely on receiving it. Here, she sensed, there would not even be mercy for children.

The men were standing over her, grinning, hands on hips. They exchanged a few sentences, others came to join them, to look down at her. One of them licked his lips, rubbing his hand up and down his stomach as if in anticipation.

But Charles had not ended his attempts to be freed. He had been slung to the deck, and was now struggling on hands and knees towards the men who surrounded Cassia, tears streaming down his handsome, bruised face. His white shirt was tattered and begrimed, his breeches torn almost in two, his hair wild.

'Please, sirs,' he wept, his hands clasped as if in prayer, 'please, *please* – if you only knew – this lady, she is an heiress. She is rich, very rich, her father will pay you any ransom you ask to have her back. I promise you this, sirs. *Please listen!*'

Brutally, one of the pirates kicked out with his foot, smashing it into Charles's face, crushing his nose to a scarlet mass, sending the blood spurting down his cheeks. He screamed, once, twice, clutching at his face. Another of the pirates slipped the dagger from his sash and advanced on Charles. At that point, Cassia stopped looking, stopped feeling. Whatever Charles had done to her, he was a human being, and he was being treated cruelly. Oh God, save us! she prayed silently, as her lover's screams rose, higher and higher, before silence fell at last.

Through the thicket of legs which surrounded her, Cassia saw Charles's inert body lying on the deck, and there was so much blood that she thought he could only be dead. She wanted to weep, but her tears were as dry as her throat, and now that the pirates had silenced Charles, they turned again to her. They laughed, nudging one another, revelling in her fear, then one stepped towards her, reaching down to rip open her bodice completely, and she saw that the others were beginning to strip off their breeches. They were lining up to – oh God no, not that! She screamed, half dragged from the deck by the grip of one of the men, who bent his mouth to her breasts and began to bite at them. The onlookers stepped closer, watching, mouths open, saliva running. All of them – they were all going to – she swallowed, her head pounding, she was going to be sick –

'*Mon Dieu, mes amies*, what in God's Holy Name are you doing?'

Cassia heard the cultured French voice, but it was the crew's reaction that told her of the speaker's importance. They leapt back from her instantly, scrabbling at their breeches, standing to attention, and one spoke to the newcomer, in French, begging his pardon, saying that they had meant no harm, that they had been carried away. Cassia, who, like all young ladies of her class, had been taught French, managed to follow the conversation.

'*Mes amies*, you know the rules. What got into you? Women must not be touched. I see them first. And what of this man?' The newcomer gestured towards Charles. The expression on the pirates' faces grew shamefaced; their spokesman asked for pardon, saying that such a thing would not happen again.

Cassia could not as yet see the newcomer fully, for she was partially screened by the men around her. Recalling their behaviour of a few moments earlier, she wondered at the authority this man (their captain?) had over them. He sounded cultured, civilized; as he approached her, surveying her with a grin on his tanned face she saw that he was fashionably dressed. Even in her bruised and shocked state, she could see he was beautiful, with glittering green eyes and silky black hair tied back in a bow at his neck. He had an air of virile charisma as well as of power and authority. He was not showily dressed, but wore a white silk shirt and beige kid breeches with black leather top-boots polished to a brilliant shine. He must have been in his cabin until now, for his shirt was untied at the neck and she could see part of his tanned chest and the black hairs springing there. He stood looking down at her for some moments, his eyes insolently drinking in her beauty, her naked breasts, her calves exposed where her skirt had been pulled back. She felt hot colour rising in her cheeks and she wanted to strike at him for the humiliation that he and his men had made her suffer. Whoever he was, this insolently grinning man, it was *his* fault. How dare he look at her like that?

She struggled to her feet, tugging her bodice together. He did not so much as offer his hand to assist her, which made her even more furious. She opened her mouth to rage at him, to tell him that she would kill him for this, and then she was overcome by such a wave of dizziness that she had to struggle not to collapse. Realization hit her. What power had she? God knows who these men were, or where they were from. They behaved like animals if given the chance – look what they had done to poor Charles – so why should their leader, for all his fine attire, behave differently? She thought of her aunt, lying ill at Penwellyn, and she began to sob hopelessly. What would happen to Julitta without her? If she did not recover . . . Tears streamed down Cassia's cheeks, and she bowed her head so that her auburn hair fell forward in a silken mass.

Captain Vincent Sauvage, descendant of a bastard son of Francis I of France, thirty-three years of age, known on the Barbary Coast as the Sea God, feared throughout the pirate world and beyond, watched the weeping girl without compassion. He was after all a slaver; there were huge fortunes to be made selling men and women to the harems and households on the Barbary Coast, Constantinople and elsewhere, and this trade was one in which Sauvage could learn nothing new.

Because of his relationship with the King of France – albeit through bastardy – he was in high favour with the French who consorted with the Barbary pirates (much to the disgust of their great enemy, Spain). Sauvage was also held in high esteem by the rulers of Islam, the Deys and Beys, and the Grand Turk himself, Hamid I, in Constantinople, for once Sauvage had saved the Grand Turk from a poisoning attempt. Thereafter he had supplied the Sultan with the pick of the women whom he abducted from every coast in Europe, putting into Constantinople every four or five months with one dozen or more voluptuous, white-skinned women to titillate the Sultan's sexual appetite. Now, Sauvage was assessing the girl who stood weeping before him, and he was thinking of the other captives in the hold, mostly Cornishmen and women, and a few children, who had been kidnapped from St Michael's Mount only an hour or so before.

The bobbing torch on the shore had alerted his look-out man as the ship was rounding the point ready to set sail for Algiers, and, thinking that they would surprise smugglers and get themselves some free brandy, they had sent out the small boat. Instead, they had captured one man and one girl, but by the looks of the girl she was worth more than a few kegs of spirit. She was one of the most beautiful females Sauvage had ever seen, for she held herself proudly despite her tears, and her colouring was superb. Her skin was soft and white as lily of the valley, her hair was flamboyant red, and her breasts, well, they were truly magnificent. Heavy, plump and rounded. He knew exactly how his men had felt at sight of her, especially after their long sojourn at sea. There was no one as radiant as this in the hold, nor had been for months.

Cassia looked up, aware of his scrutiny. 'What are you going to do with me?' she said, her voice low. 'You have murdered my friend and now I suppose you will kill me, too.'

'Kill you, mam'selle?' He spoke to her in perfect English, much to her astonishment. 'Kill such beauty, such grace? Do you think me a philistine? No, *ma doucette*, there is a far sweeter fate for you. And your – friend – is not dead. He will survive.' Turning aside, he rapped out an order to his men, who immediately disbanded. 'You will not share the hold with the scum who reside there at this moment. You will follow me.' He gestured to her to walk behind him.

'No!' she cried, but he gripped her by the wrist, pulling her along with such force that she almost lost her footing. 'Where are you taking me?' she cried. 'You cannot do this! It is against the law – King George will send his soldiers after you – you will be punished – the Lord Lieutenant of Cornwall will –'

He yanked her wrist so hard that she yelped with the pain. 'You waste your breath with all these complaints, *doucette*. No one can touch me. We have no master, no laws excepting our own, and I for myself make my own laws. Your King would be as likely to arrest me as he would a donkey . . .' He grinned, oblivious to her pain, his white teeth flashing. Cassia swung out at him with her free hand, hitting his cheek. He laughed again, dragging her through a small doorway and into a luxuriously furnished cabin. She was startled by its comfortable appearance: this she had not expected. Forgetting to protest for a moment, she looked around, eyes wide. The scent of beeswax filled the air, oaken panelling gleamed, rich tapestries hung on one wall and paintings in ornate frames on another. And surely those were priceless Bow figurines on that cabinet? Then understanding gripped her. Of course, he was a pirate, a brigand, and all this was his loot. Stolen, all these beautiful objects, from innocent, helpless people who had never done him any harm. How many had he murdered so that he could steal their property? Disgust consumed her, and revulsion. He still held her by the wrist, but she managed to turn half away from him, her mouth set. What a life he lived, preying on innocents, looting, snatching poor decent people from their homes to sell them in slave markets!

Her eyes fell on the handsome bed which dominated the room; it was richly-draped with heavily embroidered arras, there were fur rugs cast across it, the pillows were covered by spotless ivory lawn fringed with lace. Nausea rose in her at the thought of the poor wretched girls who must have been dragged to that bed and subjected to unspeakable assaults, even as he was now dragging her towards it . . .

'I will die before you touch me!' she cried as he swung her on to the bed so roughly that her teeth snapped together.

To her fury, he laughed again, standing legs astride, hands on hips, surveying her discomfiture.

'Touch you, *doucette*? Touch you? Nay, you have me wrong. No one deflowers the Sultan's gifts. A red-haired, white-skinned virgin will please him more than a casket of gold . . . and by the way you were holding off that buffoon on the shore, I am willing to vow that you are still undefiled.'

The shame of this intimate pronouncement made her blush painfully. She lowered her head, looking away, not wanting him to see her embarrassment. Then his first words broke through her shame: 'the Sultan's gift'. What did he

73

mean? Could it be that – no, he would not dare! No one could do that – it was wrong, illegal, *unbelievable*. She must ask him what he meant.

He grinned at her question. 'Are you so naive, *doucette*? We steal slaves, to sell them, not for our amusement but for a living. You will go direct to the Sultan's harem: he is always eager for new concubines, and although he has some five hundred women, he is always in readiness for more. White skins, maidenheads, intrigue him above all . . .' Sauvage spoke so casually that she could scarcely believe her ears. Concubines, five *hundred* women – and he – she . . .

She gave a little moan of horror, which he chose to disregard. Going to the cabinet in one corner, he poured brandy into two chased silver goblets, handing her one which she immediately dashed out of his grip. It flew across the cabin, spilling its contents on one of the tapestries. She recalled how she had vowed never to destroy again, and she began to sob, her body shuddering, her head throbbing from the blow she had received earlier.

Unheeding, Captain Sauvage drank his brandy, replacing the goblet on the salver. This chit of a girl was having an odd effect on him; why, he did not know. However, he had no intention of doing anything other than handing her to the Sultan once they reached Constantinople, and, until then, she would stay in his cabin or locked in one of the rooms in his house in Algiers. She was too precious to risk being damaged, or lost. If he felt in need of physical comforts, he could use one of the women in the hold, as he usually did. Big, clumsy fisherwomen who stank of the sea they might be, but they had their own particular charm. And necessity drove one to many unpalatable deeds. Like slave dealing, for example, and as to the manner in which he had begun that, he did not wish to think of it. First and foremost, he was a sea captain, in possession of a proud flotilla of vessels that pirated from coast to coast, his main ship being *The Poseidon*, which was at this moment being refitted in Algiers. A brazen Spanish galley had skimmed its stern, damaging one of the masts, and this was now being repaired. For this expedition, he was using an Algerian vessel, a polacca-chebek with a daunting array of lateen and square-rigged sails for speed and efficiency.

The girl's sobs drew his attention back to her. Her rounded white breasts were virtually naked, she seemed to have forgotten that her bodice had been ripped wide open. Her luxuriant flaming hair billowed over her white shoulders like spun silk. He noticed her tiny feet peeping out from the hem of her skirt, one of them bare, for a boot had been lost during her abduction. The sight of the delicate, shapely arch and heel gave him a strange feeling, an entirely new sensation which he could not recall having felt before. Impatiently, he tried to analyse it; then he stopped himself. The less he thought of her the better; the Sultan's delight and gratitude would far outweigh any brief pleasure he, Sauvage, might get out of seducing her. And if one had any sense, one wished to please Hamid I – not that it was fear which prompted Sauvage to keep the Sultan in good humour. Far from it, for his own position as one of the most powerful renegade sea captains alive ensured that Hamid I wished similarly to keep *him* happy. There were few non-Muslims who had attained such a close and amiable friendship with Hamid I. Sauvage kept the Sultan supplied with beautiful women, in return for which Hamid gave Sauvage free, unhindered access to those waters over which he had jurisdiction.

Sauvage realized that he had been standing staring at the girl for far too long. She had now stopped weeping, and was staring back at him, spine rigid, head high. Her jaw was clenched, as were her fists, as if she still expected to be raped. Yes, the Sultan would be intrigued by such spirit: where was the pleasure if all women were submissive in bed? Sauvage grinned at the thought of the Sultan seeing this girl for the first time, and his reactions to her Junoesque body. Hamid I would lean forward, his expression lascivious, he would run his tongue over his lips, his mouth would curve in a smile. When the girl had been led away by the other concubines, to be prepared for her place in the harem, Sauvage and the Sultan would dine and talk business, then Sauvage would be given the pick of those concubines who no longer interested Hamid.

After months at sea, with only captive women smelling of sardines and the filthy hold of *The Poseidon*, sweet indeed would be his sojourn in Constantinople . . .

'Why do you stare at me so?' Cassia cried, her eyes flashing. 'Why do you not just get it over with? You mean to rape me, whatever you say. I can see it in your eyes, your face. You are vile, despicable, the lowest vermin I have ever met!'

Sauvage arched one black brow. 'Indeed, *chérie*, there are far worse than I, of that I assure you. Obviously, you have led a sheltered youth, and have travelled little, and know even less, or you would not be misled into imagining that I am so unwholesome.' He paused. Why was he explaining himself to her in this way, trying to impress her with his integrity? What did she matter to him? Some silly chit stupid enough to meet her man in an isolated spot on the coast – she deserved all she got. Why should he feel any pity for her? She was like all the rest – like Martia . . . He clenched his fists tightly, a spasm of pain crossing his face. No, he would not think of *her*. He had vowed to forget her perfidy, the way she had deceived him repeatedly. Women were not to be trusted: they must be kept in their places: bed, or before the stove, beneath their man's heel. To allow them any trust was to invite the treachery which Martia had dealt him . . .

He said no more to his furious victim. Turning on his heel, he strode out of the cabin, locking the door behind him. Let her stew. It would quieten her temper. How dared she keep accusing him of wanting to rape her? He had better taste than that, by God!

As the door closed behind him, Cassia knew a moment of searing anger, then she sank back against the pillows, her eyes shut. She had been so sure that he would force himself upon her, and, when he had not done so, she was consumed by an assortment of emotions which she now tried to analyse. Relief was there, certainly, and bitter resentment at his mockery, but mingled with them was a surprising feeling of loss. She had been prepared to vent all her hatred and contempt in battle with her handsome captor, and now that he had deliberately turned his back on her, she felt a disconcerting sense of deprivation that she did not understand.

Her thoughts turned to Charles, viciously kicked and tortured by Sauvage's men. Charles, for whom she had longed and yearned for so many months . . . Charles, who did not care a rap for her. The bitter knowledge that her father had been right about her suitor added a fresh wave of wretchedness to Cassia's grief. To be captured and sold into slavery with a man who loved you was one thing. To be taken prisoner and degraded for the sake of a trickster who had contemptuously used your love and trust for his own ends was another. The knowledge that she had made an irrevocable fool of herself chafed Cassia's proud spirit almost more than the misery of lost love or the desolate vistas of her future as a pirate's slave.

There was no doubt in her mind that all hope of rescue was fruitless. She would never see her aunt again. Not ever. Julitta would think that she had deserted her, would imagine that she had put her lover first (for, if the story of Charles's presence at The Three Feathers was told by Bessie, it would naturally be assumed that Cassia had eloped). Sickness rose in her. To have her aunt, Bessie, all of them, thinking that she had been treacherous, was more than she could bear. She thought of Julitta waking, calling for her, of the discovery that she had gone, of Doctor Hookly trying to explain to his patient . . . She shivered, pulling the rugs more closely around her. Never to see Julitta again, never to see Penwellyn, Printemps, her friends in Cornwall, never to ride on the moors again, the sea breeze whipping her hair, the gulls crying high in the blue. Acid tears bit behind her lids, scoring her cheeks. There was no respite from grief; she must endure it though it crushed her.

Exhausted by weeping, she curled into a ball and slept at last. When she woke, silver light was filling the room. She was still alone, and she could hear the ship creaking and sighing like a living being. There was an undulating motion which had not been present when she fell asleep. They were at sea. God knows where, for she had no idea how long they had been moving. They might still be in the Channel; she really could not tell, and a glance out of the tiny window showed nothing but water and far off horizon.

She was squatting on the bed, legs folded under her, when the door swung open and Sauvage stepped into the room. White-faced, she looked up at him, dreading what she would see. He looked as clean and relaxed as the previous night – had he slept at all? Certainly he did not look tired. His eyes were as brilliant a green as she remembered them, his face as handsome. He smiled, lifting one brow arrogantly.

'Mam'selle is hungry?'

By way of reply, she turned her head away from him as haughtily as she could manage.

'I asked if mam'selle were hungry?' Jerking out his arm, he cupped her chin in one strong brown hand, forcing her to look at him. She tried to twist out of his grip but he was too powerful. Teeth clamped together, she stayed mute. 'So mam'selle is sulking.' It was a statement, not a question. She was almost driven to spit a reply, but managed to contain it. She stayed silent until he went out, then she began to cry again.

It was dark when he returned, a salver of food with him. She smelt freshly-roasted beef, Cornish cream in a huge jug, fruit, cheeses, and her mouth watered uncontrollably. He saw her expression and laughed.

'Mam'selle is still on hunger strike? Well, if so, I shall eat for two.' And he proceeded to do just that, with the air of one who had not a care in the world. Slice after slice of the juicy beef disappeared, then the cheeses and the fruit, on which he ladled lavish amounts of the clotted cream (where had he stolen the food from? she thought. The same poor people who now languished in the ship's hold?) There was wine too, and this he drank with obvious enjoyment, while she watched, her throat tightening, her lungs inhaling the delicious odours of meat and wine.

Having finished the entire repast, he wiped his mouth

78

on a lace-edged kerchief, grinned at her with one brow arched, as if to say, 'Silly girl, but you will come to your sense,' and then he left, again locking the door behind him.

She did not see him again that night. She slept a little, waking with a start, imagining there was some monstrous animal about to devour her. Curling up, she became too hot under the fur rugs, then she felt sick with hunger and had to walk up and down, taking deep breaths to stop herself from vomiting. In all, she had three hours of fitful slumber before morning and then the Captain was stepping into the room with another tray of food. To her embarrassment, her stomach gurgled, and he laughed out loud.

'Ready to submit now, *ma petite*? Or is it still war? Those beautiful breasts will shrink and hang like an old woman's, and that radiant hair will become like straw, but if that is what you want,' he shrugged his shoulders as she again refused to eat. Ignoring her, he reached for a leg of chicken and bit ravenously into it.

Cassia bit on her lips until she tasted blood. If she could go on refusing food, she would die, and then this agony would end. She would not have to think of her aunt, lonely and believing she had been deserted, of Charles's treachery, of her own terrible fate – she prayed that she would not be weak and beg for food.

She swallowed and her throat rasped. She half-closed her eyes, flinching at the discomfort. Before she could open them again, she felt a hand on her arm. Her lids flew open in shock. He was only inches from her, his breath warm on her cheek. Instinctively, she drew back, ready for battle. Seeing that she was not ill, as he had thought, he returned to the cabinet on which he had placed the tray of food and began to eat once more. Fighting back nausea, praying that her stomach would stay silent, she leaned against the pillows, pulling the rugs up round her neck. With an effort, she managed to forget where she was and to think only of her aunt; straining her mind, she imagined herself in Julitta's bedroom, looking down at the sick woman, explaining that she had never meant to leave her alone . . .

79

'Are you asleep, *doucette?*' the voice was surprisingly gentle. Her lids fluttered, but she did not respond. He sighed, as if impatient at her stupidity, then he was gone and she could relax. The first thing she saw on opening her eyes was the tray at the foot of the bed – and he had left some food on it. Ham, kidneys, eggs, and a flask of wine. Waves of hunger washed over her, to be followed by the thought that she could not, on any terms, eat food given her by this verminous slave dealer – no, she would not touch it! She would die first. But a little voice said: you will die anyway if you do not eat soon . . .

Would he notice if she ate just a little from each plate? Indeed could she bring herself to eat any of it? She reached for the dish of kidneys, but their smell seemed strong and sickly to her and she put them back. How had she ever brought herself to eat them in the past? Breaking off a chunk of bread, she dipped it in the scrambled eggs and ate that. Then she drank some of the wine. Afterwards she felt like a traitor to her aunt, as if somehow she had let her down. Sliding under the rugs, she slept.

His voice woke her. The tray had been removed but she had not heard him do it. How long had she been asleep? She had no idea. For all she knew, days might have passed. She was covered in a light film of sweat, and her head ached. 'Aunt Julitta,' she moaned, turning restlessly.

'Doucette?' Captain Sauvage was by her side, looking down at her, his beautiful face impassive, his eyes brilliant jewels. Or was it he? In her fevered mind, he was a statue in a strange heathen temple, his eyes real emeralds, glittering but devoid of feeling, and she was the offering placed at his feet to propitiate him. If she did not submit to him, her aunt would die, she would die, the whole village would be wiped out – she must submit! She tried to move towards him, but her legs and arms were like lead. She was bound as if by ropes, her arms pinioned to her sides. The jewel-eyed god laughed at her discomfiture, turning his back coldly. She was not pleasing him! Now she must die.

Vincent Sauvage watched his beautiful captive with

annoyance. Barely in his charge, and she had to fall sick of a fever. Dispassionately, he felt her pulse, placed a cool hand on her forehead. She was burning up. If he had forced her to eat three days ago this would never have happened. But thank God he had kept her here in his cabin and not in the hold, or she would have had no chance of survival.

He had learned all he knew of fevers from the inspired Arab physicians on the Barbary Coast. Mutim Benali had successfully treated raging fevers by cooling his patients, whereas others insisted on keeping the patient as warm as possible. Sauvage came to a decision; flinging back the bed-covers, taking in Cassia's beautiful body in one quick glance. How easily he could take advantage of her now, if he so wished. Cutting away her tattered clothes, he removed them until she lay completely naked, her voluptuous curves shiny with sweat. Mentally recording that he had never seen such beauty, that the Grand Turk would be stunned by such loveliness, he realized that he must begin work immediately to save the girl's life.

Sending Ahmek, his devoted body servant, to fetch fresh water, he bathed Cassia's body with strips of clean linen, then, with Ahmek's help, they wrapped the girl in wet clothes, from neck to ankles. Once, twice, her lids fluttered, she moaned, but she did not seem to know who they were or where she was. Her arm flailed, hitting Sauvage on the bridge of the nose, so that he had to bite back an oath. Ahmek grinned, his black face creasing, his huge square teeth shining.

'Slave much beaut'ful. Much please Sultan,' he said, smirking at his master. 'He much happy with gift from you. Give big reward, eh?' Ahmek leered again, winking. Sauvage said nothing, his face grim.

Ahmek had been his servant for ten years. He was totally loyal, being allowed many liberties which Sauvage would not allow his other servants. The Captain had saved the black from being massacred when he was a boy of ten and in the service of the Bey of Elum Iri who had been overthrown by his nephew, and all his family and servants slaughtered. Ahmek had been kneeling, waiting for the sword to decapitate him when Sauvage and his men, sent by the Sultan to put down the rebellion, had arrived at the Bey's palace.

Ahmek had looked up, eyes like discs, as Sauvage entered the execution chamber with his sword unsheathed. The rebels had fled, Ahmek had kissed his saviour's feet, calling him a god, blessing him for saving his life, swearing that he would serve him for the rest of his days.

The evil nephew had been captured and executed by the Sultan, and the Bey's son had been assured of his patrimony. That was one of the first tasks Sauvage had been given by the Sultan, and many more had followed it. It was not unusual for pirate renegades to be of non-Muslim origins; many were white-skinned, of English, French or other races, some were gentlemen, one had given up piracy to become an important prelate in his own lands. What was unusual was for a non-Muslim to be so highly esteemed by the Sultan.

'Yes, she is beautiful, Ahmek,' Sauvage now said as he gestured to his servant to hand him drying cloths. His face revealed nothing of his inner feelings. Since Martia, he had never let his emotions show concerning any female, whether she were slut or princess, and certainly not in front of his men – not even Ahmek.

Cassia was now dried, and her temperature a little lower. Sauvage covered her with a fresh lawn sheet. She looked like a vestal virgin, her face rosy with fever and surrounded by the tumbled russet hair, the white lawn covering her from neck to toes. So pure. So virginal. A perfect offering for a Sultan . . . Sauvage set his mouth in a grim line. He would not think of her as anything other than the Sultan's property. She was to be pampered, nursed, but only because of her future importance to the Sultan. For no other reason was he now caring for her so solicitously, he told himself.

When she was well, he would feel relief, because he had no desire to disappoint Hamid I. This superb gift which he would be able to deliver with his own hands would create an even stronger bond between the two men, between Turkey and France. This girl might even bear Hamid an heir, for, although the Sultan possessed five hundred women, he had only one son. The concubine who gave birth to the Grand Turk's son was powerful indeed, and if it proved to be this girl, then the Grand Turk would not forget.

Sauvage was ambitious. He would not deny that. The strange twists and turns of fate had mapped out his career as a pirate captain on the Barbary Coast. And he had sworn that if this were irrevocably his destiny then he would succeed in it. Reared to the story of his ancestor's bastardy, of how he might have been a prince, or even king, had he sprung from the legitimate line of Francis I, he had determined never to be in a position where others could tread on him. Only his mother might have made him return to brave the hostile shores of France, but she was dead. His one regret was that he could not, being a renegade, visit her grave. But he sent money to his cousins to ensure that there were always fresh flowers where she lay.

Strange that he should think of his mother now as he watched the sleeping girl on the bed. Perhaps it was something to do with her colouring, for his mother's hair had been reddish-brown, her eyes blue.

'Take away the bowls, Ahmek,' he snapped, his brows drawn together in a frown. When the negro had obeyed, Sauvage sat at his rosewood desk, brilliant green eyes fixed on the girl. The emergency treatment had brought down her fever, but he was insufficiently experienced to diagnose her illness; he could not say if it would return, as some fevers did. But he would be watchful. Whatever the cost, this gift must reach the Grand Turk in excellent condition.

CHAPTER SIX

'Eat? Of course I shall eat! We have to protect our investment, don't we? It is *so* important to please the Sultan,' Cassia said, sarcasm making her tone cutting as Sauvage offered her a dish of salt beef. They had been at sea for some time now, and the fresh food acquired on the Cornish coast was gone. It was back to salted meat, tough and unpalatable, and biscuits so hard they made the jaw ache. Fortunately, there was wine, and tea, although Ahmek had told Cassia that the crew preferred their rum ration, favouring this throat-scorching spirit above anything else.

Sauvage arched his brows at her tartness. When she had eaten the meat, chewing it repeatedly, and making faces, he said, wryly, 'It is good to see you so much stronger, mam'selle.'

'But of course,' she snapped. 'There will be more gold in it for you, will there not? And esteem, too. If I look thin and pale, who will buy me? Ahmek tells me that the Sultan prefers his women well-fleshed, so naturally we must ensure that I am fattened up.' She did not look at him, but kept her face stony.

In other circumstances, she would have been grateful for the way he had nursed her and saved her life – but how could she show gratitude when he had thought only of saving his investment, and had acted out of purely selfish motives? She had made friends with Ahmek – who was eager to converse with her even if his English was fractured, picked up from listening to his master over the years. From Ahmek she learned that Charles was still alive, but crammed with the other wretched prisoners in the hold. It was Ahmek, too, who had told her how carefully the Captain had tended her during her fever, bathing her and hand-feeding her chicken broth. She could not remember any of this. From the time she had eaten the bread dipped in eggs, to the moment when she had opened her eyes four days later, there was a complete blank in her memory. At first she had felt cold horror at the vision of Sauvage stripping off her clothes and bathing her – even if this vital action had saved her life. With Ahmek, it was different. He was genial, full of chuckles; she had learned that he was a eunuch, so she had nothing to fear from him. It was this fact more than anything that hastened the development of their friendship.

Sauvage sat at his desk to eat, washing down the inedible food with two draughts of wine. He did not look round at his captive and his black servant as they sat together, talking and eating, but he was listening to what they were saying.

'Captain he to inherit much great fortune,' Ahmek grinned. 'He much great friend – like son – of Captain Dash, many years now. Dash he old man, bones crooked –' Ahmek held up his hands, the fingers hooked. 'He have much great pain, cannot pirate now. He give our master his ships, his share of Barbary Coast. He retire to homeland and sickbed.' Ahmek flashed two rows of enormous white teeth, his brows moving up and down significantly.

Cassia listened, deciding that she would not sound pleased at hearing this information. Instead, she said coldly. '*Your* master, Ahmek, but certainly not *mine*.' She fancied that Sauvage made a movement of anger at her words, but she had no intention of letting him see that she had noticed. No, she would not give him the satisfaction of knowing she cared one jot for his feelings. He certainly cared nothing for hers.

Undaunted, Ahmek continued. 'We go now Algiers, you know? There Dash waits. We have much great dining, feastings, celeb-, celeb-' – his broad black face crinkled as he searched for the right word.

Sauvage turned, his face expressionless, 'Celebrations.'

Cassia did not look up; she sipped her wine with an aloof air, keeping her eyes carefully averted from the Captain's section of the cabin. If he was angry at her rudeness, then that was too bad. He would just have to be angry. She owed

85

him nothing; he was a slave dealer, the lowest of vermin; her flesh crawled when she thought of all the poor suffering wretches who had passed through his hands . . . Nor did she hesitate to say as much whenever the opportunity arose, for she knew she had a spurious safety in being so valuable to Sauvage. He could hardly damage her, whatever she did or said, after all the trouble he had taken with her so far. Sometimes he had tried to reason with her, to make her see his side of the story; often, he flung her a shrivelling look, which she would return in full measure and without fear. Sometimes their hatred of one another was an almost palpable thing in the air between them. But for this man, she would still have been with her dear aunt in Penwellyn. The loss of Julitta was a constant ache inside her.

'Ah yes, Captain-master, celebr-ay-ay' – Ahmek grinned sheepishly, shrugging his huge black shoulders. 'Much great funning,' he managed finally. Cassia wanted to smile, but succeeded in keeping her mouth still. She would certainly not let Sauvage see that she could be amused.

'Much great nice is Captain Dash – he ver' fond of our master,' Ahmek went on. 'Once, our master save his life when he chase by Spanish. Brave, our master, no fears, face four galleons with his one ship, straight on, while Dash's ship recover position. Then they two together fight Spanish. Many dead, much great loot.' Ahmek rubbed his hands together. 'Emerald, pearl, gold,' His eyes rolled.

Sauvage stood up suddenly, making Cassia start. 'That's enough, Ahmek,' he rapped, his face cold.

The eunuch's merry face fell. 'Yes, Captain-master.'

Sauvage looked at them both for a few moments, then, reaching for his spyglass, he went to the upper decks. When he had gone, Ahmek made a wry face at Cassia. She grinned, and they ended up laughing together. It was the first time she had laughed out loud since her capture, and although she must remember reality when the laughter faded, she felt better, stronger.

That night she slept soundly for the first time since her kidnapping. Sauvage, as usual, kept away during the night

– why, she did not know, for he had every right to sleep in his own bed or put up a hammock in one corner of the cabin where hooks had been placed for this very purpose. She would never have dreamed of asking him why he stayed away, of course, for that would have been tantamount to telling him she wanted his company at night. To ask him any question as to his whereabouts would display a curiosity that she had no desire to express. Curiosity meant interest, and interest was flattering, warm, caring, all the feelings which she did not want to admit she was beginning to feel for the aloof, handsome Frenchman.

He brought her in her breakfast, as usual, and she grimaced. Rock-like biscuits again, and goat's milk from one of the animals in the ship's manger. She would never get used to its musky scent, she thought, as she drank the frothing liquid hastily. Ahmek insisted that she drank it at least once a day; he said that it was a builder of strength, and she had no reason to doubt him. The biscuits were not so easy to swallow, and she found herself yearning for golden eggs in butter, and crisp toast thick with honey, for coffee with clotted cream.

Sauvage took his seat at his desk, betraying no emotion on his face. As he rarely spoke to her on these occasions, she wondered why he bothered to eat in here at all, but he always did so, bringing in each meal himself and then eating at the desk. Sometimes Ahmek joined them; sometimes not. The meals which Ahmek shared with them were, for Cassia, far lighter and happier, for he gossiped and teased her. Sauvage stayed silent, morose, whether or not Ahmek was there. He frowned on her camaraderie with the eunuch, or so she imagined, but it was only the comfort she elicited from this relationship that kept her from dwelling on her past miseries; her aunt at Penwellyn; her first love's betrayal. She had no wish to see another companion wrenched from her, for whatever reason. Sauvage could frown on them all he wished, she would go on chatting to Ahmek, hearing his sea tales, his inept jokes, enjoying his fumbling attempts at kindliness.

Half way through his breakfast, Sauvage suddenly spoke. Cassia was so startled that she stopped chewing, and stared at him.

'We are approaching enemy waters – that is, Spain. If you should hear the sound of guns, or cries, it will only be because we are defending ourselves. You must not worry that you will be harmed, or in danger. I am quite confident that we shall reach Algiers safely – as we always do.'

'Guns?' Cassia gasped, her stomach turning over.

'A little light skirmishing at the most, mam'selle. Do not alarm yourself. My men are amongst the most experienced on the high seas today. We have had ample opportunity to prove ourselves. The Spanish galleys are cumbersome and slow, they are built for grandeur not for speed. If we are fortunate, we shall capture one of them – we often do – and then we share out the prizes. This is the custom. Spanish ships often have chests of materials, silks and velvets, furs and leather goods, jewellery, spices. There may be a new dress for you – which will be a welcome change from that sheet, I am sure, *doucette*.' He grinned, eyeing the draped white linen which Ahmek himself had stitched into the semblance of a toga.

'Prizes!' she retorted scornfully. 'You mean loot – stolen loot!' She looked away from him, pushing aside her half-eaten breakfast.

' 'Tis often loot taken by the Spanish from another ship, *doucette*. And they take their turn in attacking us. Do you imagine that we prey only on innocents? Spaniards do their own fair share of looting and piracy – they are famed for it. Religiously and politically, they are our mortal enemies; they oppose the Barbary corsairs and the Grand Turk. They are callous, without principle, their lust for – for gold is immeasurable.' Sauvage's eyes had gone cold. He was remembering the Spanish Captain with whom Martia had run off, taking their baby daughter. Two years later, he had heard of their deaths in an epidemic of fever which had swept through Cadiz. Yes, he had good reason to hate the Spanish.

'Then you and the Spanish have much in common!' Cassia said icily, turning her back on the Captain, and reaching for one of the books which Ahmek had brought her. She turned the thick parchment pages without seeing the words imprinted on them. She heard Sauvage stand up, but still she refused to look at him. In her mind's eye, she imagined him surveying her, his brilliant green eyes like cold jewels, lit by a fire which burned with an icy flame, his silky black hair drawn back neatly at his neck, his shirt spotless ivory lawn, grey kid breeches, gleaming black topboots. So much the gentleman and yet . . . Her heart began to pound; she could sense his gaze boring through her. Her cheeks flushed; she swallowed, staring hard at pages she did not see.

'Mam'selle,' he began, then he stopped. 'Mam'selle, can you not look at me when I speak to you?' His voice sounded almost pleading. Surprised, she did look, to catch an expression on his face which she had not seen there before. Her heart began to pound even harder, she was sure that he would see it through the thin cotton of her toga. She tensed, waiting for some kind of onslaught, verbal, maybe even physical, and then they both heard the sound of running feet above them, and voices calling out, '*Rais* Sauvage, *Rais* Sauvage, a galley, a galley!' Then he was gone, running up on deck with light feet, grabbing his sword from the desk as he passed.

The moment was forgotten in the panic of the next few minutes. Cassia heard feet pounding on the decks above, shouts, and then the ship was turning swiftly. After long seconds, she heard the sound of thunderous explosions which shook the timbers, more shouts, musket shots. She wanted desperately to know what was going on overhead, but Sauvage had not forgotten to lock the door even in his haste. She tried to imagine what her sudden appearance on deck would have meant to the harassed crew, the Spaniards themselves. If she could somehow get up there, call for aid to the Spanish, surely they would rescue her? She stood up, walking to the door, trying it, even though she had heard the key turn. She looked at the window – what if she could prise it open and lean out to call for help? Hope soared in her. Feeling round the tiny casement, she looked for an opening, a space where she could dig in her nails and pull open the framework. Surely there was some method of opening the window? But she could find no gap, and then she saw the nails hammered into the surrounding wood and her heart sank.

Curling up on the bed, she listened dully to the noise overhead. She could only pray that the Spaniards would win, that they would capture Sauvage's ship and free her.

The battle seemed to be endless. Shots and screams filled the air. She smelt the acrid choking odour of gunpowder, saw smoke drift past the glass. Soon after that, to her horror, a body dropped past the window, emitting a blood-curdling scream before the splash of water heralded its fall into the sea. She hoped it was one of Sauvage's men – or even Sauvage himself. Please, please let the Spanish win, she prayed.

Her body ached with tension, sweat beaded her brow. She had dug pits into her palms with her nails. Still the fighting continued. If this was a little skirmish, then she would hate to hear a real battle. Her head was throbbing, and the cabin had never seemed so airless, so hot.

When Ahmek returned, she was overjoyed to see him.

'Missy not scared? No need be scared. Over now. Spanish flee. We win,' he grinned.

'I thought it was never going to end!' Cassia cried.

'Ambush, missy. One ship come first, then two more. Trick, you know?' She nodded. '*Rais* Sauvage win. What else? He always win.' Ahmek grinned again, white teeth dazzling. Bring food now. You much great hungry. Nice food – taken from enemy.'

They dined on succulent meats and luscious candied fruits dripping with molten sugar. Comfits and sugared plums followed, and there was Spanish wine to wash it down. Sauvage looked almost amiable after his success, exchanging a few words with Cassia and Ahmek, smiling to himself as he ate, discussing the battle when Cassia asked what had happened.

'The *Jesu-Maria* is one of the most feared Spanish ships, and she now lies at the bottom of the sea. It is not the first time we have fought her, but before she escaped, or we have had to withdraw. My own ship, *The Poseidon*, was damaged by her a few months ago . . . she sent a shot across her bows.' As if realizing that he had been too forthcoming, Sauvage fell silent, pouring out more wine for himself and drinking it, his face thoughtful.

'We hate Spanish. They greedy, arro-, arro-' – Ahmek's face creased, Cassia finishing the word for him. 'Yes, arro-gant. Take what not theirs – greedy hands . . .' He glanced at his master, as if fearful of having said too much. Cassia followed his gaze, seeing a muscle tighten in Sauvage's jaw. What did Ahmek mean? She must ask him when they were next alone.

Sauvage's now grim mood ensured that the celebratory atmosphere evaporated. Shaking his head, Ahmek cleared up the dishes, and took them away to be washed. Cassia curled up beneath the covers to read. She had found a book on England's Kings and Queens, probably looted, but it helped her to think of her homeland, to feel closer to her aunt. She had read five pages, forgetting that Sauvage was still in the room, when he stood up suddenly, making her gasp. He glanced at her with scorn as he walked past her to the shelves by the bed and extracted a heavy tome on navigation. Then, as if she were not there, he sat on the edge of the bed and began slowly to turn the pages. She curled into as tight a ball as she could, as far away from him as possible. She did not wish to draw attention to herself. Conscious of the unleashed strength, the virile power of the man beside her, she tried to concentrate on her reading, but found that her mind was no longer in a receptive mood. Determined to look occupied, she continued to turn the pages at carefully measured intervals. Some thirty minutes went by, and she began to ache from keeping so still. If only he would go, and yet she did not want to be alone . . .

If only he did not look so grim, so forbidding, she could talk to him as she did to Ahmek. But she feared his reactions, his anger, his contempt. She had said many vindictive things to him, all of which he deserved of course; nonetheless, not being a spiteful person by nature, she felt ashamed of having been so malicious. He had every right to respond similarly . . . She now realized that by being rude to him, she had in some strange way given him power over her. If she could apologize, maybe this power would be weakened? But that would not happen. Yes, he had been courteous but cool. Yes, he had nursed her when she was fevered, but this did not make him a good man: he was still a pirate, a slaver; he still kidnapped defenceless innocents to sell them. Ahmek had told her of the infamous *bagnios* where the slaves were kept until they were auctioned, and he had told her how the women were divided into two types, the common, and the class to which she herself belonged, *murtafa'at*, or first class. What were the *bagnios* like, she wanted to know. Ahmek had shrugged, splaying his hands, pale palms uppermost.

'Death better,' he had said. 'Dirty. No food, drink. Rats, vermin.' He had shuddered. 'Beatings, whips, cruel overseers. You glad you not have go that place. Straight to harem you go – much soft beds, cushions, silk clothes, sherbert drinks, sweetmeats. No work, much laze. Sleep, eat. *Much* lucky.'

She had not answered. How could Vincent Sauvage, who seemed such a gentleman, have anything to do with this terrible trade? She could not understand it. Piracy she could have come to accept, but slavery?

'We shall be approaching the Regency soon,' Sauvage said, bringing her out of her thoughts.

'The Regency?'

'Algiers is known by that name, and has been since the days of Kheir-ed-Din, or Barbarossa as you may know him. It means Redbeard, but there is some controversy as to whether the soubriquet belonged to him, or to his brother, Baba Aroudj. Some say that Kheir-ed-Din did not have a red beard, but only red hair, while others say that the Sultan who ruled at the time most definitely referred to him as our red-bearded Admiral. So perhaps we shall never know the truth.'

Cassia shivered. Barbarossa. The most feared pirate who had ever lived. She knew him from schooldays. He was a giant of a man in every way, and one who had become a legend in his own lifetime. So he had lived in Algiers . . . This knowledge served to inform her of the strange place to which she was being taken, a place so different from any she had yet known. The haunt of pirates and renegades, men without scruples or morals. She would never again meet normal people with whom she could make friends and share pleasant hours. She would never see England again, never know how Julitta was progressing, whether she was better now, or worse. Tears bit behind her lids; she fought their insistent pressure. Sauvage must not see her crying.

'I have no wish for trouble, and if others in Algiers see you, then there will be questions, offers to buy. I want none of that. While you are in Algiers, you will wear purdah, the black robe and veil worn by Muslim women in public. Is that understood, mademoiselle?'

Ahmek had told her about purdah, the enveloping robe and veil, and she thought that it sounded hot and suffocating in the present warm weather. How dare Sauvage tell her to hide behind a veil! She was a Christian, not a Muslim, and she was nobody's slave.

'I shall wear what I please,' she said haughtily.

'Your sheet, *doucette*?' he grinned, and she blushed, remembering that the draped toga-like affair was all she had now.

'I shall make a gown – I can sew, you know. Surely you have some bolts of cloth somewhere on board? What of the loot from the *Jesu-Maria*? You did not let it sink without first stripping its storeroom, did you?' Sarcasm hardened her voice.

'*Doucette*, if I had a full court outfit for you to wear, you

93

would still don purdah while we stop in Algiers. You have no comprehension of what the place is like – the men . . .'

'Are low vermin like you, Captain Sauvage?' she flung, trying not to wince as his eyes glittered with fury. He tossed down the book he had been reading, and leaned towards her. Instinctively, she drew back.

'Have I harmed you, mademoiselle? Have I whipped you or misused you in any way? Indeed, I thought that I had cared for you most solicitously – that I had actually saved your life. Forgive me if I came to the wrong conclusion.' In one graceful movement, he rose to his feet, and left the cabin, locking the door behind him as always.

Cassia felt ashamed the moment he had gone. But she was not going to apologize. Yes, in his own way, he had been good to her, nursed her, seen that she ate, but hadn't it all been for his own selfish ends? Had she been fat, ugly, shapeless, she would have spent the last weeks in the hold, crammed together in the dark with Charles and the other poor kidnapped wretches, manacled, never seeing so much as a patch of sunlight, vulnerable to every known disease. She thought of that carefully, of such horrors, of the trade in which Vincent Sauvage indulged, of the suffering and agonies of those whom he bought and sold like cattle. She let the full harrowing knowledge fill her mind, and then she put her hands over her face.

However much she considered the trade he was in, the fate which he had decided for her, there was something she could no longer deny. Oh she had fought it, for days now, trying with logic and reasoning to subdue it. But it was getting stronger, not weaker. Now she could barely keep it out of her eyes, her face. She felt warm when he was near; she wanted his strong arms to capture and hold her, his mouth on hers, his body crushing hers.

Slave dealer. Pirate. Renegade. But she was falling in love with him.

The heat was becoming more intense. Even late at night, it drummed against her body insistently. Shut away in this stuffy cabin she had begun to crave fresh air on her face, space to move, to walk. As they came into an even warmer climate, she thought she would melt from the heat. She could not concentrate to read; her mind felt dull, heavy. Ahmek suggested an excellent solution.

'Missy bathe?' he said one morning as Cassia was fanning herself with an ostrich feather fan which Sauvage had given her. 'Ahmek bring barrel, water, soap, yes?' His fat kindly face shone. He did not suffer from the heat, but he could see that she did.

'Bathe?' The delights of such an indulgence swiftly overcame her desire for privacy. 'Oh that would be marvellous – but can you assure me I shall not be disturbed, Ahmek?'

'Yes, missy. Master on deck two hour. You have long, 'freshing bathe, yes?'

'Oh please!'

He carried in a large empty barrel, its upper half cut away, and filled it with jugs of water. Having handed her scented soap, towels, and a comb, he withdrew, grinning, locking the door behind him. Cassia savoured the moment, dipping her fingers in the water, then her whole hand and her arms. Then she let the crumpled toga fall to the floor, and climbed into the improvised tub. The water was a little below body temperature, and very refreshing. She splashed about happily, careful not to graze her elbows on the wood, and at first a little cautious of splinters. Time passed, and she began to relax. She soaped herself all over, once, then rinsed and soaped herself again, langorously, bobbing in the suds, toes pressing against the bottom of the barrel so that she did not sink beneath the surface of the water. She unwound, at ease for the first time since she had been so roughly kidnapped. She forgot her plight, forgot what was soon to happen to her. In her thoughts, she saw only Cornish moors jewelled with flowers and heard the gentle snort of Printemps as she rode towards Penwellyn where Aunt Julitta awaited them, standing strong and hale on the doorstep.

The noise of the cabin door shocked her out of her reverie. It had opened, and Sauvage stood there. She heard his inrush of breath, heard him apologizing. She turned quickly, to reach for the towel, but it was further than she had thought and she had exposed her breasts before she reached it. Her cheeks went bright pink, she crouched in the water, willing him to go, but he did not. He closed the door behind him, and stood watching her silently. She heard Ahmek's voice outside, calling, 'No, no, master, no – missy bathes!' but Sauvage did not pay any attention. He stepped towards her, stood over her, looking down at her full white breasts. Crossing her hands, she tried to cover herself, but he took her hand and raised it to his lips. She tried to drag her fingers away, and in doing so lost her footing, plunging beneath the surface of the water, coming up gasping for breath, her eyes filled with suds. Sauvage grasped her beneath the arms, wet and slippery as she was, and hauled her out of the barrel as lightly as if she were a child.

'No – *no*!' she gasped, struggling in his arms, but she might as well have been a child for all the resistance she had against his strength. He placed her on the bed, reached for the towel and began to rub her dry. Dimly, she remembered his having done this before, but when she could not say – perhaps during her illness. Unwillingly, she began to relax, to luxuriate in the attention. He was gentle, soothing, skilled; she could not have resisted him if she had tried.

'Did you know I was taking a bath?' she whispered, her voice husky, not really wanting to speak, wanting more than anything to submit to the deliciously comfortable and yet erotic sensations she was experiencing.

'No – Ahmek did not tell me. He was standing on watch, but he had fallen asleep, and I passed him before he knew it. I daresay he will never sleep on duty again.' He spoke against her cheek, then his mouth was on her forehead, her eyes, her chin, and finally on her lips. His were silky, soft yet penetrating; she wanted them to cover all of her, to kiss her everywhere, to whisper that he loved her, that she was his because of love, and not through some mercenary trading objective.

He had dropped the towel. She did not notice. The feelings sweeping through her obliterated everything else, who she was, where she had come from, how she had got here

– that most of all. He loved her, she knew it – he loved her as much as she loved him. Joy coruscated through her as his mouth brushed past hers, to her neck, where it planted soft kisses, and then lower, and lower still. She gave a tiny moan, and he half laughed.

'You have the most beautiful neck, *chérie*. It is soft and white as velvet, so kissable, so desirable. Why have you been so cruel to me? What have I done to harm you, *doucette*?'

He did not expect an answer, for what he did next made her sigh, not speak. His hands slid down to her hips, stroking them, caressing her stomach. He kissed the smooth yielding flesh there, and brushed against the auburn triangle of silken hairs so that an electric shock sprang right through her body. She abandoned herself eagerly, silently begging him to finish what he had begun. The motion of the sea was in her head again, the waves coursing backwards and forwards, forwards, backwards, carrying her with them, bearing her up high on the waves so that she was part of the white-flecked foam, the Sea God her lover . . .

Long moments of ecstasy passed, during which she found her feeling of relaxation becoming one of tension, her whole body tightening, coiling up like a spring, accompanied by wave after wave of subtly erotic feeling. How gentle yet sure was his touch; he did not have to fight her, as Charles had done. He was no brutal monster. She was willing, impatient, encouraging him silently. She lay back, her hair spread wide on the pillow as he brought her to a new peak of excitement, and then, when he knew she could stand no more, he moved up close against her, finding the entry to her body with no difficulty. There was no struggle, no clumsiness. He was inside her, hard, warm, pulsating, and all she was conscious of was a feeling of intense heat, of being stretched to the limit. Her cheeks flushed, she went warm all over; she moaned his name, and he kissed her face and neck, whispering that she was beautiful, that she was all he had ever wanted, that he could not resist her . . .

Her heart sang. He loved her, he needed her, he couldn't

97

resist her. He wouldn't sell her now, would he? No, how could he do that *now*? He would keep her with him, they were lovers for ever. Already she was weaving romantic dreams of their relationship, their future together . . . He would find that he loved her so desperately that he asked her to marry him, they would return to Penwellyn to let her aunt see that she was safe. They would have children – they would live near Penwellyn, Vincent would give up this terrible life of piracy . . .

And then even dreams fled her mind. Something was happening to her, something which had never happened before. It was the strangest sensation, growing, strengthening inside her, like invisible hands gripping her body. She could not escape it; nor did she want to. With every movement Vincent made, the feeling increased, until she was consumed by it, as if by ropes which were tightening round her, faster, faster. She gasped, she saw him looking down at her, his emerald eyes glowing with love, then she moved against him, and he responded by thrusting even deeper inside her so that she cried out.

He was breathing heavily, moving with ever-increasing power, but her own ecstasy was rising at a faster rate and she was going to explode, she knew it, she could feel it. When it came, it was the most uninhibited moment she had ever spent. She cared for nothing in that moment except the man making love to her, and the joy he had brought. For long seconds, the bliss was unendurable, then she was released, floating gently on the tips of the waves, like a feather, light and weightless.

Having seen to her needs, Sauvage allowed himself to share in the joy. He released his control, pressing closer to her, cradling her tightly to him, his mouth on hers as his own passion reached its height. 'Cassia,' he murmured her name, and she whispered back, 'Darling,' and then they lay together, glowing with love, while the ship sped on towards Algiers and their destiny.

CHAPTER SEVEN

Ahmek could not stop grinning as he served their midday meal. His eyes rolled, his cheeks plumped, his face was split by smile after smile. To look at him you would have thought that at the least they had got married. Cassia smiled back, caught up in his infectious pleasure; Sauvage seemed not to notice, but then he was more accustomed to his servant's moods. They ate, and drank more of the Spanish wine. It had flavour, but was harsher than the French wine they usually drank. This time, Sauvage did not sit apart to eat, but shared the bed with Cassia.

They devoured a dish of fruit between them, and nuts, Sauvage selecting the choicest for Cassia and popping them into her mouth. She looked up at him tenderly, incapable of keeping the love from her eyes. She thought of Charles, and realized that she had not understood the meaning of love before. She felt ashamed of her fickleness, but she recognized that what she had believed an eternal passion was in fact no more than infatuation and the awakening of physical desire. And with that knowledge came, for the first time, the ability to forget and forgive Charles Billings's betrayal.

When her treacherous saner, self whispered that Vincent, renegade and outlaw that he was, would inevitably betray her too, Cassia found that her mind closed itself in blank terror against the possibility. Imprisoned in the warm, magical world of the cabin, she felt as though they had known each other forever, and she knew that without his tender mockery and his stern angers, his unexpected laughter and his fierce loving to light her life, existence hereafter would be meaningless.

Ahmek was at the door, laden with empty dishes, when Sauvage said, 'When you return, Ahmek, bring the black robes from the chest in the storeroom, and the veil and some sandals, too. Choose a robe which will not be too long for Miss Cassia.'

Cassia had been still lost in thought, but at these last words her head flew up. 'You still insist that I am to wear this purdah, as you call it? Why can I not wear some of the gowns which you took from the *Jesu-Maria*?'

Sauvage smiled. 'I told you, Cassia *chérie*, I want no trouble. No feuding over my slave girl. The men's passions are easily roused, and if they see your beauty while we are in Algiers I shall not get a moment's peace. Once you are in Constantinople you can indulge your need for elaborate dress as often as you wish.'

Ahmek had not moved. He still stood by the door, laden with dishes, but the smile had died from his face. Cassia too looked very pale, and her hands were gripped together as the full meaning of Sauvage's words impressed themselves upon her mind.

'You – you are still going to s-sell me?' she gasped.

'Of course, my love. What else? Did I not warn you of your fate when we were still in English waters? I do not change my mind like a weathercock.'

'But – we – we – you –' Cassia fell back, deathly white, too shocked for tears.

Sauvage shrugged. 'You did not get misled by our little moment of passion did you, mademoiselle? Lust can never be mistaken for love, surely you know that?'

'*Lust?*' she breathed, an iciness spreading through her.

'What else?' he laughed lightly.

A sound made them turn. Ahmek was standing watching them, his eyes filled with reproach as they fell on his master. His mouth now grim, he turned on his heel and disappeared, shoulders hunched.

So Ahmek had thought it too . . . She had not been wrong to imagine Sauvage loved her. Cassia in that moment felt closer to the eunuch than she did to Sauvage. She did not speak – what could she say? Her mind felt numb, she could not think straight. She had given herself to this man, she loved him, and he was going to sell her. Was he made of steel, did he not have normal emotions? She hung her head, letting the pain swathe her, while her dreams collapsed.

Sauvage tried to laugh away the cruelty. He smiled, patted her shoulder, said that life in a harem was the epitome of luxury, that she would never have to worry again. Clothes, jewels, perfume, power, would all be hers if she captivated Hamid I.

'I have no wish to captivate him!' Cassia cried. 'I am not a piece of merchandise to be bought and sold. Nor am I a whore. I am a human being with feelings and emotions.'

'You will change your mind when you are in the harem, *doucette*. Life there is tranquil, unhurried, and to the woman who bears the Sultan's son is awarded power beyond her wildest dreams, even if she is the lowest of concubines. And you will be more than that. He might even marry you – he has not yet taken his full allowance of wives under the Muslim law.'

Fury boiled in her. 'What makes you suppose I am interested in luxury, or power for that matter?'

'You wish to have power over me, do you not?' He brushed her cheek with his fingertips.

'If you call love power, then that is so . . .'

'No one has ever captured me, *doucette*, and certainly no one has ever loved me. Love is a trap for the unwary – I want none of it.' His eyes hardened, his hand dropped from her face.

She looked at him, wondering why his eyes had become so cold. She knew nothing of Martia, nor was he going to tell her. It would only give her false hope. Let her think that he had never loved anyone, nor had a serious relationship with a woman; that was the best way. Let her go to the harem and forget him – as she soon would once the indolent luxury of the life there overtook her.

'So you are wary, are you Captain Sauvage?' She held her head proudly. 'Indeed, I would not have thought it – the way you responded to me only hours ago made me think of a *real* man, a *loving* man – not an animal without sensitivity. How can one who deals in human flesh remain wary?'

She had meant to wound, but he looked as nonchalant as ever, and shrugged his broad shoulders. She could not help noticing the muscles showing through his thin silk shirt.

'Life is not love, *doucette*. Indeed, the two rarely infringe one another. I can always end this way of life if I so choose it, but to disentangle oneself from the chains of love is another matter.'

'And how do you know about the chains of love if, as you claim, you have never loved a woman?' she flashed.

He was silent only a moment before saying. 'Men talk, so do women. It is not difficult to see what misery and grief can spring from loving. Kingdoms have collapsed because of it, wars have been fought, men slaughtered. It is wise to remain on the outside, to observe yet not to be a part, lest one gets burned.'

'I do not agree. No one can be wise without first having suffered, and loving is essential to life. Love means suffering – it is the ability to experience pain.'

'You sound very philosophical, *chérie*, but if what you say is true, then I shall make sure that I never fall in love.'

'Oh you are infuriating!' she cried, struggling to keep the despair from her voice, thinking that she had lost the battle before she had even known it had begun. He was unreachable in his cool, icy tower; he had used her and now intended casting her aside.

'I never meant to mislead you, *doucette*. You must learn to take life – and people – as they are and not as you would wish them to be. If you think on this, you will realize that I am right. What happiness could you have with me, a verminous slave dealer as you have so often called me? Would you not mistrust me, doubt my every word, expect me to betray you one day? Slave dealers are not renowned for fidelity nor integrity, *doucette*.'

He gave a wry smile, and in the midst of her anger and disappointment she could not help but think how heart-rendingly beautiful he was, with his wide, curving mouth and the sadness shadowing his green eyes. One moment she loathed him, the next he moved her to tears and a compassion she had not known she could feel. But she must remind herself now that he was a slave dealer, that he had used her, and would sell her despite that as if she were no more than a sack of grain, to the highest bidder – in this case, the Grand Turk . . . and, afterwards, he would never think of her again . . . Her beautiful French Captain would be lost to her for eternity.

Tears welled, dripping down her face. Seeing them, Sauvage took her in his arms and kissed away the drops, then he kissed her mouth, holding her so tenderly that she could not have believed one bad word about him had she not known the truth. Could he really be as callous as he pretended? No, of course not! When he found out how much she loved him, how much he loved her, he would realize that they were meant to be together. She would convince him – she knew she could. If they had enough time . . . Quelling the pain caused by his words, she brightened. He would not sell her, no, of course not. He had to see that he loved her. She would show him that – she knew how to do this, for it was an essential part of her nature to be loving, warm, responsive. Soon, he would be thinking of her constantly, as she did him; he would wake with his mind filled with visions of her. When he went to sleep, she would be in his thoughts; he would dream of her every night. Just to think of him made her feel safe, protected, comforted: soon, it would be like that for him, too.

They belonged together. This was fate, although at first she had not understood. Destiny had brought them together, across the seas, the world, he from the Barbary Coast, she from London, such diverse places, to meet by the Marriage Cove where her grandparents had plighted their troth. The Sea God had brought them together – all the time, he had been watching over her, kindly convivial Neptune. She gave a little laugh, and Sauvage held her away from him so that he could look at her face.

'You are happier now?'

'You have made me happier – just to have you near me

is all I ask,' she said huskily, looking up passionately into his brilliant eyes. But she saw his gaze darken as she spoke.

'Do not live on false hope, darling. It can only lead to more pain.' His hands fell from her shoulders, his face hard. He stood up to go, with his old customary abruptness. Hurt, she watched in silence, feeling as if he were leaving her forever instead of merely going up on deck to supervise his men.

Some fifteen minutes later, Ahmek came into the cabin laden with clothes. Cassia gasped as she saw him deposit some half-dozen superb gowns on the bed. He was grinning from ear to ear, delighted at her pleasure. Thrusting his hands into the pockets of his baggy Turkish breeches, he withdrew a pile of sparkling gems, necklaces, rings, earrings, two coronals, four brooches.

'Oh, they are beautiful – are they *real*, Ahmek?' Cassia lifted up the jewels, dazzled by their brilliance. Rubies, emeralds, diamonds, glossy fat pink pearls, and a heavy gold chain from which was suspended a huge black pearl.

'They real, missy. Fine real,' Ahmek nodded. 'From Spanish,' he grimaced, then smiled again. 'We have now, so you get. You dress up, feel fine, look much splendid, yes? Captain he say.'

Tears pricked behind her lids. Despite his cool departure, Vincent had thought of her, cared for her enough to send her these gorgeous clothes and jewels: he must have known how much they would thrill her. She held one of the gowns against her cheek. It was a muted green colour shot with gold, and had a sumptuous heavy underskirt of cloth of gold embroidered with emerald and gold silks. It must have cost a small fortune, and had surely belonged to a courtesan! It was far too grand for any commoner to wear, even for a ball. The emeralds would suit it marvellously, and she hung these round her neck, looking in the mirror which Ahmek eagerly fetched for her. He chortled happily as she admired the gems, saying, 'Much great fine,' over and over, until she had to laugh, too. Then he said, 'Me go now, you try on gowns. Me come in admire when you say, yes?'

'Oh, yes please, Ahmek,' she smiled at him, thinking how kind he was and how much he had helped her to adjust to this cloistered existence. Then, when he had gone, she forgot everything except the delight of trying on the gowns and the gems, of feeling the rich sheen of them against her skin.

Two of the gowns were loose at the waist, and would need taking in; a third was tight across her breasts so that her bosom was pushed up and out revealingly, but the green and gold court gown fitted her as if it had been made especially for her. True, it was daringly low at the bosom, so that she hardly dared breathe, but the emeralds helped to camouflage this. They lay on her breasts like glittering green eyes sparking with life, Vincent's eyes . . . She shivered, putting down the mirror. She wanted him to come in now, to see her dressed like this, to take her in his arms and say that of course he had no intention of parting with her, that he had not meant the cruel things he had said. Then he would tell her how much he loved her, and needed her, but that he had been fighting it for weeks until this moment when he could no longer deny his true feelings . . .

She allowed herself to indulge in this blissful reverie for some time, until she heard Ahmek's tap at the door. Calling, 'Come in,' she posed herself in an autocratic mode, as befitted a titled lady of the court. His dark eyes glowed when he saw her, his mouth falling open in admiration.

'Missy sure fine lady,' he said, rolling his eyes. 'Captain love you now, for sure.'

Cassia smiled, enjoying the first innocent admiration she had received for weeks. She scooped up the skirt, holding it out, and pirouetting for Ahmek to see the full beauty of the gown. Again, he sighed loudly with appreciation. 'No one so much beauty on ship *ever*,' he said, making Cassia laugh, and blush a little. They were laughing together, imagining they were guests at a grand court ball, when Sauvage entered the cabin.

For a moment, he said nothing. He did not smile, nor did he greet them. He looked at Cassia, apparently oblivious to her fine apparel, then he gestured to Ahmek to go. When the eunuch had left, his face anxious, Vincent looked down at Cassia. She seemed diminutive beside his six feet three, very small and fragile. He looked at her for a long time, at her beautiful round blue eyes, so clear, so trusting, at her white velvet neck and breasts curving out of the low neckline. She coloured under his scrutiny, lowering her eyes. He saw that her lashes were dark, not auburn, and extremely thick; they shadowed her cheeks with two crescents.

'Mam'selle is radiant tonight,' he said, his voice low.

Its timbre made her raise her eyes. There was no harshness in his tone, although she had thought him angry. Yet why should he be? Had he not sent her these clothes to wear? His eyes were filled with warmth, and more – she felt a rush of excitement, of love. He *had* changed his mind! He *did* love her. When he crushed her to him, she went willingly, eagerly, silently begging for his kisses and caresses. When the priceless gown was hastily unhooked, to fall unheeded to the floor, all she wanted, all she desired, was to be held against this man whom she adored. And all she wanted was for him to love her back, passionately, tenderly, wildly.

Neither of them noticed Ahmek return, or saw his grin of delight as he carefully closed the cabin door and stood outside it, on guard while his master and the beautiful missy enjoyed the bliss of love in privacy. She was a comely girl, radiant, intelligent; surely his master would see this soon and realize that she would make him the perfect wife? Too long had his master been alone and lonely, fighting his deep need for love, true love, grieving over the deaths of Martia and their child. It was time now for Captain Sauvage to forget, to begin a new life with this girl whose eyes welled with love for him . . . yes, Ahmek knew it; he could see it plainly. But when would his master see it too? He could be very stubborn, the Captain, when he chose. Ahmek sighed, then he remembered the weeks ahead, the stay in Algiers, the long journey to Constantinople. If his master had not recognized what was staring him in the face by the end of their stay in the Regency, there would be the weeks during the journey towards the heart of Turkey when, if Allah were merciful, Sauvage would realize what he had to do. Forget Martia and her treachery. Marry Cassia. Find another beauty to go to the Sultan in her place: beauties were not hard to come by, but girls with Cassia's sweetness and generous heart were rare indeed.

Cassia barely breathed as Sauvage picked her up and carried her to his bed where he stood over her, stripping off his clothes to reveal his hard muscular body, tanned and in superb condition. His shoulders were broad and powerful, his waist narrow, and he had long, muscular legs and strong brown arms, yet his hands could be so gentle that they made her shudder in ecstasy. He had only to caress her lightly, to place his hands on her shoulders and she began to glow deep inside, the glow spreading right through her until she was bathed in warmth. Then, she was his, entirely his, for him to do with as he wished; she had no more resistance than a rose against the bee seeking pollen. With a sigh, she curved against him, her arms rising round his neck and pulling him down to her.

'Vincent,' she sighed, then she said no more for he was covering her mouth with his kisses, gentle yet sure, bearing down on her, harder, and harder still, until she could not wait. 'Take me, take me,' she sighed, and he kissed her brow and face, her neck, her breasts, keeping her waiting until her mind cried out for the deepest intimacy. Still he did not enter her, but kissed her, over and over, with feather-light kisses, stopping occasionally to look down at her and smile, noting her reactions. He did care for her, oh he did; she knew it! How could he be so gentle, so considerate, and not love her? Lust was brutal, self-seeking, impatient: she had learned that with Charles.

It seemed to her that hours had flown past, yet still he had not committed his body to hers. He was rousing her to a peak she had not known existed, a peak which was enthralling, blissful ecstasy. She would not wait any longer – she begged him to make love to her now, *now*. Laughing gently, he obeyed, sliding into her, hard and forceful, so that she became him, was part of him, and they were one being, their souls joined.

Slowly he moved, and the glow inside her became a fire, her face burned, her breasts tingled, she sighed and curved against him, conscious only of one thing, that she need not fear his taking his own selfish pleasure without regard for her. She could respond, writhe, plead, sigh, dig her nails into his back, kiss his neck, his lips, but nothing would make him lose control until she was totally satiated. Then and only then would he allow himself to be satisfied.

No one could convince her now that this was lust. He could have bedded any of his captives in the hold if all he had needed was physical stimulus. But he had sought her, and given her gifts, then been unable to resist her when he saw her in the gown. He had put aside his determination to keep her virginal for Hamid I, because, discovering he loved her wildly, he could not prevent himself making love to her as he was now doing. She had never known such bliss, such happiness – they had been fated to find one another across the seas, and now they would be inseparable for all time. Laughter rose in her throat, accompanying the sensations which were springing from other parts of her body to conjoin in the waves of orgasm that seared her, spangling her mind with a burst of stars, gripping her in hands which were more powerful than any possessed by humans.

Vincent watched her, his eyes tender. Her head twisted from side to side, her eyes were half-closed, her cheeks rosy. Her nails scythed his back as she gasped his name, her breath hot on his face. Feeling the first gentle grip of her muscles against him, he paused, waiting, allowing her to surge against him, pulling him to her with desperate arms, her face pressed close to his as she moaned, whispering his name again, 'Vin-cent, ah, Vin-cent,' and then she was quiet, thinking it was all over. Laughing, he began to move inside her, so that her lids flew open in surprise, her mouth curving, and then he was taking her into the realms of a world which she might never have known about had he not been her lover. Twice, three times, he allowed her to reach orgasm, and only then did he release his control and move into her with a wild desire, saying her name, that he loved her, that she was his. Then it was over, and they slept in one another's arms.

CHAPTER EIGHT

Cassia stood on deck as the ship neared Algiers. She had been allowed out of the cabin, but she was heavily draped in black robes and veil like a Muslim woman. At first she had refused to wear them, but Sauvage had said, simply but firmly, that she would not be allowed out of the cabin until she put them on. Seeing that a fight would be useless, she had obeyed.

The blinding light of the sun was hurting her eyes, weeks in the cabin having accustomed her to dimness. And the heat was searing; already she dripped with sweat beneath the heavy shroud of clothes. But she had learned something. Although, in purdah, she was virtually sexless, nothing showing except her hands and her eyes, the crew were already giving her lecherous looks, and making comments in their guttural tongue. Ahmek stood by her all the time, arms folded, muscles bulging, and when the comments became too raucous, he glowered at the offenders until they retreated, chastened.

'They been at sea much long time,' he explained to Cassia. 'Like beasts now. Take no notice of them, missy.' He grimaced.

'I won't, Ahmek, although I don't know what they're saying, of course, but I can tell from their expressions that it's not very nice!' Her voice sounded muffled behind the yashmak, her breath and the heat had already made the material damp, and it clung unpleasantly to her nose and mouth so that she had to keep lifting it off her face in order to breathe. But she was so delighted at being released from the cabin at long last that nothing could deflate her – not even Sauvage's grim expression as he passed her now and again while organizing their coming in to land.

Why he should look so grim she did not know, but he did, and it was none of her doing. He was determined, despite everything that had happened between them, to go on with his original plan to give her to the Sultan; he had said so in no uncertain terms. Coming as it had after the last few days of happiness, she found his determination crushing. They had been through every phase: she had argued, cajoled, reproached, still he refused to change his mind. She had done everything except plead with him and that her pride would not allow. That he still would not admit they were meant for each other, she found mystifying. Why, why, should he be so adamant about selling her? She felt that she would have a better chance of staying with him if she were old and ugly. As it was, she felt that he was deliberately putting her from him with stoic purposefulness because he found her irresistible – and it was this side of him that she found so puzzling. Why insist that she go, why not submit to fate and keep her beside him? If she put this to him, he laughed it off lightly, telling her that he had never made her any promises.

'I am not a marrying man,' he would shrug. 'If you thought that, then you were weaving womanish dreams. My life is the sea, and there is not room for anything else. My time is fully occupied as it is, and soon I shall be governing Captain Dash's territory as well as my own. The last thing I shall want is a woman round my neck.'

His contempt had stung her, but then he had grinned, placing his hands on her shoulders. 'This way, *doucette*, you will mean far more to me than any woman. If we stayed together, the result would be inevitable. Disillusionment would set in, we would quarrel and see one another's faults, the bad side of one another. We would start to make illogical demands on one another, become petulant, reproachful. Our relationship would tarnish rapidly, as the best ones do, from familiarity and boredom. When you go to the Grand Seraglio, I shall remember only your sweetness and your beauty – the loving times we shared. There will be nothing to mar my memories of you.'

'Boredom? Familiarity?' she had retorted. 'Those sound to me like the plaints of someone greatly lacking in imagination! Are you bored with the sea, with piracy? No, of course not, yet you have lived this life for ten years have you not? Why then should you grow bored with me, or I with you? If something is worth taking up, then it is worth preserving. Not to appreciate what one has been given, but to relinquish it callously is a great crime, Captain Sauvage. Those who do not feel proper gratitude, lose what they have.'

He had not grown angry at her words, which well he might. Instead, he said, 'But did I not tell you from the start, little one, that we were to lose one another? Constantinople is your fate, and mine is the sea. Nothing can alter our destiny.'

'On that I agree entirely – no one can alter it. Yes I too believe in fate, but I believe that we are destined to be together.'

'And I say that we shall part. You will become a royal concubine, perhaps even a wife, and I shall stay as I am, in the life which I chose ten years ago when . . .' he stopped, his eyes clouding and she waited for him to go on.

When he did not, her impatience to pursue the argument made her say: 'So we each believe differently at the moment? Perhaps that also is fate. Who is to win, Vincent?' She looked at him with sad eyes. Perhaps because he realized how much he had upset her, he did not meet her gaze.

'Fate will win of course, sweetheart. It is as likely that we shall share a life together as – as that fur rug will grow legs and run back to the forest from whence it came –' he gestured to the beaver coverlet on the bed.

Her shoulders dipped. She turned away. Pride and anger warred with a resolve not to be defeated by the obstinate arrogance of any man, and a desperation lest her second love should prove as ephemeral as her first. Sauvage's rejection had touched her on the raw in the two most vulnerable parts of her soul – her yearning for love and her stubborn inability to concede victory in a fight.

Her hands gripped the deck rail. She did not see the shimmering cornflower blue waters, nor Algiers in the distance, a crammed hive of buildings seemingly held together by thin air, some fifteen thousand houses or more, so Ahmek had told her. Such a little city, and so many houses, so many people and slaves – Christian and pagan. Nor did she notice the harbour basin in front of the city where the pirates anchored their ships, the long, narrow mole built by Barbarossa wending its way out into the sea to enable more ships to be anchored. Cassia saw none of this but only Sauvage's brilliant green eyes, his face soft with love as he bent to kiss her, and then she imagined their parting, the agonizing loneliness which would follow. Never to see him again, never to be held and loved again – how could she endure it? Life would be a cold and meaningless charade without him.

'Beautiful, isn't she?' She had not heard him come up behind her, to place his hands on her shoulders, his palms warm against the cloth of her robe. 'Barbarossa made her what she is today, carving shape and order out of chaos. See that tower at the end of the mole? He designed that, and fortified it with three hundred cannon. There are gateways into the centre: on the landward side is the Bab Azou, through which everyone must pass to get into the city centre. West, there is the Bab el Oued, for merchants, and leading from the city to the mole is the Marine Gate. East is the Gate of the Fishermen through which the fishermen reach their boats, and where we repair our ships. Those taller minarets you can see belong to the mosques and the Dey's Palace, the Jenina.'

'There are fishermen here?' She was thinking of Cornwall, of the kindly, ruddy-faced men who had come round the point to Morbilly Cove that day, when Charles and she were making love. How long ago that seemed. A different world. A different Cassia.

'The Mediterranean is rich in marine life, with fish of a far greater size than the sardine.' He grinned, but she could not share his amusement. She felt numb, unable to laugh or be cheerful, unable to drink in the ivory and indigo beauty of the scene before her. All she knew was that his hands burned her where they touched her flesh, and the searing heat of the sun, the piercing light of it, served to make her feel faint. Could she ever adjust to this debilitating heat, to the warring emotions within her?

'Lucien is here.' Sauvage pointed to a longboat scudding through the waters towards them. 'He has come to take you ashore.'

'I will not come ashore with you?'

'Lucien takes the prize captives ashore. It is better that way, for everyone. There will be many sightseers watching out for our arrival, and if they see I have someone so exceptional in my company, they will pass the word round. I shall be besieged with buyers. The Dey will send his men to offer a price for you. That could prove very embarrassing, for the Dey is a man of pride. To refuse him would make life very difficult for me here.'

'But I am completely disguised in these clothes,' Cassia persisted.

'They will know, by the very fact you wear them, that you are something out of the ordinary, *doucette*.'

'Where will Lucien take me?' Cassia watched the longboat approaching, saw its oarsmen guide it up the ship's side, heard the dull thud of wood against wood. A rope ladder was flung down, and a young man appeared on the deck. He had a pleasant face, and he was neatly dressed in plain but well-cut coat and breeches.

'To my house, of course,' Sauvage replied absently, then his hands fell from her shoulders and he strode towards Lucien, his face alight. She saw the two men embrace one another, as Frenchmen do, and exchange a few words in their own language. She was too far away to catch every word. Then Sauvage was introducing her to the newcomer and she was looking up into laughing blue eyes.

'Mademoiselle Cassia Morbilly, Lucien d'Arbigny,' Sauvage said. 'Lucien would you please take Mademoiselle Morbilly home, and see that Fleur takes care of her well. She is wearing purdah, as you will have noticed, for obvious reasons. Do not leave her alone for one moment until you are safely indoors, and speak to no one of her existence. Understood?'

'Understood, *mon capitaine*.' Lucien grinned, giving a mock salute. 'Mam'selle,' he half-bowed to Cassia, who automatically responded with a graceful courtsey.

She saw Lucien's brows rise a little – was he surprised at her elegant form of greeting? Perhaps he was accustomed to uneducated whores, or dull peasant women, and had not expected this response from one of Sauvage's slave girls? If so, he was in for more surprises – but how difficult she found it to be herself when only her eyes showed! Lucien had no idea what she looked like, what sort of girl she was. She could be pockmarked, buck-toothed, black, yellow or brown-skinned for all he knew.

Lucien gestured to her to follow him to the longboat. She turned to bid Sauvage goodbye but he had already left to go about his business. Feeling bereft, wishing he would come with her, she followed Lucien to the hempen ladder and he slowly helped her down it. She found the descent quite hazardous with the heavy, voluminous robes wrapping themselves round her legs, and her veil falling in her eyes. She had to keep pushing aside the material so that she could get proper grips on the wooden slats of the ladder, but eventually she was seated in the now rocking boat and the rowers picked up their oars and headed for the mainland.

They swept through the brilliant blue waters towards Algiers, the hive of white-washed houses growing closer, larger.

'They look something like a Roman amphitheatre, do they not, mademoiselle?' said Lucien smiling.

Cassia looked from the shore to Lucien. 'An amphitheatre, m'sieur?' she said in French, and felt a thrill of pride as she saw the surprise again on his face.

'Why yes, do you not think so? All those houses built so close together, elevated one above the other, just like a classical theatre – myself, I have always thought so. Of course the spires of the mosques and the Jenina – that is, the Dey's Palace – rise higher, but that only serves to make the scenario more interesting, would you not agree?' He brushed back a tendril of blond hair that had fallen across his forehead.

She wondered how he had escaped serious sunburn with such a fair skin, but of course she did not dare ask him – she barely knew him. He seemed pleasant enough, though, and she would guess that he was of good family. She felt relaxed in his presence, and he seemed eager to talk, in a light cheery vein that she found infinitely heartening. She had enjoyed her exchanges with Ahmek, but he was after all of a different race and creed, and spoke such limited English. She felt that she could trust Lucien d'Arbigny, and that she could confide in him.

'Yes, it is a very interesting scene, monsieur, and very welcome after the long weeks I have spent shut up in Captain Sauvage's cabin.' She spoke, then realized how her words could be misconstrued and she blushed hotly, grateful for the first time that she was veiled.

Lucien did not seem to have noticed anything wrong. 'Ah, so you were fortunate indeed, mademoiselle – you must be very special to the Captain. I do not recollect his having done that before . . .' Lucien's blue eyes sparkled.

Was he teasing her? She could not say, knowing as little of him as she did. She pushed back the veil which was now unbearably hot. Strands of silky auburn hair escaped from their bonds and a few inches of very white neck were revealed. She saw Lucien staring, and hastily tucked the hair away. Although the look in his eyes had been of admiration, or curiosity, but not desire, she suddenly remembered Sauvage's warnings. How did she know what manner of men these renegades were? They might look and behave quite normally, but who knew of their secret predilections? She thought of how normal Charles had seemed to begin with . . .

Lucien must have sensed her withdrawal, for he leaned back, surveying the sea and the now fast approaching city, and they spent most of the remainder of the journey in silence.

The harbour was shaped like a dish, and it was packed with every hue and size of craft. Galleys and the more exotic Algerian ships, polacca-chebeks, flaunting their generous array of lateen and brilliantly coloured square-rigged sails, and some ships of which she had never seen the like before. Lucien, seeing her interest, told her that these were Turkish vessels, a *mahovna* was the name of the single-masted sailing barge, and the ship with the gaff-rigged mainsail, foresail and two jibs was called a *tchektirme*.

She chuckled at mention of these nautical terms, unable as yet to relate them to the correct sections of each vessel. She expected that if someone were patient enough to instruct her, she might learn them all eventually. Then she was struck by a thought: if she were going to the Grand Seraglio, she would not need to know such things. Indeed, any knowledge at all would be useless. What she had learned from Ahmek about harems suggested that the emphasis was entirely on the physical charms of women. Her mind would atrophy; she might as well be a simpleton. Her heart sank. She had an alert interest in so many things; the thought that she would not be able to exercise it was unbearable.

The boat thumped against the landing stage so violently that she was flung forward; Lucien gripped her by the arm to steady her, a smile of apology on his handsome, snub-nosed face. And then she had no time for sadness or feelings of isolation, for Algiers and all its drama was upon her.

The smells were the first thing she noticed, despite the yashmak she wore. Packed humanity beneath the searing sun, sightseers, beggars, sailors, all crowded together watching, craning their necks to see – what? The approaching ship with Sauvage in it? If so, he must be very well-known here. The beggars made her feel sick. She felt faint as she noticed their deformities. Some of them were armless or legless, and there was one with no eyes at all, not even scarred sockets. All of these ragged people clamoured for alms as she stood on the jetty waiting for Lucien to join her. Children gathered round too, their hands extended for money, their big dark eyes shining with hope. She wanted to give them something, she looked at Lucien pleadingly, but he shook his head.

'You would be crushed to death in the stampede if they saw you had any money. Besides we are supposed to be discreet, not attract attention by distributing largesse.' He waved his hands at the children, speaking some foreign words to them. They glared, and some shook their fists. Now their beautiful luminous eyes were narrowed, with hatred. Slowly, they began to withdraw.

How they smelt! She had never known such a smell. Unwashed bodies and clothes, greasy lank hair; some had open wounds which were festering – and so many were suffering from diseased and scarred skins. Could it be smallpox? It looked far worse than anything she had seen in England. Instinctively she shuddered, and Lucien took her arm.

'If you can bear this, mademoiselle, then there will be no more of such experiences for you. Indeed, I had not expected to find anyone here at this time of day. They have obviously been warned of Vincent's approach. Come, we go up into the oldest part of the city now, to the Street of the Golden Moon, where the Captain's house is situated.'

'What is it like?' Cassia asked, following Lucien and the oarsmen through the crowd.

'Very pleasant. You will like it. There is a beautiful harem for lady guests, with fountains, potted palms and trellises entwined with vines and exotic blooms. The furniture is of the best, so is the wine and food.' Lucien laughed, his eyes twinkling. 'Mademoiselle will have no complaints.'

And will I not indeed! she thought, but had the sense to keep silent. Awed by the sights and sounds of this unique city she followed the men through a square, an enormous gateway, and into the narrower streets which wound their way though the centre of the city. They had reddish baked clay walls, very high, and the upper rooms of each house had terraces constructed roughly from slim tree trunks lashed together.

Everywhere there was clamour and bustle, stalls lined the streets and were heaped with fruit and vegetables, fish, meal, bolts of gaily-coloured cloth, hand-made shoes and bags and beads. Many of the street vendors attempted to engage their attention, thrusting their wares into the faces of Lucien and the other men, holding up strings of beads and pointing to Cassia, then to Lucien, as if to say, your lady will love these. But he treated all the vendors in the same fashion, smiling, but showing by his undaunted expression and cool manner that he would not be buying today. Some of the vendors then became abusive, making crude gestures and spitting after them. Others shrugged, or donned expressions of contempt.

They were now walking up a very narrow, twisting street, overhung with timber terraces and virtually empty of passers-by. No traders stood here, and they saw only a thin, moulting cat with a bent spine and one eye missing. Then they were emerging into a pleasant square with white-washed walls and lattice-worked baskets in which were blossoming shrubs and fern-like miniature trees. A fountain sang in the centre of the square, its surrounds made of prettily-decorated green and gold tiles, and tubs of fronded ferns had been placed on the three steps leading up to it. Here it was cool and shaded from the direct heat of the sun. It was the sort of place where one wanted to sit and be peaceful. Cassia looked eagerly at the fountain, wanting to let its spray fall on her face and hands, but Lucien said they could not stop yet.

Two more corners and another short walk found them in the Street of the Golden Moon, and now Cassia could see the house where she was to spend the next few weeks. It had a flat white façade, looking like the other houses in that street, but inside it was spacious, cool, and beautifully decorated. Standing in the tiled hallway, where walls and floor were sparkling white, she immediately felt refreshed. Trellises stood in each corner, and flowers with enormous heads of scarlet and yellow had been trained to grow up them. She could smell the heavy scent of lilies but could not see them. She guessed that they were behind the trellises.

Servants scurried forward to welcome them, bowing low, taking their outer clothes, and leading the oarsmen to the servant's quarters. Lucien waved to Cassia as a young Turkish girl escorted her up the stairs. The girl's eyes glittered with curiosity, her black hair glossy with oil and plaited with blue and white beads and cord. She wore a chemise of fine linen dyed red and blue, baggy silk trousers, or shalwar, with an elaborately embroidered tie belt, and a yelek, a bolero sewn in blue and red silks and buttoned just below her breasts. On her feet were flat slippers with gold cord rosettes on each toe.

'My name is Fleur,' she told Cassia with a smile of great sweetness as they mounted the stairs, and then said no more, although her eyes continued to devour her companion.

She showed Cassia through a section of open trelliswork and into a large, airy room hung with white linen cloths embroidered in green and white. The floor tiles were blue, green and white. There was no furniture except for a carved bench.

Motioning to Cassia to be seated, Fleur went to what looked like a plain wall, lifted one of the hanging cloths and revealed a flat white cupboard. From this, she took a handful of delicate clothes, and then she gestured to Cassia to follow her through another concealed door and into the apartments which Cassia recognized from Lucien's description. So this was the harem created for Sauvage's slave girls! It was indeed a sumptuous suite, spotlessly clean, smelling of jasmine and lilies, white fur rugs on the floor and beds, hanging lamps engraved in many colours suspended from the ceiling. Fleur smiled, handed her the clothes, then spoke again in her flawless French.

'Mademoiselle will be brought water to bathe. Rest then until dinner. The bell is there if you need anything.' She pointed to an engraved brass bell which emitted a high tinkling note as she shook it.

'Thank you, Fleur,' Cassia smiled, but the young girl dipped her glossy black head as if to say, I am only a servant here, I need no thanks, and then was gone, moving silently on slippered feet.

Cassia was alone for some ten minutes before two black men brought her the tub of bathwater. They wore baggy shalwar and scarlet boleros, and she guessed that they must be eunuchs or they would not be waiting upon her in the harem. There was a flask of scented oils, a pot of unguent, and a selection of sweet-smelling soaps with the bath. The two eunuchs disappeared, without a word, and she remembered what Ahmek had told her about the privileged position these men had in the harem. They were the only men allowed in such a place, because they could not seduce or attack the concubines, nor get them pregnant. Most of these eunuchs were also very strong, a valuable asset if one wished to ensure the safety of one's wives.

Making sure that the door was locked, Cassia stripped off the heavy purdah with a sigh of heartfelt relief, and stepped into the bath. It was bliss, and she sank into the frothing, scented waters, adding more oil and lathering her hair with jasmine soap. For some forty minutes she sat there soaking, her hair swathed in fluffy white towels, not caring that the water had cooled, then she stepped out and dried herself vigorously before massaging in the rich, creamy unguent. Afterwards, she felt very sleepy and curled up on one of the plump, cushiony beds, where she fell asleep in seconds.

It was dark when she awoke, and the sound of revelling came from a far off section of the house. Shouts, laughter and eerie wailing music came to her ears. For a moment she thought she was dreaming, and then she realized that Sauvage and his associates must be dining and celebrating their return. She wondered if Captain Dash were here; she wanted to see this man who revered her lover like a son and who was leaving him all his ships and territory on his retirement. She wanted most of all, however, to see her lover. Barely half a day had elapsed since she had left the ship, but she had missed him dreadfully and was aching to talk to and be near him.

She got up. Her hair had dried in the heat while she slept, and curled round her face and shoulders as though it had been treated with heated tongs. She found a mirror and surveyed her face in it. She looked refreshed and her eyes were clear. She wondered what she was expected to do now, knowing, as she did, nothing of the customs in this house. Did Sauvage's slave girls assist at mealtimes, or would they be guests? Perhaps Turkish customs were kept here, in which case she would be expected to stay in her room. She thought about this, then came to a decision. No one was going to keep her shut away any longer. She had spent too many weeks in that airless cabin – now she wanted to be a part of life again.

She picked up the clothes Fleur had given her. They consisted of a jewelled waistcoat that barely fastened across her breasts, and a long, loose gown of ivory silk embroidered with silver and azure roses, with silk-fringed sleeves which hung to the floor. She put these on, enjoying the feel of the delicate, feminine finery. There was a bracelet of engraved silver, and silver beads which tinkled as she moved. A long cord sewn with pearls was, she presumed, for her waist. The slippers were made of soft white leather decorated with big silver rosettes.

Once she had dressed, Cassia went to the door to look out, and saw the two eunuchs, faces impassive, arms folded across massive chests. Her heart sank. A prisoner again! She had hoped that Ahmek would be guarding her, if there must be a guard while she was here, but she had not seen him yet. Perhaps he was even now enjoying the dinner after the long voyage – he deserved it but, come to that, so did she. She was no Muslim woman reared to instant obedience and subjugation. She would do as she wished.

The two eunuchs did not attempt to halt her as she passed them, her silk robe drifting in the breeze caused by her movement. She held her head high, not looking in their direction. But she heard their bare feet shuffling after her as she headed towards the noise of the celebrations. Opening one or two doors, she glanced inside but did not see revellers. Then she came to a flight of wooden steps and these led on to a terrace. Suddenly she was in the midst of the assembly, two drunken sailors were asleep in the bushes, three more gazed up at her with bleary eyes from where they had sunk to the floor in a semi-stupor. The eunuchs came closer to her now, but still did not try to stop her.

Those must have been the ordinary seamen, for now she came into view of the revellers, seeing them through an arcade of twisted trees. The wailing music was deafening, and a row of voluptuous dark-skinned girls were dancing to it. Their hair was long and loose, black and glossy as oil, their bodies were naked, sweat gleaming in the light from the lamps and tapers. On their wrists and ankles hung tiny silver bells which rang as they twisted and dipped in the sensuous rhythms of the dance. Cassia experienced a moment of acute embarrassment at the sight of their naked bodies, and then her eyes were drawn towards the table at which Vincent Sauvage and his guests were sitting. Her heart began to pound as she saw her lover deep in conversation with an old man sitting next to him. Vincent's companion was vividly dressed in an orange, yellow and apple green doublet, breeches and a shirt across which was tied a silken sash. He had many gold rings on his twisted, deformed fingers and shaggy white hair and brows. That must be Captain Dash, she thought. How old he looked, and yet his eyes were a clear, light blue. He was the first at the table to notice her presence.

She saw him point her out to Sauvage, whose face darkened. He stood up angrily, strode across to her, and gripped her arm so that she almost cried out with pain.

'Why are you here? How did you get out?' he barked, his brilliant eyes boring into her. Just to be near him was worth his anger, she decided, as remembered experiences flowed through her.

'I came to join you,' she said defiantly, head thrown back.

'Will you join us then? Take off your clothes and dance with these *houris*?' His voice was biting.

'If you wish,' she dared him, her hands rising to the buttons of her waistcoat. At once, he pushed her back into the shadows, his face alight with fury.

'You would be torn apart when the dance ended!' he growled. 'How dare you come here! Were you not shown your place?'

His choice of words was most unfortunate, for Cassia flung her arm out, trying to loose his grip, and when she could not, she made her hand into a fist and struck at his throat and jaw.

'Yes, I was shown a place, but it was for Muslim women, and I am a Christian. My place is not shut away in a harem.' Her blows increased, but appeared to make not the slightest impression.

'My men and my guests fully expect all women in this house to behave like concubines. Are you prepared for that, mademoiselle?' His eyes seemed to cut through her, with ice, with flame.

'Are you saying that they would rape me? And that you would stand by and let them do so?'

'I told you I want no trouble!'

'Nor do I, but only a chance to be a part of life again. I cannot bear to be shut away.' Despite her efforts, tears welled in her eyes and dripped down her cheeks. Angrily she dashed them away with her free hand.

His grip loosened. He looked down at her with eyes which were suddenly softer. Startled, she heard a querulous voice behind them.

'Vincent, who is this charming young lady? You are going to introduce us? Surely she is English?'

The speaker was Captain Dash, who was now smiling happily at Cassia. This talk of her being attacked by Sauvage's guests was just so much nonsense she decided.

'Yes, she is English,' Sauvage replied reluctantly. 'But

she is my captive and she is destined for the Grand Seraglio in Constantinople.'

'Ha, so she is to be a royal slave? Fortunate girl, fortunate Hamid.' Dash stepped closer, moving with a hobbling gait, a stick in each hand. He looked Cassia up and down, as if examining a horse, and then he said, 'Yes, too good by far for the Dey. Certainly she must go to the Sultan. He will be overcome.'

'I am banking on that,' Sauvage said grimly.

'You always were an astute fellow,' Dash grinned, now leaning on Sauvage's arm for support. 'Young lady, you have my good wishes for your new life.'

Cassia opened her mouth to retort, stunned at the way in which these people accepted slavery so coolly. She imagined Sauvage at a dinner in England, introducing her as his slave. There would be a riotous reaction to such a statement. But Sauvage and Dash were heading back to the table, she was forgotten. Now she realized how foolhardy her appearance here had been, born as it was of her desperate need to be with the man she loved.

Sadly she turned to go back the way she came, the eunuchs silently following her. She did not see the eyes that watched her greedily until she was out of sight. They belonged to Nathan Dash, brother of the Captain who had just been speaking to her. Nathan was twenty years younger than his brother, and he was also healthier, stronger, and more avaricious, but he was not, as he dearly wished to be, the heir to his brother's pirate empire. Captain Dash had never trusted his brother. For one thing, they had different mothers and Nathan's mother had ousted the Captain from their father's home. For another, Nathan had never been reliable. He was unscrupulous, a man who stepped in when others were in dire straits and cleaned them out ruthlessly.

When the Captain had heard of the fortunes to be made on the Barbary Coast, he had left the farm, which was running at a loss, intending to make enough money to give his mother a good home. Five years later, when Nathan had paid a sly visit to his stepmother to find out how the

Captain was doing he had followed him out to Algiers to tack himself on to his retinue. Always smiling, always convivial to everyone's face, Nathan deceived many. But beneath, determined to snatch all he could, at any cost, he was an evil man. Whatever his brother planned, he pretended that those plans were his. He had his own little band of followers who revered him, such was his surface charm, but there were many who had learned never to trust him. He had one enemy, one man whom he loathed and abhorred with every particle of his being, a hatred sired by jealousy, envy and greed, now exacerbated by the fact that this man, Vincent Sauvage, was to inherit the Captain's empire.

Seeing Sauvage stride across to the girl standing in the shadows, Nathan Dash had watched with narrowed eyes. Who was she? Why was she here? During that evening he made enquiries, discreetly, learning of the girl kidnapped off Cornwall, and intended for the Sultan's harem: a special gift from Sauvage to Hamid I. Nathan Dash began to plan, being driven not only by hatred of Vincent Sauvage. Now, there was another fire burning within him: a desire for the beautiful red-haired English girl, so cool, so voluptuous, yet so innocent-looking. He wanted her – and he would have her. And, if by doing this, he injured Sauvage and his brother, then that would be all the more satisfying.

Nathan Dash leaned back, a goblet of Burgundy in his leather-brown hand, his coal-black eyes secretive. His long thin nose like a hawk's jutted out over the tangled black moustaches that were badly in need of combing, and he wore his hair wild and loose, some strands being plaited and tied with scarlet bows. He had an unfortunate eruption of the skin which covered him in unsightly scaly patches, some dry, some oozing. It was an ailment which he shrugged aside, unaware of its loathsome origins, its contagious qualities and eventually fatal outcome. His followers were an even more extraordinary sight, some without fingers on one hand, or having lost eyes in duels or wild skirmishes. One had had his jaw broken and it had set so badly that his mouth was where his right cheek should be, and he could not chew. Their total acceptance of their ringleader's physical offensiveness was perhaps the worthiest quality they possessed.

Nathan Dash's mind buzzed with plans. He would wait and watch; he would discover Sauvage's plans, and he would in some as yet unformulated way baulk them, ruining his intentions to delight the Sultan. If he, Nathan, could somehow get his hands on the girl and give her to Hamid after he had used her himself, of course, would that not be a brilliant coup? He suppressed a sly smile, lifting the goblet to his scaly lips, concealing the look of gloating delight that now stamped his features as he imagined climbing on top of the beautiful red-head and satisfying himself on her body.

Cassia walked back to her suite slowly, shoulders drooping, the sound of revelry fading behind her. She saw nothing as she returned to her prison, not wanting to see, not caring. The eunuchs padded behind her like two great black panthers, but she did not heed them. Having found the right room, she went in and promptly curled up on one of the beds to sleep. A little later, Fleur brought her a tray of food and only then did she realize that she was ravenous.

Thanking the Turkish girl, she looked at the food. It was rice mixed with onions, raisins, mutton, and currants, cooked in oil and garlic. The smell of the garlic was not tempting, but she was so hungry that she ate quickly. On a dish beside this were six or seven squares of a strange, rubbery confection, some pieces white some rose pink.

'What is this?' she asked Fleur, who was standing waiting to take the tray.

'It is *Rahat Lokum*, mademoiselle. It is made from white grapes, or mulberries crushed into a pulp, to which is added some semolina flour, rosewater, honey and the kernels of apricots. The name means "giving rest to the throat", and you will see that this is truthful.' Fleur beamed.

Cassia picked up one of the pink pieces and put it into her mouth. It was delicious, tasting of roses, and she reached for a second piece and then a third, offering Fleur one. The young girl shook her head in refusal, saying, 'Not for me, for our guest,' which made Cassia smile despite herself. So she was a guest here, was she?

'Does anyone else help you?' Cassia asked. 'With your work, I mean.'

'Oh yes, but other girls wait on table tonight. I did not go for I am serving you, mademoiselle.'

'Would you rather be there? I can look after myself, you know.'

Fleur looked horrified. 'I have been instructed to look after you, mademoiselle. *Rais* Sauvage told me this. I would not dare disobey him.'

'Oh, of course, you are a Muslim, aren't you.' Cassia sighed, trying to imagine English women displaying this submissive obedience with their men. How tedious it would be for everyone concerned.

The *Rahat Lokum*, or Turkish Delight, was soon finished, and Fleur brought more at Cassia's request, again refusing to have some.

'The Captain did say you could eat today?' Cassia asked sarcastically, but Fleur shrugged, smiling helplessly, and Cassia immediately felt penitent. It was this girl's way of life and she must not jeer at it.

'What was the rice mixture called?' she now asked, eager to make normal conversation.

'Pilaf, mademoiselle, such as the Sultan himself eats. It is a favourite dish, and very popular amongst Turkish peoples. We who are far from the capital like to have as many Turkish foods as we can, to remind us of our ruler.'

'How did you come to be here, Fleur? Were you kidnapped too?'

'Kidnapped? Oh no. I am daughter of old friend of *Rais* Sauvage. He died, my father, by Spanish hand, and *Rais* Sauvage promised him as he lay dying that he would care for me like a daughter of his own. This he has done, since I was eight years of age. One day, *Rais* Sauvage will choose a good husband for me. When I am ready to marry.'

'You are not betrothed yet?'

'What is that?'

'You have not found a man who has offered to be your husband?'

'Oh no, not yet. I am too young. But I am happy here. *Rais* Sauvage is kind. He always brings me a gift from wherever he travels. This time, it was a necklet, look.' Fleur held out the long chain of silver links which hung round her slender neck. 'When Allah wills it, my husband will appear.' The girl smiled. It was not the first time that Cassia had seen this benign acceptance of Allah's Will. Ahmek too had displayed it. Although Allah was a strange God in every way to a girl reared as a Christian, Cassia could not help thinking that such faith and trust put many Christians to shame.

'Who taught you to speak such excellent French, Fleur?' Cassia asked, but thought that she might already know the answer.

'*Rais* Sauvage. When he was ill, with a small wound, I nursed him. He taught me French as he recovered. It was good, because before that I spoke only one language. It is good to speak more than one, is it not?'

'Definitely. I don't know where I would have been if I could not speak French. You and I would not have been able to talk, would we?' Cassia handed the now empty tray to the girl, who half-bowed, her glossy black hair swinging forward. 'When will you come again, Fleur?'

'Later. I bring you sherbert. It is delicious. Then in the morning I shall see you again. I sleep not far away. Down the passage. Do not fear anything, for Kol and Ulek are outside to guard us. All night. They are devoted. They were saved by *Rais* Sauvage years ago from the slave market. Terrible place –' Fleur shuddered. 'They are very grateful now. But a little simple yes?' she pointed to her head. 'They are brothers and are both simple.'

Cassia grinned at this. She had thought that the eunuchs' flat, squashed features were part of their racial inheritance, but she now realized that she had seen such features on the faces of retarded children in London.

When Fleur had gone, Cassia thought about Sauvage's penchant for saving people. Was there no end to their number, Ahmek, Kol and Ulek, Fleur? And why did he not wish to save her in the same way? These others had been rescued from the very life which Sauvage seemed determined to make her endure. Did he think them better than the woman to whom he had made love? This thought angered her, but she was too tired to work it out to its conclusion. The delicious pilaf had made her sleepy, and she drifted off into dreams, to be woken later by Fleur who had brought her a drink of sherbert.

After the two girls had talked for a little while, discussing Sauvage and his way of life, his friendship with Hamid I (during which conversation Cassia learned nothing new) it was time for bed, and to her surprise she slept immediately. Her dreams were wild and vivid, and in them a huge hirsute man with a steepled crown was taking her by the hand and leading her down a rocky beach to the sea, the waves were rising higher and higher over her legs and thighs, her waist, her hips, but she was not frightened. She was smiling up at the man, willing and eager to be taken deep down into his watery kingdom.

CHAPTER NINE

The next morning, Lucien visited her, his face wreathed in smiles.

'You have slept well, mam'selle? Is there anything I can get you?' Taking her hand, he kissed it lightly. If he were surprised to discover such beauty had been concealed by the black robes of the previous day, he did not show it, nevertheless there was admiration in his twinkling eyes.

'I slept for hours, thank you, and Fleur has looked after me well. I did not realize I was so tired. But I have one complaint, I was not allowed to join the festivities last night, m'sieur.' She pouted.

Lucien swallowed. 'Mam'selle is surely jesting. You dine with those pirates, those cut-throat brigands? *Mon Dieu*, they would have – have –' he swallowed again.

'What would they have done?' Cassia looked up at him archly.

'I – well, they are not like your countrymen. That is, not like your countrymen when they are in England, for of course Captain Dash is English. Life here changes them. They become – inhuman, wild, unprincipled. They have too much power. They see women as toys, playthings – they do not respect them.'

'Does this include yourself, m'sieur?' Cassia hid a smile.

Lucien blushed lightly. Then he grinned. '*Mais non*, mam'selle.'

'I am pleased to hear that, for I feared that there were no real men here at all.'

'You do not think that such men are real? Indeed, to me, they are all too substantial.' He made a face.

'I was referring to their customs, m'sieur. No real man would wish to keep a woman subjugated. Only a man who has doubts about himself and could not face a full, complete relationship with a woman would desire to keep her shut away in a harem, to be taken out, like a toy from a cupboard, when he wishes to play with her . . .' Cassia could not help but look contemptuous. Lucien did not realize that she was speaking specifically of his master, and not of the Turkish peoples generally, for she had realized that Turkish customs seemed to work quite well for them.

'You seem to have something there. Yes, you could be right. *Mais helas*, what do you think of me, for I have no *amoureuse* at all, in a harem or out of one.' He grinned again.

'If you must know, m'sieur, I find that something of a relief,' Cassia rejoined. She liked this fresh-faced, uncomplicated young man who was obviously gently reared. How had he come to be in this savage place, under her lover's thumb? Dare she ask him outright? She dared.

'How came I here?' he replied. 'It is a long tale, and not for such tender ears as yours.'

'Now I really must know,' she teased. 'If you do not tell me I shall be most offended.'

Lucien gave a little cough, bunching his mouth as if in thought, then he began to speak.

'My parents were the Comte and Comtesse d'Arbigny, great friends of the late King of France, Louis XV. But unfortunately they died together, of smallpox, leaving myself and my sister, Gentiane, orphaned. We were raised carefully, by the King's orders, and placed in the household of the Comte d'Ellerbonne. When my sister was married to the Comte's son, Gerard, it seemed that all was well. They were very happy, blissfully content it seemed. However –' Lucien sighed, his happy grin vanished – 'my dear sister suddenly died. I was told that she had had some female complaint of a serious nature, due to a pregnancy which went wrong. Please, mademoiselle, are you sure you wish to hear all this?'

Cassia was by now intensely curious. 'Please go on, I am very interested indeed.'

'I knew no better for some months – a year in fact – and then, quite by accident, I heard a rumour. At first I thought it malicious gossip, nothing more, but in fact, it was the truth. Gerard had had my sister murdered so that he could marry one of his mistresses, Fiona, a Flemish girl, blonde, brazen, who was carrying his child. That marriage had been kept secret from me, and I was deliberately misled over the whole matter. You can imagine how I felt when I discovered this. My poor sweet sister, only seventeen years old, so much in love, to have been cruelly murdered to make way for that hussy!' Colour flamed in Lucien's face. 'I went at once to Gerard's home, and faced him with what I had learned. He did not deny it. He was quite shameless about it, but as he said, how was I to prove he had harmed my sister? As he pointed out, women die every day in childbirth and with feminine complaints. I challenged him to a duel, of course, wanting to kill him there and then. But he had the audacity to refuse my challenge. Imagine how I felt when I remembered how my sister had adored him!'

Cassia put out her hand to touch his arm, her eyes misted. 'Do not go on if it upsets you so much, m'sieur.'

He swallowed. 'I must finish the tale now. Gerard saw me out of his house, I swear that he was grinning. I heard a voice call softly to him as I stepped out into the carriage-way – it was Fiona, his Flemish whore. I could have killed them both at that moment, but the door was slammed behind me. Two nights later I returned. Gerard invited me into his study, and we talked for a few moments, in the same vein as before. Then suddenly he stood up, tore at his shirt and jacket, and began to cry loudly for help. He snatched up a dagger which lay on his desk, and cut his arm with it, once, twice. I could not believe my eyes. He is mad, I thought, quite mad! I did not understand, you see.

'Then Gerard fainted – whether it was assumed or genuine I shall never know, but when his servants rushed in, he looked up and said that I had tried to kill him. "He has tried to kill me with that knife!" he told them. "Help me, he is mad!" those were his very words. Immediately, the servants pinioned my arms and held me until the authorities arrived. I had as much chance as an idiot of convincing them of the truth. I was taken away; there was a trumped-up trial at which my brother-in-law bore false witness against me, and I was sentenced literally to hell, the most notorious fortress-prison in France; the Château du Diable.'

Lucien got up, paced up and down the room, took out his kerchief and wiped his brow. 'The savagery there, the cruelties perpetrated in the name of the King, defy description, but worst of all was the Governor, a man of noble birth who should have behaved honourably. But he did not. He took bribes from those who were in a sufficiently fortunate position to offer them, and the rest – we poor mortals – were starved and lashed, and racked. It was there that I met Vincent Sauvage, my greatest friend, the greatest friend any man could have.'

'You were falsely accused? That man lied and condemned you to prison? As you say, he is insane. Your poor sister.'

'Oh, Gerard is dead now, or I would not look so happy for most of the time, mam'selle. He died of a malignant growth while I was in the Château du Diable, so I think you could say that justice was done.' Lucien gave a short laugh.

'And what happened when you were released?'

'I was not released. I was sentenced to a very long term of imprisonment, and I know no one anticipated that I would survive the years in that living hell. Few do. Were it not for Captain Sauvage, I would indeed have died there. He organized our escape brilliantly, down to the last detail. We would have got away with little mishap had I not been bitten by an adder, and in my already half-starved condition, I became very ill. Captain Sauvage himself cut the wound and sucked out the venom, but even so, I lay fevered and too weak to move.

'But instead of leaving me, as others would have done, the Captain stayed to look after me. He erected a rough hideout in a tree, and carried me up to it on his back. Then he trapped rabbits and cooked them over an open fire, and gave me the broth until I was strong enough to chew the meat.

'I raved with fever for most of the time, but he never lost patience with me. Of such are saints made, mademoiselle. And then the authorities caught up with us, just as we were about to move on out of the forest. Sauvage saw them coming from his look-out farther up the tree, and he immediately set about distracting their attention while I escaped alone. They took him: I watched him being led away.' Lucien's face twisted. 'He would not listen to my pleas but insisted on sacrificing himself. There was nothing I could do except make sure that his sacrifice had not been wasted. But imagine how I felt after that. Oh, most unworthy to be alive and free while he, my brave saviour was back in hell!'

'It must have been very troubling for you – I know how you must have felt.' Cassia wiped away a tear. 'Even I, in England, heard of the Château du Diable. A most dreaded place, it is said that no one ever leaves it alive. People say that it is better to die than to go there.'

'That is so. And I would have died there, tortured, if Captain Sauvage had not helped me to get away. Yes, he let them take him so that I could escape!' Lucien paced up and down, fists clenched. 'Do you know what happened to him, mam'selle? They took him to the galleys, for five years. Five years of unendurable torment.' Lucien sighed deeply. 'Life in those slave ships is purgatory, the men are lashed, fed on dry rusks and sour gruel, discipline is kept by the most barbarous punishments such as the cropping of noses and ears – and he suffered it for me.'

Five years. Cassia wiped away more tears. This was a new world to her, one of vicious spite and inhumanity to man, horrors too terrible to grasp. And her lover had sacrificed himself to let young Lucien go free . . . He could not have been more than a boy at the time, and Sauvage would have considered his life to be of more importance than his own. Yes, she felt that instinctively. Then, having served his five years of torture, he had taken up piracy and slavery: to revenge himself on a world which had so ill-used him?

Maybe. Or to expunge his own private suffering? She could not say for sure, of course, but as she thought of Sauvage's past, and how she had reviled him, more tears welled in her eyes, tears of pity and empathy and love.

Seeing them, Lucien believed that he had caused her distress, and he hastily sought to apologize, taking her hands in his.

'Oh, *chère* mademoiselle, forgive me! I should never have told you of this!'

' 'Tis not that, do not think it. That such horrors are accepted as normal, that is what appals me. In England, I never dreamed such cruelties existed. Slaves and punishments and savage methods such as these to deal with mankind. It is hideous!'

'But it is my fault for telling you of it and making you weep. It is just that you are so easy to talk to, and I have never really spoken of this fully to anyone before, excepting the Captain. Also, I can never resist telling people how he saved my life.' Lucien's boyish grin was back.

'I can understand that. If only I could say the same!' her mouth twisted. Had she truly come too late to save Sauvage, to make him her husband? It would seem so now that she had heard his story. A man treated like that would put up barriers between himself and the world which had condemned him to suffer. Ineluctable barriers.

Lucien went only after he had been assured she was recovering from her tears. It was not until he had gone that she remembered. Her absorption in his story had made her forget completely the one question she should have asked at the start.

Why was Vincent Sauvage imprisoned in the Château du Diable?

The days were all very much the same in the house in Algiers. Cassia had adjusted to the peace and silence of her suite, the solitude broken only by visits from Fleur. It was then that Sauvage called on her unexpectedly. Bowing stiffly he said, 'I believe that you are bored, Cassia? Is that correct? You are eager now for a little *divertissement*?'

She looked up at him, thinking of all she wanted to say: Where have you been? Why have you ignored me the past few days? How can you be so cool when we were lovers – do you think I am here to be picked up merely when you wish to make love to me? Instead, hating herself for appearing spiritless, she nodded.

'As I thought. Today you come with me to the Bedestan, the slave market in Algiers. It will be salutary to see what you are missing. But for me, you would have been there now, in the bagnio, sweltering in the heat and dirt, scratching at vermin in your ragged clothes and hair, cowering beneath the lash . . .'

'And is that so?' She drew herself up to her full height. 'Indeed I had thought that, but for you, I would be at Penwellyn, in Cornwall, England, with my dear Aunt Julitta, living happily in peace and contentment.'

Was there no end to his arrogance? – He seemed to see himself as her saviour instead of as her gaoler, which he surely was. Did he think he could ignore what had happened between them? Remembering how they had lain in one another's arms, sharing the most searing passion, whispering of love, she felt her face go hot. But if he wished to play this game of icy detachment, then she would show him that she too could play. If he thought that she would fling herself on his neck and sob, then he was to be rudely surprised. The blood of Morbillys and Joliths and O'Claires flowed in her veins; she was passionate, she needed love, but she was proud too.

Sauvage did not reply. He glanced round the chamber, asked where her outdoor clothes were, and then ordered her to dress.

She reached for a flowing lemon silk caftan embroidered with silver lilies, but Sauvage shook his head.

'Your outdoor clothes, *ma chère*. Has all I told you been wasted? Where is your Muslim robe and yashmak? You will wear those.'

'I have to wear that hot, suffocating thing? How would you like to –'

'Thousands of Muslim women do not complain,' Sauvage interrupted.

'They know no better, but I do. And who would listen to their complaints if they shouted them from the rooftops? No one listens to women here!' Her voice was bitter.

'Only imbeciles complain about the rules that keep them safe and secure.'

'So I am a fool then! What proof have I that wearing purdah will stop me from being attacked? You will be with me, anyway, and I am sure some of your men will be coming with us – Ahmek too?'

'They will. However, unless you wish to be auctioned, put on your purdah, Cassia. The Dey is a greedy man. If he hears of your beauty, he will want to know where you are going, and why I have not told him of your presence here. I would not wish to see you end up in his harem.'

'And would you let me?'

'It might be that I would have no choice. The Dey is in control here, he is appointed by the Sultan, but while he has great authority, he is also his master's rival.'

'And he has authority over Christians too?'

'Most certainly. There are thousands of Christian slaves on the Barbary Coast, and the Dey has mastery over those in Algiers itself. Religion is irrelevant in a slave, he has no rights, no needs. After the slaves have been bought in the Bedestan, they must appear before the Dey, who, if he takes a liking to any of them, has the right to buy them at the same purchase price as that of the first buyer. So you see, his authority is all-encompassing. He, with the aid of the Janissaries, rules this area most competently. We do not wish to alienate him. That would be most unwise. Now please dress.'

Sauvage turned his back while Cassia, seething with silent rage, donned the black robe and pinned the yashmak over her face. But for her blue eyes she could have been a Muslim woman.

They left the quiet, cool suite and were soon out in the Street of the Golden Moon where Ahmek and other crew members awaited them. Cassia smiled at the eunuch, then remembered that he would not be able to see her smile. Instead, she touched his arm and dipped her head in greeting. His eyes sparkled down at her.

Keeping a respectful distance between *Rais* Sauvage and his slave girl, the crew members followed them through the city streets, down twisting high-walled alleys and into slightly wider streets; but not even the wider ones were anything like the pleasant paved streets she knew in Orchard Square and the rest of London. Here, it was as if the builders had cared for nothing except keeping the sunlight off the people, making the walls as close together as possible so that, even at midday, there would be shade somewhere. Of course the narrowness and the total lack of hygiene combined to create odours and sights which Cassia found nauseating, even though her yashmak shielded her from the worst effects. She glanced behind at Ahmek. He did not seem to be perturbed by the mound of fly-covered dirt and rubbish which they had just bypassed. He would be accustomed to this, of course. One could get used to just about anything, it seemed. She thought of her life in London, of the spotless silk gowns, the scented kerchiefs and ribbons, lace fans, the priceless pearls her father had given her, the social engagements and tea drinking, the way one man, John Morbilly, had mercilessly governed his minute household. If they only knew . . .

She gave a little gasp as a beggar thrust himself at her, hands extended, pale palms uppermost. He wore a huge, filthy turban, and a tattered robe encrusted with dirt. She could not take her eyes from his face. His nose had been eaten away by some loathsome disease.

Faint with horror, she watched as Sauvage pushed the man aside, snapping some words at him. The man fell back, hatred in his eyes. She thought she would feel much the same if her entreaties were rebuffed with such harshness. She wanted to throw money to all the beggars she saw on the way, especially the poor, half-starved children with their enormous velvet-dark eyes, but she had no money, and Sauvage would not have let her anyway.

The Bedestan, the slave market, was between the Gates of the Bab el Oued and the Bab Azoun; she could hear the babble, and smell the scents long before they came in sight of it. The men with them drew closer in ranks, so that she and Sauvage were protected, and he put his hand on his dagger, as if expecting trouble. Ahmek folded his arms and looked fierce.

First, Cassia saw the men who were standing, chained together, against one wall. They looked healthy, proud, well-built – and they had fair complexions and some had blue eyes. Could they be English? She looked more closely at them; yes, they could have been men from Cornwall, except for one or two who had the dark straight hair and deep-brown eyes of the Celt. Now that they were closer, she could hear a whispered word or two – they were Scottish. But at that moment, one of the Janissaries lashed at them viciously with his whip, and their talk subsided.

'Those men are from Scotland,' she said to Sauvage, in a horrified voice.

'There are many different races here, *doucette*.' He half smiled at her naiveté. 'Why are you shocked? There will be Cornishmen and women sold here today – had you realized that?'

She felt herself go cold, then hot. He could not mean – oh no! She bit on her lip, wondering if she could get away before she had to see her own countrymen sold like cattle. But they would bring her back, even if she managed to escape the little knot of sailors protecting her.

'The – the captives in your hold?' she whispered hoarsely. 'You mean you brought me here to see them being sold?' He nodded. 'Will – will Charles be with them?' Her heart pounded in an absurd fashion as she waited for his answer, reproaching herself for her callousness in not asking before.

'No. He was bought almost immediately by a Turkish merchant who thought him handsome with his gold-streaked hair and full mouth. I would guess that he is now being fêted and accorded every honour. Handsome male slaves are very much in demand here.'

'You mean the women are also allowed to have harems of men? But surely that is against the Muslim law?'

'It is. I did not refer to male slaves for women, *doucette*. These are *garzones*, and they are strictly for the male harem owner.'

Cassia felt her cheeks flush; she went very quiet for a time. She had never dreamed such things existed, nor how they worked in practical terms. Her mind throbbed with imaginings, but she could not guess at what went on between two men, the *garzone* and his owner. Charles would bask in admiration, and perhaps he would discover a certain power. She hoped so for his sake.

Sauvage had thought all along that Charles Billings was better suited to men than to women, but he would not have said this to Cassia. The man was fortunate that he had gone to the house of Mustapha Seremith, for Seremith was extremely indulgent with his *garzones*, as long as they pleased him in the particular ways he preferred. No doubt Charles would learn those ways rapidly, and adapt himself to his new way of life.

The sale was progressing, and Cassia watched in silent dismay as bands of slaves were ushered into the centre of the Bedestan, whips singing on their shoulders, gutteral voices snarling commands to them. Some of the slaves were in reasonable condition, but most were bedraggled and bowed. A few were coughing uncontrollably, and one had blood dribbling down his chin as if he had suffered from a lung seizure. Others wore filthy ragged robes, or tattered loincloths, and cloths bound round their heads; many were bearded and had long, unkempt hair. Others were clean shaven and had red, gold or brown hair. Cassia looked searchingly for Cornishmen and women, but could not see any she could identify as such until Sauvage pointed them out to her.

Following his gaze, she saw a dozen or so men and women,

clean and standing straight. No one was lashing them with whips, or screaming at them, but they were manacled with a chain looped through each metal wristband so that none could escape alone.

These were the captives from St Michael's Mount, her fellow countrymen, to be sold here in this stinking market! She felt tears welling up, and as no one could see them through her veil, she let them fall, to be absorbed by the material of her yashmak. Poor wretched creatures, torn from their families and the beautiful Cornish countryside, to be brought to this pirates' lair and sold to Muslims who would use them as slaves. Had she lived in Morbilly longer, had these poor villagers not been abducted, she might have met them, talked to them, discussed the weather, their children, her aunt's health.

Again she was assailed by the extraordinary details of her plight, swept up as she had been from such normal, placid surroundings, to be brought to this incredible place where everything was so different, religion, morals, beliefs, customs. A place where men were bought and sold like pots and pans at a fair, as if they had no souls, no say in the matter. Where women were subjugated . . . she thought of Fleur, but then was forced to admit to herself that Fleur seemed inordinately content with her lot. The Turkish girl was virtually a prisoner, yet she was not in the least rebellious. Cassia could not help but remember her own great rebellion when she had lived in Orchard Square and when, by comparison, she had been so very free.

Screams brought her out of her reverie. She saw a woman running, a baby in her arms. One of the Janissaries – the soldiers specially trained to help govern Algiers – had assaulted her, and she had struck him, then tried to escape with her child. There was a mad scurrying chase, the woman screaming wildly, clutching at her infant, running clumsily towards the far end of the Bedestan. Cassia watched, barely breathing, nails digging into her palms, too shocked even to pray.

It ended horribly. The woman tripped and fell, the baby,

jolted from her arms, dashed its head against a wall. It lay still in its own blood, and the Janissary, helped by his fellows, picked up the mother and dragged her back to the market, pulling her along the ground by her hair and wrists until her back was a bloody pulp and she became unconscious with the pain. No one took any notice of the dead baby.

Cassia could not see for tears. Her shoulders shook with sobs and she blessed the concealment of her veil. She did not learn what happened to the woman for she was taken away, and Sauvage's slaves were next to be sold. No one lashed them or shouted insults while they were standing before the crowd of purchasers, and she was to learn from Ahmek that *Rais* Sauvage did not allow anyone to mistreat his slaves. He always gave strict instructions that his captives were to be properly fed, receive medication if necessary, and soap and water to wash.

Cassia felt that the sights and sounds of the Bedestan would be forever imprinted on her memory by the time Sauvage told her they were to go home. So much misery and degradation, people huddled, shivering, chained together, no food or water brought to them however many hours they stood in the decimating sun awaiting a buyer. And the methods of examining the slaves . . . the brutal manner in which the women had their breasts and teeth inspected, hands being thrust up their skirts, their buttocks pinched and kneaded. And if the men were being bought by someone like Mustapha Seremith, they too were handled, being roughly caressed to see if all their parts were in good working order.

Cassia was sickened but fascinated by this, watching with startled eyes but unable to look away. She did not find it hard to imagine herself amongst the group of slaves, being probed and pinched by prospective buyers, her breasts bared, and worse . . . The thought made her hot with shame. How near she had come to this degradation, she thought. Then she immediately stamped out that thought, for wasn't that why Sauvage had brought her here, so that she would realize how much she owed him? No, she would never be grateful, *never*! She loathed him! But for him, she would still be at Penwellyn, safe and content.

She was very quiet on the return journey, conscious that Sauvage looked at her frequently, his face inscrutable. Was he hoping for signs of warm gratitude on her part? Perhaps he expected her to fall at his feet and kiss them? She gritted her teeth on the words which she longed to say, for this was not the place to speak them. They passed through the narrow, now darkening streets, the smell of decay and rotting refuse even more nauseating after the day's blazing heat, and on upwards to the Street of the Golden Moon, and still she remained silent, walking like a black shadow in her purdah, eyes downcast, every inch the submissive Muslim woman.

Vincent had not expected her to remain silent. He had anticipated dawning realization in her eyes, then frank gratefulness, when she saw how the slaves were treated. But she had not said one word to him, and now she was silent: not at all like her usual spirited self. He would never admit it, but he had come to enjoy their heated exchanges, the acerbic repartée she dealt out. Why did she not say something now? He would have welcomed even an insult, anything but this muteness.

When they reached his house, he touched her arm, saying, 'We dine alone tonight, Cassia, just you and I, so you may wear what you wish. I have sent the trunk of gowns to your room in case you want to wear one of them.'

She looked up at him, astonished, and did not know whether to assent eagerly or stay cold. Those gowns she loved, dinner alone with him – was he trying to win her over now? For a moment she felt a rising excitement at the thought of dining with him just as if they were a married couple. Then nauseous visions of the slave market filled her mind. Her hands trembled slightly as she replied.

'I shall be pleased to have the gowns, although I cannot say as yet whether I shall wear them or not. It depends entirely on how I feel tonight.' She sounded capricious, which she had fully intended, but her eyes were on his face when she spoke. She was hoping to see some reaction, hoping that he would remember when she had last worn the green and gold gown, so that she could show her contempt, but apart from a shadow flickering across his face, to be expertly dismissed, she saw nothing. If he had indeed forgotten what had gone between them, then he needed to have his memory jolted sharply. And she intended to do that tonight.

She went in, to find Fleur waiting for her.

'What time will dinner be served?' Cassia asked her.

'Late mademoiselle, but do not fear that you will miss it. I shall come to tell you when it is ready. You must dress, put on the beautiful robes from the trunk in the corner of your chamber. You will find it there now. I looked at the robes while you were away. You are lucky, mademoiselle.'

Cassia thought she saw Sauvage's intentions. He, too, wished to indulge his caprice. He imagined that he could make love to her as and when he wished, discarding her in between times and forgetting that she existed. He thought he only had to invite her to dinner, send her the trunk of gowns, and she would be his willing *amoureuse*. If that were so, then he was due for a great surprise. She would dine with him, dressed in the green and gold court dress; she would smile and nod sweetly, appear pleasant and responsive, and then she would rebuff him coldly without the slightest show of emotion. What would he say to that, she wondered?

'Mademoiselle?' Fleur was looking at her, head on one side.

'Oh, I'm sorry, Fleur, I was thinking. Do you like the robes? Would you wear one if I gave it to you? Look, there's a yellow brocade one here, which is too small for me. Take it if you like . . .' Cassia delved into the trunk, lifting out the buttercup-yellow gown with ivory overskirt trimmed with azure velvet bows.

Fleur's face glowed. 'For me, mademoiselle? Truly for

me? Oh you are very generous. But I wonder if I have the courage to wear it?'

'The courage? Of course you do! Take the gown, and look, here are some yellow slippers and a fan to go with it.'

Fleur, face shining, bowed her way out of the room, clutching the gifts. Cassia went to one of the mirrors and began to comb her hair. She would dearly have liked a bathe after taking off the heavy robe, but Fleur had brought only a bowl of water and soap. Deciding on a thorough wash, she proceeded to scrub herself all over. Her emotions see-sawed.

Should she or should she not let Vincent make love to her tonight? Suddenly, irrationally, she wanted him to, yes, desperately, more than anything she wanted his arms around her, his mouth on hers. Oh to pretend that today hadn't happened! Then she thought of the way he had ignored her in the past week, not to mention his coldness when she had interrupted the dinner party, and she longed savagely to punish and hurt him. She tried to balance her thoughts.

Resignation of a sort had come to her in the last few days, partially extinguishing the blithe optimism that was her nature, dulling her resolve to fight. Vincent was still going to sell her to the Sultan, he had no intention of letting their relationship deepen, he had no feelings for her other than those of lust – had he not told her so repeatedly? Today merely proved that she should be thankful.

So what would she gain by letting him make love to her tonight, except the doubtful pleasure of being in the arms of the man she loved, and a temporary assuagement of the ache of longing within her? Oh yes, she admitted, she needed him! It was now over two weeks since they had last made love, and it had seemed an eternity to her. Not even the colour and clamour of Algiers, or the horrors of the Bedestan today could change that. She might hate and detest him, but she never ceased to yearn for his touch. Misery and doubt churned within her.

She had washed and combed her hair until it fluffed out

into bright russet curls round her face and shoulders, then massaged into her body the scented oils which Fleur had given her. Should she wear the green and gold gown, or would it look too obviously like an invitation? Finally she decided on a gown of delicate lavender lace, tying it at her waist with a silver-embroidered sash. She selected silver-embroidered slippers and a silver lace rosette for her hair, then she surveyed herself in the mirror. Yes, she preferred English clothes to Turkish, and, recognizing this, she knew she ought to make the most of the ones in the trunk before they arrived in Constantinople and her choice became limited.

She raged inwardly. How dared he do it? With an effort of will, she checked her rising temper and excluded thoughts of her future to think calmly of the coming night.

She was ready for dinner, and feeling brighter. Perhaps he had asked her to dine with him because he had something special to tell her? Of course! Why had she not thought of that earlier? Her heart began to pound unevenly. He had obviously tried to keep away from her, but now, realizing that they were meant for one another, he would tell her so tonight. He would implore her forgiveness . . .

Fleur came at nine in the evening to escort Cassia to the room where Sauvage was to join her. A table was spread with dishes and platters of food, two chased goblets encrusted with jewels stood by a flagon of wine. There was a central table arrangement of fruit and exotic blooms, and the food was a generous selection of both English and Turkish dishes. One oil lamp lit the room, suffusing it in a romantic glow. Cassia felt an increasing joy. Such a discreetly-lit room, an exquisite dinner, wine, she in her beautiful lavender gown: how could Sauvage fail to relent? They would spend the next few hours eating, drinking, talking, and then . . .

'Where is *Rais* Sauvage?' she asked Fleur.

'He will not be long, mademoiselle. One of the concubines fell ill. He is ensuring that the physician arrives before he leaves her.'

'Concubines? But I thought all his slaves were sold today?'

'Oh, not the slaves he sells, mam'selle.' Fleur smiled, her face innocent, for she was unaware of the effect her words would have on the English girl. 'She is one of the concubines *Rais* Sauvage always has here, in his harem.'

Cassia swallowed, a strange dizzying feeling sweeping through her head. 'He – he has a harem of his own? For – for his own use?' Her voice rasped in her throat.

'But of course.' Fleur looked genuinely puzzled. 'All the wealthy men have harems, you knew that, surely? Mademoiselle feels all right?' she asked, as Cassia fell against the wall, a hand to her throat.

'I – yes,' she struggled for composure. Her lover, the man she had wanted for her own, had a harem! That was why he had not visited her since they had arrived in Algiers. Why should he when he had his pick of willing, voluptuous creatures all skilled in the arts of pleasing their master, girls who belonged to him, body and soul, and were obedient to his every whim . . . ?

You fool, she thought, you stupid little fool! He would have no reason to marry you when he has his pick of women from the world over . . . A harem of his own, furnished with beauties whom he had chosen himself. Somewhere in this house, his own seraglio that he could visit at any time of the day or night . . . Oh, you imbecile, Cassia Morbilly! She felt weak, ill, there was a twisting pain behind her breasts.

She stood there, clutching at the trellis, in the beautiful lavender gown, the silver rosette in her hair, while the pain gnawed at her heart and tears rolled down her cheeks.

CHAPTER TEN

Thirty minutes later, Sauvage arrived. He was dressed in a sapphire-blue brocade jacket and satin breeches, and he looked so devastatingly handsome that Cassia wanted to throw herself into his arms, forgetting the resolution she had made in the past half hour.

He grinned. 'Mademoiselle has not been too bored waiting? I am sorry to be so late. It was unavoidable – one of my slaves was ill.'

Cassia glared at him. So he dared say so much, and yet conceal the truth? How arrogant he was.

'Male or female?' she said coolly, straightening one of her rings with an insouciant air.

Sauvage flicked her a glance. 'Female.' He poured out wine for them both, Cassia sipping hers, not tasting its sweetness. Her hand gripped the goblet tightly. She would have liked to throw it at his head.

Fleur served them, piling their plates high with pilaf and beaming at them both as she did so. The English girl's tears had amazed her; she had not really known why Cassia wept. In Islam, girls did not weep over men because they owned harems. Only the poorest Muslim men did not have concubines. Why there should be tears Fleur did not know. If Mademoiselle Cassia secretly loved *Rais* Sauvage, she should have been happy because tonight he had chosen to be with her. In Islam, a husband could choose a different wife or concubine for each night, or none at all, and it was a great favour to be selected. The Koran said, *Your wives are your field: go in, therefore, to your field as you will.* Was this life not easy and safe while girls were protected and cushioned against hardship? That was why Muslim law advocated a man taking more than one wife: so that there would not be a surplus of impoverished women when wars drastically reduced the male population. Yes, as Fleur saw it, life was easy for Muslim women. It was their men who bore the hardships, the anxieties, the risk of death. She could imagine no other way of life.

Cassia was reluctant to drink, the wine, not wishing to lose even the slightest control of the situation, but the pilaf was rich, oily-sweet, and the wine stronger than she had thought from its pleasant taste. The lamp in the room seemed to glow with a stronger, almost eerie light, every noise sounded louder. By the time Fleur brought them each a dish of fruit and one of *Rahat Lokum*, Cassia knew that she had drunk too much. Fighting to steady her movements, she ate some of the Turkish Delight, her head carefully lowered so that Sauvage would not be able to catch her eye. He had tried to do so, throughout the meal, but she had kept her eyes averted. Nor had she responded to his attempts at conversation. If he wished to think her uncommunicative, then that was too bad. He did not hesitate to be taciturn when he chose, so why should she?

Finally, he said, 'Are you not feeling very well, Cassia?'

'I feel very well indeed, thank you,' she said coldly.

'Then what is troubling you, *doucette*?'

'Nothing. Nothing at all. What makes you think I am troubled?'

Her hand moved clumsily, tipping over her goblet so that wine splashed on the table. She blushed hotly, and Fleur hastened forward to mop up the liquid.

Sauvage arched his brow. 'Perhaps the lady is not happy here, but wishes to be in the Bedestan with her countrymen? That can easily be arranged . . .'

'How dare you threaten me!' she cried, eyes flashing. 'Do you think you have only to mention the slave market to me and I shall become smiling and submissive? I am not frightened of you, m'sieur, oh, no, not at all! And I think your threats are beneath contempt.' Cassia rose angrily, her chair falling over with a loud crash. She wished immediately that she had not got up so quickly, for her head whirled and when she tried to make a dignified exit, she stumbled over the fallen chair and would have fallen headlong but for Sauvage's grip on her arm. She looked up at him furiously, her head spinning, then tried to thrust him away. She did not succeed, for his fingers were like manacles. 'Let me go!' she cried and he obeyed so suddenly that she swayed, and would have collapsed into his arms had he not caught her again.

'You have put something in my wine,' she accused.

'Indeed not, *doucette*. I have no need to do such a thing.'

'Then why am I ill? I –' her eyes blurred, Sauvage's face misting.

'Perhaps mademoiselle has drunk too much of the wine? It is very strong – I think I advised care.'

'Indeed you did not! You chose a strong wine purposely to – to –' she realized how arrogant her accusation would sound, but it was clear to her that this was why she was now in such a lamentable state.

'To what?' He looked at her steadily, his brilliant-jewel eyes inscrutable.

'To – I –' She fell silent, taking her seat again, head lowered.

Fleur finished serving them, bowed and went to her bed. The lamp flickered, glowed, and flickered again. Was the oil running out? Sauvage finished his meal, apparently regardless of her stony face. Finally, she said:

'I feel better now.'

'I am pleased to hear that. It is always troubling to see a beautiful woman ill.'

She swallowed an angry retort. He had classed her with all women, when she wanted to be the one and only woman to him. 'I believe that is why you were late tonight,' she went on, daringly. 'Because one of your "beautiful women" was unwell.'

Sauvage raised his brow. 'Aminia, you mean? She is often ill – she suffers from pains in the head.'

'How that must annoy you, to own a concubine who cannot always be available. How infuriating to have to consider her first, now and again, before your own selfish pleasure,' Cassia riposted.

'I see that you are cross with me, Cassia,' he mocked. 'Would you have me a monk?'

'There is an enormous gap between being a monk and a lecher. Most men contrive to stay somewhere in between.'

'And what makes you think I am not?'

'Who could own a harem and be a monk?'

'So you believe that possession of something makes one self-indulgent? Would this also apply to fields, *doucette*? Would you say then that a man who owns many fields is inevitably to be a farmer?'

'No – I did not say that. But why does a man need a harem if not for his lechery?'

'I cannot speak for others, *doucette*. For myself I own a harem – a little harem – because the girls in it would be worse off elsewhere. And, being Muslims, they consider it an unhappy state to belong to a man and yet not be bedded by him. Aminia, for example, would feel it a personal insult if I did not treat her as a desirable woman.'

'Then you have your work cut out, Captain Sauvage.' Cassia rose, her face icy, and turned to storm out of the room.

Sauvage stood up immediately. She found him barring her exit.

'I had not realized, *chérie*, that you were the opposite of Aminia.'

'The – the opposite?' She struggled for composure, but he was very close to her and her senses had begun to swim.

'Aminia would be insulted if I did not find her desirable. You it seems are insulted because I do find you desirable. Very desirable.' His eyes glittered. She could not take her gaze away from his.

'There is more to desire – and love – than coupling and then going one's separate ways, Vincent! When a woman is loved, taken to bed, she begins to dream. She wants constancy, to know her man is nearby, to know that she can build a home and bear children in loving peace and security. Any man can desire a woman, desire is a fleeting, selfish passion. It never puts the lover first, and, when it is over, the lovers do not think of each other again. Love is totally different. It never fades, it is constant, unselfish, devoted.'

He listened without interruption, but still barring her way. She felt better now that she had spoken what was in her heart: somehow cleansed. She did not care if he found her odious now. Eyes unflinching, she stared up at him, silently daring him to disagree.

'I cannot say that I have come across this unselfish, unfading emotion. Those of my friends who are married do not particularly display it.'

'Perhaps you do not have enough friends then? And denying that something exists does not cancel it out! It is well known in my homeland that the King and Queen are devoted to one another, and a very happy family. That is just one example of the love I am talking about.'

'But it would not do for a king or queen to allow the people to think otherwise, would it, *doucette*? Obviously they will put on a happy front to keep their country content. Who knows what lies behind that façade?'

His cynicism infuriated her, and she said so. He gave a half laugh. 'Cynicism, *ma petite*? Do you not mean *realism*?'

'Are you saying that it is more realistic to think the worst than to think the best? Surely that is illogical, and, yes, cynical. Nothing is always bad, and nothing is always good. I prefer to see good where possible.' She had not considered his past when she spoke, but now she thought: How can he see good when he has been a prisoner in the Château du Diable and served five years as a galley slave? That would harden a saint. She wanted to cry, 'I did not mean it – I understand.' But how could she when his face was so forbidding, his eyes so cold?

'If you are happier that way, then so be it, *doucette*. But it is hardly self-protective is it? You have seen only the best in a man before, disregarding the worst, and the consequences were unpleasant for you, were they not? Have you not found yourself burned, and now wish to stay away from the flame?'

She fancied there was a certain pleading light in his eyes, and wondered why it should be there. Was it simply that he wished to have the relief from responsibility he would feel if she were also cynical?

'M'sieur, I have loved, and am not ashamed of it. No indeed – even though I discovered that he was worthless. 'Tis infinitely sweeter to have loved, to be able to love unstintingly, than to be so warped that love is impossible. Not even in the most fearful of nightmares would I wish to be so cold and selfish that I could not love. Love means the ability to be hurt, did you know that?'

He sighed, his eyes closing. 'Yes, *ma chère*, I know it. I have known it longer than you.'

She was startled. 'Then why do you argue with me? Why do you speak so cynically of lust and desire?'

'Do I? Perhaps I cannot help it. Perhaps I am cursed to speak thus for the rest of my life.'

'For the rest of your – nonsense! How can you say such a thing?' Her hand reached out, and clasped his arm.

'It is easier for me to say such things than to think as you do, Cassia. Where is the sweetness in my life? Where are the happy memories for me to recall? I have none – only bitter thoughts of revenge and hatred. If you had suffered five years in –' he stopped, turning away, his teeth gritted together, a muscle clenching in his jaw.

'Five years in the slave galleys?' she finished for him.

'How did you find out?' His face was suddenly forbiddingly dark.

'Lucien.'

'He had no right.'

'He is your good, devoted friend so he has every right to speak loyally, reverently of you and of what you did for him when you helped him to escape. He loves you.'

'Love. Is that *all* you can speak of?'

'Would you have me talk of hate and malice and revenge? Are they so preferable to love? Surely you cannot see the world in such a twisted way?'

'Twisted? Yes, that is how I see it. I am twisted, too, by

life, by circumstances. So you see, *ma chère mademoiselle*, you cannot help me. I am beyond help. If you were to devote the rest of your life to me, I could not, would not, change!'

The romantic dinner was over. Vincent Sauvage strode out of the room without a backward glance, leaving Cassia to clasp her arms round her waist to quieten the pain growing there. She should have known from the way the evening had begun that it could only finish badly, but she had been unable to extinguish her hopes.

She had begun the night by crying, and now was crying again, silent tears rolling down her face, unquenchable tears bitter as acid. Hot, angry tears that reproached her for not adhering to her plan, for allowing her feelings to show. She told herself roughly that she did not care, that he was not worthy of another thought. And then she imagined what he was doing now. He would be with his concubines, they would be stroking his face and kissing him, and helping him to undress. In her mind's eye, she saw their beautiful golden-brown bodies, plump and naked, and Vincent's inevitable response. His slave girls, his property, willing, eager to satisfy every whim. Disgusting . . . horrible, she would drive him from her mind . . . How she hated him!

The oil lamp finally guttered and went out, plunging the room into blackness. Cassia stayed where she was, still weeping, seeing with bitter clarity all her folly. Wishing that Vincent Sauvage had never laid a finger on her. Longing for the storm in her heart to subside so that she could be indifferent again.

It was after midnight when she heard the door of her harem suite closing gently. Immediately she sat up, her skin prickling. She had been in bed for about an hour, and as far as she knew Kol and Ulek were on guard as usual. It could be anyone, one of the pirates . . .

She choked back a horrified gasp as footfalls approached her bed, then she opened her mouth to scream.

'You are awake?' It was Sauvage's voice. She nearly fainted with relief and then pulled herself together angrily.

What did he want? Why had he come here like this? She lay there, staring unseeingly into the darkness, pretending to be asleep, willing him to leave the room. But her involuntary movement at the sound of his voice had betrayed her.

'So you are awake. Were you lying there in darkness thinking of how cruel I was to you? Forgive me, *doucette*, please forgive me.' Vincent took her hands and kissed them. She could hardly believe her ears. He had come here in the middle of the night to apologize to her?

'Will you forgive me, *ma chère*? Say you will. I cannot rest until you do.'

She did not speak for a few moments. Sauvage continued to kiss her hands, her arms, then he began to plant kisses on her face, gently, tenderly, until he came to her mouth. Obstinately she clamped her lips together, promising herself that she would bite him if he continued this probing, insistent, passionate kissing that sent waves of sensation coursing through her tense body.

'Go away,' she said fiercely, 'Leave me be.' But her words were drowned as he slid his arms around her and whispered against her mouth:

'*Petite*, all you said tonight was right. In my heart I know it, but I cannot admit it. I have built a life here which I could never have without the motivation of revenge which has driven me now for years. And if I admit that I was wrong, that revenge is wrong, I shall then have to face what I have done in the past. The misery and degradation I have caused . . .'

She put her arms round him now, pulling his head on to her breast, feeling the anger and the hatred evaporating at his words, thinking of nothing but comforting him. Whatever his past, whatever her future, he was sorry for it now and needed her love. She could no more withhold her loving comfort than tell him to leave.

'You are sorry. Nothing else is necessary. Once you have been repentant, all is forgiven. You can be a new person now.'

'Ah no. It is too late. Look at what I have done to you. I took you away from your home, your aunt.'

'You saved me from being raped, if I remember right.'

'Don't mock, *petite*. You loved him.'

'Only until that moment when he went berserk and tried to force himself on me. I had already decided I could not leave my aunt, she was too ill, but Charles said that he would take my virginity, and make me pregnant so that I would have to marry him.'

'I did not know all of that. *Pauvre petite*,' he kissed her forehead and cupped her neck in his hands to kiss her mouth again.

'So really you saved me, you see.'

'Your aunt . . .'

'It is true that I have grieved deeply over being torn from her, knowing that she would think I had deserted her. But I have forgiven you my darling. Long ago.'

'It was a way of life. I had no choice. Like Lucien, I can never go back to France. Renegades are unwanted, even in their home towns. He, poor boy, has had the same wretched experience of the law as I. We could never change now.'

'I do not know why you were imprisoned. Can you tell me?'

'It is not a pleasant thing to discuss. I would rather you did not know.'

'If that is what you want. Tell me at your leisure, darling.'

He sighed, his arms tight round her waist. She cradled him lovingly, warm with the delight of his nearness and the very fact that he needed her. There was nothing sweeter than this in all the world.

It was natural that their kisses became more passionate and that he slipped into bed beside her, stroking her breasts and telling her how much he loved her. Then he pressed against her, she put her arms right round him to pull him close, sighing as she felt his powerful response. Gently, he slid between her legs, making her moan with delight and

157

pull him closer. She knew that she had missed his love-making, longed for his caresses, but even knowing this, her own response amazed her. She seemed to melt into him, and he into her, she could barely catch her breath as heat raced over her skin, gushed through her body. He felt incredible inside her. He was her, she was him. Such power, such hardness, and he knew exactly what to do to thrill her – it wasn't studied or forced, it just happened naturally. And while he was scything through her, taking her will-power, her resistance, he was kissing her ears and neck and lips, her breasts and wrists and arms, gentle, loving kisses. Those sweet kisses affected her as much as his body inside her, for they were thoughtful, tender; they told her that he was thinking of her and not just of his own pleasure.

As before, he took his time, there was no hurrying. She relaxed, floating high, suspended on hot velvet clouds, knowing that she could sigh, or moan, relax limply for a few seconds when overcome by love, or respond with wild-ness, and that he would understand and be in accord with her in every way. How safe she felt with him – as if they had been lovers for eternity.

When her pleasure began, he knew at once. '*Doucette*, I am with you,' he whispered, 'be happy – enjoy yourself. Take all the pleasure you want. If I can bring you such delight, I ask no more.'

Her head moved from side to side, she gripped his forearms, moaning his name, once, twice. 'I'm here, beloved,' he said, and then she gasped out loud, and again, her breath drawing in with a rush, her eyes closing, scarlet flooding her cheeks. He smiled as he watched her bliss, and she opened her eyes to see him looking down at her, his face alight.

'You feel wonderful,' she sighed, bathed in glowing warmth. 'Are you a god, or human?'

He grinned again. 'Human. At least, I think so.'

'Then I would hate to mate with a god – it would kill me!' she teased, at which he clasped her tightly in his arms, caging her, and moving more fiercely so that she began to climax again, and this time, having forgotten nothing which could give her pleasure, he finally forgot himself.

It was dawn when she awoke. She was alone. Had it been a dream? Had he really come to her in the night?

But no, her body ached, and her neck was bruised from his kisses. She sighed, blissfully, then turned over and went back to sleep. She would see him today, she knew it, and they would be happy for all time.

He would have to get rid of his harem, of course.

CHAPTER ELEVEN

Nathan Dash was in bed with one of the whores he had picked up from the backstreets the previous night. He was governed by periodic impulses, to go out at night and pick up the commonest prostitutes he could find. It was not that he was short of women – far from it – he too had his harem, some thirty girls of many different races, all huge breasted and broad-hipped, girls who were accustomed to his perversions. It was the thought of novelty, of debauchery, that took him out, every few weeks, to pick up some girl, lure her back to his rooms and force her to submit to his inclinations. One or two of the girls had been able to teach him a thing or two; one he had beaten brutally because she had told him he was a dirty, vile old man. When she had collapsed to the floor, semi-conscious, her teeth broken, he had done what he wanted to do and she had not even known what was happening. After that, he had wanted to do the same thing again, at other times, but even he knew he was treading on dangerous ground. One of the girls had died, and he had rowed her out to sea and was about to cast her overboard when he was again overcome by his strange lust. He had kneeled over her body, trying to keep the boat steady, and when he had finished, his face covered in sweat, he had tipped her into the sea like a bale of garbage.

When that was over, he was filled with self-loathing, until the lust began to grow again.

He realized that he was very fortunate living in Algiers, with his successful half-brother to back him. Captain Dash did not love nor even like him. But they did have the same father, and blood links could prove powerful in times of need. Nathan had often resorted to dropping his brother's name when necessary. Usually it got him what he wanted. He had built up his own little fortune over the past few years, a fortune that would have been larger but for his extravagance. He wanted only the best for himself, and he always got it. Sumptuous clothes and jewels, rings, earrings, gold chains for his neck; he indulged himself in all these, and, every few months, at great cost, he would completely replenish his wardrobe.

He had never loved a woman nor been married. As far as he knew, he had no bastards: that was entirely due to his peculiar perversities. The way which procreated children had never attracted him; he sought to be different, and what better way to be different than this? Men had never pursued him, and even at his most frustrated he had never considered them an adequate substitute for females. There had been an incident when he was twelve – an older man had tried to seduce him, but he had run off, leaving the man furious and red-faced, with his breeches round his ankles. When he had tried to chase the boy, he had fallen over and bruised himself. Nathan had laughed about that for months. It still amused him to think of it now and again. No, it was women he liked – or rather, did not like, but needed. The girl lying beside him now was asleep and snoring, her tattered black hair spread across the pillow. She had decayed teeth, a scar on her breast where a lover had bitten her in a frenzy, and she had not had a bath for months. But she had been willing, which was what really mattered to Nathan. She had known what he wanted straight away, and given it to him. They had wrestled and thrashed about together on the bed, sweating and clawing at one another, and when it was over, they had slept, exhausted.

Thinking of that, Nathan found his body responding. He touched himself, caressing the hardness growing between his legs. This was the one part of his body that was not rough or scaly, but satiny and shiny and he thought it beautiful. He considered himself well endowed, he had no doubts on that score. Many of his women had remarked about his size – none had ever grumbled at his being too small. His fingers moved rapidly, he squirmed. The girl gave a loud snore, and rolled against him. He put out a hand and twisted her left breast until she woke.

'Look at that. Nice isn't it?' She nodded, sliding down the bed to accommodate him. 'No, not that. Turn over,' he ordered and she obeyed meekly, face pushed into the pillow. He mounted her, entering her so roughly that she groaned, and he twisted her breasts in his hands as he began to move more quickly. She climaxed savagely, as did he, and they collapsed together on the bed. Half an hour later, waking from a light doze, Nathan ordered the girl to get out. She did so only after he had punched her in the face.

When she had gone, he began to think of the girl with the virginal face and the Earth-mother body. From England she was, like him, kidnapped off the Cornish coast by Captain Sauvage, brought here on her way to the Grand Seraglio. He wanted her. He had never been so obsessed by a woman. The thought of doing to her what he had just done to the whore made him shudder with anticipation. His hand returned between his legs, and began to caress. Cassia, beautiful red-haired Cassia with the hydrangea-blue eyes and the ivory skin, such full heavy breasts and tiny waist – and those rounded hips . . . He gritted his teeth, brows drawn together.

He was going to have her. He had not changed his mind. Since that night at Sauvage's home, he had been besotted with the idea of bedding her, every whore he laid was Cassia in his mind. But he had to be careful. His half-brother and Sauvage between them had sizeable authority in Algiers. Sauvage was as close to the Sultan as a non-Muslim could be, and anyone who harmed him would be dealt with by Hamid – horribly. For some days, Nathan had mulled over various plans for ridding himself of his enemy. Poison? Too difficult to administer secretly and without trace. A dagger in the back? That would bring down Hamid's wrath on them all. A duel? How could he engineer such a method with the man who was shortly to inherit his half-brother's empire? No, it was very awkward. But he wanted to avenge himself on Sauvage and get the girl at the same time, and as he always got what he wanted in the end, he was not dismayed by the lack of an immediate plan.

He awoke during the night with the right idea in his mind. He would get his men together, and they would disguise their vessels under the Spanish flag, attacking Sauvage as he left Algiers on his way to Constantinople. It was so simple that he could have cursed himself for not thinking of it sooner. They would lie in wait for Sauvage's ship, *The Poseidon*, and attack it, taking its crew by surprise in friendly waters. Who would expect the Spanish to be lying in wait so near Algiers? Surprise would be his main weapon, and the second would be force. His men were bloodthirsty, ruthless, and dirty fighters. He had no fears that they would be beaten back.

He grinned, then laughed out loud. They would take the ship, *The Poseidon*, one of the finest privateers on the Barbary Coast, and they would take the girl and Sauvage's other slaves. All of Sauvage's men must die, of course, so that no one could carry the tale. And he, Nathan Dash, would have Cassia. He knew what he would do with her. He was going to chain her up on his bed, face down, and keep her there for as long as it suited him.

He imagined her soft round buttocks like velvet, and her beautiful white back, the tumbling russet hair, her screams and pleas, her struggles which would be to no avail because she would be manacled. My God, he thought, it's happening again. He looked down, barely able to believe what he saw. He knew he was virile, but the frequency and force of this was surprising even him. He would have to get one of his concubines in, or maybe two. He rang the bell by the side of the bed and ordered one of his servants to fetch two girls from the harem: any two, it did not matter which.

Aminia was dead. Cassia heard this from Fleur, who spoke with tears in her eyes.

'*Rais* Sauvage is sad, so sad, for Aminia is one of his

favourites. She's been here five years. She loved *Rais* Sauvage.'

'Was she very young?' Cassia asked.

'Not very. Twenty, maybe, she herself did not know. It is tragic.'

'*Rais* Sauvage is very upset?'

'Yes, mademoiselle. He blames himself. Yet it is not his fault. Aminia has had pains in her head for a long time now. For two years. Physicians have been helpless. Only cutting her head open would have saved her, and yet that, too, would have killed her.'

Cassia felt sorry for poor Aminia, but now knew why she had not seen her lover since the night he had visited her after their dinner together. Two days had passed since then, and she had had no word from him. Naturally she had thought the worst. She had stormed and wept, she had devised wild and complicated escape plans, she had also prayed, but at last, in the face of her utter helplessness, a strange ennui had overcome her. If Vincent had been there, no matter how remote or ill-tempered, she could have fought for what she wanted, but faced with his silence and his absence, her confidence and courage began imperceptibly to seep away. Gripped by a deep sadness, she lost her appetite; her face became pale and hollow.

She was, mentally and physically, resigning herself to life in Grand Seraglio, when Fleur brought her the news of Aminia's death. But why had Vincent not sent her a note? Just a few words to explain about the concubine and to say that he would see her as soon as possible? It would not have hurt him to do that. How loving and tender he had been with her two nights before, and yet she'd had to suffer this unnerving silence.

'Will you tell *Rais* Sauvage that I am very sorry about Aminia and send him my condolences, please, Fleur? Ask him to come and see me when he is feeling better – please?'

Fleur's coal-black eyes slanted. 'Come and see you, mam'selle? But he is not here. He has gone to do penance in the great mosque of *Sancta Zita* in Imuma. The mosque is famed as a place of penance, you see. He went there straight away when Aminia died.'

'Imuma? Where is that?' Cassia's hands were gripped together. So he was not even here in Algiers – suddenly how alone she felt.

' 'Tween here and Bougie, mam'selle. Not too far. A trip of a few hours. But it is a long penance there.'

'And he did not leave any message for me?'

'No, mam'selle.' Fleur's eyes held empathy now. Poor, troubled English girl, strange to ways of Islam, she suffered too greatly for love. She did not have trust in Allah. Allah loved lovers; he would bring them together when it was His Will and not before.

Cassia sighed, the ennui falling over her like a shroud. She felt cold and dispirited. Tears welled, but did not fall out of her eyes. Instead they stayed inside; she wept, but inwardly. Somehow, despite the knowledge that Vincent was bound to return, she felt that this episode was the last act in the drama. Despite the fact that he professed not to care for women, but only to use them, Aminia's death had clearly affected him deeply. Of course, Vincent would have been a Catholic in his homeland, even if he had dropped his religion when he became a renegade, and Catholicism applauded true penance and confession. Perhaps Aminia's death had reminded him of his early years, of all that he had abandoned, and he had been obsessed by this sudden need to make amends to God? Something told her she had found the true reason for his absence. Nevertheless, she felt desolate. And what good was penance, if you did other things which in their turn would require penance, so that you had to make your confession yet again?

To love her, as he had done, to make love to her, raising her hopes, and then to go like this . . . Surely that would offend God as much as anything? Ah Vincent! She lowered her gaze seeing pity in the eyes of the Turkish girl. Although she was very young, Fleur knew more of life than Cassia did. Fatalism, that was what the Muslims practised. At first it had seemed far removed from the English creed, but

Cassia had come to realize that fatalism was also part of true Christianity. Trusting absolutely in whatever God brought. Would she ever have such strength and courage to practise it?

Lucien came to see her two days later. He looked very serious and Cassia immediately asked him if he had news of Sauvage.

'News? No, he has gone to Imuma – Fleur told you, did she not? I asked her to. I think.– well, you know how I feel about the Captain, but in leaving you as he did I think he behaved thoughtlessly to say the least. I could not have done it!' Lucien flushed as if this criticism of his friend were being wrenched from him.

Cassia put out her hand and touched his arm. 'I do not think for a moment that you would have done, Lucien. The Captain is a strange man, driven by needs and motives we could never understand. How complicated he is. Just when I think I begin to know him, he shows yet another side and I realize I shall never know the truth about him.'

'We leave for Constantinople the moment he returns. Before he left for Imuma, he gave me orders to prepare, to have everything ready for our departure by the time he gets back from *Sancta Zita*. *The Poseidon* is in readiness now. She was being repaired here, and has never been in better shape.' He lowered his eyes, for Cassia had gone very pale.

'He did not say anything else to you? Nothing – about – about me?'

'No, mademoiselle. I am sorry. So sorry. If only I could do something.'

Cassia sighed. 'I know that you would help me if you could. But how could either of us dissuade Captain Sauvage from the course of action he is so irrevocably set upon? And yet I thought, I hoped . . .' She turned away to hide her tears. 'Oh, you cannot know how I have suffered, thinking he loved me, and that we would be together! Instead, he continues with this plan to sell me. Not even in my craziest dreams could I have imagined such a thing – being sold to a Sultan. Me, a Cornish girl!' Cassia put her hands

166

over her face and sank down on a bench. Lucien sat beside her, his arm round her shoulders, letting her weep, her head against him.

'Lucien, in the absence of information to the contrary, I can only assume I am still going to the Grand Seraglio – oh, but if you had heard what he said to me before he left for Imuma! How could he say those things and *still* sell me? Is he driven by some demon? I just do not understand.' She wept again, Lucien stroking her hair. He opened his mouth to tell her something, then closed it again. Would it help her to know of Martia? He pondered over this for some minutes, then finally he said:

'The Captain has not had happy experiences of love, mademoiselle. He has trusted two women, and both betrayed him. He made me swear never to speak her name again, to anyone, but I think, mademoiselle, that it would comfort you to know this. Why he behaves as he does, that is. You see, soon after he came to the Barbary Coast, he fell in love with Martia Stainesbury. She was the widow of an Englishman, a silk merchant, who had lived here for six months before his death. When he died, she was left penniless, and with no method of returning to England. She came to Captain Sauvage for aid, having heard that he was sympathetic to those in desperate need.

'She was very beautiful, Martia. She had yellow hair and grey eyes, and a smooth white skin. She knew that if she did not get a protector soon, she would be in serious danger from the Turks. I myself think her husband was insane to bring her to this area, but then he was a greedy man. He wanted to make his fortune in England selling the silks he had bought here at a low price. He did not want to be separated from his bride, so he brought her too. Maybe he did not know how dangerous it is here for women – especially for beautiful ones. Anyway, she threw herself on the Captain's mercy, he was moved by her plight, and gave her a suite in his own house.'

'In this house?'

'Oh no. His previous house, which was much smaller

and more modest than this. He very soon offered to marry her, and she accepted. He told me that she was sweet and virtuous, totally unlike the girl he had known in France who had ruined him.'

'He married her?' Cassia was stunned by this news.

'Yes. They had a child. A beautiful child. But as you know, life here is hazardous, and Sauvage had his work cut out to keep his position here. He had to spend long absences from home, and Martia became bored.'

'She did not travel with him? I would have!'

'She suffered very badly from *mal de mer*, and also, there was the child. She said that life on board was not suitable for a little girl.'

'I would not have said that. A man and his wife should be together.'

'I agree. But it seemed that after Martia got her wedding ring, her protector, and her child, she did not wish to exert any energy on her part to keep them.'

'And what happened?'

'The Captain was delayed while in Constantinople. He was trying to buy some rubies for his wife. The famous Smiling Sun rubies. The Sultan had agreed to let him have them at a special price in exchange for two dozen concubines. Sauvage could have provided any girls, but he went out of his way to find two dozen particularly handsome women. That was what took him so long. At last he returned with the rubies, but when he got back, Martia was not here.'

'She had been kidnapped?'

'Nothing like that. She had run off with a Spanish captain – a man who had called on Sauvage to seek employment with him, had been entertained by Martia in Sauvage's absence, and had fallen in love with her. She had not resisted his advances. In fact, so her serving women said, she had spent many hours alone with this Spaniard – nights, too – and neglected her child. Then, only days before Sauvage returned, she ran off with the man. They went to Cadiz, and he apparently went back into the Spanish navy, giving up his plans for a pirate's life.'

'So she betrayed Vincent – she must surely be the most stupid creature ever born.'

'Was. She died. There was an epidemic of fever in Cadiz – and she and the child both died. The Spaniard too. It was about six months after she had run off, and before Sauvage could trace them. He found out about their deaths when he discovered where they had gone. By then they had been dead for some months. He told me of this, when he returned from Spain, and he abjured me never to speak of them again – to him or to anyone. Until this day, I have not done so, mademoiselle.'

'Poor Vincent. How he must have suffered. To lose a wife and child like that . . .'

'You will promise me not to mention this to the Captain?'

'Of course. I give you my promise, Lucien. But there may be no need for promises. It is possible, you realize, that I may never speak to him again? He will return from Imuma, and put me in the hold of *The Poseidon* and that will be that.'

'Mademoiselle, I do not think so. I am sure he loves you.'

'Maybe he does, Lucien. I feel that in his own unique way he does love me. But what good will it do us? He fights it – he rejects it, as if it is some sort of loathsome disease, and not the most beautiful emotion in the world.' Cassia sighed deeply, wiping her eyes. 'To run from love, as Martia did, as he is now doing – what can we do for them, for people like that? What is wrong with them, Lucien?'

The young Frenchman shrugged his shoulders. 'If only I knew mam'selle, I would tell you. But I do not, *helas*.'

At that moment, Fleur came in, bringing mint tea and sweetmeats.

Lucien jumped up to take the tray from her, at which she laughed sweetly, her cheeks going pink. Even in her unhappiness, Cassia noticed the girl's pleasure at Lucien's gallant gesture. She looked from the Turkish girl to the young man, and back again. Was it possible that love was blossoming here, and she had not even noticed it?

Cassia did not feel like eating, but she drank the refreshing tea while Lucien and Fleur chattered together. How voluble the usually quiet girl was in his presence, and how gracefully she used her tiny, shapely hands when she spoke. What an adorable bride she would make for Lucien. Perhaps after all some good would come of this whole unhappy affair.

The next three days were the most depressing Cassia had ever spent. She could not eat; she hardly slept. The hours seemed to weigh on her like boulders, and she felt as if she were in prison. She would never be free, never see her lover again, never be happy again . . . Misery held her in a cruel vise. She had little power to free herself. Fleur and Lucien did all they could to lighten her hours with chatter and Fleur brought her especially tempting meals, but she ate only a little fruit.

'What shall we do with her?' Lucien sighed, and Fleur held out her hands, palms uppermost, shaking her head from side to side.

'There is no cure,' Cassia said. 'Perhaps I do not wish to be cured? Perhaps I want to be like this. To be otherwise would mean that I did not love *Rais* Sauvage, and to love him is all I ask of life.'

'Mam'selle speaks like a Muslim now,' Fleur smiled. 'Allah watches over *Rais* Sauvage, and you too. As he watches over me and Lucien.' She glanced at the Frenchman, her cheeks pink. 'Allah has a special place in his heart for lovers, for those who give unstintingly of love.'

'It is so with our God,' Cassia said. 'He preaches love above all things.' Then a thought occurred to her. 'Lucien are you still a Catholic?'

Lucien looked surprised at her question. 'I have forfeited my religion. Since I took up this life, I am unworthy to practise Christianity. I am to become a Muslim.'

'Ah.' Cassia gave a little smile. She knew that the Koran forbade the marriage of a non-Muslim to a Muslim woman. Fleur had told her so. Muslim men could take non-believers to their beds, but not the women – although in fact some did disobey this law, much to their shame, Fleur had said.

'Did you have any particular reason for asking?' Lucien now asked.

'Oh no.' Cassia smiled mysteriously, the thought of love between these two comforting her a little. Whatever might be denied her, at least they would have some happiness. If only Vincent could have been like Lucien, but of course she would not have loved him if he were. Perversely she did not want Vincent to change, she wanted him as he was, however many problems that made for them. Many years before, Shakespeare himself had said, *Love is not love which alters when it alteration finds.*

And so the hours dragged on, and then Lucien returned to say that everything was made ready for the voyage. All they now required was the presence of Captain Sauvage. Cassia had packed her belongings in the chest that had held the Spanish gowns, and Fleur had given her combs and rouge, bath oils and unguents for the journey, along with towels, scented soap and nightrobes. Cassia had accepted them gratefully, but had thought wryly that she would not need any of them if she were packed in the hold in semi-darkness, on a narrow, unpadded bunk. She packed the Muslim robe, then unpacked it, for of course Sauvage would want her to wear this on the way to *The Poseidon.* Having done these things, she sat waiting. When would her lover return? And what would his reaction be when he did?

CHAPTER TWELVE

The mosque of *Sancta Zita* was cool and spacious. Its high, pale walls rose above thickly carpeted floors and it was built in the shape of a crucifix, like most mosques. Sauvage could not say why he had thought of this church as soon as Aminia had died. *Sancta Zita* had sprung into his mind and he had felt compelled to come here. He had been a good Catholic before he had been imprisoned in the Château du Diable, but incarceration there, followed by years in the slave galleys, had eradicated Catholicism from his soul. Somehow, he now found Allah more benevolent than the God of the Christians. Allah was called the All-Merciful, the All-Powerful, and that appealed to the man who had been treated without mercy, the man who had found himself powerless after his imprisonment for murder.

Lucien had come out of his abortion of justice with a far more optimistic outlook than Sauvage, but then Lucien had not been dragged back to the Château du Diable to be racked and beaten before being taken to the slave galleys. The fact that both he and Lucien had been imprisoned for similar crimes had always been a powerful link between them. But if Lucien were innocent of the murder of which he was accused, Sauvage was undoubtedly guilty.

The girl involved was his first love, Marisa, the daughter of the Mayor of Villy-sur-Mer, a township near Perpignan. Marisa was pretty but wilful. Vincent, young as he was then, saw only her sweetness, knew that he adored her. He had no doubt that they would one day marry. Six or seven months passed, his mother met Marisa but they did not care for one another. It was unfortunate, although Vincent did not see why the problem should not soon resolve itself. But Marisa was impatient, she became querulous and complained of the delay. If Vincent had been older, more experienced, he would have seen she was not for him, but he was young and naive.

Marisa goaded him unceasingly. She spoke of her other suitors, Georges and Claud, and said one of them would marry her tomorrow if Vincent did not. Finally, Vincent agreed to elope secretly with her. Carefully he made all the arrangements and arrived, as arranged, beneath Marisa's window one night. He had two good horses waiting, and a box full of all that they would require for their elopement.

He stood beneath her window, wondering if he should wait a short while before casting stones up at the pane, since he had arrived a little early. Then he heard Marisa's laughter, and next a man's deep voice, the tones sensuous. Her father was away, she had no brothers, her mother slept at the opposite end of the house. Who then was in her bedroom at this late hour?

Vincent took hold of the trailing ivy which blanketed the house, and was soon standing on the balcony of Marisa's room. Drawing aside the curtains which fluttered busily in the night breeze, he saw his beloved lying on her bed, her shift pushed up around her waist – and a man bending over her.

Something exploded in Vincent's head. Reaching for his sword, he advanced on the couple.

Marisa screamed a warning to her lover, who looked up, his eyes dilating. It was Georges, the man whose name she had so often used as a threat to Vincent. Georges jumped up, reached for his sword, but Vincent did not hesitate. He attacked the young merchant head on, fighting furiously. Within a few moments, Georges was dead, his heart pierced by Vincent's sword.

Marisa had fallen on Georges's body, sobbing and wailing. She glared up at Vincent, her face convulsed with venomous hatred.

'You have killed the man I loved,' she had snarled.

Vincent had stared at her, speechless. His betrothed, the girl he was to have married in a few hours' time, not only had a lover, but she did not love him. Her treachery worked

173

its way through to his mind, his heart. It was the beginning of seven years of hell for him. The authorities arrived; he was dragged away.

Marisa was, throughout the entire hasty trial, his cold-eyed accuser. She did not mention that they were to have eloped. She swore that Vincent had told her he would kill Georges to prevent his marrying her. It seemed there was no lie she would not tell to have Vincent convicted. What might have been forgiven as a crime of passion was condemned as pre-meditated murder.

Growing colder and colder, he had listened to her testimony, heard his sentence: life imprisonment in the Château du Diable, and he had been led away to his fate.

There, during the two-hour weekly exercise period the prisoners were allowed in the Château yard, he had met and befriended Lucien. They had managed to communicate in signs and whispers, for the guards were merciless regarding contact between the men. Lucien had told his story, and Vincent responded with his. A close bond had been immediately forged between the two young men.

Remembering, Vincent sighed, the serenity of the mosque settling around him. He still did not know why Aminia's death had so deeply affected him. Yes, she had been a favourite of his, but why had he been assaulted by such a tangle of emotions when he saw the breath depart from her lungs? He had thought of Marisa and Martia, and Cassia, and he had known in that moment that he was going to betray Cassia just as surely as Marisa and Martia had betrayed him. He could not help himself. And he did not know why.

It seemed that *Sancta Zita* did not want him to know, either. She ignored his prayers. He remained uncomforted. Reluctantly he began the return journey to Algiers, knowing that all he wanted to do was get to Constantinople and hand over Cassia to the Sultan. After that, the devil could do with him as he wished: he would no longer care.

CHAPTER THIRTEEN

Algiers was fading behind them, a dream that had not come true. Ahead of them lay the ruins of Carthage, the African coast, Sicily, Greece, the Aegean, Syria and finally Constantinople. They would stop only to take on water and food.

Cassia was given her own cabin. She was not put in the hold as she had feared. Lucien and Ahmek had escorted her to *The Poseidon* and she fancied there was pity in their eyes. She had seen nothing of Vincent. Lucien brought her books and Ahmek brought her meals. Her door was always locked. Fleur had wept when they said goodbye, and she had been moved to tears also. She knew that she would never see the gentle, sweet-faced Turkish girl again, but she had wished her every joy on her wedding day, and Fleur had blushed and lovingly kissed her on each cheek.

In the first two days of the voyage, Cassia reached the nadir of despair. Helpless, betrayed, she wept, and could only sleep when exhausted from her tears. Ahmek took away the trays of food untouched, making clicking noises of disapproval with his tongue, and finally he said that she would fall ill of a fever again if she did not eat.

'Perhaps that is what I want. Then I shall die,' she had whispered.

Stunned, he had stared at her, the tray in his hands. 'Missy want die when all life to live yet?'

'Life? Slavery, you mean! That is as good as dying.'

Ahmek had gone, his face dejected. It was not easy to stand by and watch his master ill-treat this girl who loved him. Ahmek wanted to shout at his master and curse him for being a fool, but how could he do that to the man who had saved his life and whom he had worshipped for so many years? On the other hand if he stayed silent, this poor young girl would die of a broken heart and that would not be good for her or for his master. *Rais* Sauvage needed love, more than any man perhaps. Ahmek knew this, but *Rais* Sauvage did not. If this girl died, then *Rais* Sauvage would die too, if not bodily, then his heart would die and he would be a cold shell.

Unable to speak, unable to think of a plan that would bring the girl and his grim-faced master together, Ahmek prayed and prayed to Allah the All-Merciful. She the All-Powerful. He read about Muhammad, posthumous son of Abdullah, and his love match with Khadijah had been Muhammad's only wife until her death when he was fifty, and he had always kept her memory sacred although he had taken other wives afterwards. Ahmek prayed that the happiness of the great Prophet would somehow be visited down the centuries to *Rais* Sauvage, and that he would unbend before it was too late and realize that he could not live without Cassia.

Sauvage sat at his desk with his head in his hands. Torn by conflicting emotions and doubts, he found that he both wanted and did not want Cassia Morbilly. French justice and his own recklessness had forced him into a way of life that he dared not now abandon. He was a criminal, an outlaw from any civilized society. And the sea was in his blood. Rover, pirate, renegade sea captain – Vincent Sauvage was not a fit husband for any woman.

He remembered Martia – so loving and confident to begin with. So disdainful and cold later. After a few years of marriage Cassia would long for the comfortable domesticity of an English home, children, a conventional husband. Vincent Sauvage knew that he would feel fettered and constrained by such a life. Far better to let her go now than to make promises he could not keep. If he could just get this voyage over, as quickly as possible, and leave her with the Sultan then he would not have to drive himself, trying to block out her image, the memory of their love-making. At night he could sleep only after drinking deeply of wine. If he did not drink, he knew he would go to her cabin and beg her forgiveness, take her in his arms, and, in the climax of their passion, ask her to be his wife.

It would be as good as stabbing himself with his own knife if he did so. He was no callow, foolish youth now but a man of nearly thirty-four and so many people depended on him. He could not let Captain Dash down, nor Lucien. Nor Hamid. If he had been in a more logical mood, he would have realized he was being absurd. The Sultan did not even know Cassia existed and to him she would be just another woman. He had five hundred concubines already. But Sauvage was in a supremely illogical frame of mind. On one level his lonely existence cried out for Cassia, for her trusting love, her uninhibited passion and her courageous spirit. On another, he despised what they had shared together as merely the satisfaction of physical desire. He knew guiltily that when he was in her arms he was prepared to swear undying love, but that as soon as he left her side, the old yearning to be free possessed him. Asked whether he loved her, he would have said yes. Asked if it were significant, he would have answered no, not in the very least.

Where the point of UllahKeli butted out from the mainland like a gigantic jaw, Nathan Dash was waiting with three heavily-manned ships. The point provided ample concealment. He could see but not be seen. He knew that Sauvage was an adversary to be feared on sea or land, and he was prepared for a terrible battle. That was why he had brought three ships with him. His men too were prepared for a violent encounter. Some were his, body and soul, others were mercenaries or men who had reason to wish Sauvage dead. Dash had calculated that his trinity of ships should be enough to take on *The Poseidon*, especially as the attack would be a total surprise, coming as it would in friendly waters. It was dusk, and Dash had selected a spot he knew well, but which was not overlooked. No one would know what had happened to Sauvage and his ship. The inevitably fierce battle would be over swiftly and Dash and his ships could return to Algiers with their plunder, and the stolen slaves. If his half-brother the Captain ever found out who had killed Sauvage, he, Nathan, would have his throat slit from ear to ear, or worse. That must never happen.

The look-out on *The Poseidon* spotted the three ships as they rounded the point, but they were sporting the Algerian flag. Nothing to worry about there. These were friendly waters. They were chebeks too, with their vivid striped sails, a common sight here. He turned his gaze away, looking towards the sapphire oceans and the setting sun that flamed in gilded orange and liquid honey. The setting sun always made him feel romantic. He thought of his woman, a sensuous widow, who waited for him in Constantinople. She was rich, she was willing, and he asked no more. he was thinking of her white breasts, her cream thighs when the first cannon shot smashed into the side of *The Poseidon*.

There was chaos. The three enemy ships glided towards them like water rats, sleek and low in the waters, their speed catching *The Poseidon* unawares. She too was fleet, but the cannon shot was shredding her side and a gaping hole had appeared before she could raise the speed for evasive tactics. All hands had to concentrate on dealing with the damage; each sailor knew exactly what to do in such emergencies, but now more explosions were heard, one following fast upon the other. Cannon balls whistled through the air smashing against *The Poseidon* while she struggled to rally, reeling about in the waters as one of her masts shattered and plunged down onto the deck. Dash's ship slewed into position ready for boarding that of Sauvage, he stood in readiness watching the destruction, hearing the cries of the wounded and dying with a gleeful sneer on his lips. A scimitar gleamed in his right hand, a dirk in his left. He had daggers tucked in his boots and his belt. All was going as he had planned. *The Poseidon* was dying. Should her Captain still be alive, he would take him on in single combat, his aides standing by, of course, to protect him should the fight not go favourably.

Surrounded by the three enemy vessels, *The Poseidon* wallowed in the seas, taking on water through the hole in her side, now too ravaged to attempt to rally. Dash's men flung out three landing boards, then he and his crew swarmed onto the dying ship like ravenous cockroaches in search of a feast.

When the first shot rang out, Cassia jumped to her feet, a scream on her lips. She remembered only too well the horror of battle on the other ship, and did not know whether to scream for help, or to hide. Panic gave way to sense. She was in Sauvage's ship. No one would get the better of him. But just in case, she dressed in her purdah and kneeled by the bed to pray. When her cabin door burst open, she was prepared for the worst, but it was Ahmek, with Lucien behind him.

'It's not going well, mademoiselle.' Lucien was deathly white, and a spreading scarlet stain stood out on his white shirt. Cassia gasped, hurrying forward to tend him, but he said, 'No! There is nothing you can do – Nathan Dash is attacking us, with three ships. Sauvage sent me to get you. You are to hide in his cabin. There is a secret panel. Not until the battle is over must you come out. Is that understood?' He winced. She saw him struggling for control.

'Yes, yes, of course.'

Hastily she followed the two men to Sauvage's empty cabin. Lucien touched a scroll of carving and a stretch of panelling slid open silently. Inside was a tiny, dark cubbyhole. Lucien almost pushed her into it, and then the panelling slid back and she felt as if she had been entombed. He had said it was simple to open from the inside, but she still felt terrified. What if she died here of starvation? Tears came to her eyes, but she controlled them. She must not make the slightest noise until the battle was over.

In her hideout, she heard every sound, as the wooden panelling acted as a noise conductor. The screams, the cries, the moans of the dying; she pressed her hands over her ears to try and shut them out. The fighting seemed to go on for hours. She thought of the slaves in the hold, the special women Sauvage was taking to the Sultan, the ones he had been gathering together for this voyage. Poor creatures, how they would be suffering not knowing what was going on. She was too scared to pray, her mind would not formulate the words. She shivered, swallowing with difficulty for the dust was thick. Sailors would not have thought to dust the cubbyhole.

Cramp seized her leg and she nearly cried out with the pain. She could not stretch out her leg nor could she move to rub it. Tensing, she tried to will away the agony but only half succeeded. 'Oh, Vincent, Vincent where are you?' she moaned.

It was much later that she heard what must be his cabin door crashing open and then his voice, sibilant against the panelling.

'Don't make a sound, don't say a word!'

Then she heard strange voices, and the clash of steel in the cabin and was filled with cold horror. The fighting went on and on. In God's name, she thought, how many is he fighting? She imagined the flashing steel blades, his flesh being pierced, his blood gushing, she saw him dying on the floor, and sobs rose in her throat. Thrusting her knuckles into her mouth, she shut her eyes.

Someone slammed against the panelling, and she heard the thud of a body falling. His? She all but screamed aloud. She heard a groan, and then there was a silence so eerie that her nerves grew ragged. She must know what had happened! *She must!* Touching the little carved button to her right, as Lucien had told her to do, she watched as the panelling slid open and then she saw Sauvage lying on the cabin floor, in a spreading pool of his own blood. She flung herself on him, crying out his name, heedless now of danger, caring for nothing but the fact that he was mortally wounded.

She was sobbing his name, over and over, begging him not to be dead, when Nathan Dash stepped into the cabin, grinning evilly, his eyes on her breasts.

She knew then that she had never experienced despair

or grief before. Those pale sadnesses were happiness compared to this.

Nathan Dash stepped towards her, tearing open her robe with one huge, scaly hand, his leering face contorted with lechery. At the sight of her milky white breasts, he turned scarlet. She thought he would rape her there, over her lover's body, but he did not. Instead, she was locked in the cabin for some hours, after Vincent Sauvage's body had been carried out by three of Dash's men. Slumped in a corner of the cabin, too shocked to cry, she was white as bone, barely breathing. Now and again she felt sick, but was too weak to respond to the feeling. *He is dead, he is dead*, she kept thinking. The man called Nathan Dash had murdered her lover. She recognized him from that night at Sauvage's house, and from details Ahmek had given her. He was the man who plaited his beard with red ribbons and fancied himself Sauvage's equal when nothing was further from the truth. Oh God, why did this happen, why, why?

She stared at the bloodstains on the floor, where Sauvage had died. She crept across the floor on hands and knees and touched the blood, dipping her fingers in it and weeping, then she looked round to see if there was a dagger with which she could kill herself. There was nothing. The cabin had been stripped bare. She could hear the shouts of the men on deck and in the storeroom looting and searching. She thought of her gowns, and jewels, and knew she would have given them up a hundredfold to save her lover's life.

One hour later, Nathan Dash unlocked the cabin door and strode in, grinning, his slimy green teeth exposed. He came over to her, putting his hand under her chin and twisting her head to face him. Licking his wet lips, he ran a hand over himself as if in anticipation. She felt faint with horror.

'Well, my little dove, we are together at last,' he leered. 'I planned it you know, all of this. To get my revenge on that filthy scum, Sauvage. You should see our treasures — and the slaves we have now. I'm rich! *Rich!*' He hummed a little song to himself, his eyes half closed as he watched her reaction. He is insane she thought, quite insane.

'You look very white, my dove. You cannot really be so upset? What good was he to you? He was going to sell you to Hamid, wasn't he? I won't do that, little honey. I'll keep you for my bed. That will please you will it not? You don't know what a man is really like yet – wait until I . . .' He then uttered a stream of obscenities which so sickened her that she felt her gorge rise. Dash stepped back hurriedly as she made a retching noise.

'Ill, eh?' Now he had gone pale. 'I don't like sickness. Not got a rash have you?' She stared at him dully. 'Well, keep away until you're better. *Then* see what I've got for you.' Just in case she doubted him, he pulled open his breeches to show her. She turned her head away, disgusted. He moved as if to approach her, then thought better of it. She might be feverish and he had a dread of fevers. She did look pale. He had plenty of time anyway. His men could carry her on to his ship, and then, when he had her in his house in Algiers, he could show her what it felt like to be swived by a real man.

As far as she knew, they were all dead, smiling young Lucien, happy, kindly Ahmek, Sauvage's devoted crew. All slaughtered by this stinking pig who had brought her by night to his house in Algiers and who was keeping her existence secret from everybody. The women slaves taken from the hold of *The Poseidon* were now in the hold of Dash's ship, *The Incubus*, which would soon be on its way to Constantinople. Dash was selling the women to Hamid, saying that he himself had gathered them together especially for the Sultan's delight. He bellowed with laughter every time he mentioned this to Cassia.

Cassia waited in dread for the time when Dash lost patience with her. She had pretended illness for two days, but he was getting angry. He had sent for two physicians who had pronounced her healthy. She knew that as soon as they reported to him, he would be here. But she was ready. One of the physicians had a slender dagger, of Turkish design. He had used it to prick the soles of her feet to assess her reflexes. After he had done this, he put the dagger on the side table for a few moments. When the two men were conferring with one another, Cassia slipped the dagger beneath her pillow, praying they would not notice its absence. They had gone a few moments ago and so far no one had returned to claim it.

Thirty minutes later, Dash appeared, laughing out loud.

'Thought you'd trick me did you, little minx? Well, I know about your game now – and you're not going to escape me this time.' He flung off the robe of dazzling colours, green, scarlet, blue, yellow and white, which he had been wearing, and she looked in dismay at his sickeningly repulsive body. It was scaly all over, dry scales in parts and wet eruptions in others, marks all over him, everywhere, only one part was still smooth. He looked like some monstrous gargoyle whose stonework had been pitted and scarred by centuries of wind and rain.

Fear made her forget everything for a few seconds and she shrank against the pillow, hands over her face.

'Scared are you? Well I am big, I must say, but not too big,' he snickered. 'It'll only hurt pleasurably, of that I can assure you. Come, my pretty.'

He leaned over her, there was saliva pouring down his chin; she could smell his foetid breath. He was very aroused; she looked at his excitement with a sense of suffocating dread. She would not have wanted so much as to brush past such a man in a crowd, and here he was naked and aroused, about to rape her . . . She gave a cry of horror, and reached for the knife. He saw the flashing steel and bellowed, jumping backwards but not before the knife had slashed down his forearm. Blood shot out all over the bed, all over Cassia. Dash screamed, like a wounded animal, shrieking for his guards to save him. They ran in, and pinned Cassia's arms behind her back.

'Bitch, whore, you'll pay for this! I was going to be nice to you, and make you my chief wife, but not now, you vicious little bitch. Yes, that's what you are, *bitch*, *bitch*, *bitch*,' his voice rose to a high pitch, he swayed, one of his men supporting him, another binding his arm hastily with a torn-up sheet. Dash sank down on the bed, still cursing Cassia, telling her what he thought of her unprovoked attack.

She watched as if in a dream, beyond feeling. When, a little recovered from his first shock, Dash stood up and smashed her in the face with his fist, and then slammed his fist into her stomach, she felt little pain but only relief at losing consciousness.

She came to in what must be a ship's hold. It was dim and airless and smelled foul. Women were bending over her, their faces alarmed.

'Where am I?' she groaned, then winced at the pain from her bruised jaw and stomach.

'On yer way to the Sultan, duckie,' one of the women answered. 'Kidnapped ye, did they? Us too. Buggers they are. Took me off a wharf in London itself. 'It me over the 'ead and tied me up. Didn't know nuffink 'til I comes round in an 'old. Bloody maniacs, should be locked up!'

'Shut up, Dolly. She doesn't want to hear all that.' The speaker was also English, a motherly looking woman with fluffy pale hair and protuberant pale eyes. 'How do you feel, love? They flung you right down here, cruel they are. We thought you was dead for a minute. You been out for ages.'

'Get 'er a drink, Angie,' Dolly urged, and one of the women standing near a barrel reached for the wooden stoop and held it to Cassia's lips. She drank greedily, and then fell back.

'Where does it hurt, love? Tell Angie, come on, do. I got good hands for rubbing ills better.' Angie smiled, rolling up her sleeves and Cassia explained that she had been punched in the face and stomach.

'Who did that ter yer, the brute? Dash was it? We 'eard 'is men talking as we were brought 'ere from Sauvage's ship. Couple o' us can talk their language. Terrible shame about Sauvage, did yer know? He might be a slave trader but he warn't evil. Fed us well, didn't 'e, girls?' There was a chorus of assent at Dolly's words. 'Since this Dash fellow took over, we ain't 'ad much worth eating.'

Cassia winced at the mention of her lover's name, but Angie thought it was the pain as she set about examining the girl's bruises and gently rubbing them. A nightmare, this is a nightmare, yes it is, it's not really happening, I'm dreaming, Cassia said to herself as Angie massaged her stiff body. Vincent is still alive, and this is just a nasty dream. In a minute I'll wake up, and he'll say, 'Good morning, *doucette*,' and then I'll smile at him and he'll take me into his arms . . . Tears rolled out of the corners of her eyes.

'Not hurting you, am I, love? Don't mean to, anyways. Shout if I do,' Angie said.

Cassia barely heard. She was far away in her dream world, enjoying a waking dream in Vincent's arms. While she was there, nothing could hurt her, not Nathan Dash, nor Angie's strong, skilful hands.

They were well out to sea before Cassia felt strong enough to get up from her rough bed on the straw sacking which served as the women's mattresses. Her bruises were healing, but she was not too sure about her heart. It was the plight of the women that stirred her into action. They had been in one hold or another for weeks now, seeing no light, and, since Dash took over, they had eaten no fresh fruit, no wine, but only sour gruel that upset their stomachs. The water in the barrel was finished and when they requested more they were cursed.

One of the women was near her time, and suffering from continual back pains. Another had dysentery, another a quartan fever. No one could have continued to listen to their groans and tears; someone had to do something, and Cassia felt it must be she. She felt responsible for the plight of these poor creatures. If Vincent were still alive, he would have cared for them better than Dash. As he was dead, she must look after them. She took the gold chain from round her neck and bribed one of their guards with it – he would get the chain when he had brought them two barrels of fresh water, she said. He spat, and cursed them, but he brought the water. He also flung a few loaves down the hatch, and the women grabbed at them greedily, holding the fresh bread to their noses and inhaling its delicious smell before tearing it up and dividing it amongst themselves.

Liz, the pregnant woman, was given the best food they could get, and she was touchingly grateful. Poor Margaret, who had the stomach upset, could not eat at all and vomited even after sips of water.

'You must keep drinking all the same,' Cassia told her, 'or you will waste away.'

Margaret obeyed, although her stomach frequently rebelled, and after a few days she seemed a little better.

'You are a good nurse,' Liz said as Cassia rolled up some sacking to make her a back rest. 'I feel a little happier now you're here. Can I call my baby after you if it's a girl?'

'Of course.' Cassia lowered her eyes to hide the emotion she felt at Liz's words. To have a baby named for her . . . what could be more touching? They needed comfort, all of them. The hold was bleak and suffocatingly hot; there was nowhere to wash, and calls of nature had to be attended to behind a strip of sacking nailed up in one corner. This was particularly embarrassing for Margaret, who spent much of her time behind that tattered curtain. If only they had some soapy water and brushes, Cassia thought, but knew her hope to be in vain. The sort of men who crewed Dash's ships did not clean their own quarters let alone those of their prisoners.

The gold chain gone, there was nothing left with which to bribe the guards. For two days, no one lifted the hatch to peer down at them, not even to hiss vulgar comments. The women lay stretched out, singing or talking, or sleeping, one or two praying, Liz making plans for her baby – plans which she knew very well would never reach completion. Cassia asked her about her husband.

'He was a sailor – worked hard all his life, and dreamed

of having a son. But we never had none, not in twelve years of being wed. He went away on his last voyage before retiring to take up farming. Left me with his mother in their cottage by the sea – pretty little spot, Swallow Cottage, it's called. I was real happy there. Then I went out walking this day – on me own – and they came up the beach like a bunch of demons and took me. I screamed and struggled, but who would hear in that isolated place? I thought of Jim, my husband, and the baby he'd never see now and I just wept for days after they put me in the hold in that other ship. Poor Jim.' Liz's eyes were bleak, but she had cried all her tears.

Cassia recognized a frightening resignation in the pregnant woman – and realized that they were suffering similarly. She told Liz and the others how she had been kidnapped – but she did not mention Charles. Somehow it all seemed so long ago now, and his part in it so irrelevant. Nor did she mention Sauvage, for how could she in all honesty mention her relationship with the pirate who had abducted these women? They did not know him, except to recognize that he had not been an unkind master, but he was, after all, the man responsible for their plight.

A soft voice interrupted their talk. It was that of Xenobe, a Turkish girl who had hitherto said very little. She was tiny and slender, and her huge dark eyes were like black pearls. Now she spoke up, saying, 'We go to very different lives. All of us. Different from what we have known. Some better, some worse. Some will find happiness, others sadness, but whatever is given shall be returned.'

Cassia looked at the girl, her eyes wide. Was she a prophetess, a seer?

'I see you staring at me, mistress,' Xenobe smiled. 'But you believe what I say, yes? Not like some people who sneer at me and curse me. Oh I have been cursed for my gift, wherever I have gone there have been those who curl their lips at me. Let me tell you, mistresses, that those who sneer at my gift will never be happy. Never.'

There was a silence after she had spoken. Liz put her

hands over her swollen stomach, Margaret lay very still, her face ashen. Angie and Dolly looked at one another, brows raised.

'You been quiet, Xenobe,' Dolly then said. 'Not 'eard you speak for days, and now you tell us this.'

Xenobe lifted a slender, fawn-coloured hand. 'Before you speak, remember that those who sneer will never find happiness.'

Dolly said, 'Huh!' and turned her head away, but Cassia observed Xenobe with wondering eyes. A seer – the French called them pythonesses – sorceresses – women who had the gift of foretelling the future. She had heard of an old cottager in Morbilly who had told fortunes. She herself had planned to visit her. However much she wished to look at this talent logically, she could never decry it. Who knew what marvellous gifts these women had been given? And who was she to sneer at them? She went to Xenobe and smiled at her.

'Tell us what you see, Xenobe. For all of us.'

Xenobe's black-pearl eyes closed, her face relaxed, then tightened, her mouth seeming to squirm across her face. A spasm of anguish creased her brows and then she said, 'Long voyage, great journey across seas of world. Over oceans. Long, long, weary voyage.'

'Huh, as if we don' know that!' Dolly said disparagingly but Angie nudged her and told her to be quiet.

'Great fortunes ahead. The Sea God . . . The Sea God . . . Love, love, the Sea God loves . . .' Xenobe's eyes flew open, but she did not seem to see the women. She stared at and through Cassia, in a way which made the Cornish girl shiver, then slowly her eyes became normal again. 'What did I say?' she whispered.

'You spoke of a long tiring sea voyage, and then you mentioned great fortunes, and the Sea God, and love. "The Sea God loves", you said, and then you stopped.'

'I felt – for a few moments – as if he were here. It was frightening!' Xenobe shuddered.

'Who was here? Who did you feel was here?'

'Why – the Sea God, of course. Poseidon.'

Cassia drew back at the name of her lover's ship. Was he with her then, as spirits were said to be for some time after their deaths? Was his soul clinging to her, yet she could not see or hear it while Xenobe could? Oh why, why, had he been killed? She bit on her lips until she tasted blood, and Xenobe watched her, as if she knew.

Liz said, 'Come on, Xenobe, you haven't said much. If you're a seer, tell us what you see.'

Xenobe sighed. 'It is gone. I see no more today. Another day. Tomorrow.'

The women settled, one or two grumbling at the sudden evaporation of this little excitement. Cassia slept fitfully, thinking of Vincent near her, invisible but present all the same. If only he could be seen, if she could pull him down into her arms and kiss him, over and over.

Xenobe's voice came out of the dark. 'You think of your lover. He think of you too. Always he thought of you, night, day, night again, his mind filled with you. It was love. Deep, strong love. Love survives even death, separation.'

'It is good to be able to think that,' Cassia sighed.

'Think it because it's true. Listen to no other words but mine. When gods love, their loves are protected, safe. Whatever happens, you will survive.'

'Survive? Alone? What sort of living is that?'

'You speak like one who has lost her lover. But that will change. I tell you this so it is true. All will be returned. But you must trust and hope and be patient. I can say no more.'

'How can I have him back? He is dead, *dead*!' Cassia muffled her tears for fear of waking the others.

'Love never dies,' said Xenobe in her infuriating, oblique way. 'Love never dies. It survives. I told you, so it is true. Trust and hope. Be patient. See not the now, but what will come. You understand?'

'I think so. But that is too hard a thing to ask of me.'

'If you not suffer a little, be tortured a little, you will not deserve reward. Nothing is given for nothing.' Xenobe closed her eyes suddenly and slept soundly for the rest of that night. Cassia lay awake on the hard boards of the floor, her shoulders aching, her hips bruised, her heart too, willing Vincent to come to her, to be near her, to be alive again. She felt now that she would settle for the Grand Seraglio, accept his indifference and forget their loving if only she could know that he walked the earth again.

CHAPTER FOURTEEN

They had lost all track of time. They were beginning to forget who they were. Stale bread, hard biscuits and strips of salt meat were cast down at them as if they were lions in a cage, and never frequently enough they were given water. Their fevered dreams were of grassy shores and seagulls wheeling in the blue, the lap of cool waves and darting silvered fish in curling streams, of roast beef and succulent fruits dripping with juice, of frothing milk straight from the cow. After appearing to have recovered a little, Margaret became worse. She was so weak that she could not even crawl behind the sacking curtain, and Cassia and Angie had to carry her there. She could barely speak, and finally could not even swallow water for her throat seemed to constrict as soon as the water touched her lips. She died eleven days after the ship left Algiers, and all the women wept over her thin, still form. The guards took away the body, cursing the women as they did so and kicking out at them cruelly. Margaret had been like a sister, and now she was to be flung overboard so coldly. It was a terrible feeling to know she was dead and that she would not have a proper Christian burial, although they had prayed as she lay dying.

The hatch was hardly shut behind the men carrying away her body when Liz gave a groan of agony.

They all looked at her, and she nodded. 'Yes, this is it – oh, what am I to do? Oh Jim, Jim, I want you!'

The cleanest material in the hold was Cassia's chemise, and this she proceeded to tear up. Fortunately they had two full barrels of water, but no soap. Liz was in labour a day and a night. She suffered, the women suffering along with her. Some of them had birthed children of their own and helped Cassia with the labour, but finally Dolly took Cassia aside and said that she was worried.

' 'Tis taking too long. 'Tain't normal lasting so long.

Babe might be dead. Stillborn. Ask me, 'twould be better if it were.'

Cassia drew in her lower lip. Dolly might be right, but surely a living babe would be better than a dead one? She asked her if there was anything she could do.

'Not that I knows of. 'Taint much yer can do if everything's going well and midwives is present. If a babe's stuck, it's stuck.'

At that moment Liz screamed, and then she screamed again. Blood gushed from between her legs, and she collapsed back against the sacking pillow, unconscious.

'Oh my God!' Cassia cried, hurrying to the woman's side, and attempting to staunch the flow with the torn material of her skirt. She worked quickly, praying all the time, but Liz stayed unconscious and the blood continued to gush. Soon the woman lay in a spreading pool of her own blood. In Cassia's mind's eye, it was Vincent she was aiding, Vincent lying dead on the floor of his cabin. Tears drowned her vision.

' 'Taint much we can do now,' Dolly whispered. 'She's gonna die.'

'Oh no!'

'Look at all that blood. And it ain't stopped yet. She can't have much left inside 'er.'

When Cassia had packed all the cloths between Liz's thighs, she kneeled by her, holding her hand. How cold she felt, and her lips were blue. How could God be so cruel? Why did He let women suffer like this? All the time they suffered, in anguish, pain and agony while men went on with their smooth, untrammelled, carefree existences. 'Oh God, it is not fair!' Cassia whispered.

Liz gave birth to her daughter at dawn of the following day. She opened her eyes, gave a little moan, and her baby slipped into the world in a sea of blood. Some twenty minutes later, Liz died. Ten minutes after that, the baby died too.

The deepest misery gripped all the women. They thought of Jim coming back from the sea expecting to find his wife and child, and instead there would be nothing. Just his mother waiting in her little cottage. Liz would have disappeared into the blue. Her husband would never be sure what had happened to her.

Nor would Aunt Julitta know what had happened to her niece. Vanished. Gone. Like a puff of smoke blown away by the wind. How many hundreds, thousands, disappeared in this way every year? It was incomprehensible until it actually happened to you.

And all for greed. For lust and sex and men's desire. Sold into slavery, to labour, or to languish in a harem. Either way, it was a fate which appealed to none of the women present. How could men have consciences and go on letting this happen? But perhaps they did not have consciences? Perhaps they felt only lust and need of a woman, and cared not how they obtained that woman? But no, thinking about it, Cassia could not condemn Vincent in this way, nor Lucien. They both had suffered, felt guilt – if anything too much guilt – and had tried in their own way to mend matters. But it was they, and not the truly evil ones, who had died. Nathan Dash and his men, savage beasts all of them, were still alive, still wreaking havoc.

A light hand touched her arm. It was Xenobe.

'You have least to worry you of those present here,' she said. 'So why do you look so anguished?'

'*Least?* If only you knew the truth, Xenobe! A truth I can never talk about here, not with you or the others. Look at these women – Margaret dead and now poor Liz and her baby. And it's all my fault – all of it. Just as if I myself kidnapped you all from your homes.'

'So you take on a burden which is not yours? Is that not arrogance, Cassia? Can you really say that Allah – or your God – wishes you to be bowed by this great burden when you have contributed nothing to our suffering? Surely you have helped us all?'

'I am responsible! I cannot tell you how, but surely the fact that I feel responsible means that I am?'

'Or could it mean that you have a distorted sense of

responsibility, Cassia? You are like those who feel that they have caused badness, and thus must try to heal that badness, but in fact you have not done this. You have healing hands, a natural gift for reassuring and cheering people. Use that, and it will make you happy.'

'Happy? I shall never be happy again!'

'My dear, there is one sure way to gain happiness, and that is to think of others, to put them first, to love, to care. If you do these things – which are a very part of your own nature – you will find happiness. There are some who search the world over for happiness because they do not realize that happiness is inside one's self – if you know how to find it. Look no further than yourself, look in, not out, my dear. To be selfish and expect happiness is like trying to kindle a fire with bars of iron and wondering why the flames will not leap.'

Cassia sighed. 'You are very wise, Xenobe, and I think I believe what you say – it strikes true, anyway. But what opportunity shall I have in the Grand Seraglio to practise this unselfishness, this love?'

'Why, my dear, there are people in a harem are there not? Many people, eunuchs, wives, concubines in their hundreds. They are not without feelings and emotions, just like us. Some will need cheering or praising or consoling every day.'

'So you think this is a great plan and I am meant to go to the Grand Seraglio as a sort of saviour?' Cassia gave a wry smile.

'Maybe. I cannot say. Allah is as mysterious in His ways as is your Christian God. But I know that harems are places of discord and sometimes of grief. I have lived in one . . .'

Cassia's eyes opened wide. 'How did you get out?'

'When my master died, he left orders that we were to be freed. He was very generous. Some leave orders that their wives must die with them. How fortunate I thought myself. But you see I am trapped again – I was kidnapped, after being free for one whole year.'

'Had you no vision of your being kidnapped?'

'I cannot use my powers for my own gain. That is unthinkable. It would bring more harm on me than good. No, I was surprised to say the least when I was sold into the harem by my brother who cared for nothing except his own avarice. By the time I was ten, there was nothing I did not know about the arts of love. My late master was old and very fat. He liked little girls, but fortunately his liking was stronger than his ability to put his feelings into action. He would sit me on his knee and undress me slowly, and caress me, and then he would ask me to do things to him that would bring him pleasure but which did not entail any great effort on his part. I became highly skilled; I could bring him intense pleasure without his ever entering my body.' Xenobe smiled, her black-pearl eyes like polished satin.

Cassia listened, a flush spreading across her cheeks. She wondered what Xenobe knew of Hamid I. As if reading her mind, the Turkish woman mentioned his name.

'He is petulant, and moody, Hamid, but he is generous too and so rich. Also he has but one son and for a man who has five hundred women in his harem this fact must be terrible to live with. Turkish men dote on their sons, and a Sultan especially must have many strong male heirs. Boys die so easily – especially when there are jealous women who wish to have their sons on the throne. Poison is employed as casually as rouge.'

'Poison? They poison one another's sons?' Cassia felt a chill course through her. What manner of place was she going to? She had been told her life would be easy, tranquil, pleasurable, but this was a new and frightening aspect of the Grand Seraglio, and she did not like the sound of it at all.

'Why does Hamid have only one son? Have the others been poisoned, Xenobe?'

'Oh no. It is simply that he has been unfortunate. Allah has denied him other sons. There is another heir living, however, a male relative of Hamid's. Unlike previous male claimants to the throne, he is not kept hidden away, imprisoned in the *Kafes* – the Princes' Cage. In there they are allowed few visitors, occasionally they may have women, but these must be old or barren women, for there cannot be the risk of one of these men siring a son. Should this calamity occur, the woman and the baby will be put to death at once.'

'Put to death!' Cassia breathed.

'Muhammad III, the eldest son of Murad III, had his nineteen brothers put to death, and had seven of his father's concubines sewn into sacks and drowned in the Marmora in case any of them were pregnant.'

Cassia slowly digested this shocking information, and then she said: 'So the princes, the heirs, that is, were kept in a cage for fear that they would overthrow the ruling Sultan. That alone is a terrible thing – imagine their frustration, their fear.'

'Imagine the fear of the Sultan himself, my dear. To have, say, twenty men all clamouring for his throne, and all those men possessing mothers who would do anything – *anything* – to see their sons on that throne. You see, the most powerful person in Islam after the Sultan himself is the Sultan-Validé: the mother of the Sultan. It is she who has the true authority and reverence, not the Sultan's favourite wife.'

'I had been led to believe otherwise. I was told that the Sultan's favourite woman could enjoy much power.'

'To a point. And certainly she will if she mothers a male heir, but otherwise, as I said, it is the Sultan-Validé who dominates the palace. But imagine her fears, too, for there might be twenty or more boys all seeking to supplant her son. And they all have mothers who, like she, would do anything to see their sons in power. Poisoning, strangling, drowning, or whatever quick and silent method they can think of.'

'I see. How do they live with themselves afterwards? They must lie awake at nights, or have terrible nightmares.'

'Not they, my dear. It is a way of life. There is always a beautiful woman to bed, or drugs and herbs to lull the senses; so much to do, and so little time. My own late master, the Bey of Bamlik, with his own hands strangled his three brothers and his father's favourite wife, as soon as his father died. She was pregnant you see. They had called her the Star of the East, her beauty was legendary and she was respected and revered, but when her husband died, she was without protectors. She and her sons were murdered, swiftly, silently one night, and then my late master could rule without fear of a coup that would lose him his little throne. Extraordinary, is it not?'

'Horrifying, Xenobe. It really is. It seems incredible that no one opposes such cruelty and corruption. I cannot understand why the people do not rise up in disgust and prevent one man seizing such power.'

'You will have to accept this as normal when you go into the Seraglio, my dear. You must never show surprise or shock, or comment on things which alarm or dismay you. Say nothing, mask your face. Beware of eunuchs, they are like spiteful children. Trust only yourself. Friendship can be the pit of the serpent.'

Eunuchs . . . Cassia thought of Ahmek. He had died on *The Poseidon*, his cheery laughter stilled for all time. He had not deserved to die, her jolly, heartening friend. So far, he was her only experience of a eunuch, but she had heard of others who were not so kindly as he. He had been castrated when he was a little boy, and thus had adapted better to his barbarous deprivation. Those who were castrated late, during puberty or after, took it very badly. Many died, sometimes as many as twenty-nine out of thirty who had been brutally castrated. Ahmek had told her of this, explaining that those who did survive were intent on revenge and this revenge could take many and varied forms: greed, amassing fortunes and power, a lashing, cruel tongue, acts of savage cruelty to others. At the time, she had thought perhaps he was exaggerating a little.

But now Xenobe, too, said the same. Cassia realized that she would have to tread very carefully indeed once she arrived in the Seraglio. Already she felt taut and uneasy.

And really all she wanted to do was curl up and go to sleep, never to wake again. Life was worthless, a dark, empty chasm, without Vincent. Whatever Xenobe said, whatever she herself did, how could joy ever return now? It had died when Vincent died, ebbing out of her as his blood had ebbed out of him. There was nothing left for her except the burden of going on alone.

The days became a blur of heat and discomfort and hunger. They were living on stagnant water and stale bread, they had rashes and sores on their mouths, and their teeth were loose. Time was lost. They had no idea what day or month it was; soon they forgot the year too. The hold smelled like an animal's den and they could do nothing about it. In time too they ceased to care. Hygiene and its importance faded as if it had never been.

Sometimes they talked of home, and their favourite foods and what they would do if they were freed, but gradually these talks became fewer and fewer. Weariness set in like a poison, and nothing mattered except the next lump of stale bread or fragment of iron-hard biscuit. One day fresh fruit was flung down at them, a huge mound of it, luscious fruit even if it was bruised and battered by the time it reached them. They had a feast, and then suffered for it with upset stomachs, but some of their sores healed and Cassia's teeth stopped bleeding for a few days. Their requests for information from the guards went unanswered as always. Xenobe remonstrated with the Turkish sailors, also to no avail. They cursed, or spat, or leered, but they never told the women where they were, what day it was, or how long it would be before they reached Constantinople. Weary resignation set in, and sleepiness. One woman complained of painful arms and legs, and she died in the night, silently, stiff and cold to the touch by the time the others awoke. Like Margaret and Liz, her body was hauled out unceremoniously and cast overboard.

The sailors who had kicked out at them as they carried away Margaret and Liz's bodies barely looked at the women now. They must look ghastly, filthy, bedraggled, unwholesome. Even sailors long at sea could not be tempted by them. This in itself was both a relief and an anguish.

They felt degraded, lacklustre. They were no longer desirable women but merely objects which would be sold in the slave market in Constantinople. Dash would not get much gold for them in this condition, mused Cassia. He would be fortunate if he could sell them for a pittance. How stupid to let them get into such a filthy, bedraggled state.

As the men were disappearing up the hatch, Xenobe called out something to them in Turkish. It sounded angry, irate, accusative. When the hatch had closed, the others asked her what she had said.

'I told them they were fools for letting us get like this. I said who would buy dirty slaves who were ill and half-starved? If they wanted gold, I said, then they should let us wash and feed us properly.'

'Good for you, Xenobe!' Cassia smiled. 'You were brave, they might have come back and beaten you.'

'I am not afraid.' Xenobe shrugged.

The astonishing thing was that the men took notice of her words. They brought food for the women, and watered wine, and from heaven knows where they found soap and threw that to them. Ten buckets of cold water were lowered, and a hip bath of battered metal.

It was like a miracle. The women gaped at first, then began to tear off their ragged clothes, and one by one they bathed in the water, lathering themselves thickly, laughing, throwing the slippery balls of soap at one another and making jokes about its being Christmas. Cassia watched them, her face bright. They were like little innocent children delighting in a gift – if only she could set them free, let them go back to their homes. If only she could go back.

When they had all bathed, soaking for hours in the tub, and had washed their clothes and hung them to dry on nails jutting out of the uneven timbers of the hold, they sat round totally unabashed by their nakedness and ate more of the food. The meat was tough and so salty it made their gums sting, and the cheese was maggoty, but it was so marvellous to taste cheese again that they brushed off the grubs and ate it hungrily. Their clothes did not take long to dry, for the hold was always too warm, and now that they were in an even hotter climate, they steamed. After sluicing the floors with the soapy bathwater, and luxuriating in the scent of the soap which eradicated some of the malodour they had been forced to accept, they lay down to rest, a little happier than before.

That they should have reached such a pass! Cassia thought. To be so happy because they could wash – how low they had sunk in the previous weeks. She wondered if indeed the men had taken note of Xenobe, or if they always did this for their captives as they approached Constantinople? If they did, it seemed inane to her that they should let their slaves die through neglect and starvation. Surely the whole point of slave trading was to make money, and bodies brought no money whatsoever. Did they get some kind of malicious pleasure out of eating and drinking their fill up on deck while thinking of the captives ravenous and sickly below? If so, they were devils. The women had spoken well of Vincent, he had seen to it that they could wash and were fed properly. Also, he sent them the ship's doctor if they fell ill. She was sure that his reward would be a hold full of healthy, hardy slaves when they reached their port of call. As it was, Dash had already forfeited over half a dozen women on this journey and those who were left were very weak.

Dash had boasted to her of his prowess; he had said that when he sold her to Hamid, the Sultan would remember his gift and be his good friend. He obviously wanted desperately to impress the Sultan. Why then had he let them get into this abominable state, unless perhaps it was revenge for her wounding him? But to gain such a petty revenge out of spite was to harm himself too, for the healthy, spirited redhead he believed would impress Hamid was now very pale, very quiet. She would need all of her willpower to face her enemies when she was taken off this ship.

A few more days passed before the horrifying voyage was over. They were in Constantinople, the hatch was being thrown open and blazing sunlight shot at them like living flame. They staggered and blinked and had to keep their eyes tightly shut. Holding hands for support, they waited, trying to adjust to the light. The guards ordered them up the step ladder, and, with fumbling, trembling hands and feet they made the slow ascent.

A crowd of sailors waited on deck to see them, their faces twisted with disgust and repulsion. They spat at them, and jeered, and shouted obscenities which made those who could understand Turkish flush with embarrassment and shame.

Cassia tried to pretend the men were not there. She mustered all her dignity and walked carefully, trying not to sway, towards the rope ladder which would take them into the waiting longboat. One or two of the women fell, and there was a burst of coarse laughter.

Xenobe helped one of them, Cassia another. They managed to get into the longboat without serious mishap, without one hand having been extended by any of the crew to help them. Dash watched the little procession from the poop deck, his face tight with bitterness. He was still recovering from his wound, nursing himself with excessive care. By his side was a young girl, no more than eleven, and he was pawing her as he observed the women's departure. The little girl had her hand between his legs and was fingering him.

Cassia saw, and immediately turned away her head, sick with revulsion. That man was a devil; he should be killed. If she could get her hands on him, she would murder him herself, for what he had done to Vincent and to these poor women. If only her knife attack had not failed – she would not have minded dying at the hands of his men after she had killed him. 'If there is a God who is seeing this, let Him watch over us and keep Dash away from us,' she prayed as she settled herself in the rocking boat, with her head lowered.

They must have been one of the most ragged and pallid

groups ever to arrive in Constantinople. Cassia glanced up once to see where the boat was heading and saw a city not unlike Algiers but larger, more commanding.

'That is Seraglio Point,' Xenobe whispered, 'the Bosphorus opens there, and higher up you can see the Suleymaniye Mosque. Between are Aya Sofya and Sultan Ahmet. That building which looks so massive and rock-like is the Topkapi Saray, and beneath that, along the Marmora shore, you can see the old Byzantine seawalls.'

'It is beautiful,' Cassia said reluctantly, thinking with tears in her heart of her arrival in Algiers, when Vincent was alive and she had been so joyous with hope and love. All that was now gone forever.

'Do you know how it began, this beautiful city?' Xenobe asked.

'I know nothing of it at all,' Cassia said. 'Only what you have told me.'

'Many centuries ago, the sea-god Poseidon used to stable his horses under the Aegean Sea, and his son was called Byzas. It was Byzas who went with a group of Megarians to the shores of the Bosphorus, in about 658 BC, and there they founded Byzantium, which was the old name for Constantinople, of course.'

Cassia barely heard the story. 'Poseidon, Poseidon the Sea-God,' rang in her head, repeatedly, until she felt dizzy, bemused. The Sea-God had stabled his horses beneath the Aegean, so close to this great city, and his son, his own son, had founded Constantinople.

'You are wondering how I know all this? The Grand Vizier at my old harem was very fond of history. He talked for hours about his country. There was little else for me to do except listen and learn. This city was conquered by various Greeks, the Athenians, the Spartans, and the Macedonians. It was even a province of Rome at one time. In 330 BC, the Emperor Constantine chose it as the centre of government for the Roman Empire, and it took its present name from him.'

'So it was Christian once.' Cassia sighed. 'If only that

were so now, I would be feeling much happier.' (But no, how can you ever be happy now that he is dead? said a little voice in her mind.)

'You think that Christians are blameless, my dear? I know those who can tell a different story. It does not automatically follow that because men are followers of your prophet Christ they treat women gently, you know. Nor men, either. You have said that castrating men is a terrible thing, and yet did you know the Popes also do this?'

'The Popes?' Cassia took her eyes from the beautiful harbour of Constantinople to stare at Xenobe.

'The Sistine Chapel in Rome needs choirboys whose voices are sweet and golden, to sing hymns to your God. How do you think their voices stay thus? Magic? No, they are castrated, my dear. Ever since Sixtus V, in 1590, Christian men have been mutilated by Christian men to make their singing voices more beautiful.'

Cassia did not argue. Xenobe had no reason to lie. She had nothing against Christians.

'And what of the way you treat witches, my dear? They are hounded and tortured and burned at the stake, they are stripped and searched for marks where Satan has suckled them, and if so much as a mole is discovered, the women are condemned. One hundred years ago, the Archbishop of Salzburg sent ninety-seven women to the stake because cattle were dying in large numbers. In 1630, the Bishop of Bamberg had nine hundred witches and sorcerers put to death, and, about the same time, the Bishop of Wurzburg was responsible for twelve hundred dying similarly. At Wittenberg, in 1591, it was still being debated by a Christian council whether or not women are really human beings at all.'

Cassia listened, absorbed what Xenobe was saying. Of course the Turkish girl spoke of Germany and Rome not of England, she did not think women were barbarously treated there – not now at least. Perhaps life spent shut away in a harem was preferable to being burned at the stake? As yet she did not know. Somehow, she could not see life as worth living if one was not free, if the man one adored had been horribly slain.

'Tears, Cassia?' Xenobe's delicate fawn face was all concern.

'I – I was thinking of the man I love – loved. He was murdered. I saw him die.'

'Poor child. Allah's mercy is without limit, without constraint. He will know of this. He will be watching over you. He asks only that you bear so much, and when you have borne all that you are able, He will deliver you. Believe me, I know.' Xenobe was once more her visionary self, the knowledgeable historian retiring behind the black-pearl eyes and exquisite features.

The women became silent as the city once legendary as the heart of Byzantium came into full view. They saw, as they came into the Sea of Marmora, the Blue Mosque of Sultan Ahmet, and, a little in front of it, Sancta Sophia, the Church of the Holy Wisdom, a sulphurous yellow colour, begun in the 530s by Byzantine architects. Flanked by tall spiked minarets, its massive central dome and supporting half-domes give it the appearance of a far more modern building. On the opposite side of the city was the Golden Horn, an estuary some seven miles in length, and curving round its point was the Bosphorus, another channel about sixteen miles long which separated Constantinople from Asia. But it was the brooding, murky yellow church which drew Cassia's eyes.

Xenobe saw, and commented. 'Sancta Sophia has eight green marble columns from Ephesus itself, and eight porphyry columns that Aurelian once used in a Roman temple – originally they came from Jupiter's temple at Baalbek – there is a bronze door which is over one thousand years old – do you not find that intriguing, my dear?'

Cassia would have done, under different circumstances, and she said this. Xenobe smiled mysteriously. 'Maybe one day you will find this marvellous, whatever you are thinking now.'

The harbour was packed with craft. The caiques belong-

ing to the local people, the Bosphorus boats with their dipping bellies which seemed to vanish into the sea itself,
barges, rowing boats, bobbing confidently on the waters.
Here, the centuries had been at a standstill, here the power
of the past had not dimmed. The spirits of the great war-
riors and conquerors who had each in turn made this place
his home were still here, earthbound, vigorous as ever. It
might be ruled by Muslims now, the nucleus of Islam, the
home of the Grand Turk, but Christian heroes still haunted
this magnificent city.

'See there, the Blue Mosque?' Xenobe was pointing,
Cassia's eyes following her hand. 'Where the hill begins to
slope down to the Sea of Marmora? That was built in the
middle of the seventeenth century, and it has six minarets.
The only mosque in Constantinople with more than four . . .
it caused great consternation in Mecca, for their great mosque had only four minarets.'

'How did they resolve their problem?'

'They added two more to the mosque at Mecca. Me, I
think it would have been simpler to pull down two at the
Blue Mosque. But then men always choose the most difficult way. They do not have the agile minds like women.'
Xenobe grinned. 'Inside, the walls are covered with tiles
in green and blue faience. I went in it once, after my master
died, to give thanks for my freedom. If I could choose one
mosque and one only to have seen in my lifetime, it would
be the Blue Mosque.'

The longboat was coming into land. Men in soiled white
breeches looped between their legs, and tattered shirts baggy
at their waists, were watching, some shouting and pointing,
open mouths revealing jagged, broken teeth.

'They love visitors – maybe it is because they had so
many in olden days,' Xenobe said. But now the pirates
crewing the longboat were intolerant of the women's talk.
One spat at Xenobe and fired a stream of abuse at her. She
closed her mouth immediately and drew a piece of ragged
veiling across her face. Remembering Algiers, Cassia did

likewise, hunching herself into the dirty, tattered robe which was all she now had in the world.

The longboat had to thrust its way against the pier, so many were the craft at anchor there. Eager hands caught the mooring rope as it was cast on shore and then the boat rammed against land. One of the pirates jumped out to secure the rope, and then the women were being herded out of the boat and into a group round which the sailors stood guard, faces grim.

Cassia wondered what would happen now, but she dared not speak to Xenobe. Those daggers tucked in the pirates' sashes were huge and glinted in the sunlight. One of the pirates hastened away, and returned some thirty minutes later with an enormous black man. By then the women were faint with the heat and desperate for a drink. One or two looked ready to collapse, but the negro did not display any pity for their condition. He made the pirates line up the women, then he waddled past them, one by one, his tiny berry-black eyes piercing them, his mouth a slit of disapproval. Some words were exchanged, then some more. Still the negro looked sour, the pirates more impatient. Finally one of the pirates said something which sounded accusative, at which the negro squared his massive shoulders which were like the sides of a whale, black and glossy. His pudgy hand, gemmed with dozens of rings, fell to the curved dagger at his scarlet sash.

'Trouble,' whispered Xenobe. 'Stay still.'

The pirates' spokesman stepped up to Cassia, tore the veil from her face, then ripped open her tattered robe with one brutal movement. She flinched, struggling to pull back her robe, but her hands were knocked down with such swiftness that she winced with pain. Pain sang through her wrists.

The huge negro stepped close to her, peered into her face, palmed her breasts and stomach, then her thighs. When his fingers probed between her legs she prayed that she would not faint. His nails were long and cut into her. She wanted to strike his fat, smug face but knew he might kill her if she did. The fingers continued to probe her, wriggling, squirming like living worms. Heat flamed in her face; sweat sprang out on her brow. Suddenly her tormentor grinned, spoke again in his squeaky, girlish voice. The pirates seemed to relax. Cassia was pushed forward, and so was Xenobe and two other women. The rest were kept in a little group, and Cassia saw one of the pirates reach into the boat for a rope with which to bind the women's wrists together. Where were they going now, the women who had shared the long trip here? She had thought that all of them would be staying together, going immediately to the Grand Seraglio, but no, only four of them had been selected by the eunuch, who was, Xenobe whispered, one of the assistants of the Kislar Agha, the Chief Black Eunuch of the Grand Seraglio.

The negro, his protuberant lips shiny with saliva, cracked the hippopotamus hide whip which had been tucked in his sash beside the curved dagger. The four women jumped, huddling together, too terrified to look up to bid their friends goodbye. The women who had not been chosen for the Sultan's harem were being dragged off to the open slave market, and they called their farewells as they went.

'Be happy, we shall not forget you!'

'Give my love to Hamid!' Angie called out cheekily, her face white, fear in her eyes despite her spirited words. 'Look after one another!'

'We will listen for news of you – be clever girls and give the Sultan the sons he wants, then we shall know you are his favourites!'

Cassia started to lift her head to call out goodbye, to take a last look at her friends, but the eunuch immediately cracked his whip, catching her a stinging blow on the back of the head so that she gasped with pain and bit on her lips to suppress her tears. To see her friends dragged off like that, like animals, not even to be able to say a proper farewell . . .

'Do not weep,' Xenobe whispered. 'Do not let them see

you have feelings. Be brave. Say nothing. Keep your eyes lowered.'

Cassia was too overcome to reply. She had not been through this before, like Xenobe. She knew so little; even after all she had endured, the barbaric heartlessness she encountered could crucify her anew.

The huge, barrel-bellied negro whirled his whip once, twice; the women shuffled round, to face the way they must go, towards the Sultan's palace. Behind them was the great expanse of sapphire sea, the speedwell-blue skies, life, some semblance of freedom – a great freedom if it were to be compared to what was coming.

The citizens of Constantinople stepped back hurriedly at the sight of the massive black eunuch with his waddling yet autocratic gait. He was not afraid to walk alone in the streets; he was a servant of the dreaded Kislar Agha, who was feared and held in terrified awe, whose powers were greater than any man's at court excepting the Sultan himself. No one tampered in any way with the Kislar Agha or his servants, not even the most menial. He was the confidential messenger between the Sultan and his Grand Vizier. He was the commander of the corps of Baltaji, or halberdiers. He was entitled to have both eunuchs and women as his slaves.

'He is the only man allowed to approach the Sultan at any hour of the night or day,' Xenobe managed to whisper as they made the best speed they could in their weakened state.

'We might even be going into the Kislar Agha's harem – I know little of the man except that he will be corrupt and avaricious: they all are. Nathan Dash gave his men orders that we be given to the Sultan in his name as personal gifts. He will wish that he had been well enough to do this himself, for I guarantee that his name will not be mentioned again. You will see.'

Sure enough, after a breathless trek through the winding streets, across parks, and yet more streets, they arrived at the Sultan's palace and there the negro – not at all breathless despite his bulk – introduced them to another eunuch.

'Already Dash is forgotten,' Xenobe whispered. 'We are to be bathed and groomed, as a gift from the Kislar Agha himself – carefully selected after great thought – to be given to the Sultan.' Her eyes glittered.

They were exhausted, hot, tired, and aching from head to toe. Cassia's stomach was rumbling, her throat was parched. After a brief wait in the little cubicle where the first eunuch had deposited them, they were greeted by a group of women who entered the cubicle on silent feet, their shalwar billowing as they walked.

Five of the women spoke Turkish, the sixth, to Cassia's astonishment, spoke English with a cultured accent. She did not dare ask the Englishwoman where she was from, for fear of anger or punishment, but she stared at her, noticing her blue eyes and brown hair. The woman did not appear to notice her scrutiny.

The women stepped through a trellised screen with the new slaves following. Then began what seemed like another endless trek through dark and musty corridors until they stepped into a beautiful, high-roofed, room of white marble – the bathrooms for the harem.

Despite the incredible size of the palace, the harem quarters occupied a comparatively small area, situated next to the eunuchs' quarters, the school for the young princes, and the courtyard of the Sultan-Validé – the mother of the reigning Sultan. Also in this section was the slaves' hospital, the kitchens, and notorious cage where the older princes were incarcerated. Beyond that were garden and the hall of circumcision. Everything a king could want was in these walls, sometimes in triplicate or more, bathrooms, bedrooms, gardens, libraries, a first, second, third and fourth court each with its own strictly designated character and atmosphere.

The first court was barred to no one who wished to enter, being of an almost public nature where there was only one rule: that of silence. In the second court, or court of the divan, which was considered the stepping stone to majesty, there was a deeper silence, a reverence, and here were fifty solemn guards protecting the gateway from the first court. Over the gateway was the great creed of Islam: *La ilaha ill-llahu, Muhammad rasul allahi: There is no God but Allah, Muhammad is the apostle of God.* Here foreign ambassadors were ensconced while waiting, sometimes for days, to see the Sultan, and here also were the dungeons where those people were cast who had displeased him. In the third court, an even more profound silence reigned. Here, where the throne room and libraries of the Sultan, his treasury and private apartments. The fourth court had superb views of the Marmora and the Bosphorus, and tranquil verdant gardens where, after all windows, doors and gates had been securely locked and barred, the women of the harem were allowed to stroll. Here also were the tulip gardens of Hamid III, these slender graceful flowers an unusual sight amongst the lush scenery.

Every room, every court was designed for the glory of Allah and of the Sultan. Marbles, tiles, faience, scroll work, ivory and mother-of-pearl, Chinese porcelain, golden domes, designs of pomegranate flowers and scarlet-beaked birds were only a few of the brilliantly decorated items in the palace. The Sultan at any time he chose might see it all, but few of his wives and concubines would ever see beyond the harem quarters, and the gardens of the fourth court.

Prisoners of love, Xenobe had called the harem women, but where was the love? How could one man love five hundred women and keep them all happy? Cassia realized that she was thinking in the western way, that here, in Islam, love was not considered essential for happiness in marriage. But to her, it was and always would be. Yet with Vincent dead, she could never love again, nor wish to be loved by any man. She did not imagine that the Sultan would expect her to love him – revere him, yes, but nothing else. If she could just keep in the background, stay quiet and be obedient, with luck she might not be noticed. Hamid had five hundred women to choose from, so he might take months, years even, to find out that she existed. That thought brought her some small relief.

The women were handed washing requisites and told to bathe. When they were ready, they were to be inspected by the Kislar Agha himself.

CHAPTER FIFTEEN

They were clean, sweet-scented, and robed in caftans of
fine, floating silk embroidered with silver, gold or moss-
green flowers. Embroidered, backless slippers encased their
feet, and scented oils of musk and jasmine billowed from
them as they moved. After the horrors of Nathan Dash's
ship, this was paradise – or would have been had they not
dreaded the approaching visit of the Kislar Agha. While
the other concubines were helping them to bathe, handing
them soap and oils and towels and lathering their hair for
them, they spoke of the Chief Black Eunuch in respectful,
awe-filled tones.

'No one has more power here excepting Sultan Hamid
himself,' one said. 'He is trusted with secrets and he is
allowed to go anywhere he pleases in the Seraglio. No one
ever dares to question him, or resist his wishes.'

'You are warning us to obey him?' Cassia said.

'More than obey: worship, respect and revere!' the girl
replied, her light green eyes shining. 'I am Circassian, and
women of my race are prized here for their beauty and
comeliness; however, I am not exceptional. There are many
lovelier than I.' She smiled, her light green eyes entrancing
against cream skin. Cassia thought she was enchanting,
and said so. The girl, Emanda was her name, lifted her
shoulders as if in apology. 'No, no, there is something about
me that is not favoured. But it does not make me anxious . . .'
she smiled again, handing thick warmed towels to Cassia
and helping her to rub herself dry.

Emanda said more than the other attendants all put
together, some of whom frowned at Cassia as if she were
unwelcome. She thought that Emanda's failing might be
to gossip too much. But as for beauty, she was truly eye-
catching.

A susurrus of whispers rang down the corridors towards

the bath-house and immediately the concubines became pink and flustered, hurrying to tidy the room, to arrange the folds of the women's gowns to perfection. And then the room was filled with people. Small, neatly dressed slave-boys with scarlet or emerald turbans on their heads. Black and white women robed in flamboyant caftans, their faces autocratic but captivating. Three young, extremely hand-some negroes wearing furred gowns, their flowing sleeves edged with jewels. They looked bored, sullen, they pouted and gesticulated like women. Cassia could not help but stare when they came near her, for their faces were painted, their mouths outlined in crimson; eyelids emphasized by silver and gold paint. She drew back, but to her relief they did not come any closer. How strong was their perfume – musk and patchouli, chokingly heavy.

Behind the bevy of attendants, concubines and *garzones*, stood a huge, flabby-faced black man with broad cheek-bones, thick lips, large brooding eyes and a thick squat neck. On his head was a steeple-shaped headdress covered by a hanging veil; his robe was of finest silk, dotted with crimson circles, and his outer robe was heavy with fur, despite the heat. Trailing sleeves reached the floor like cur-tains on either side of his immense, protuberant stomach. Strangely, his hands were tiny and slender, his small feet covered by white kid boots. He did not look terrifying. In fact, to Cassia, he looked cheerful, benign. She breathed again.

The Kislar Agha strolled round the newly-bathed women, his face benevolent. He looked at them from the back, the side, the front; he stuck his tongue in his cheek and made humming sounds. He touched Xenobe's hair and he placed a gentle hand on Cassia's chin. Otherwise, he did not embarrass them as his assistant had done in the harbour. He was no monster, Cassia decided. This was not going to be so terrible after all.

It was at that moment that one of the small slave boys slipped on a piece of soap which had not been tidied away. He tried to save himself, but failed, and tumbled into one

of the baths. As it was now emptied of water, he fell heavily
onto the marble base, lying motionless, colour ebbing from
his face. Cassia's immediate instinct was to run to him,
down the steps into the bath to see if he were badly hurt.
She moved, but immediately felt the lash of a whip round
her ankles. Pain blurred her vision.

The Kislar Agha had produced a whip from his jewelled
belt, and, after lashing her ankles, was setting about the
inert boy in the bath. Once, twice, he lashed the child, who
remained very still, and then, obviously furious, the Kislar
Agha gestured to one of his men to lift the boy up and carry
him away.

Xenobe managed to whisper: 'The boy will be drowned.
He has interrupted his master's precious routine and must
suffer for it. It is obvious that Allah meant the boy to drown
(so says the Kislar Agha), or he would not have made him
fall in the bath. Now he is to be sewed in a sack and flung
into the Marmora.'

Cassia, listening, went pale. 'Drowned for something
which the poor child could not help? Oh no!'

'Ssh,' Xenobe warned. 'They will notice us.'

The interview was over. Surrounded by his colourful
train, the Kislar Agha part swayed, part waddled his way
out of the bath-house. As he went, the concubines flung
themselves down as if worshipping him. Anxious not to
offend, Xenobe and the others did likewise, but Cassia was
most reluctant to prostrate herself. Finally, at Xenobe's
desperate behest, she did, but not before she had caught
the eye of one of the women accompanying the Chief Black
Eunuch. Tall, ramrod straight, with pastel-blue eyes and
glossy yellow hair wreathed round and round her head, she
stared hard at Cassia, her mouth unsmiling. She seemed
to be deep in thought, pondering. Cassia felt a chill run
through her. Hastily, she lowered herself, hoping that the
other women around her would conceal her from the eyes
of the yellow-haired one.

'Who is she?' Cassia hissed to Xenobe.

'I am not sure. It would seem that she is one of the Kislar

Agha's favourites, but . . . well, there is something special about her. She has great dignity, did you notice? It would not surprise me if she were not close to the Sultan in some way. If so, we shall soon know it.

'Odalisques, that is what we are now,' Xenobe whispered as the women were led to their quarters to be shown which beds were theirs. 'Now we must consider ourselves mistresses in the arts of love, for they are the only arts which we shall be allowed to practise here. We must be temptresses, angels, lovers, houris, all these things rolled into one, if we intend to keep the Sultan's interest and thus make our lives more comfortable.'

'You speak as one who has been trained to live this life – obviously you do not find it disquieting as do I,' Cassia grimaced.

'But we must make the best of things – would we weep and moan and feel the lash of the whip on our breasts? Surely not. Now that we are here, we must adapt. Do not come to grief while trying to ride a strange horse without a saddle and bridle, Cassia. Make your own saddle, take up the reins in your hands, firmly. Show your strange horse who is mistress.'

'I fear you waste all your good advice on me,' Cassia sighed in the now darkened room as they prepared for sleep. 'I am beyond advice.'

'Never!' said Xenobe. 'You will be chosen for the Golden Path, and those who walk it must be prepared.'

'That sounds like the path to heaven – what do you mean?'

'Those chosen to keep the Sultan company at night walk the Golden Path to his chamber. You will walk it, Cassia. I see, I know.'

The pythoness was speaking again, Xenobe's voice had become slurred, indistinct. Cassia turned her face into the hassock beneath her bed, knowing that she was about to weep. The Golden Path . . . to the bed of a man she already loathed because of his effect upon her life during the past months. Ever since the night of her abduction, the Sultan's name had hung over her head like the Sword of Damocles. Now, if Xenobe were right, that sword would soon fall on her. She could not survive it. To have to bed with some strange man – even if he was Allah's Vice-Regent on earth – to be encased in his arms and forced to submit to his lovemaking . . . such thoughts filled her with repugnance. She felt physically sick.

'Oh Vincent, Vincent,' she wept. 'Why did it have to be like this? Why were we parted so cruelly?'

To be so helpless, so vulnerable and alone. And in a land where everything was different from her childhood, religion, morals, customs, beliefs. It was as if she had stepped through a secret door, where everything she had once known was reversed. But there was no going back. She could not find that door again, to step back into the land she had once known so well. Vincent was there, she could see him in her mind: tall, strong, his emerald eyes glinting like jewels, his mouth curved in a smile. Broad-shouldered, his waist so slender, his charisma no less pale because she held only a mind-image of him. The picture was so strong she could almost step into his arms. Catching the image, she held it, was almost in his embrace when the picture clouded and vanished. He was gone. Grief and pain overwhelmed her. At that moment it was as if she had just learned of his death again.

So acute was the pain that she winced, tensing herself, curling into a tight ball as if fending off a blow. Without him she was soft, vulnerable flesh. She had no power, no strength, no motivation. To die would be a blessed relief. She knew now how people took their own lives, because living caused them far more agony than dying. Dropping into the pit of tears, she did not trouble to swim.

Next morning, she woke feeling strained and unrested. Her eyes were swollen, her skin blotched. Xenobe looked at her in alarm. 'Why this sadness, Cassia, when we are out of that black ship and safe now on shore?'

Cassia did not feel like replying. A weight seemed to

hang on her mind. She wanted to hide away in a corner, and sink into apathy. Now she did not even imagine the sight of Vincent approaching her – a favourite dream in which she had indulged.

'Think of your Christ Jesu at the gate of the palace,' Xenobe said. 'Think of him, picture him in your mind, strongly, and then say to him, "Welcome back, my love, my sweet love". Do this, Cassia, for great happiness!'

But before Cassia could reply, they had a visitor: the tall, yellow-haired woman who had stared at Cassia the day before. She glided into the room as if floating, her shimmering blue caftan starred with diamonds and gold filigree work. Her beautiful rounded breasts were naked, for her gown was split to the waist, and round her nipples were glued tiny diamonds. Her yellow hair was loose today, and her pastel blue eyes carefully painted with silver. At the corner of each was stuck a tiny diamond. Having surveyed the women silently for some time, she smiled. Her face was transformed. Deep dimples showed in her cheeks, her teeth were white and even, her eyes twinkling.

'Sweet virgin maidens – how we welcome you to the Seraglio. It is pleasing to see such proud beauty.' She looked directly at Cassia, 'and such exotic beauty,' she looked at Xenobe. 'There will be a place here for all of you, you will see. Do not fear that any of you shall not have the chance to rise to certain heights if you wish it. The heights you can select for yourself, but you must make the climb unaided. The chance is there.' The woman smiled again, then said. 'I am Kadine Mimosa. Here, many of us take the name of a flower. It is the Turkish custom for women. I shall also be your translator, for I speak many languages. If you desire anything, ask me. I wield no whip, nor do I have a lashing tongue.' Her eyes twinkled.

Xenobe immediately said, in Turkish, 'When shall we see the Sultan, Your Highness?'

'Ah, when he is ready, my impatient one. There is no haste. You must learn much before you may even look at him. And those who share his bed must be very special, highly-trained, schooled in every way. I am sure however that you will be good pupils. You look bright, but you, my English one, look very pale this morning.'

Kadine Mimosa tilted Cassia's chin gently with her hand, speaking now to her in English, much to her surprise. So far, she had spoken perfect French, then Turkish, and now English.

'I – I slept badly, Your Highness,' Cassia said, low-voiced.

'We have medicines here to solve every ill, my sweet one. Also to make you sleep, to wake you, to make you happy, sad, lusty,' she twinkled. 'Do not fret, ring the bell and ask Aisha or one of the others to bring you a phial of deep sleep. It is so simple. It is like paradise here, my beautiful ones, as you will discover. Anything you want can be yours, if you are good, if you please your royal master.'

Anything but the one man she really wanted, thought Cassia, her mouth twisting.

'To show that you have discarded your past, and now belong to the great Sultan Hamid, you will forget the names you have gone by until now. Each of you will be given a new name, that of a flower or perhaps a beautiful feature you possess, as is the custom. You,' she pointed to Xenobe, 'will be called Black-Pearl because of your eyes, and you,' she pointed to each of the others in turn, until reaching Cassia where she thought for a moment or two before saying, 'I think that you must be called, Briar Rose, for you are an English beauty yet I suspect that there is more than one thorn in your nature: pride. Yes?' Mimosa smiled gently. 'Or is it some secret sadness?' To Cassia's relief, she did not seem to expect an answer for she called one of the concubines and rattled off some instructions to her.

When Mimosa had gone, Xenobe turned to Cassia. 'She wanted to know if I was Turkish – the Sultan does not sleep with his subjects, did you know? She said that the harem women come from Georgia and Circassia, Syria, Rumania, England, Spain, France, Italy, but never from the lands over which the Sultan has jurisdiction.'

'And what did you tell her?'

'The truth of course. I said that my nurse was Turkish and that was how I knew the language so well, but that my parents were Arabic.'

Cassia looked at her. 'That is the truth?'

'But of course.' Xenobe flushed.

'It is just that you speak so fluently . . . Turkish I mean.'

'How would you know?'

Cassia grinned. 'Of course, I would not know, would I? I am sorry to have doubted you, Black Pearl.'

The use of that name made Xenobe laugh. 'Finding out who is and who is not a subject of the Sultan is not as easy as it sounds. Originally the Ottoman Empire was quite small, but it spread to Bulgaria and Greece, Smyrna and up towards the Black Sea by the mid-fifteenth century. Then Mohammed II conquered Serbia, Bosnia and Albania, Wallachia and Armenia. Selim I took Egypt, Jerusalem, Damascus and Haleb, and Suleiman the Magnificent added Algiers, Tripoli, Tunis, Hungary, Moldavia and Baghdad. But Austria reclaimed some of its lands quite recently in fact, and Russia is also battling for part of its country back. So you see, it is all very complicated.'

'I do admire your memory, Xenobe. You are so clever.'

'It is nothing. We Arabs are famous for remembering.' Xenobe winked mischievously.

At that moment, some half dozen attendants appeared, bearing boxes and carved containers in which were rouges and henna, scented oils, hair ornaments and every possible artifice to ensure instant, dazzling beauty. Now were to begin the meticulous lessons of the *Academie de l'Amour* which were essential training for those who one day hoped to catch the Sultan's eye.

Xenobe knew something of the training for she had once, in more modest circumstances, undergone it, but here everything was done in such splendour, on such an awesome scale that she must learn all over again whether or not she liked that idea. Her pleas that she knew how to make up her face and paint herself with henna were brushed aside by the determined concubines. Language difficulties arose, as these attendants did not speak Turkish, and Xenobe searched in vain for one who knew a smattering of English. No one did. Finally she gave up, her face taking on a look of long suffering. Cassia watched Xenobe being stripped of her simple caftan, thinking how unique her friend was when uttering her eerie prophesies, but how human she became when annoyed or frustrated.

Xenobe was to be used as a model for the others present. At this moment they were joined by other newcomers to the harem, a dozen girls and women, who were also to go through the Academie. Xenobe was made up, with care and dexterity, until her beautiful fawn skin shone like satin, and her eyes assumed the appearance of an Egyptian Queen's, slanting, carefully outlined in kohl and silvery-green paint. Her thick black hair was brushed out and plaited with silver and green ribbons, and she was liberally doused with attar of roses. Then, seated, her palms and feet were painted with henna, to colour them terracotta. At the end of the specified time the henna was removed and there were the shapes in orange, on her hands and feet.

Cassia noticed that some of the attendants were covered in designs, flowers and leaves and zigzags, in this colour, and she realized that they were stencils made with henna. Xenobe now looked mysterious, alluring, and extremely beautiful. She had also sighed a few times, impatiently, but was apparently resigned to the process. She did however give a start when one of the attendants advanced on her with a pair of silver tweezers. To Cassia's astonishment, she saw her friend being plucked with the tweezers until all the hair from the region between her thighs was taken out by the roots. It became painful, and Xenobe grimaced and begged for breathing space. Her discomfort seemed to amuse the concubines very much; they giggled and smirked. Finally, Xenobe was painted with henna in the plucked area, and then she was allowed to rest.

'I shall never be the same again. I feel as if I have sat in a bath of scalding water.'

Cassia held her friend's hand. 'It must have hurt terribly – what a thing to do. Shall we all get that treatment?'

'It would seem so,' Xenobe said ruefully. 'I did not have to suffer this in my former master's harem.'

One by one, the others were treated as Xenobe had been, being groomed and painted, plucked and oiled, until they presented a very different picture indeed. Some were given thick black brows which met in the middle over their noses – a sign of great beauty in Islam – and their lips were painted a brilliant red. Cassia did not like the thick black kohl that made her eyes feel heavy, and the greasy lip paint soon smeared. She longed only to be left alone so that she could remove it all and be herself again. But they were not to have peace. The next weeks were filled with lessons, some of them simple, some complicated, some startling. Deportment was vital, for grace, dignity, and self-control were essential in the harem. Many times over, each new girl practised walking along the Golden Path towards the Sultan, for she must be prepared should he select her. Any who stumbled, waddled, or faltered would bring down the Grand Turk's wrath not only on themselves but on the *Academie* tutors.

Cassia learned how to make a deep, steady obeisance, right down to the floor, head lowered. She might have to remain in this uncomfortable position for a great length of time, for she could not arise from it until her royal master ordered her to do so. Gradually, her joints became supple, and the position ceased to be such a bone-crippling experience. Some of the concubines could assume this position for hours at a time without feeling in the least stiff.

Bathing seemed to take up much of the day. The bathhouses were extensive, and the concubines spent hours in the water. Cleanliness was a part of their Muslim religion, and it also helped to keep them cool. Cassia was delighted to be able to bathe so frequently, and found this one of the most satisfying things about her new life. In England, washing was a ponderous matter with servants heaving great jugs of hot water up the stairs, and a metal bath screened from the draughts which always seem to chill the bather however carefully the screen was positioned. To bathe in winter was to risk a cold or fever, so few took that risk. Here, there would have been chaos if a woman refused to bathe.

As the days passed, Cassia began to relax a little, and the dread of her meeting with the Grand Turk faded. Now she could not recall the tensions she had once felt whenever she thought of him; nor the terror with which his name had become synonymous. Hamid, Emperor of the True Believers, Shadow of Allah Upon Earth, ceased to exist for her. He was a name, a shadow in truth, he had no substance, no form, and this pleased her more than anything. This was what she had prayed for, anonymity, peace, the freedom to withdraw from life.

Mimosa arrived, walking swiftly, yellow hair slapping against her silk-clad back. Her pastel blue eyes looked so innocent, so youthful, one could not believe that she saw all, knew all.

'Briar Rose is not happy,' she came up to Cassia who, recently out of the bath, was plaiting her hair.

Cassia looked up with startled eyes. 'Not happy, Kadine Mimosa? But I am content,' she lied.

'Contentment is for old women and sheep, my dear, not for young beauties. Those gifts which Allah has given you must not be veiled from your royal master. I have spoken highly of you, very highly. I have whetted the Sultan's appetite, his curiosity. He wishes to see you.'

A coldness filled Cassia, trickled through her mind, to her back and down her legs so that she felt weak.

'You are not pleased?' The Kadine leaned forward, her face intent. 'Do you argue with the ways of Islam?'

'Oh no, it is just that . . . I – I cannot explain it, Kadine Mimosa.'

'I was shy once, but when our master's eyes fell upon me, I accepted it as the will of the All-Merciful and I now have two royal daughters. Do you not wish to bear our master a child? It is a great honour, and he needs an heir. Since his infant son died, he has not been replaced. If you bore him a son, you would become a Kadine like myself – you would have your own suite and servants, and great authority here.'

Cassia took a deep breath. 'I do not wish to have a child.'

The Kadine stepped back as if threatened by a blow. 'You – you do not want a child? But all women want children! It is Allah's Will – that is how He created us. Your God too says the same. How can you resist the great plan?'

'I did not ask to be brought here. I did not want to come here. I was kidnapped, stolen, brought here under duress. You have no right to keep me here. I am English, *English!*' Now that the flood had begun, she could not stop it. With tears racing down her face, Cassia told the Kadine what she thought of the harem, and the prisoners of the Sultan. Mimosa listened, hands linked in front of her, and then, when Cassia finally became silent, she gripped her shoulder.

'Come with me, my dear. Come, follow me.'

Surprised, Cassia obeyed. The Kadine took her to the nursery suite, and showed her two baby girls lying asleep in their cradles. Both had black hair but their skins were snowdrop white. Their tiny mouths were the colour of pink *Rahat Lokum.*

'My daughters,' Mimosa explained. 'Tulip and Noanda. Are they not adorable? Do you not desire to bear such adorable children yourself? To hear them call you mama?'

Cassia had no wish to hurt Mimosa – it was not she with whom she was angry. She said that the little Sultanas were sweet, and that the Kadine must be proud of them, but that she, Cassia, did not feel that life here in the Grand Seraglio, with or without children, was for her.

'I was raised a Christian, in a land where a man has one wife only. Even to have a mistress is considered shocking, scandalous by most people, but here, a man has as many women as he can afford. Five hundred for one man, I find that so disturbing . . . It is not what I would have wanted, ever, to be one amongst many, I –'

The Kadine interrupted. 'Ah, so Briar Rose seeks the foremost light? She does not wish to be a minnow in a lake, but a mermaid in a tiny pool? I see. I see.' And now that Mimosa thought she had seen, nothing would deflect her. Cassia tried to correct her, but failed. Mimosa took her back to the harem quarters, and returned to her own, in the suite of the Kadines, which was separated from the courtyard of the Sultan-Validé by the first Kadine's own chambers, these being directly beside the Golden Path which led to the royal bedchamber.

There, Mimosa pondered for some time. Slaves brought her *Rahat Lokum* and sherbet, but she waved them away saying that no one must disturb her, for she was thinking. The slaves knew of Kadine Mimosa's thoughtful moments; she had often had them before. She went over the matter of the stubborn English girl, wondering what would be the best for her. Briar Rose was so proud by nature and stature; she held herself well, she was not afraid of anyone. (Or if she was, she hid it superbly.) And although she declared herself English, and reared to the ways of the English, it seemed to Mimosa's skilled eye that Briar Rose was possessed of great sensuality.

All her life Mimosa had dreamed of entering the Grand Seraglio. To her, it was the fulfilment of her fantasies, her ambitions. She was not alone in this, for many girls grew up with this ultimate desire. She had thought that she would bear the Sultan a son, for his little boy was frail, and she longed to be the Sultan-Validé herself, to enjoy immense riches, power, authority. Any Sultan would have served, she did not mind which as long as he reigned supreme. She was now twenty, her skin still supple and satiny as when she was a child, and her pastel blue eyes continued to entrance the black-eyed, swarthy-skinned Turks. Her beauty was held up as an example of perfection in the Seraglio and she did not quibble about this. But in her wisdom and astuteness, she knew that she would one day be too old to please, for who would choose a mature woman when thousands of tender young girls were at one's disposal?

Mimosa had given twin girls to Hamid – but of girls he had plenty. It was a son he now urgently wanted, for his little boy had died. It was a great disgrace to have five hundred women and no sons, and each daughter born to him filled him with further despair. So Mimosa had almost toppled when her daughters were born; she knew that Hamid was beginning to tire of her. But she believed that she could keep in his favours by presenting him with exceptionally beautiful concubines whose grace and seductiveness outweighed those of the average odalisque.

Mimosa, in her years in Constantinople, had learned that a man can either be entrapped by a woman herself, or by the women she procures for him. This was how she herself had come to the harem, purchased as a gift for the Sultan by his then favourite. There was no eye-scratching here. To please one's master by bringing him such a gift kept his eyes gratefully upon you, too. Instinctively Mimosa realized that she could make Briar Rose into the perfect gift for Hamid – and by so doing earn his delight and gratitude.

It was not that he was deprived of beauty – far from it. In fact, he was steeped in it. But like all things, straightforward beauty could become boring if one had too much of it. Concubines by the dozen scrambling at his feet and desperate to please were in great abundance. Hamid would not expect anything different, until he got it . . . And if the English girl bore him the son which Mimosa had failed to do, she would be mother to the boy who was second in line to the throne. As Mimosa well knew, sons were delicate creatures. They were born fragile and few passed their first year. Anything might happen to young Selim, Hamid's nephew, who, according to Turkish law, was his heir, for Selim had already been poisoned once by an ambitious Kadine. Fortunately, he had recovered, but now his health was delicate. He was pale, introspective, and it was said that his recovery was a miracle which would not be repeated should such a thing happen again.

Everyone loved Selim because he was gentle and had no temper. No one wished to see any harm come to him, but Hamid must have sons. There was a place waiting for the mother of the Sultan's first living son, a sacred place, as first Kadine, and, when Hamid died, the first Kadine would become the Sultan-Validé. If Selim did not survive.

Mimosa smiled, her full red lips curving upwards. She stroked the sumptuous silk brocade of her voluminous caftan and held out her hand to admire the rubies and sapphires that glowed on her tapering fingers. To poison Selim was something she had not yet considered, but to find a girl who would captivate Hamid above all was surely an act of great sagacity? It would increase Mimosa's chances of remaining in favour, for, if she did not in the meantime bear a son, the girl she had introduced to Hamid might well do so. Either way, she had little to lose, and it might be the making of her. The alternative was to sink back into oblivion, condemned to a lifetime of sipping sherbets, eating sweetmeats, and soaking in scented water.

Mimosa rose, smoothed her jewel-encrusted caftan and glanced in the mirror to see that her hair was neat, her face immaculate. There was only one she feared more than Hamid, and that was the Kislar Agha, who was the keeper of the harem, and provider of concubines for the Sultan. How was she to step on to his terrain without offending him? His face was cherubic, his anger maniacal. He had been known to strangle an errant slave boy with one hand. He had stamped on the neck of an unfaithful concubine a few months before, breaking her spine so that her head lolled back and her mouth gaped open as if she were laughing at him. Incensed, he had stamped on her face, again and again, until her features had become a bloody pulp.

Mimosa knew the Kislar Agha's predilection was for young, nubile boys. He must be placated with a gift, or gifts, of boys who pleased him so much that he smiled upon Mimosa even more than he now did. After, she hoped, he would allow her to direct Briar Rose's career in the harem.

CHAPTER SIXTEEN

The Kislar Agha sat upon a vast brocade cushion, his eyes dulled by the effects of opium. He was dreaming of himself and four, sweet-faced boys, virgins until now, whom he was schooling in the arts of pederasty. He could see their slender, silken bodies, flat stomachs and narrow hips, their soft mouths like velvet, their small, satiny buttocks as they prostrated themselves before him. His drugged dream continued, he lay back, breathing slowly, stentoriously. At these moments he was at his most vulnerable, which was why his faithful slaves now stood round his room on guard.

When one of them opened the door, he did not hear it. Nor did he see Kadine Mimosa tiptoe in, holding by the hand a small boy of about nine years of age. The boy was beautiful, his face fresh and innocent. His eyes were large, luminous and silver-grey, his hair a thicket of gilded curls. He was a little too plump but it did not detract from his charisma. He was the sort of boy who brought out a mother's instincts, who made childless women long to have their own baby. His name was Paule, but Mimosa had already renamed him Hyacinth, the name under which he was to introduce himself to the Chief Black Eunuch.

The opium dream was increasing. Now it was more realistic than reality. Before the Kislar Agha stood a beautiful yellow-haired woman and a small boy whose face was blanched with fear, his eyes dilated, lips parted.

'Great one,' said the yellow-haired woman, 'I have brought you a gift, a little flower called Hyacinth – is he not pretty? He longs to win your love. He is very frightened, but that is because he does not yet know of your kind and generous nature. Will you accept this gift from your true friend, Kadine Mimosa, who has gone to such great lengths to find you this little flower to warm your bed?'

The Chief Black Eunuch blinked, rolled his eyes, sat up

straight, staring hard at the woman, then at the boy. Saliva filled his mouth. The boy was clad only in a tiny loincloth of red silk, his favourite colour. He always wore red, and his slaves and apartments were decked with it. The Kislar Agha's fat black fingers tingled to tear away that red loincloth and take the naked boy upon his knee. A trickle of saliva rolled down his chin. He felt a very familiar stirring in that place which, for some eunuchs was *sandali*, completely clean-shaven, and, for others, devoid of the ability but not the desire. He was fortunate. He was a *thlibias*, or *semivir*, and thus considered safe to be trusted with an entire harem of women. He could never fertilize any of them, but he could enjoy sex whenever he wanted it, for the vital instrument of love remained. He felt desire like any man – more, perhaps – and he was free to indulge. But not for him the love of women. (Unlike some eunuchs who were allowed to marry but were then forced to take up work elsewhere.)

'My name is Hyacinth,' the boy's voice squeaked and cracked as he spoke. 'I am nine years old, and I am a gift from Kadine Mimosa, your devoted friend.'

'Well-learned, Hyacinth,' the Kislar Agha nodded. 'Come and sit upon my knee. I will not hurt you. I am a kindly, gentle man.' He grinned, and at that moment his face looked so jolly and benevolent that one could not imagine him any other way.

Mimosa began to breath again. Her gift was accepted. But now she must say a few more words.

'O great one, Hyacinth has two friends. He also has a brother. They are adorable, and one is only seven years old. He has heard of you, and wishes to meet you, but his mother refused to let me buy him. She is an honest, hardworking woman, and says the seven-year-old is too young to leave her. But I think that I can persuade her when next she visits me. She brings me trinkets and bolts of material. One day she came with Hyacinth and I knew at once that you would love this boy.'

The thick black lids of the Kislar Agha rose so that he

could survey the serene, unblemished face of Kadine Mimosa.

'What do you wish in return?' he said, his voice slurred with passion, for Hyacinth was now sitting on his lap, directly over his instrument of love which had risen like a bar of iron and was throbbing most painfully.

Mimosa then told him about her plan for Briar Rose. He listened, sighed, nodded his head up and down and squeezed Hyacinth harder against his lap.

'It is done, Kadine. The agreement is made. Let Allah be my witness.'

Mimosa smiled joyfully, made a deep obeisance as a sign of her gratitude, then hurried back to her suite. She began at once to prepare carefully chosen robes, jewels, scents, unguents and hair oils for Briar Rose. The Sultan never saw his women in the same robes more than once; they changed constantly to hold his attention. Briar Rose would be no exception and each outfit would be planned to perfection. For his first sight of the new concubine, a caftan of shimmering ice-blue slit to the naval to reveal her cool cream breasts, for his second sight of her, a caftan of buttercup-yellow silk dewed with diamonds . . . Yes, there *would* be a second sight, Mimosa was sure of that. This concubine would not be taken up, bedded, and returned to the anonymity of the harem. All her instincts informed her that Briar Rose had a great destiny ahead of her, and that she, Mimosa, would be her well-rewarded friend.

Briar Rose did not show any delight in Mimosa's efforts on her behalf. Her indifference drew shocked cries from the other concubines.

'Not grateful for the Kadine's plan!'

'She is a sullen, wicked girl who does not realize how fortunate she is!'

'If only I had her chances!'

'If the Sultan could only see her sulky face he would order her to be whipped!'

Briar Rose listened to their remarks with a singular passivity. She did not wish to enter this cattle market, this ritual of the plumpest cow being chosen for the bull. It was unseemly and unsavoury . . . she would fight Kadine Mimosa the whole way, and, with luck, possibly the woman would give up. With five hundred others to choose from, there was a chance that she would soon tire of Briar Rose's contumacy.

In the next few days there were storms such as the harem had never seen before. Briar Rose insisted over and over that she would not be groomed, would not be made up, would not be schooled in the secret, intimate ways to please Hamid. No, she would fight, and she would resist. Mimosa would have to find another victim.

'But you are no victim, my sweet one,' Mimosa said with the patience that as yet showed no signs of deserting her.

'You will be the victor, if you will only desist from these efforts to deny your great kismet, your destiny. First Kadine, just think of it – and one day Sultan-Validé: it is every woman's greatest desire but only you will achieve it!'

'Why not you?' Cassia flashed angrily.

'I have birthed my daughters, as you know, but there is no sign of another child, not after all these months. Besides, my monthly emissions are few, and growing even less frequent. The court physicians say it would be unlikely for me to have another child while this state of affairs continues.'

Cassia thought her turn of phrase amusing, and smiled despite herself. 'State of affairs' just about said it all, here in the harem.

'You think it amusing that I shall not bear a son for our master?' Two spots of colour spoiled the ivory beauty of Mimosa's face.

'Oh no, no, forgive me, I did not smile because of that.'

Mimosa relaxed, then realized that the new concubine had actually smiled – at long last – and that she, Mimosa, had become angry when in fact a smile was the very response she had been desperately seeking to evoke.

'You have a beautiful smile, Briar Rose. Your eyes light up, your teeth are so white. Your whole face shines. The

Sultan will be entranced by you. He is so sad, so sunk in gloom since his little son died. You can cheer him, brighten his hours, perhaps even make him laugh again.'

Cassia did not reply. She had not imagined Hamid unhappy. Surely such a wealthy, powerful man would be content? This was a new picture of the Sultan, as a man bowed by grief. She could not help but feel a pang of sympathy for him. All his money and affluence had not bought him tranquillity.

But she would not be drawn into more than sympathy. There were hundreds of girls here who could delight the Sultan, and make him smile again. Why should she become involved? She was still mourning her beloved Vincent, and she knew that she would never get over his death. Wherever she went, however old she became, she would think of him, long for him, and want him back beside her.

'Do you not wish to become a queen? How can you stay so cool when so much is offered you?' Mimosa's exasperated tones brought Cassia back to the present. 'May Allah give me patience with this stubborn child!'

But Cassia was learning from these Muslims. She said, 'What if Allah does not wish me to become the Sultan's wife? Perhaps He wishes the Ottoman heir to be born to another woman, one who will soon arrive here, or who is already here? Had you considered that, Kadine Mimosa? Perhaps I am fated to behave reluctantly to make way for this as yet unknown queen?'

Mimosa licked her shiny red lips, her eyes lowered as if she were visualizing a scene in her mind. She was not called Mimosa the Thoughtful One for nothing. Tick, tick, went her mind, as she considered what Briar Rose had said, and then her mouth curved into a smile.

'I do not think Allah has selected another. I am sure he has selected you, my dear. You are – were the unknown one. I saw you in a dream I had some months ago, before you arrived here. I saw your blue eyes and auburn hair, your stubborn chin, and there was a crown hovering over your head in my dream, and an infant in your arms.' Mimosa half-closed her eyes, but she was still watchful, waiting to see how the English girl would react to this disclosure.

Cassia shrugged. 'That dream could have been of anyone – even the Virgin Mary with the Infant Jesus.'

Anger flickered momentarily across Mimosa's smooth face. The obstinacy of this girl was driving her to a fury that she had not known she possessed. To fight her fate, when there were hundreds, thousands who would leap at just such a destiny! How could anyone be so obtuse? Was it something to do with her being English – were they particularly mulish? Mimosa heaved a sigh, flinging wide her jewelled arms, and paced up and down the room for a few moments to quieten herself. If only it were she being coaxed, how eagerly she would leap at this brilliant chance. She felt like taking Briar Rose by the neck and beating her beautiful head against the wall.

Instead, she finished her pacing, having breathed slowly, deeply, and turned a beaming face to Cassia.

'I do not think so, my dear. I think the woman was yourself, and the infant the next Ottoman Sultan.'

'The next Sultan? But what of Selim?' Cassia asked, astonished.

Mimosa realized that she had spoken too hastily. Collecting herself, she said, still smiling, 'Selim is sixteen. However many sons he sires, by Turkish law it will be the eldest male relative of his Uncle Hamid who takes the throne after him. That will be your son, if you co-operate, my dear. And then, ah, such glory, such magnificence, such power will be yours.' Mimosa lifted her tapered white hands into the air, her face thrown back, eyes shining.

Cassia did not know what demon possessed her as she answered, but there was Morbilly and Jolith in her face as she jutted her chin and said, calmly, resolutely: 'No.'

Mimosa did not trust herself to remain. Turning on her heel, she left Cassia without another word.

The rumour began hesitantly, gathered speed and soon became full-blown: Hamid was to visit his harem. The visit was, as always, supposed to be a complete surprise but in fact his concubines were well prepared. For him to see them all stunningly beautiful, immaculately groomed and dressed, when he thought he had taken them all by surprise, would increase his esteem and thus the esteem in which he held them. He must think that his women were at all times soaking in scented waters for him, massaging themselves with unguents, perfuming their bodies, shaving and applying henna to their intimate parts, coiling their hair with jewels, just for him and him alone.

'It is not a simple act to choose a new favourite,' Xenobe told her friend. 'For all his power, the Sultan cannot just walk into his harem and pick out a bedmate. There is a long, complicated ritual. Frankly, if I were a man, I think that by the time the ritual were over, I would have lost my ardour.' She giggled, her slim fawn hand over her mouth. 'It is always supposed to be such a great surprise, the visit, but we know of it long beforehand and prepare accordingly. Usually, the Sultan will be received in our midst by his mother and his chief treasurer, but of course there is no Sultan-Valide because Hamid's mother is dead. He is over fifty, you know. *Did* you know?' Xenobe quirked her black brows at her friend.

Cassia shook her head. 'Somehow I had imagined him young, strong.' Now to her picture of a sorrowing king was added his age, fifty, an age when a man might well have reached a desperate point if he wore a crown but had no male heir.

Xenobe continued. 'He is strong enough, from what I hear, but very pale-skinned, almost deathly white, and the contrast of his black beard is startling. Those women who have slept with him told me of this. I thought it best to find out all I could about him!' She smiled. 'Better the devil you know than the devil you do not know – do you have that saying in your country?'

'Oh yes. So he is past fifty, without a son, and very sad. What else should I know?'

'I was telling you about his visits, wasn't I? The Kislar

233

Agha will be here, of course, to show him round, and there will be a grand reception, either here, or in the apartments of one of the favourites. Before that, we must line up, heads thrown back, hands crossed on our breasts, so that the Sultan can examine us. With his eyes, of course.' She giggled again. 'All his family come to watch, Kadines, daughters, past favourites (they are called Ikbals) and the Guzdehs. You will be a Guzdeh, my dear. It means "she who has caught the eye of the Sultan". Then Hamid will sit down on a divan, with his chief treasurer and chief eunuch, and the odalisques – that is us – will file past, one by one, while the Sultan admires them at a leisured pace.'

'Just another cattle market,' Cassia snapped. 'I saw cows and sheep herded that way in markets in Cornwall, all spruced up and brushed, to catch the eye of prospective buyers.'

'You sound so bitter, my sweet, but you must remember that Hamid does not have to buy us. He already owns us. It is true that he can do anything with us that he chooses – absolutely anything. Although he is not as cruel and savage as Mahomet III – for which we must thank Allah and your Christ Jesus – he can be terrible when he is angered or rebuffed. It is unthinkable that you rebuff his advances, Cassia my love . . .' Xenobe leaned closer, whispered. 'It would mean your death. I am not jesting. Let me tell you of Mahomet III. When Murad his father died, he left twenty sons including Mahomet. Mahomet arranged immediately to have his brothers circumcised, according to the law. They were all eleven or under, handsome, adorable boys. They came to kiss their brother's hand, and he then told them that he wished them no harm, but that they must go into the next room to be circumcised. Surgeons waited, and when they had performed their operations on the innocents, each boy was taken into yet another room where he was strangled with a bowstring – which is the accepted method. Next day, the nineteen little bodies were laid out in their coffins, and Mahomet went to inspect them just to make sure that they were dead.'

Cassia was white. 'But that is dreadful – you told me before about the murders, but how could he have done that in such a callous, cunning way – was he a monster, a madman?'

'But, my dear, how do you think Mahomet got away with it?'

'Got away with it? I do not know.'

'I shall tell you how, my sweet. Because it is the law. Yes, the law. I can see you are amazed. To prevent insurrection and war caused by disputed successions, a law was passed many years ago, the Zanan-nameh it is called, which gave a Sultan the right to murder his heirs. The law stated, quite frankly, that all those who came after Mahomet the Conqueror (who made the law) should have the right to execute their brothers in order to ensure the peace of the world. That is only one story I can tell you, my dear. Purposely I have not mentioned the fates of some of the concubines who have lived here in past centuries. We do not want you shaking like a windblown tulip when you meet Hamid, do we?'

'I cannot countenance such brutality,' Cassia said. 'It is unbearable, sickening.'

'But we have no say in it, my dear. All we can do is try to deflect that brutality from our own selves.'

'It is blackmail. "Do as I say or I shall have you strangled." '

'Yes, that is so, and, like the Zanan-nameh, it is the law here. Tell me, would you attack the law of England, would you take on your men of law there and berate them? What is the penalty for trying to prevent law being done in your homeland? Yes, I see I have made my point. You would not dream of flouting English law, so you must not flout Muslim law either. You must try to accept it as a law that is as viable and legal as those you have in England. Seeing it as brutal and outlandish will only bring you pain in the end.' Xenobe stroked her friend's cheek, smiling at her with soft, pity-filled eyes. 'Do not think me a traitor, my sweet, when I say obey the Kadine and submit yourself to the

Sultan's caresses. There are ways of dulling one's senses so that one need know little of what happens. I did that, the first time with my late master.'

'Drug myself? But I know nothing of drugs.'

'But I do, and I am sure that the Kadine knows a great deal about them. Kadines and Sultan-Validés are experts with opium and with other methods of increasing or decreasing the senses. You will be given an opium drink, and you will know nothing, until you wake next morning.'

'But what chance will I have then to captivate the Sultan? Surely a deadweight will not intrigue him?'

Xenobe grinned, her teeth glossy white. 'Oh, you will react, my dear, do not fear that. But you will remember nothing of what has happened.'

'That sounds, well, odd to me. I do not see how it can work.'

'Be assured that it does. And am I to take your interest as proof of your having changed your mind?'

'*No!*' Cassia said vehemently. 'No, never. I would rather be strangled!'

'My sweet, you talk such nonsense.' Xenobe sighed, her eyes sad.

'But I mean it, Xenobe. I truly do. I would far rather die than go to bed with that old – old monster!'

Xenobe winced. 'Keep your voice down. These trellised walls are sewn with ears all listening agog. To speak thus is treason. Think what you like, but never, never say it.'

The arrival of a bevy of concubines wishing to bathe brought an end to their private discussion. The women stared hard at Cassia with narrowed eyes, chattering beneath their breath to one another in their own language. Their gazes were fixed on her as if she were some sort of two-headed beast.

'They say you are crazed, mad,' Xenobe translated. 'That you need your head breaking open to see what is wrong inside it. They say only fools and imbeciles repulse the wishes of the Sultan. One of them thinks that you will be sentenced to death for your rebellion.'

Cassia drew her eyes away from the women to stare down at her hands. She looked very pale, very beautiful, but so serious in that moment. There was no sign of the brilliant-eyed spirited sixteen-year-old who had once been wildly in love with Charles Billings, nor of the more mature but still radiant girl who had loved – still loved – Vincent Sauvage. Now her beauty was ethereal, as if painted on delicate porcelain, as if there was only the exquisite shell, but nothing beneath. She thought of the murdered princes, strangled by their own brother's deaf mutes, and of the other hideous tales Xenobe had told her. Then she thought of Vincent dying in a pool of his own blood, and of the fiendish Nathan Dash. She could never relinquish her identity, her independence, while Nathan Dash was still loose in the world, not while she still hungered for revenge on him. To be shut away here, in a scented prison, was intolerable. And yet . . . Dead she would be unable to avenge herself on the man who had slain her lover.

But to bed with a stranger, a gross, lecherous man like Hamid I. How could she do that and remain true to herself? And there was no one here with whom she could discuss this in the way she needed, for, although Xenobe was close to her, she saw life in such a different way from Cassia.

'Someone has taken my rouge pots and jasmine oil!' This cry was heard from the adjoining chamber, and one of the concubines, Aletha, came running into the bath house, her eyes wild. There was uproar, at once, every woman present wishing to state that she had not been a thief, that it must be someone else. Cassia watched and listened, thinking that they were like restless, vindictive animals when they were upset. And such minute things upset them.

'Well, well? Where are they? The rouge was a gift, a special gift from our Padishah. If I tell him that someone has stolen it, his wrath will descend on you all.' Aletha glared at the assembled women, her teeth bared.

Xenobe, who was translating for Cassia, said that the Padishah was another of Hamid's many illustrious titles.

There might well be the most terrible reprisals if, as Aletha, claimed, his gift to her had been stolen.

'Say nothing, Cassia, my dear. Protest your innocence by all means – but do not criticize whatever happens next, however much it shocks you. Aletha is a jealous, spiteful creature. It is months since she slept with Hamid and he only sent for her once. If he gave her a gift, I am a crocodile!'

The Kislar Agha himself came to sort out the furore. All the women were lined up, their robes searched by the Kislar Agha's slaves, their rooms ransacked for the rouge pot. By the end of the search, a pile of some two hundred rouge pots lay on the floor before Aletha, but she had disclaimed them all.

'Mine is not here. It has a tiny red mark on the base – I shall know it as soon as I see it,' she cried, tears beading her slanting brown eyes. Aletha had Oriental blood, and her skin was like yellowing cream, thick and smooth and soft, her eyes sloped, and were very deep-set. Her hair was shiny and black and she wore it in a long plait. She was very much overweight, since she devoured sweetmeats incessantly from dawn to bedtime.

'Anyone would think she was Sultan-Validé the way she is carrying on!' Xenobe whispered. 'Look at that outraged face of hers – phah, she is an idiot. The Kislar Agha won't stand much more of this, I promise you!'

As if he had heard Xenobe, the Chief Black Eunuch suddenly gave a bellow of enraged impatience.

'Women – women, control yourselves! This is a waste of everyone's time. I have important business to execute for our Sultan, the Emperor of the True Believers, and I cannot keep him waiting. Kadine Mimosa will take over now.'

A glance passed between Kadine Mimosa and the Kislar Agha; neither Xenobe nor Cassia missed that look.

'They seem in league – they were friends before but now they are more. It will not be sexual, of course, for the Keeper of the Rose lusts after little boys, not women. I wonder what they are up to. It seems to me that Mimosa is desperate to become Sultan-Validé. While there is no actual mother to hold that title, it is a case of fighting it out between themselves for power.'

'Mimosa wants me to fill the role,' Cassia said. 'She says that the Sultan is tiring of her, and that she is unlikely to have more children, as her monthly emissions are growing fewer. She wants me to find favour with the Sultan, and become powerful through her alliance with me.'

'But the Kislar Agha would never allow that. He is the Keeper here, and it would be his business to –' Xenobe stopped, thoughtful. 'She has bribed him. In some way, she has bribed him so that she has a free hand with your fate. Yes, that is it. Oh I am experienced in the ways of harem intrigue, my sweet, do not look so surprised. Also, of course, there is my gift. It has deserted me of late, but then it usually does when I have much to occupy my mind.'

'Oh, Xenobe, if only I could be free again – back in Morbilly, riding across the moors and watching the gulls wheeling above me! This stifling, scented atmosphere is so suffocating.'

'Sssh, the Kadine speaks,' Xenobe interrupted.

'Women of the harem, this matter is trifling and petty and far beneath the concern of myself. I shall ask our Sultan if he gave this gift to Aletha and we shall then get to the centre of the trouble . . .'

'Oh no, no, please, *please*!' Aletha cried, falling to her knees at Mimosa's feet. 'Oh, forgive me, forgive me, Kadine! I lied. I lied! Our master did not give me the gift. But I had a rouge pot and it has disappeared. That was the truth, I swear it.'

'You witless, stupid creature,' Kadine Mimosa snarled, lifting her foot and bringing it up sharply beneath Aletha's yellow-cream chin so that her head snapped back. The snapping noise echoed throughout the chamber and Cassia felt an icy chill prickle over her skin. Aletha's head tilted, she stayed in her kneeling position for a few moments then keeled over, a deadweight. Turning her back, Mimosa swept out of the room. The other concubines returned to what they had been doing. Nobody went near Aletha.

239

Cassia went as if to approach the fallen women, But Xenobe pulled her back.

'No, no, you must not be seen to sympathize with trouble-makers. She will be all right. She has only fainted with the pain.'

'But that terrible noise – what if her neck has broken?'

'It hasn't. Kadine Mimosa is an expert at such modes of punishment. I saw her do the same with a slave a few days ago. He spilled sherbet on her gown. He recovered, and he has a stiff neck, that is all. Aletha will recover too. Come, you must be more philosophical about these things, my dear.' Xenobe drew her away, but Cassia came reluctantly for Aletha's body looked so stiff, so lifeless. She would never have thought the serene-faced Mimosa capable of such violence. Oh she was learning fast about harem life!

The next few days were all bustle. Bathing, then bathing again, and continually massaging their bodies with unguents, oils and creams, each concubine vied with the other to make her body more soft and sensuous. When Hamid visited, it would be she whom he chose, having eyes for no others (or so each odalisque thought). Competition and rivalry ran high, reaching an almost hysterical pitch. Glances became cold and hostile, and as fast as one girl discovered a new style for her hair or for the way she wore her robe or jewels, others would copy, so that in the end there could be no originality. When Hamid came, he would see an ocean of faces all painted the same, bodies all wearing similar robes, feet all encased in the same jewelled slippers. And so many women had dark hair and eyes, brown skins. Auburn hair was extremely rare, and blondes were treasured like rubies. One small but unusual feature, hair a slightly different shade, eyes a little larger or more luminous, mouth a little fuller, softer, might catch Hamid's eye, and that would be all that was necessary for the odalisque in question to be prepared in readiness for his bed that same night. (And it did not matter if she had spent the entire week beforehand in the baths, in to the baths she would go again, to soak for hours, such was the Muslim obsession with cleanliness. They prayed at least three times a day, always before washing their hands, face and feet, a ritual which they called ghusl. The concubines spent much of their time in the baths, even when they knew they would not see their Sultan. Imagine the stringent cleanliness demanded of those who would share the bed of the Emperor of the True Believers.)

Throughout the preparations, Cassia merely obeyed mindlessly. She did not complain nor did she argue or criticize. What did it matter if she bathed until her skin was crinkled, until even the soles of her feet were white? And she had no objection to trying on different gowns and robes, slippers and headdresses. Mimosa hovered by her constantly, her face rapt, her smile omnipresent. She brought Cassia rare scented oils to douse her body, and a box of paints for her face, and told her to experiment with the application of these.

'I can teach you nothing about grace, my dear, for you know it all. Such natural composure is rare, and a delight to my eye. Think how it will please our master.'

Cassia said nothing. She smelled each of the little phials of perfume, chose one she liked and applied it liberally. The commingled scents of a myriad flowers filled her nostrils, honeysuckle, jasmine, roses, lilies, hyacinths. Mimosa smiled and nodded happily. Perhaps the English one was at last learning the lesson of submission? When Hamid saw the flowing gold-red hair, the blue eyes, so unusual, so lovely, he would lust after the girl. Mimosa had no doubts about this. He would lick his lips and perhaps some colour would fill his bone-white cheeks. Then he would cast his yaglik at her feet, his kerchief, to show that he had chosen her, and Briar Rose would be the Favoured One, having her own suite, her own slaves. Once, this had been Mimosa's lot, and she had not wasted her time. She was a Kadine because she had borne the Sultan two daughters, and although she would never lose this title unless she committed some crime against him, she did not have any influence now where she most desired it: with Hamid himself. It would be Briar Rose who would open the door to ultimate power.

241

CHAPTER SEVENTEEN

The sound of the vast golden bell rung by the eunuchs threw the harem into confusion. No matter how many times each concubine had dressed her hair, examined herself in the mirror, daubed herself with ambergris, musk or jasmine, now she set about doing it all over again. The Great One, Allah's Emperor, was en route. The golden bell was the announcement of his approach.

Xenobe looked flushed and excited, her black eyes glowing. She wore a fragile lace entari, an elegant gown that left her fawn, silken breasts bare. Its colour was eau-de-nil embroidered with silver and it was caught at the waist with four black pearl buttons so that it fitted very tightly, displaying her slender lines to perfection. The sleeves hugged her arms to the elbow and then hung to the ground in two silvered fantails. The hem of the entari was edged with arj, rich gold-silk braiding. On her black hair she wore a fotaza, the pert little harem cap like a pillbox, with a long gold tassel swinging from its centre. Her mouth was rouged, her eyes painted with kohl, green and silver; she looked superb, and Cassia prayed vehemently that Hamid's eye would fall on her friend and not on her.

There had been a long, arduous debate about Cassia's outfit. Should she wear a caftan, to preserve her entrancing modesty, or an entari to display her full white breasts? Mimosa pondered on this, first deciding one way, then the other, until Cassia felt exhausted. Finally, she was dressed in an entari of ivory Brusa brocade embroidered with crimson full-blown roses. Her hair was brushed until it gleamed, and plaited with seedpearls and white satin ribbons and a crimson silk fotaza was placed on her head. She wore the yemeni, too, an exquisitely embroidered muslin kerchief beaded with rubies and pearls, which was intended to keep the fotaza from falling off the back of the wearer's head;

and also a yashmak, the veil which could be drawn across the lower half of the face. (Only she knew that she had chosen the yashmak because she intended to pull the veil across her face just before Hamid reached the audience chamber. If she did it surreptitiously, she hoped that Mimosa would not notice. Suitably veiled and hidden in the crowd, there was no chance that Hamid would be able to see her face.)

'You look like a rose still blooming on its bush,' Mimosa cried, throwing up her slender white hands which were starred with dazzling jewelled rings. 'That skin so velvet-moist – how fortunate you are to have that famed English complexion. The heat of Turkey soon dries up the flesh and makes it wrinkled like the hide of a goat.'

Cassia said nothing, wishing that the audience were over and Xenobe chosen to be the new favourite while she returned to anonymity again, to dream of Vincent and their loving.

Mimosa was radiant in lemon silk hung with azure-blue silk tassels and gold braid. She looked like a brilliant beam of sunshine with her yellow hair cascading to her knees. Cassia could not understand why she was not still Hamid's first choice. What a discontented creature he must be, possessing so much beauty but remaining unsatisfied. She imagined that any Englishman born would have been more than content with Mimosa as his one and only wife.

The Chief Treasurer of the harem arrived, flustered and puce-cheeked in his haste. He stood at the doorway to the harem, awaiting the Sultan's arrival, every nerve tensed to make the studied obeisance. Normally, he would have been accompanied by the Sultan-Validé, but there was none at this time. And since the First Kàdine had recently lost her infant son she was not expected to put in an appearance. It was said that she was still grieving deeply.

The Kislar Agha arrived next, billowing on his tiny feet like a fully-rigged sail, his robe orange silk starred with emeralds and his tall conical hat a brilliant green draped with an orange veil. He seemed tense, flinging a brief glance at Mimosa. She smiled back tranquilly.

Cassia heard the voice echoing down the corridor, the voice of the eunuch announcing the approach of the sovereign.

'Behold our Sovereign, Emperor of the True Believers, Shadow of Allah upon Earth, the Successor of the Prophets, Master of Masters, Chosen of the Chosen, our Padishah, our Sultan. Let us worship him who is the greatest glory of the House of Osman!'

The entourage burst into the harem like a bevy of peacocks. Cassia stepped back involuntarily, hands clenched. She was so apprehensive that she nearly forgot to raise her yashmak.

The women lined up, arms crossed on their breasts, heads thrown back while Hamid slowly made his way amongst them, staring without appearing curious. Cassia stood frozen, hardly daring to look at him, hardly daring to breathe, praying that he would go away quickly, quickly.

And then Aletha, spiteful to the last, tugged at the long gold tassel on Xenobe's cap. Xenobe cried out, for Aletha had pulled some of her hair. A shocked gasp filled the audience chamber as Xenobe struggled for composure while Aletha assumed an expression of vapid innocence, eyes wide and shining, quite sure that now she had drawn the Sultan's eyes in her direction (for she stood next to Xenobe) he would choose her.

But Cassia stood on the other side of Xenobe, and, as the Sultan stepped towards the little group, she felt faintness gripping her and fought for self-control.

Hamid eyed Aletha, briefly, so briefly as to be an insult, and then his eyes lingered on Xenobe, long, contemplatively. She did her very best to hold his gaze, thinking of her friend's distress, caring neither one way or the other that Hamid should select her.

Hamid drew his eyes from Xenobe and saw one of his concubines — his very own property — daring to wear the veil before him. Veils were to be worn in public, before strangers, but never before one's royal master. Another sigh of astonishment ran round the room as Hamid stopped before Cassia, his eyes narrowing, his bone-white face becoming even whiter.

Cassia looked into the narrow, dark eyes of the Sultan. They were heavily lidded, as if he were exhausted and had not slept for many nights. His nose was wide at the tip, and very long, his mouth thin, curving down at the corners, giving him a disdainful air. His beard was spade-shaped, thick and bushy, with a little v cut in its centre at the base. His thick black brows were arched, so that he looked surprised as well as aloof. Cassia, seeing smears of black on his cheeks, realized that he dyed his beard, that Allah's Shadow upon Earth was really an old man trying to look young, an old and frightened king without an heir. But it was his pallid skin that held her eyes. She had never seen such whiteness.

In that moment was born the only feeling she could give the Sultan. Pity.

Hamid stared into the hydrangea-blue eyes fringed with silky dark lashes, gazed at the immaculate creamy skin above the yashmak, and then he reached out and tugged the veil from Cassia's face.

Another gasp filled the room, passed from mouth to mouth, as Hamid continued to examine the face of the English girl, apparently unable to take his eyes from her face. Xenobe, watching, horrified, saw that his eyes held those of Cassia's like a mesmerized snake. It was as if, in labouring so fervently to repel, she had done the very opposite.

Then, lifting his hand, Hamid dropped his kerchief at Cassia's feet, and at last drew his gaze from hers to leave the audience chamber for the reception which Mimosa had prepared for him in her own suite.

Now that he was gone, Cassia shook from head to foot, her teeth clattering together. Xenobe held her by the arm, propelled her to a seat, tried to comfort her.

'It won't be as bad as you think – I am sure of it my love.

245

Please, please, do not cry so. He is not an ogre; he has no perverted desires. He is a lonely man, sad and bereaved. He needs someone who will love and understand him, comfort him and stroke his brow. Here, all that the women think of is bringing their master sexual satisfaction. How many, I wonder, see him as a man who has other, deeper needs? You can be that one, my dear, and see what a power you will have to help others then! There is cruelty here and injustice. You can alter that if you have influence with the Sultan. Hear me, my love, and know that I speak true.'

Cassia did not reply. She continued to weep in her friend's arms, while, round them, the other concubines stood, whispering or staring, some devoured by envy, some perplexed by Cassia's grief.

Aletha clamped her lips together, digging her nails into her palms. She fought the desire to attack her rival, to bite and scratch at her face, for she knew that would mean immediate, vicious punishment. Aletha's mind was peopled with dreams and delusions. She believed she was the Chosen One and that she always would be, but that others, malicious and greedy, strove to keep Hamid's attentions from her. Now, she knew that Briar Rose was the one she must destroy so that Hamid would look at her, Aletha, again. But the destruction must be done with finesse, so that no hint of it could be traced back to her.

Blood oozed where Aletha's nails split the soft flesh of her palms. The nerves in her face jerked, a flicker coursed across one eyelid. She stared at Briar Rose. In her mind's eye, Aletha saw the new favourite crushed, damaged, lying beaten and lifeless upon the floor, while Hamid, his face alight, took Aletha into his embrace and whispered that he had always loved her, and only her, and that she was now his First Kadine.

Intent upon Cassia's distress, Xenobe failed to intercept Aletha's venomous glances. When the worst of the tears was over, Xenobe drew her friend to a quiet spot far from the audience chamber, and there they stayed together, not speaking, not having to speak, each picking up the other's thoughts. Later, they went to one of the windows and looked out at the gardens, seeking peace in nature. They could see the Bagdad Kiosk, built by Murad IV after his return from that city, its tiled walls shining in the sunlight, the lotus motif predominating, with coloured marble and circular inlaid medallions on white. Above it a gilded dome was supported by arches, and from its centre was suspended an ornate gilt ball on a long chain. Inside, the building was tiled in shades of blue and green against a white background. Floral designs rioted on the walls; pomegranate flowers and enormous leaves stood in two-handled vases in the panels on either side of the fireplace. Birds flew and glided in brilliant plumage, their beaks scarlet. Round the edges of the main room stood handsome divans beside which were cupboards inlaid with mother-of-pearl and ivory, the windows were traceried and looked on to the broad marble terrace, a havuz or pool, and, beyond, the Hall of Circumcision. Xenobe, being highly perceptive, saw all and memorized. Cassia did not even smell the commingled scents of the luxuriant blooms so carefully nurtured in the gardens.

With Vincent beside her, she would have been as perceptive as her friend. Without him, she had no wish to see.

They kept away the *Academie* tutors for as long as possible, but eventually Mimosa and her entourage found them, and hurried them to the bath-house where Cassia was stripped, soaked, and lathered repeatedly. Gowns and jewels were brought, and Mimosa became flushed and excited while trying to decide which one Cassia should wear. It was not easy, for she suited them all to perfection, whatever their colour or style. In blue-green she looked like the Earth-Mother, in white. she was Diana, in cream and gold she was Aphrodite, in black fringed with gold, Minerva.

Desiring to make the most subtle impression, Mimosa hovered between blue-green and cream and gold, but finally decided upon the latter. Virginity was always impressive, even to a man of Hamid's experience. With her hair unbound, and strewn with pearls, Cassia looked goddess-like. Mimosa knowing the Sultan better than many, knew that he would not notice the sadness in her eyes, but would be dazzled by her physical appearance.

Xenobe squeezed her friend's arm tenderly, sending silent messages of loving comfort. Cassia was grateful, but she could not suppress her wretchedness at the thought of betraying Vincent with her body, if not her mind. She told herself sadly that soon she would be able to call herself an adulteress.

Mimosa handed her the goblet of wine and she drank it without thinking. It would bring some small oblivion, and that she needed. After a few moments, she seemed to hear Xenobe's voice in her mind.

'When Fate has brought lovers together, nothing can separate them, not death nor disaster, nor any mortal or immortal act, for their souls have joined, they are one. One. The love of the body is transient, but the love between souls is immortal. This is true. I know it . . .'

And then Mimosa was leading her to the apartments of the Sultan-Validé and through into the courtyard which led to the Golden Road towards Hamid's bedchamber. At that point, Mimosa stepped back. Cassia stood for long moments, her senses swimming from the drugged wine, then, knowing that she dared not hesitate any longer, she took her first steps, alone, along the Road.

By custom, the Sultan would be in bed when his chosen favourite arrived. Hamid was there now, waiting, eyes closed, pretending careful disinterest. He had been through the ritual a myriad times before, until each time blurred into the next and the whole became one. Nothing stood out in his memory, every girl was much the same as the next. They all dressed the same, wore the same facial artifices, smelled the same, blushed and giggled the same. Few said more than a brief, awed sentence to him. Some were so stricken by his proximity that they fell silent as mutes. Now, he saw them only as vessels for the son he craved. They would all remain pale, characterless statuettes until one became pregnant and bore him his heir and then that one would become his First Kadine, his treasured favourite.

He did not realize how, in seeing nothing and wanting much, he was totally isolating himself from happiness, caging himself as he had been caged in the Kafes for over forty years until his predecessor's death. Those terrible years of mindless incarceration would not free him of their talons. He was still, in his heart, in the Kafes, the Prince's Cage, shut away from life, from hope and promise. Released, he had become Allah's Vice-Regent, and the shock of the change had been intense. Now, riches and incalculable power were his, yet still he was deprived of what he most wanted: an heir.

His solitary confinement had borne a little fruit. His own sufferings remained so vivid in his memory that he had given his nephew Selim his freedom, and allowed him to live normally in the world. Selim was movingly grateful, a devoted nephew.

Hamid's thoughts roved freely in the limited sphere of his Kafes-bred mind. Deprived of loving arms, of parents, family, nurse, he could have been a vegetable – many were. He had not slept with a woman until he became Sultan in his middle years. It was an experience that had nearly destroyed him, so traumatic had it been; but girl after girl had helped to eradicate that first memory. Now, they were all the same, scent, hair, painted eyes, shaven bodies, mute and mindless reactions.

If Mimosa had given him a son, he would have been loyal to her. He knew that he was capable of cleaving to one woman, but the circumstances must be special: she must be loving, sensitive, and fertile with sons. Hitherto, Allah had denied him this last. Hamid, being one of the faithful, believed he must obey the wishes of the Great One. But now he had reached a crossroads.

Believing himself strong, invincible, self-sufficient, Allah's Vice-Regent upon Earth lay curled in his vast bed waiting for Briar Rose.

The Sultan's bedchamber was rococo in style, ornate, lacquered in gilt, or worked in marble, every inch lavishly designed. Louis XV furniture covered the floor. The fountain, chimney-piece and dais were alive with wriggling scrollery. It was a fitting frame for a man who had been shut away like a leper for over forty years of plain, severe, unornamented subsistence. The drapery, the ornaments, the flowers and gilt and smooth marbles were all necessary for Hamid's peace of mind, regenerating his thoughts and keeping his memories diverted from the past. He liked his women ornate too (but what Sultan did not?) and although he was wearying of their sameness, he was not growing tired of his bedchamber nor of his throne room and royal bath in which he found a deep gratification. They, more than any mere woman, could express the uniqueness of his personality.

He was bored, even before he heard the door being carefully opened. He knew every move of what would now ensue, knew it by heart, but despite his mental dejection, his body, conditioned as it was to this sensuous ritual, was already beginning to respond.

Cassia had been instructed as to how she must behave in this most sacred room. She must walk slowly to the foot of the Sultan's bed, lift the coverlet and raise it to her forehead and mouth as if in genuflection, then she must carefully ease her way up the bed from its foot, until she lay level with Hamid. Meanwhile, two eunuchs would be standing on guard outside the Sultan's door, there would be absolute silence maintained in all the quarters nearby, and it was forbidden to watch the favourite as she approached or left the royal suite.

Knowing all of this did not give Cassia courage. She wished herself far away from here, anywhere but in the Seraglio, anywhere but on earth. In the great bed which she was now almost touching lay the black-bearded, white-faced man who was her destiny, her unchosen destiny and with whom she had no affinity. He had not even caressed her yet, but she felt raped, unclean, tainted.

The effects of the drug were already beginning to wear off, for Mimosa had given her only enough to pacify her along the Golden Road. She had never intended that her chosen victim should be in a stupor by the time she reached Hamid's bed. He would not be pleased with a rag doll, nor would he remember such a girl. Whether Briar Rose fought, screamed or responded with passion, she must be remembered by Allah's Vice-Regent. In memory lay power.

Attar of roses wafted in waves around Cassia's face as she lifted the coverlet, touching it against her forehead and lips. The room seemed to spin a little, her vision clearing as the drug's effects receded. She saw patterns, shapes, colours so bright that they dazzled. Lamps glowed like flames, gilt gleamed like seams of gold. Her legs would not move, her muscles were constricted in a vise, she was crippled. Managing to kneel, she insinuated herself under the coverlet, up the bed, slowly, in terror, something hard pushing against her as she came level with the Sultan. He was ready for her, waiting, pulsating, but he did not speak. He wore a voluminous robe of smooth silk, parted down the front and held open by his manhood. He said something, which she did not catch, and she dared not reply for fear one did not ask the Sultan to repeat his words. He moved, and the scent of attar of roses billowed around them; his mouth was on her cheek, her eyes, he pushed against her, crushing her close, and she felt tears biting against her lids because this was wrong, he was not Vincent, she did not love this man, nor want him.

Struggling for control, she let Hamid kiss her wildly, continually. He seemed overcome, impassioned by her face and body, unable to speak sensibly. He sighed and panted, gripping her tightly in his arms. He was immensely strong; his fingers were manacles, his limbs hard and heavy. He rolled on to her, pushing her legs down and apart. She cringed, forgot to breathe, went limp, let him do what he wanted, her only defence withdrawal, while she silently begged Vincent to forgive her.

*

251

Afterwards they sat in bed drinking sherbet made from ambergris, and Hamid stroked her arms and breasts, his narrow dark eyes glittering. He had said nothing, and she was glad, for she would not have known what to say to him. Did one praise insincerely, utter endless compliments? No one had told her how to deal with this problem, and she had not thought to ask. Now, having used her body, Allah's Vice-Regent seemed content, but in need of her company. He smiled, nodded, gesturing to the eunuch to replenish her jewelled goblet, but she saw that, despite his awesome dignity, his eyes were sad. Grief was etched into the fine lines of his face, it darkened the flesh beneath his eyes, but he had good teeth, his skin was soft. He reeked of attar of roses, which she found delightful on a woman but disturbing on a man, and he moved with slow, studied gestures, as if he thought he were being constantly watched and must always be at his best. She wondered if his forty years in the Princes' Cage had made him that way? The heirs were watched as closely as lunatics, guarded, haunted, by slaves.

An hour passed, and still Hamid had not spoken to her. She became ill at ease, once or twice opening her mouth to speak then thinking better of it. She seemed to recall someone saying that one did not speak first in the presence of the Sultan, but only after he had begun a conversation or given permission for one to say something. She wondered idly if she would be punished for introducing conversation, and what the punishment would consist of. She realized that her thoughts were wandering on inanities but she found it hard to concentrate. This was partly attributable to nervousness, and who could blame her for that? To have been put to bed with a total stranger, a great, omnipotent ruler, yet a man who had spent over forty years of his early life in a cage, and who treated women like toys. It would have made any but the steeliest of women ill at ease.

To prevent those first words from being uttered, she thought of how she had come to this strange place, and inevitably her mind returned to Vincent. She felt as close to him as if he were with her, watching over her. In a strange way it became harder not easier to accept that he was dead. The more bizarre her experiences of the present, the more she took refuge in the past. Sometimes she told herself sternly that she must cease to conjure him up in her mind – it was so painful coming back to earth. Sometimes, as now, she felt it would be worse agony not to have such a secret place in her mind to retreat to.

Hamid leaned towards her suddenly, his salt-white face brushing against hers. He had long, powerful fingers and he now stabbed them into her flesh as he gripped her again, pulling her close. She found herself twisted neatly on to her back, her legs pressed open, her body invaded. He had the skill borne of great experience, and yet it was the least arousing experience Cassia had ever had. It was as if Hamid were alone, as if she were not even in his thoughts let alone in his arms. The conclusion came swiftly and it was over. Allah's Vice-Regent lay panting on his side. She was forgotten. Tears came crowding, but she fought them, praying that he would sleep now and leave her alone. He had touched her body but not her heart. That was, and always would be, Vincent's.

Lying there, as the Grand Turk began to snore, Cassia faced her lonely destiny, feeling as if she were lying on a chilly mountain peak alone, with the storms of night thrusting against her.

CHAPTER EIGHTEEN

'What happened? Tell me everything – did it go well? Was he gentle? Tell me, my love!' Xenobe clasped her friend's ice-cold hands, looking into her eyes with love and concern.

Cassia shrugged. 'There is nothing to tell. It was over quickly, he did not speak, nor did I speak to him. We drank sherbet made with ambergris, and he looked at me as if I were a statue which had suddenly come alive, and then he made love to me again. After which, we slept. No,' she added, 'you could not call it making love. It was one-sided, clinical. He cared nothing for my responses nor for my feelings. No, it was not love.'

Xenobe drew her to a seat by the fountains where bubbling waters sang.

'He did not touch your soul? Well, my love, you must be glad about that at least. Would you not have been confused if he had stirred you? Confused, and guilt-ridden?'

Cassia looked up, surprised. 'How well you know me. You see so much. Yes, it would have been a betrayal of my dead love if Hamid had roused me. As it is, it really seems as if nothing happened. He is no great lover, and his refusal to speak cancelled out any chance of our relationship blossoming – for which I am heartily glad, of course.'

'Do not be too sure of that, my love. He rarely speaks, so I have been told. Some say it is his long stay in the Kafes – that such an incarceration inhibits speech. I was told that infants who are placed in there have been known to remain mute all their lives. Perhaps it is not that, of course, but just one of his peculiarities – to which, being Sultan, he is perfectly entitled. My own late master could not bear any light when we were bedding. Always we must be in total darkness, or he was incapable of playing the man. Perhaps Hamid finds silence conducive to sexual activity? Maybe he does not wish to build a relationship with a woman.

Considering his long imprisonment, perhaps he cannot build such a relationship at all?'

Cassia pondered on that for a while, watching the fountains bubbling, trying to accept that the Sultan might not be finished with her, that he might indeed send for her again. She had left his presence in the accorded fashion, after he had left the bedroom to go into the next room to dress, leaving his previous day's robes with her. She was then supposed to take all the loose money in his purses. If exceptionally pleased with her, the Sultan would send a gift of jewels or robes from the next room. Xenobe now asked if Cassia had received such a gift.

'There was plenty of money in his purses, but I left it. He sent me a gift, yes, a bolt of crimson silk embroidered with gold roses, but this too I left on the bed.'

'You did not take the money or the gift?' Xenobe gasped, sitting back with her mouth open in dismay.

'I would have felt like a common whore being paid for my body. Taking money for sex – no, no, ask me anything but that.'

'Oh, Cassia, my love, sometimes your naiveté troubles me. You could have used the money to buy presents for the infant Princesses, you could have made your own life more comfortable. If you had brought the bolt of cloth and let others see it, your position here would have been immediately improved.'

'Are you so sure of that? What of the jealous ones? Aletha? I am sure that she would have tried to steal the gift, or damage me in some way. Her eyes glitter like blades in the sun. She has the most terrible temper. I do not want discord.'

'There will always be discord where so many women fight over one man, my love. I am sure that the possession of the gift would have made your life easier, not worse. Mimosa would have been pleased, for one, and now she will be furious. To refuse a royal gift is almost a crime – what will you say to her?'

'I have committed another offence, have I? Well, I acted

on impulse, but then it is not easy to plan one's every move. Mimosa will be angry, you say. Well, she will just have to be angry then. There is nothing I can do now.' Cassia looked almost defiant, and certainly not afraid.

'No, I suppose not – except try to look penitent when she comes to upbraid you.'

'As to that, you know I can only be myself, Xenobe. I am not sorry that I left the money and the gift. Would you ask me to be a hypocrite?'

'No, but for your own sake . . . Take care, my love, my dear love, take care.'

A rustle of sound, many voices raised in comment, alerted them to the arrival of a visitor. Kadine Mimosa bore down on them like a yellow-crowned wraith.

'Gossiping together again? Always together you two – why is that? You are not sisters. It is not that you prefer women to men is it, Briar Rose? Is that it?' Mimosa peered at Cassia closely, her eyes bright speedwells of curiosity.

Cassia felt the heat flowing into her cheeks, her throat tightening and going dry. Huskily she managed to whisper that she was perfectly normal, and certainly did not prefer women to men in that way.

'That is all right, then.' Mimosa stood back, hands on hips. 'How did your night pass? Did it go well? Did the Sultan enjoy himself?'

'I imagine so.'

'You imagine so? Can you not tell me more details? Did he take you once, twice? Did he become very excited and tear off your clothes? Come, girl, tell me all!'

Cassia turned a deeper pink. She had not expected an inquisition of this sort. Conscious of faces peering round arches and through trellises, and of the many ears stretched to hear her replies, she said that the night seemed to have passed amiably enough.

'The Sultan seemed content. He – he made love to me twice. He left me money and sent me a gift. He did not speak to me, however. I do not think that I truly pleased him.'

256

'Oh, he does not say much at the best of times. That is nothing to worry over. Where is the gift? What was it? Have you counted your money? Was it a lot?' Mimosa rubbed her hands together in excited anticipation.

Cassia licked her lips. 'I – I did not bring the gift with me. And I left the money behind.'

There was such a prolonged silence after her pronouncement that she began to feel chilled. Mimosa's smile had frozen and now was shrinking from her face in slow, jerking movements. A nerve jumped beneath her left eye. Once she opened her mouth to speak, then shut it and then opened it again. Eventually, she collected herself, but her words came out as a squeak.

'You will have pained Hamid greatly. How could you be so cruel, you wicked evil child? Is there no compassion in your heart? To reject the Sultan's gifts! Oh, Allah, have mercy on this erring child, this witless, foolish creature!' Mimosa pressed her palms together, eyes raised to heaven.

'I did not mean to hurt His Majesty – I truly did not think of it that way. It was merely, well, I did not wish him to think that he must reward me for sleeping with him. I do not see why he has to pay his concubines for that privilege. Is he not our great Sultan and master? Why then should he pay?'

Mimosa's shocked expression faded. A sly, contented look began to spread over her features. 'Briar Rose, you have heartened me. Truly I had thought your heart was stone, but now I see your heart is like the velvet of a beautiful gown, soft and overflowing. Your sentiments are touching. Hamid will weep when he hears what you have said. I must tell him quickly before he finds out about the rejected gifts and imagines that you hate him.' Mimosa swirled on her heel, leaving behind her the pungent odour of roses and hyacinths.

'What did I say?' Cassia looked helplessly at Xenobe.

'Something original, my love, which is as rare in this place as the waters drying up in the fountains and the women losing their voices.'

There are some things which one cannot escape. They are a destiny of a different sort from that of love. Often, they are unpleasant, even unbearable, but in facing them one can learn strength, reach maturity, and find the ability to stand alone. As she walked along the Golden Road again a few days later, Cassia thought that something of that nature must come out of her experiences in the harem, or her whole life would have been fruitless.

Again it was silent, again she walked alone, seeing no one, not even a guard.

She wore a loose transparent robe of silvered lamé tissue, so fragile that it billowed like curtains in the wind as she moved. Her hair was oiled and scented, and dressed with rubies, and she had been washed so many times that her skin felt tight. Beneath the robe her body had been massaged and creamed, and rubbed with pungent oils; she had been stripped of body hair and henna was painted between her legs and on her palms and the soles of her feet. Not daring to think, wanting only to turn round and go back but knowing that too much lay at stake, she continued to walk. Mimosa, Xenobe and so many others would be at risk if she behaved in a rebellious fashion. All of them in some strange way depended upon her; how could she let them down, even though the combined weight of her immense responsibilities was crushing her exuberance? She remembered the days when Vincent and she had been lovers, the spellbound, magical quality of their loving, and knew that for the rest of her life she would never feel like that again.

Hamid was waiting for her, lying on his side, his head cushioned on a pillow so that he could watch her entry. She caught the glitter of his eyes in the lamplight, but pretended not to see. Approaching the end of the bed, she had begun to lift the coverlet, to crawl upwards until she reached his side when he sat up, a pleading look in his eyes, and gestured to her to get into bed in a normal fashion. She kept her eyes averted as she obeyed. He was naked but for a collar of emeralds the size of poppy seedpods, and his long dark hair hung to his shoulders in shiny strands. On his forehead hung a gold chain, from which was suspended one enormous ruby. He smelt as before, of ambergris and attar of roses, one spicy, one sweet. Looking up, she found that she had not imagined the pleading light in his eyes. He seemed to be silently begging her to guess what he was thinking and feeling. Only an extremely isolated man could expect others to possess such depths of insight. It should be Xenobe here, not me, Cassia thought, as she slipped into the silk-veiled bed. The chill of the silk made her shudder; it was like stepping into dry, cool waters that were much too deep for her. She had not liked it the first time, nor did she now. Her overriding reaction was to leap out, to run as fast and as far as she could. Quelling this, she lay down beside the Sultan, her muscles rigid.

The next two hours were as silent as the first time. Hamid seemed overwhelmed by her nearness. He kissed each of her fingers in turn, then her palms, her neck. He sighed over her mouth and breasts, visibly moved by them. His hands were soft as a woman's, and as light, yet his fingers possessed an almost frightening strength, and he knew exactly how to use them. But Cassia's soul was far away with Vincent where no harm could befall her. Hamid would never possess that, whatever he did – not even if she bore him a child. This conviction gripped her as the Sultan proceeded to take her with a ferocity that would surely have delighted Mimosa or Aletha.

Cassia became increasingly conscious of just how much the Sultan was striving to impress. Somehow, his feelings were softening towards her; she could sense it. She had so little to judge by – he might be like this with all his women, or at least with those whom he bedded more than once. His emotional involvement might be intense, but short-lived. Possibly it all revolved round his desire for an heir; if so, she was merely, in his eyes, the vessel which he must fill with that heir. It was a cold thought, and yet she welcomed it, for Hamid would ask only that one thing of her, that she provide a son. He would not demand her love.

An hour, two hours passed. Hamid, beaded with sweat, was about to embark on his third onslaught upon her body. She observed him with a detachment for which she was grateful. It was so enveloping that she seemed to be standing outside herself watching the scene.

Gasping, his limbs convulsing, Hamid finished, falling back on the pillow to drift immediately into exhausted slumber. Cassia lay awake for some time, thinking of the nights of love she had spent with Vincent, trying to block out this night with those earlier, rapturous ones. Her mind called out to her lover, begging him to come back to her, to be alive and not dead. If he could but step into this room now and take her up into his arms and carry her away, far away to safety and a life with him.

She did not adjust easily to her new position as favourite. Others bowed and kneeled before her, sought to attract her attention, brought her gifts, asked her favours, but it did not touch her. She was not Cassia Morbilly any more but a strange, empty creature who could laugh and talk, eat and sleep, but no longer feel. Perhaps during that night when she had longed to be with Vincent, her soul had gone to him, and she would never have it back? If so, she could not say that she was troubled. To be the old Cassia, awash with suffering and the fires of grief had not been pleasant.

Xenobe watched her closely, uneasy at this transformation. It was too high a price to pay for being Guzdeh, in 'the eye'. She remembered the spirited Cassia of old, who had been a pillar of strength and hope in the hold of Nathan Dash's ship, who had fought so determinedly against her absorption into harem life. Her friend had gone along the Golden Road as one person and had returned as another. What had happened to her in the Sultan's room?

Not for the first time, Xenobe wished that the eye had fallen upon her, if only so that she could save her friend.

It was about this time that Cassia had a strange visitor. At first, she thought it was a child, so *petite* and fragile was the veiled figure which stood before her. Then the yashmak was removed by a tiny, jewelled hand and Cassia saw the face of Manina, the favourite of Selim, Hamid's nephew. Manina did not often show herself about the court for, although Hamid was sufficiently forward-looking to allow Selim a freedom which would have been denied him in previous eras, neither Selim nor his concubines flaunted their existence unnecessarily. He and his harem lived quietly, rarely appearing unless invited. In all the time that she had been in the Grand Seraglio, Cassia had seen Manina only twice and that from a distance.

The favourite of Selim made a deep obeisance, remaining on her knees before Cassia. Silence fell. Manina seemed to be waiting. Cassia did not know what was expected of her. The silence lengthened, and then Manina looked up entreatingly and said, in a low, trembling voice:

'O Most Beautiful One, Most Favoured One, might I, humble Manina, be allowed to speak privately with you?'

Cassia frowned. Privacy in this place? They were surrounded by her own attendants, and Xenobe was sitting close by sketching one of the intricate designs on a painted vase which had caught her eye. It was virtually impossible to be alone here . . . and yet, was she not the favourite now? Whatever she wanted, she could have. Wondering what Manina would have to say, Cassia dismissed her women.

As soon as they were alone, Manina flung herself face down before Cassia, tears rolling out of her almond-shaped eyes. She sobbed as if some great tragedy had just befallen her, and only after much prompting could Cassia persuade her to get up.

'Tell me what is troubling you,' she said. 'Can I help?'

'O Great and Favoured One, it is my beloved, Selim. His health is as delicate as that painted vase –' she pointed to the vase which Xenobe had been sketching. 'More than once he has survived dreadful poisoning, but still he lives, although now his health is fragile. I fear for him most dreadfully. I fear that he will die before he can become Sultan. Hamid is old; he has had his life. It is time now for Selim . . .' Manina's pale green eyes glowed as she spoke.

A coldness crept over Cassia. She sensed danger; a trap. But before she could speak, Manina went on:

'Selim is more disheartened with each passing day. He has no joy in living now. It is said that he will never beget a son. Is that not a great tragedy?' Fresh tears rolled out of the pale peridot eyes. 'I have tried so hard to give him a son, but to no avail. He has sired none, nor any daughter. People speak of a curse upon Hamid and his nephew because both are without sons, did you know this? Men must have sons. Even the poorest of men must have sons. It is unthinkable that they do not.'

'But I do not see how I can help you, Manina.' Cassia finally managed to interrupt the flow of words and tears.

'Do you not? Oh, do you not? Selim will make a brilliant Sultan. He is kind and generous and wise. He wishes to reform and to make good the ills which are destroying our society, those ills which Hamid encourages. Selim wishes to free the slaves from bondage and make the lot of women easier. He wants to bring to an end the cruelties which abound in the harem. You know of these, I think?'

So word of her discontent had reached even the ears of Selim and his followers. Cassia nodded, her uneasiness increasing.

'Then please, please, O Favoured One, make it possible for Selim to rule now, while he has the strength. Think of all the suffering which will be ended, the evils and ignorance put to flight. You could be the one who is our saviour – if you act now.'

Manina paused, looking around her. Then, her voice even lower, she said, 'I have something in this phial which will make Selim Sultan and free thousands from a terrible bondage. You are a Christian – Selim promises that he will free all the Christian slaves in the *Bagnio* if you do this. Oh please, Most Beautiful, Most Favoured One! Think of them . . .' Manina's voice was soft but insistent. In her outstretched palm lay a phial of some murky fluid. Cassia stared at it, overcome by the strange feeling that she had heard this woman talking like this somewhere before, that she had been faced with this dilemma in another time, another place. She knew that could not be true, however. What a risk this woman had taken coming to her like this. Cassia could so easily have denounced her, thus condemning her to a hideous death. How she must love Selim to endanger her life in this way.

Cassia felt admiration, but she also felt fear. What thin ground they were all treading on in the Grand Seraglio, even the favoured ones. She believed that she could almost feel the ice beginning to crack beneath her feet, the lapping of chill water around her ankles.

Manina saw her expression. 'You will not help us? But only you can be the divine instrument! Only you are allowed so near the Sultan. He trusts you, no one else. You see him alone. Do not be afraid that he will suffer, for the liquid in this phial kills instantly and without pain. Nor will there be traces of it when he is dead. It will be as if he has suffered from a choking of the heart.'

When Cassia did not answer, Manina went on, more coaxingly. 'O Great One, I had heard that you desired to be free above all things, that you hated life here. With this phial, you can be free, for Selim would free you too!' Manina's eyes were peridots, round and shining.

For long moments Cassia stayed silent. She, a murderess? Yes, but free! And free all those slaves in the city, the harem. The concubines would have easier lives, and all because of her . . .

It was a judgement of the harem's insidiously evil atmosphere that she could contemplate murder so coolly. Enforced imprisonment had made her desperate, so desperate that instead of loathing she felt a rising excitement at being able to destroy Hamid, the ogre who had blighted her existence for far too long.

She imagined herself tipping the phial's contents into Hamid's sherbet, handing him the goblet, watching him swallow the poison made sweet by the flavouring. He would convulse, turn white, his eyes would bulge, his breath rasp in his throat. He would clutch at his heart, the sound in his throat becoming the death rattle. Then she saw herself leaving the harem, after Hamid's death, with Xenobe beside her. They would turn to take one last look before walking to freedom. There would be no regrets.

Manina, watching, saw the anticipation in Cassia's eyes, and a little shiver of joy coursed through her.

'As I said, O Favoured One, there will be no trace, no symptom of poison. I have searched the land for such a concoction, and this is it, here in this phial.' Again she extended her hand.

Their eyes met and held as Cassia took the phial, enclosing it in her palm.

'Put it in his sherbet. He likes the ambergris flavouring strong. It will disguise the poison.'

'Yes,' Cassia replied, her voice a sigh.

They exchanged a conspiratorial smile and then Manina turned to go. She glanced back once to look at Cassia. 'You will not betray me?'

Cassia shook her head.

Wishing Allah's blessing upon her, Manina slipped away. Cassia did not see her again.

For the remainder of that day, despite her apparent willingness to comply with Manina's wishes, Cassia went through torment. Could she kill another human being? Could she coolly put poison into anyone's drink and watch them die? But if it meant her freedom, and the freedom of all those poor suffering souls in the *Bagnio*? She would be able to return to Cornwall, taking Xenobe with her, and Aunt Julitta would be overcome with joy to see her again. Waves of longing swept through her. How she wanted Cornwall and her Aunt and all those beloved familiar things again. To ride on the moors, to watch the sea in all its phases, to feel rain against her face and see the seabirds wheeling high above her. Fresh air and sunshine, wind, storm, she craved them all. She would fling her arms round Printemps's neck and weep for happiness. To think of it brought her such an intense delight that she forgot where she was, forgot the prison of the harem, the events which had brought her here. Nothing existed for her in those moments of reverie except her Aunt, Penwellyn, and freedom.

They would all be hers if she destroyed Hamid.

The thought of what she would have to do to gain her freedom brought her out of her reverie, and she bit on her lips, as anxious as if she had already committed the crime. Murder. Even if he did not suffer, it would be cold-blooded murder. She could kill in terror, as when she had defended herself against Nathan Dash, but could she kill in cold blood? But if she did not, she would be here in this scented, loathsome prison for the rest of her days. She would never see Julitta again.

She would do it. The next time she was summoned to Hamid's bed, she would tip the poison into his sherbet! She had decided finally, when fresh waves of doubt consumed her. How could she live with herself after murdering him? She would not be able to rest, to sleep, to smile. Always the crime would be on her mind, bedevilling her. And yet, if she did not, she would be bedevilled by her imprisonment in the harem. Whichever course she chose, life would be hell.

She walked along the Golden Road with the phial securely tucked into the mesh of jewels at her breast. It seared her skin, and yet the phial was cool. Soon, she was going to be free, and so was Xenobe, and all the poor Christian slaves whose lives were as hellish as hers would shortly be released. Soon, she would be on her way to Aunt Julitta at Penwellyn. Murderess or no, how could Penwellyn fail to comfort her? The people she left behind in Constantinople would bless her name; she would be their saviour. Those who knew that she was responsible, would call her the One Who Slew the Ogre, and they would revere her memory. Gentle Selim would rule Islam and evil would be forbidden.

The people would cry, 'The Sultan is dead! Long live Sultan Selim!' and Manina would be First Kadine.

Together, she and Selim could reform to their hearts' content. The harem, the city, all Islam would be transmuted. A thrill of delight at being responsible for this made her increase her step. She felt like an avenging crusader.

Freedom. Freedom waited impatiently for her.

The royal bedchamber was heady with attar of roses. As before, Cassia trod softly to the foot of the royal bed, genuflecting before sliding under the silken coverlet and snaking her way up the bed towards where Hamid lay, apparently sleeping. As he made no move, she lay beside him, her heart thudding, the phial burning her breast. Time passed and she grew fearful. Was the Sultan ill? She must have sighed, for his eyes flew open, black coals against his startlingly white face. She felt his hand against her thigh; how strong was his grip considering that he had never had to exert himself throughout his life. Steeling herself, she let him paw her body while she shrank inside herself. How could she face this for the rest of her life?

When he gestured to her to remove her clothes, she slipped them off with care so as not to dislodge the phial. He murmured something to her in Turkish; she had no idea that he spoke of loving her, of needing her, that he praised her above all women he had ever known. Yet there was something in the timbre of his voice which moved her, which made her doubt what she planned to do, but only for a few moments, before her resolve returned. Tonight she would be free!

After he had used her, she rose to pour out their sherbet, pretending to curse as she trod on her discarded clothes, flinging her jewelled bodice angrily across the room so that it fell on top of the carved table where the sherbet stood in its jewelled flask.

Her heart was pounding so noisily that she could hardly breathe. Sweat broke out on her forehead. She wiped her upper lip with her hand as she walked to the table to pour out the drinks. She reached the table, and picked up the flask with a trembling hand. It almost slipped from her damp palm and she gripped it tightly, a tremor passing

266

along her arm. She was going to kill Hamid. The man who had just been kissing her and panting over her body was going to die. In a few moments, he would be dead and she would be a murderess.

Slowly, carefully, she reached for the phial, her back to the Sultan. Moving gracefully, she tipped the contents into Hamid's goblet, watching the murky fluid vanish into the scented, sugar-sweet depths of his favourite drink. I am a murderess, she thought, but is it not a crime of necessity? I am going to kill a cruel despot. Then I can go back to Penwellyn.

She carried the goblets to the bed, and kneeled beside Hamid. His eyes were closed again and he seemed to be lightly dozing. She placed his goblet at the side of the bed and began to sip her own drink. How sickeningly sweet these Turks liked their drinks. Hamid opened his eyes, and moved into a sitting position. She arranged his embroidered pillows for him to rest comfortably, and then she reached for his goblet to pass it to him.

Any moment now, she would be free. She kept saying that, over and over, so that no one was more surprised than she when she jerked her hand, spilling the sherbet all over the pillow. Pretending to be shocked at what she had done, she begged Hamid's forgiveness, speaking in French, cowering before him, as if awaiting his blows. But he did not strike her. Instead, he raised her chin gently with his hand, and looked deep into her eyes, a sad smile on his lips.

In halting French, he said, 'Do not be afraid, my beloved. I would not harm *you*.'

Tears came into her eyes at his gentleness, and at the thought of what she had so nearly done to him. Whatever had made her spill the poisoned drink, she gave thanks to it now. She had not wanted to be a murderess.

It was some two weeks later that Hamid complained of pains in the stomach, and the word spread round that he was ill. At once an invisible net seemed to descend upon Cassia. She was the current favourite – Hamid had looked

267

at no others for weeks now. If she were pregnant with the heir, then she would be Sultan-Validé one day. For this, she must be watched, nurtured, preserved from all harm until the child was born. Although Cassia had hotly denied it, the entire court was convinced that she was already pregnant.

Gloom enveloped the Seraglio. Mimosa watched Cassia like a hawk, and the Kislar Agha or his servants hovered close by. She could not walk from one room to another without being followed by a gaggle of people. There was barely time now for secluded conversations with Xenobe and this she missed most of all.

'It will not be the same when you bear the heir,' Mimosa said, 'You will have so much power then that you will be like a female Sultan here – all the Seraglio will bow to your will. You will be worshipped and revered.'

Cassia did not answer, but sighed, looking down at her hands. Mimosa had become accustomed to this response from her protegée, and knew better than to comment acidly on it.

'Hamid wishes to see you within the next hour. He is very ill – do not look shocked when you see him. Tell him that he will recover, that you know this.'

'You want me to lie to him?'

'No, it is no lie. Black Pearl says that his illness will not be fatal. That is true, is it not, Black Pearl?'

Xenobe nodded. 'You did not tell me this,' Cassia said. 'Why not?'

Xenobe shrugged. 'I did not think that you would believe it.'

'But surely you know –' Cassia stopped. Of course her friend would not have wished to depress her by saying that the Sultan would recover. Cassia had seen freedom in his death, for she did not think that she was pregnant, and when a Sultan died, his harem was disbanded.

'It does not matter,' Mimosa hissed. 'Black Pearl says that he will recover, and she has told me other things that have come true. I believe her. However, we must conform

268

to harem rules, and so you will be treated with the deepest reverence while Hamid is ill. You will smile at him, and say that you love him, and then you will say that the gods have spoken to you telling you of his recovery.'

'The gods?'

'Yes, it will sound more valid that way. He would not expect you to mention Allah's name, and if you mention the name of your god, Hamid will be sceptical. Now please, no more questions. Trust me, for I know best, Briar Rose. Was I not right about your becoming favourite?' Mimosa swept out without waiting for a reply.

'How is it that she can be so thoughtful and yet not think of the most essential points?' Xenobe watched Mimosa's retreating back, so firm and straight, swathed in crimson and gold silk. 'She truly deserves to be Sultan-Validé, if only as a reward for all her schemes.'

'You do not see that destiny in her stars? If you did, it would relieve me of much pressure.'

'No, I do not see such a destiny for her. She has attained her greatest height and will go no further. But you . . .' Xenobe's eyes were now turned full on her friend, their glossy blackness dimmed by the mistiness of the seer. With an effort, she brought herself back from the future, as if she did not wish Cassia to know what she had seen. She looked pale, strained, where only moments before she had seemed radiant.

Cassia would have asked her what was wrong, but the Kislar Agha was bearing down on them like a huge pan-oplied elephant garbed for ceremonial duties. He trundled across the floor, his black face swathed in frowns, while his mouth incongruously curved upwards. He was doing his best to conceal his distress at his master's illness.

Bowing his head on its stubby neck, he beamed at Cassia and gestured for her to follow him. She obeyed, glancing back once at her friend, whose face was still pale and anxious. What had Xenobe seen in the future? The Sultan's death? But no, of course not – she had predicted his recovery. Further conjecture was made impossible by their entry into the state apartments. Here the silence was penetrating in its intensity. The huge royal bed was draped with dark curtains, physicians clustered nearby, their faces fearful.

Cassia approached the side of the bed, her eyes expressionless. She was terrified lest she betray shock or dismay at what she was to see. Slowly, she let her eyes move towards the Sultan, her hands clasped so tightly together that she could feel the bones.

Hamid was white as hawthorn blossom, his skin transparent, the hollows beneath his eyes black crescents. His breathing was shallow but rasping, and a fine veil of sweat covered him. His hair was lank, his beard heavy with sweat. The smell of attar of roses was drowned by that of sickness, and fever. Cassia tried not to inhale too deeply; she had smelt that rank, acid odour in the hold of Nathan Dash's ship. Then it had preceded death. Poor Hamid, she thought, so rich, so omnipotent, and yet when death knocked, he must open the door. She wanted to say, 'Poor Hamid, don't be afraid,' but he would not understand. She wanted to nurse him, but knew that would be forbidden. (And if he should die, she would be punished – unless of course she were pregnant.)

She stood looking down at the man who was her destiny despite all her efforts to elude him. Pity encompassed her, but she was dry-eyed. He had been gentle with her. He had no idea of the torment through which she had lived because of him. In his isolated existence, Hamid could not guess at half the realities of life, the pains, the suffering. And yet, even if he had known, would he not have put her through the same torment? She believed that he would. Poor sick King, pallid as drifting snow, weak as an infant.

What would her life be without him? She could scarcely imagine an existence now where there was no Sultan to fear. These past weeks were engraved on her heart, much as Calais was said to have been engraved on the heart of Queen Mary Tudor when she died. Hamid had terrified her, chased her, caught her. He was the very symbol of her slavery and her bereavement. She could never rest while she was still a prisoner in his harem. Yet, when he died, something of her would surely die with him.

She caught herself up. Mimosa had ordered her to speak of recovery, and she must do that. She had no wish to be malicious, not even to this man. But how would she communicate with him? She did not even know if he spoke much French. Agonized, she looked around for help. Was there no interpreter? But no, they were alone. Even the Kislar Agha had waddled away while she was contemplating the dying Sultan. Fear caged her. She must speak to him, cheer him if she could, but how?

Speaking in French, she began haltingly.

'Your Majesty. You are ill, and I know that you must feel wretched. I feel for you badly, oh, if only you knew how! But I am so confident that you will get better. I feel that very strongly. You are greatly loved, and you have so much to do. It is unthinkable that you do not recover. *I will not let you die!*' Leaning forward, she took one of Hamid's cold white hands in hers and raised it to her lips. His anguished eyes caught hers, a tear trickled down his cheek. He moved his lips – he seemed to want to say something. The veins bulged on his forehead, his eyes dilated. His lips trembled, opened, trembled again. And then, in a hoarse, faint voice he spoke to her in stumbling French.

'Sweet Rose, you have – moved – me. I have been alone – yet – now I am no longer alone because you are mine. You – have touched – me, deeply. You were – sent by Allah the All-Merciful to be the mother – of – of –' he paused to cough, some colour coming into his cheeks then draining away leaving him even paler. His eyes half-closed, Cassia waiting in silence for his next words, his hands clasped in hers.

'The – mother of my son – my heir, who will, after Selim, my nephew, be Sultan. This is Allah's Will, there – is – is no doubt. Now – that – I know this – I can be at peace. My mind is free of fear. I – am – free – of – fear. Briar Rose, there – is a new feeling – in my heart. It is so – new that I cannot put any name to it. You will help me to put a name

271

to it. When I am – well.' He coughed again, then said, 'Send in my doctors now. I will tell you when to – to – come again.'

Humbled, Cassia left the royal suite, seeing no one on her walk back down the Golden Road. She did not think that she had misunderstood the emotion in his eyes; it was pleading and devotion, both of which, in his usual healthy state, he would never have dared display. Yet he had shown them now to her, because he was beginning to rely on her. She stopped, her robes swaying around her feet and clasped her hands to her face. The knowledge was intolerable.

CHAPTER NINETEEN

The Sultan continued in his semi-comatose state for more than a week, during which time Cassia barely had a second to herself. Even at the most intimate times she was watched, or else someone stood close by, with half-averted eyes. When rumour circulated that Hamid was rallying, there was no one more delighted than she.

Mimosa brought the affirmation of the rumour, her face rapturous.

'You see, Black Pearl, you were right! He is going to get better – the pains have gone and his fever has dropped. The physicians say he has only to get back his strength and he will be himself again. Oh, gratitude a millionfold to Allah the All-Merciful!' Mimosa clasped her hands together, eyes heavenwards.

'I knew that he would recover,' Xenobe said happily. 'I just knew it. It is not his time to die. Many will die before him. We both, Briar Rose and I, were confident that he would fight the fever successfully. We must celebrate now, must we not? There must be feasting and dancing in honour of our Sultan.'

'I have ordered it already,' Mimosa nodded. 'The concubines are preparing their robes. The court poet is composing verses which give thanks to Allah, and the Sultanas are going to dance for their father as soon as he is sufficiently strong to tolerate their antics.' Mimosa smiled indulgently, thinking of row upon row of exquisite princesses in their bright silken robes and tasselled headdresses. Hamid would be enchanted. If only there were a son to stand beside his bed during the entertainments . . .

She looked inquisitively at Cassia, first at her face and then at the swell of her breasts. Cassia knew what she would say next.

'And you, Briar Rose, you will be present also. Hamid

273

has ordered it. He wishes to ask you a certain question. It would be to your eternal benefit if your answer could be yes.'

Cassia felt the heat wash over her cheeks, but managed to maintain her composure. Embarrassing as Mimosa's words were, at least she was to be spared a public questioning.

After Mimosa had gone, Xenobe said, 'My love, you are in high favour now. You do not even have to accept Mimosa's officiousness. You can retaliate. You can refuse to speak to her at all until she mends her manners. It is not seemly that the favourite of Allah's Vice-Regent be treated like an erring child. You must show her who is favourite; it seems to me that she imagines herself to be that one and not you.'

'She, the favourite, but . . . ?' Cassia paused, considered. 'Yes, there is something in what you say, Xenobe. She is very high-handed. She enjoys keeping us all under her thumb, but especially me.'

'She must greatly fear that one day you will stand up for yourself and show that you have a mind of your own. If you do that, she will lose her power over you and her own authority will vanish. Do you realize, my love, that her only power here is through you? It is not right that she should treat you so haughtily. Do not allow it!' Xenobe placed her soft fawn hand on Cassia's.

'You are a good friend. I shall heed your advice. I always do. But if I do not seem to take it yet, do not grow angry with me, will you? I still need time to adjust to being in the eye.'

Xenobe smiled. 'Grow angry with you, my love? Not in one thousand years.'

The harem was never happier than when preparing for a royal visit or festive event. The women flung themselves into their plans for the thanksgiving celebrations with an enthusiasm that was an astonishing contrast to their customary daily lethargy. Those who could dance with the greatest inspiration devised costumes of brilliant-hued silks which whirled around them like living flames as they twisted and turned to the music created for them with oude and tambour. Eerie, undulating music like nothing Cassia had ever heard before.

The dancers were graceful and sinuous, but their faces remained expressionless while their slender hands curled and dipped in the air, their heads moved from side to side like a cobra's, their hips swaying while the silvery tinkle and clink of their gold and silver jewellery rang in the ears of the watchers. All of the Sultanas would dance. Their troupe was led by the eldest Princesses, and followed by the most skilled concubines who would complete the entertainment in a more worldly fashion. Watching, Cassia saw the concubines become beckoning houris, their sinuous movements suggestive of sexual congress, their voluptuous breasts and thighs barely concealed by the twists of transparent silk. If this did not revive Hamid, then nothing would, she reflected wryly.

Mimosa circled the dancers and stood before Cassia.

'Briar Rose will dance for the Sultan?' she said, apparently assured that she would receive yes for an answer. Cassia reacted with a startled air.

'Dance? *Me?* But I have never – I do not think . . .' Then she remembered Xenobe's words and strove for composure, for some sharp retort that would send Mimosa on her way.

'One does not know what is possible until one tries. You have a natural grace. You are incapable of clumsiness. Also, that sensuality which I see so carefully concealed can be allowed a freer expression during the dance. It would please Hamid greatly . . .'

Cassia licked her lips, looking away, keeping Mimosa standing, waiting for her reply. It was a first tenuous step to wielding authority.

Finally, spurred on by Xenobe's words, she smiled mysteriously, and said, 'I shall think on it.' Then she turned

275

her back on Mimosa, as if to get a better view of the rehearsals.

'You did well my love!' Xenobe whispered when Mimosa had gone. 'Her face – you should have seen it! But she is due for this – she is altogether too arrogant. She must learn that gentle coaxing wins more than cold command.'

'She is not all that bad,' Cassia said generously.

'No one is so marvellous that they cannot be improved one way or another.'

Aletha was determined to be more splendidly dressed, more vividly attired than anyone else. She had created a startling headdress based on the pillbox and adorned with huge curling feathers and gold fringes. Her robe was slit down the front and tied at her elbows with gold threads so that when she lifted her arms in the dance, her voluptuous body was revealed completely naked. A diamond was fixed in her navel, her nipples were painted gold and gemmed with tiny pearls. Strings of seedpearls hung beneath her heavy rounded breasts, drawing the eye as she moved. Her eyes were painted into fantastic ovals of gold and green, and her thick black hair was loose like a waterfall down her back. She cast many triumphant glances in Cassia's direction, but they failed to alarm the favourite. If Aletha wished to deck herself in such a daring fashion, then she should be free to do so, and if she should attract Hamid's eye and become the new favourite, then Cassia would be the first to congratulate her.

Cassia noticed how Xenobe went out of her way to avoid Aletha. She would never allow the Envious One to come near her, nor would she ever speak to her. Cassia reflected that this was most unlike her easy-going, laughter-loving friend and resolved that once the festivities were over, she would ask Xenobe to elucidate the mystery.

Mimosa was determined that the favourite would dance for their royal master. No protestations from Cassia would deter her. The dance could be brief, but it must take place.

Cassia would receive all the help she needed from the more experienced dancing girls, one of whom was Aletha.

Cassia knew that she had never done anything intentionally to offend Aletha and yet the one-time favourite never failed to take advantage of any moment when she could glare at her maliciously. Those glinting lights like dagger blades in the sun that flashed from Aletha's eyes were not a product of Cassia's imagination. The girl was jealous to the point of being unbalanced, and her vanity was awe-inspiring. She carried a mirror on a chain at her waist, and constantly admired herself in it, smiling into the glass while rearranging her hair and veils. Only when she was gazing at herself did her eyes soften. At all other times, they seethed with envy. Careful of her position in the harem, she agreed to show Cassia how to dance but inwardly she raged with hatred against the English girl.

Xenobe was helping to design Cassia's costume. It would not be boldly revealing, but high-necked and its beauty would lie in its billowing silken folds which would be of many colours blended into one another like a rainbow. While the sewing women made up the gown, Cassia took up residence in the new apartment, that as favourite she was now entitled to. The apartment consisted of three large rooms, one a bedroom, and the door leading to them opened off the Golden Road. The rooms were beautiful, they were both spacious and elegantly furnished. The bedroom was rose-pink and silver, with French furniture of the same period as that in Hamid's bedroom. Rose-pink singing birds with silvered feathers flitted and darted on the pink silk-hung walls, and a silver nymph rose out of the centre of the fountain, her arms filled with carved roses. Attar of roses from some hidden source filled the air. She now had her own eunuchs to guard her, serving women to wait upon her and bathe her, to care for her clothes and bring her sweetmeats and sherbet. Although these servants were entirely her own and for no one else's use, she immediately instructed her servants to wait upon Black Pearl, as if she were their mistress too.

The most agreeable aspect of her new apartments was the peace and seclusion. She and Xenobe could retire there whenever they pleased, for hours at a time, resting or talking, trying on gowns and jewels, eating, or practising their dancing. Xenobe danced with a sinuous, inspired grace and a natural gift for rhythm. At first Cassia was tense, stiffly unhappy at shedding her reserve, reluctant to be drawn out by the music, but gradually her natural grace asserted itself and she found herself moving in a way that, in her former life, would have made her hot with shame.

'You dance like a water nymph!' Xenobe grinned. 'It is as if your limbs are weightless and you sway in the sea's waves . . .' Having said that, she suddenly went very pale, her mouth hanging open, her hand raised to her face. Cassia, gyrating with ornate flourishes across the floor, smiled, but was too absorbed to notice her friend's pallor. Nor did she take note of the silence that fell between them for some time after that. Breathless and hot, she sank on to the brocade pillows heaped in one corner of the room, and fanned herself with one hand. A slave girl hastened at once to her side with a wide, feathered fan and began to cool her.

Refreshments arrived, sent in by Mimosa. Pistachios, crystallized ginger and slices of melon chilled by snow, with hot black coffee to follow. Cassia was glad of the chilled melon, which was refreshing, but she had not yet begun to like her coffee black.

Xenobe did, however, and drank three cups full, one after the other, as if in great haste. She was as cold as the melon, for she had suffered from a dreadful premonition a few minutes before. Drinking the hot coffee with her palms curved round the tiny, fragile porcelain cups, she hoped that it would warm her. It had been a short fragment of vision, but its incompleteness had made it all the more shocking. She knew of old how her gift worked. There could be no hurrying it. Scenes came in their own good time. If she strove to see the rest of the vision, it would disappear, perhaps forever.

Cassia did not suspect anything. In the days that ensued

she became totally immersed in her dance rehearsals, and in the process she found herself relaxing more and beginning to enjoy herself. It was true that the Turkish mode of dancing was far removed from that of the West; the aim of a harem dancer was to arouse and titillate her royal master; every step, every movement must be directed towards that goal. Repelled by the principle, Cassia nevertheless found it impossible not to succumb to the alluring rhythms of the music. Her body took over from her mind, until by the day of the thanksgiving celebrations, no one would have guessed that she had not been a harem dancer all her life.

There had been some trouble with Aletha, whose acerbic advice was not kindly meant, but Xenobe had put an end to that by making a veiled allusion to her own gift for prophecy. She told Aletha that she could read thoughts quite clearly, especially when they were malicious.

'That girl is totally unscrupulous,' she told Cassia. 'She lies, she is cunning, and she has delusions. Beware of her, my love. Have nothing to do with her. Her mind is unhinged, she exists in a world of her own making. I recall another like that, at my late master's court. She was for the most part left to her own devices, more out of fear than for any other reason. And then one day she went into the nurseries, a knife in her hand, and stabbed baby after baby before she was discovered and stopped. It was terrible. Her face was twisted out of all recognition; she said Allah had told her to massacre the innocents, and that she was His handmaiden.' Xenobe shuddered. 'Those poor little dead babies – I dreamed about them for months afterwards.'

'I will heed your warning, Xenobe, but I can't look on her as anything more than a jealous, stupid woman. I can't see her resorting to violence.'

'Oh, you English, you are so cautious of passing judgement!' Xenobe was exasperated. 'Would you defend a poisonous snake that bit the ankle of your child? No, of course not. Treat Aletha like that snake, or she will bite.'

The little Sultanas in their exquisite new gowns were clamouring for attention. Mimosa was superintending them, her face shining. For all her overbearing manner, she adored children and they seemed to love her. The rest of the harem was busily putting the finishing touches to their outfits, the musicians were warming up, when they heard the noise of the Kislar Agha's approach. He stepped into the harem, beaming broadly, his big, square teeth like pieces of white *Rahat Lokum*. His new favourite, the boy Hyacinth, clung to his hand. The child was dressed in scarlet silk, and his face was painted, his neck and ears studded with jewels, his tiny fingers stiff with rings. Behind the Chief Black Eunuch and his favourite was a throng of smiling, gaudily-decked courtiers and servants.

Hurrying forward to greet them, Mimosa ushered them into the harem. The Sultanas were running up and down giggling and seeking out particular friends. The noise became a hubbub, and finally Mimosa had to clap her hands loudly, twice, before silence reigned. Then, each group started to assemble as they had during rehearsals, and the cortege began to wend its way towards the Sultan's chamber.

Hamid was lying, covered in furs, on a gold velvet chaise longue in his main audience chamber. He looked deathly white, and the grey roots of his hair were beginning to show. His hands on the fur rugs shook slightly. Cassia, seeing his pallor and the sunken eyes, could not help but wonder if he were fit to enjoy the festivities.

Hamid saw her then, and half rose from his cushions, with a smile and a slight gesture with one hand. She smiled back, then blushed at being singled out for his greeting.

A few yards behind her, Aletha drew in her breath with an angry hiss, clenching her hands into fists. There was that imposter Briar Rose, walking ahead of her, the true favourite, while she, loyal and devoted, was forced to trail behind amongst the ordinary concubines. Briar Rose would suffer horribly for this indignity, and soon. Aletha vowed, her face crimson with fury, that she would have the English girl exposed for her crimes, and when Hamid found out the truth, he would take Aletha as his First Kadine, his only Kadine.

Unaware of the seething hatred in the mind of Aletha, Cassia walked towards the Sultan, the concubines streaming behind her like a bevy of variegated butterflies. Each of them genuflected before Hamid, who nodded if he felt disposed, or surveyed them with bored disdain. Frequently his eyes roved towards Cassia, who stood now to one side, arms crossed on her breasts, waiting for the moment when the last concubine had made her obeisance, at which the first notes of the music would strike up. As soon as this happened the little Sultanas began their dance, hands linked together so that the smaller ones would not lose their balance when the steps became more intricate. Hamid watched his daughters with half-closed eyes, his mouth curving upwards. When they had finished, he instructed one of his servants to fling them handfuls of money. Giggling and squealing, the little girls scrabbled about on the floor for their reward.

Next was the dance of the concubines led by Aletha in her spectacularly-revealing gown. She cavorted with energy and not a little beauty, tossing her hair and swinging wide her arms to show her naked creamy curves, and finished her steps by casting herself down at the Sultan's feet in one swooping movement.

Then it was Cassia's turn. Dry-lipped, trembling inwardly, she took up her position to wait for the notes of tambour and oude played for her by the musicians of the harem, eunuchs who had been blinded so that they would not see the Sultan's women.

There was an electric silence from the entire court as she dipped and swirled her way round the floor on tiny, light feet. Her hands curved and twisted like streamers, her body seemed weightless as each note of the music lifted her high into the air and then down again. Hamid did not move at all while she danced. Rapt with admiration, he devoured her with his gaze, but when she finished, and knelt before him, he took her hand and kissed it before giving her a collar of emeralds for her reward. Eyeing the enormous gems with startled surprise, Cassia whispered her thanks and withdrew slowly to the back of the room.

The strain of the past few days combined with the generous gift made her feel unduly exhausted. She felt desperately in need of peace, somewhere to lie down and think.

Xenobe looked at her with concern. 'You are very pale. Do you feel all right?'

'I must lie down. I feel drained,' Cassia confessed in a whisper.

'Go to your room. I will stay to answer questions should the Sultan want to know where you are. But he looks tired himself – I should think he will send us all away soon. Go and rest my love, and recover your strength.'

Cassia slipped out, thankful that no one appeared to see her leave, for all eyes were focused on the entertainers now performing alarming acrobatic feats in the centre of the floor. Retracing her steps down the Golden Road to her suite, she stepped inside her room with eager relief, leaning back against the closed door, eyes shut, legs weak.

'*Doucette!*'

The voice was a living dream. She was so tired that she was imagining his voice, his special name for her . . . Shivers of bitter-sweet delight coursed through her flesh. She sighed, bit on her lips, kept her eyes closed to savour the dream.

'*Doucette! Chérie, chérie!*'

She opened her eyes. That voice was not in her dreams.

Vincent stood facing her on the opposite side of the room, his face alight, his arms held out to hold her.

CHAPTER TWENTY

'Vincent, Vincent! But – I don't understand! Am I dreaming? Is it really you? Oh, can it be?' She sobbed and laughed, ran into his arms, gazed up at him through tear-blinded eyes, felt his arms caging her so tightly that she could not breathe, did not want to breathe. She thought she would die of joy. The pain was too beautiful to bear. Happiness sang in her heart, her mind, her soul. Her lover was alive, *alive*, he was here now, holding her, kissing her, telling her that he loved her, that he had always loved her, that they would never again be parted. Words that she had scarcely hoped to hear when she knew he was alive.

'Oh, my darling, but I am a prisoner here – how can I ever escape? I am as helpless here as if I had chains at my ankles!' she cried.

'But I got in, *doucette* – despite the guards and the eunuchs, didn't I? So that means I can get you out. I shall – as soon as I can – there is no need for you to doubt it. My beloved, these past months have been purgatory without you.'

She looked up at him, more closely now, seeing fine lines beneath his eyes, around his mouth, and silver streaks in his jet-black hair. He was thinner, and yet his eyes burned as brilliant an emerald as ever before, and they were incandescent with love for her now. She could feel the love beaming from them; it was palpable in the air between them. How had he got into the Seraglio? It would have been easier to fly! She asked him, but he kissed her, then said that it was simply a matter of tactics and timing. He had been trying to get in for days, ever since he had reached Constantinople, and he had befriended a guard by giving him generous bribes. It had been this same guard who told him of the harem's preoccupation with the celebrations, and who had explained that everyone would be in the Sultan's audience chamber on this particular day. While they were there, Vincent had slipped into her room and concealed himself until she came. The guard had told him how to get there.

'But it seems impossible – like magic. I still don't know how you did it, darling. Oh my love, I have been only half alive without you!'

'And I without you, *doucette*.' He led her to the bed, lifting her up in his arms to place her gently down again, himself beside her. They kissed, then kissed again, then Cassia asked her lover how he had managed to survive his wound.

'Dash had me flung overboard, thinking me dead, but the chill of the sea revived me. A fisherboat came by just as I was sinking beneath the waters for the third time, too weak to hold out much longer. They pulled me on board and took me to their village where there was a Turkish galleot in some difficulty moored just off the coast. When all the villagers came to the shore to see the catch, they saw me instead, but I was too ill to take much notice. With them were some of the people from the Turkish galleot, and one of them – to my great good fortune – was an Arab physician, a highly skilled man who took one look at me and had me taken to the ship. I was by now fevered, but I was determined to rally, so that I could get back to rescue you. I imagined terrible things – Dash raping you, beating you. I can tell you I was the most restless patient.'

'There was so much blood where you lay – I did not think you could possibly be alive. I was so sure that you were dead, darling. I touched you – I dipped my hands in your blood.' Cassia shuddered, and was immediately pulled even closer to her lover.

'My poor *doucette, ma chère*! God forgive me for what I put you through. It was all my fault – all of it. If I had left you in your Cornish cove . . .'

'If you had, I would never have been more than half alive for the rest of my days,' Cassia whispered, her throat husky. 'Hold me darling, hold me! Tell me you love me, tell me, tell me!'

'We shall never be parted again. I promise you. Once I

get you out of here we shall return to Algiers and be married at once. You see, my dearest love, when I knew that I had lost you, I realized just what a worthless thing my life had been. I dealt in slaves because I hated the world. That evil career brought me to you and then it took me away from you. If you will forgive me and come too, I shall give up everything and start a new, clean life far away. I have friends across the Atlantic.'

'Forgive you . . . go with you . . . ah, darling! But do we have to go back to Algiers?'

'I must sort out my affairs, *doucette*, and see that Captain Dash knows what his half-brother has done. Nathan must be punished. I myself intend to challenge him to a duel. And we shall need money, which I can get in Algiers. Then we shall leave this area – we want no reprisals from Hamid, who will surely want his favourite back.' Vincent kissed her, and chuckled. 'To think that I lost my beloved and found her again when she was the Grand Turk's favourite.'

'You – you are not jealous, my darling?'

Vincent pulled away from her a little so that he could look into her eyes. 'You had no choice. You were forced into it, just as I was forced by events into my life of piracy. No, no, my love, I am proud of you – of what you have made of your life since you were kidnapped by Dash.'

Tears came into her eyes as she nestled her face in her lover's neck. 'Hold me, Vincent, hold me so tightly. I wanted to die when I thought you were dead, darling. I begged to die with all my heart. You would never have believed the fight I put up to resist my fate in the harem. I infuriated everybody here. But finally I had to accept their plans for me, and give up my freedom. It was not easy, and I could not forget you. All the time I felt as if I were betraying you, and being unfaithful, yet I would say to myself, "How can I be unfaithful when my love is dead?" The tears I wept – you would have thought me mad if you had seen me!'

'Mad, my little flower? My own sweet love? Do you think I did not grieve too, thinking you were being brutally treated by that fiend while I was too weak to save you? I suffered torment, unbearable agonies, while the galleot was repaired, and then wended its way back to Bada-Alhim, which is roughly forty to fifty miles from here. I was too ill to protest, and realized that without the Arab's skilled care, I would most probably die. So I could do nothing. In Bada-Alhim, I was put to bed in the Palace of the Pasha – for it was his own personal physician who was tending me. Can you imagine my astonishment at finding myself in a royal bed? But little concerned me except getting back my strength so that I could find you and be in your arms again.'

'You are now. We have each other again.' She hugged him. 'But how did you find out I was here?'

'The Pasha has a sister, a very independent and proud young woman by the name of Jasmina. She is widowed, and thus has more freedom than most Muslim women. Also, she is the Pasha's favourite only sister and so he indulges her. Well – she decided that she wanted to marry me.' Vincent pulled a face. 'She proposed to me, on the condition that I would become a Muslim. As gently as I could, I told her that I was in love with you, and that you and I were betrothed. She asked your name and all about you. I told her that you were Cornish, and something of the way we met – but not the full story. When I mentioned Nathan Dash, she went white. She seemed to know something about him. But she would not tell me what it was. I questioned her, but she refused to say, and then she admitted that she had bought some jewels and gowns from him, and that he visited her at court every few months with wares to offer her. This time, he had brought her the jewels and two of the gowns which I gave you – the Spanish booty, remember?'

Cassia went cold, thinking of her clothes being sold by the repulsive Nathan Dash.

'When Jasmina showed me what she had bought, I told her to whom they belonged. She was ashamed. She told me that she would send out her spies to discover what Dash was up to, and where he had hidden you. But it took some time, and then I had a relapse of the fever – I lost many

286

days through that. When I came to, I was weaker than before. I could not understand it. I had never felt so wretched, and all the while I longed to get to you.'

'Jasmina nursed you?'

'Devotedly. I am much in her debt.'

Cassia listened, feeling uneasy. This woman, rich, powerful, obviously accustomed to getting her own way, had behaved like an angel with tenderness and generosity. Had she felt no anger at the rejection of her proposal? It was unnatural to be so saintly. If Jasmina loved Vincent, would she behave so selflessly, nursing him, finding out the whereabouts of his betrothed so that he would then leave her to marry another woman?

Quelling her jealousy, she pulled his head down to hers, cradling his neck in her palms and kissing him soundly. In response, he kissed her throat and breasts, her face, and mouth again, then, as their passions climbed together, in sweet ascendancy, he entered her body and began to move within her as she clung to him desperately, barely able to catch her breath. He whispered repeatedly that he loved her, that he would get her away from the Seraglio and make her his wife. Cassia felt dizzy with ecstasy, her mind swimming away from her body with elation while her body burned with love. He crushed her against him so fiercely that she became part of him, fire coursing through her, even as far as her breasts, causing a rapturous agony from which she thought she might not recover.

'You – are – hurting –' she gasped, knowing that he would understand that the pain was ecstasy, that she did not wish him to stop. 'Oh – it – is beautiful . . .'

'We were made for each other, my darling. I knew it from the moment I set eyes on you. What a fool I was not admitting it! But I admit it now, *doucette*, oh, how I do admit it! I have been starved for you, ravenous with longing. Nothing could feed me but your love.'

'And now you have it, my darling. You always did,' she added with a grin. 'Even when you would not admit that you loved me, I loved you!'

'You are wiser than I. You are not afraid to accept things unquestionably, my love.'

'But now you are wise too.'

'If love makes me wise, then I am the wisest man in the world!' he laughed. Then they forgot to talk, for passion governed them. Everything was forgotten, the harem, the Sultan, their long separation, the fear of being discovered. Love, clamouring for first place in their attentions, had its way.

Later, they slept briefly in one another's arms like babies, relaxed and content. When they woke, it was dusk, and a sickle moon lit the skies. Smiling, they kissed and made love again, more slowly this time, sensuously, with infinitely tender passion.

It was then that they heard the revellers returning from the Sultan's suite. One of the little Sultanas had overtired herself and was wailing. Two of the concubines were having a noisy dispute over some trivial matter. It was only when the noise died down that Cassia could relax again. She knew that no one would dare disturb her except for Xenobe, and if Xenobe believed her friend to be sleeping, she would not waken her.

'Will you stay tonight?' she pleaded.

'I want nothing more, but my friend the guard expects me to leave at midnight. He will be waiting for me then, to show me out. There is a secret passage, and he knows the way.'

'So you won't stay?' Disappointment dulled her voice. When he went, it would be like losing him all over again. She would think she had imagined this incredible visit, the lovemaking, the promises.

'If I did, it might be for ever, *doucette*. No, we must be careful. Say nothing, and behave as if everything is normal. I will return as soon as I have devised an escape plan that will not endanger your life. My guard was easily bribed, but if I can tempt him, so can others. We shall not be safe until we are many miles from Constantinople.'

He kissed her again, and again, warm, firm lips caressing

her neck and breasts, vowing to love her for all time, and then, reluctantly he withdrew from her arms and stood up to dress. He wore a voluminous dark, hooded robe, which he now arranged so that it concealed his face. Cassia flung herself passionately into his arms.

'Take care, my darling. Come back for me soon. I shall be waiting. Oh, how I shall be waiting!'

They exchanged one last sweet kiss, and then Vincent went out the way he had come, via the balcony into the next room and from there along a side passage to the place where the guard would be waiting for him.

Cassia sank on to her bed, shivering with cold and fear, gripped by loneliness. She wished she had insisted on going with him, but if they were seen, there would have been a hue and cry, the entire court would have hunted them down. Vincent would have been hacked to death, and she with him.

She lay down and tried to rest, but her thoughts were incoherent, and when she sank into fitful sleep she dreamed that she and Vincent were running away, hand in hand, while vicious wild beasts pursued them. She woke with a jolt, beaded with sweat, her heart thumping savagely.

Someone was in her room . . . Had Vincent come back? Eagerly she sat up, whispering his name into the gloom. Someone moved, a billow of ambergris scent wafted towards her. One of the concubines come to see if she slept?

'Who is there? Who is it?' she called.

Still no answer. Alarmed, she moved to jump out of bed and as she heard the rustling movement of someone seeking escape without being seen, she called out for the guards. They came immediately. It was not difficult to catch the interloper. The lamps were lit, for Cassia to see who her night visitor was.

Aletha.

'What do you want?' she asked the scowling concubine. 'You gave me a fright sneaking into my room in the dark.'

'I did not sneak in, Briar Rose. I have been here for some

time.' Aletha looked meaningfully at the English girl, her eyes black slits of venom.

Swallowing, Cassia said: 'And why did you come here?'

Aletha moved, reached out a hand to point at the emerald collar that lay on Cassia's dressing table where she had flung it when Vincent took her into his arms. 'I came for that, Briar Rose, that collar which is rightfully mine, for *I* am the favourite, not *you*.'

Cassia breathed a sigh of relief. If Aletha was going to rant in her usual crazy fashion then she was safe. They were all accustomed to hearing her talk like this. The terror which Cassia had felt at her earlier words drifted away.

'Take her away – do what you usually do in such cases,' she said to the guards, suddenly weary, and longing to be back in her bed.

'Who do you think you are giving orders to, you *Nazrani! Nazrani! Nazrani!*' Aletha screamed, biting savagely into the arm of the eunuch who stood on her left. He let out a yelp, raising his hand to strike her. 'Are you going to let this crazy Christian order you about?' Aletha cried, her face twisted with fury. 'She is nothing, nothing. If the Sultan hears that you have mistreated me, he will have you all executed! Do you hear me?' She glared at the guards.

Ignoring her tirade, they began to drag her out of the room, but she struggled wildly, screaming, 'Briar Rose, if you do not listen to me, I will tell them your secret! Do you hear, Briar Rose? *I will tell them your secret!*'

Cassia was not imagining the cold rushing winds that roared in her ears, nor the weakness which made her sink on to the bed. What did Aletha know? Could she possibly have seen Vincent leaving?

There was a commotion in the corridor outside. She could hear Mimosa's voice asking what was happening. Then she came into the room, taking in the scene at a glance.

'What is happening? What is this nonsense?' she asked Aletha.

'The *Nazrani*, she has had her lover in here. I saw him,

I saw him leave! He went out on to the balcony and into the next room. I came in here to get the emerald collar which is rightfully mine and they were there together on the bed, making love. They did not hear me come in, they were making such a noise . . .' Aletha's face contorted as if in disgust. 'I slipped behind the tapestries until he had gone. Oh, he was here a long time, and I listened to their plans. This *Nazrani*, oh, she is a false and evil creature – did I not say that she was, long, long ago, but you, you are so stupid you do not listen.'

For once, Mimosa's composure deserted her. Scarlet flooding her cheeks, she raised her hand to strike Aletha, but the concubine stepped back, twisting out of the arms of the unwary guards. Mimosa's blow glanced aside, narrowly missing one of the eunuchs.

'You are the most vicious creature I have ever known!' Mimosa snarled. 'You cause nothing but trouble here, you upset the peace, you tell lies, you –'

'*Ask her!*' screamed Aletha. 'Ask the *Nazrani* if she lay with her lover tonight. They spoke together in French so I understood what they said, and how they made love!' Aletha made a crude gesture with her two hands, to show what had taken place on the bed. 'He is coming back for her, the one she called Vincent, he is coming to help her escape.'

Mimosa lowered the hand that had been raised to strike at Aletha again. She was breathing deeply, almost panting, her teeth gritted together.

'You have no proof of this, Aletha, we have only your word, and your word is frequently false. How could we believe such tales? No man has ever found his way into the harem – it is unthinkable that anyone could get in. If you wanted to discredit Briar Rose, you should have thought of a more plausible tale.'

'But that is just it, Kadine, I would have done if I had been lying, but I am not. It is true, *true*! Look at the bed, look at her body – you will see. You must look,' Aletha screeched.

Mimosa bit on her lip, one part of her wanted to silence the jealous concubine, the other remembered the punishments meted out to those who were unfaithful to the Grand Turk – and to those who in any way aided the unfaithful. If there were something in what Aletha was saying, if she ignored it, and later it was discovered to be true – she flushed again at the thought. Hamid's heir not of his flesh but conceived by some interloper, her own disgrace, Briar Rose's disgrace – death for both of them.

It was not easy to decide, for she had always needed time to make up her mind, but Aletha sounded convincing. Bargaining for time, Mimosa sat down and told Aletha to retell her story.

Cassia listened, paralysed with dread. How could she get out of this situation? She would have to lie, to stay cool and laugh away Aletha's accusations, but in her present state of alarm, that would be virtually impossible.

Mimosa listened to Aletha, and then bade her be silent. First looking round the room, she then stood up and went out on to the balcony to search it. Returning, she said, 'There is absolutely nothing to be seen out there, nor in here, Aletha. To satisfy you, we shall of course have the harem searched and everyone will be questioned. But that is for the morning. And until then, no one must speak of this – do you understand?' Mimosa peered into Aletha's face, her anger all the more frightening because her expression was so tranquil.

'As you say, Kadine, but if you would only search now.'

'If Briar Rose has had a visitor tonight, he will hardly have stayed around to be caught will he? I think the morning will be soon enough.'

Aletha went away, head bent, followed by the eunuchs. Mimosa turned to Cassia.

'I shall not speak more of this now. If it transpires that you have been unfaithful to our royal master, I with my own hand would joyfully kill you. If you have not, then I shall beg your forgiveness for doubting you. Until tomorrow, sleep well.' And with that, she swept from the room.

Cassia bent over her hands, shuddering from reaction. The whole scene had been a terrible nightmare, it had blown up like a storm, and she had been helpless to prevent it. Xenobe had warned her against Aletha, but how could she have known that the concubine would dare intrude into her suite? And to think that Aletha had seen her with Vincent! 'Sleep well,' Mimosa had said – how could she sleep?

The punishments for infidelity in the harem were barbarous. If only Vincent had taken her with him they could have been riding to freedom at this very moment!

She did not sleep, of course. She lay in bed, tense with dread, attempting to capture an elusive peace of mind. She thought of her lover escaping, then returning for her, and finding her too closely guarded to rescue. If Hamid had a trap laid for Vincent when he returned . . . She shuddered, biting on her hands. This place, she thought with fear, she wished she had never been near it, she wished there was no such city as Constantinople, no such place as the Grand Seraglio.

Dawn bathed the sky, and Cassia lay on her back staring up at the carved ceiling where cherubim flocked and roses rambled. The silence of the harem was eerie and unsettling. She could imagine she was the only person alive there, that everyone else was dead. How could she get a message to Vincent to warn him? There was no one here she could trust with such a letter – everyone was immovably loyal to Hamid, either from adulation or terror. She, too, had been fearfully loyal until the previous night.

She sought to examine the possibilities of Aletha's story being discredited. What proof did the concubine have? None really, only her word which was notoriously false. Her troublemaking tactics were well known; people stayed out of her way or ignored her tirades. Even the Kislar Agha treated her with contempt. If Cassia remained very cool, very dignified, there was every chance that she would get through the day's inquisition safely. It would take all her acting ability but so much was at stake if she failed: she would never see Vincent again, he would be captured when he tried to help her escape; he would be horribly punished in the savage ways adored by the Turks.

The stretch of the Bosphorus beyond the walls of the Grand Seraglio was filled with dead bodies tied in sacks, bodies of concubines and favourites who had displeased their masters. Even minor offences had been known to merit death by drowning – let alone faithlessness.

If she were found out, she did not see how she could evade death.

Mimosa came for her early, followed by a retinue of guards and courtiers. In the audience chamber of the harem, the Kislar Agha and more courtiers awaited them. Aletha, her face glowing with triumph, stood between two eunuchs, waiting to give evidence.

Cassia sat quietly while the court began its routine, the charges were called out, and the witness, Aletha, told to relate her evidence. Excitedly, the concubine did as she was bid, her voice breathless. When she had finished, there was a taut silence. The Kislar Agha was the first to speak, for the Grand Vizier had ordained it so.

Cassia could not understand what was said, the Kislar Agha was speaking in Turkish, and the Grand Vizier was questioning Aletha in the same language. How could this be called justice, she asked bitterly, when the accused could not understand what was being said? The questioning went on for some time. Looking from one face to another, Cassia struggled to assess their reactions but it was not easy, for court proceedings were always carried out with immense composure. Mimosa looked particularly expressionless, her hands gracefully linked on her knee, her eyes for the most part downcast.

Some time elapsed before the Kislar Agha spoke to Mimosa who then stood up to interpret his verdict for Cassia. She said that the proceedings were informal, for as yet there was no evidence except the accusation of Aletha, whose word could not be trusted. However, after this hearing, the rest of the court would be questioned, especially those who protected the security of the Seraglio.

Informal? thought Cassia with an inward grimace. If this was informal, then she would not like to be present at a serious case. Having spoken, Mimosa returned to her business elsewhere, the courtiers dispersing slowly. Cassia sat for a time thinking, her legs too weak to bear her weight. Xenobe came up to her and smiled, touching her cheek.

'Oh my love, if only I had been with you last night, I would have been able to protect you now. I thought you asleep, so I did not disturb you.'

'You thought me asleep? So you know the truth?' Cassia whispered so that no one could hear.

'I do. I saw the return of your lover some weeks ago, in a vision.'

'But why did you not warn me?'

'What could I have said? Your lover will return from the dead and visit you here in the harem? Oh surely, my love, you know of old that it is not easy to tell premonitions – and besides, what if I had mistaken my vision? And if I had told you, would you have believed me?'

'You are right, of course. I always seem to be so obtuse about your gift. Oh, Xenobe, what am I going to do?'

'Exactly what you are doing. Go about your business looking as beautiful, cool and innocent as you can, giving the lie to Aletha's crazed rantings. I am amazed that anyone listened to her – it is only the fact that the harem is obsessed with fidelity that she has had any listeners.'

It was true. The harem became demented when fidelity was in question. During the next few hours, it seemed that all the souls of the dead, murdered for faithlessness, and their babies, sired by men other than the Sultan, would be roused. The Turks were thorough, and cruel. If they doubted a guard's response, they tortured him. This time, however, Hamid had ordered no torture. He wanted to learn the truth. He did not want men forced into lying by their sufferings.

'Do you realize how fortunate you are, Briar Rose?' Mimosa said, her face cold. 'If our Sultan were well, he would have officiated at your hearing, and he would not have been so patient. You might have been condemned outright.'

'For being innocent?' Cassia replied coolly. 'Surely not. That is not how we go about things in England.'

'England? Our justice is excellent here. The Sultan, being Allah's Vice-Regent upon earth, has an unfailing gift for searching out those who lie.'

'Then let him question Aletha,' Cassia retorted boldly, 'After that, he will have no doubts as to who is lying.'

'You are very brazen,' Mimosa said. 'If there is any truth in her accusations –'

'I know, you told me before: you will kill me yourself,' Cassia said wearily.

When she had gone, Xenobe took Cassia's hand. 'You are in great favour, my love. That is obvious. You would have been sentenced to death without a hearing if you had been one of the lesser concubines. Hamid's pride is deeply hurt at the moment. Last night he gave you an emerald collar, and publicly acknowledged his affection for you. Now he has been told that you met your lover only moments later. He must care for you very much not to have ordered your immediate punishment. Women here are in such huge supply that they can be put to death in their hundreds – as some have been – and there will be thousands more to fill their places.'

'Should I ask to see him alone?' Cassia said miserably.

'That would never do. Such a request would scream of guilt. There was one who did such a thing some years ago – she was a favourite, very lovely, her name was Iris. It was discovered that the son she had borne was not fathered by the then Sultan. There was, as you can imagine, the most awful furore. She begged to see the Sultan alone, but he would not hear of it. She was beheaded, in the courtyard, as she stood weeping and beseeching him beneath his window. Her son was flung into the Marmora.'

'And the father of her son?'

'Do you really want to know?'

Cassia said that she did.

'Each of his arms was tied to a stallion, each of his legs to two more stallions, and then the horses were stampeded in different directions.'

Cassia was deathly pale. Her shoulders slumped. 'How do we get a message out to Vincent? I just do not know what to do.'

'There is nothing we can do except carry on as before. Any untoward movement or action will be noted immediately. And we must stay together night and day. Then you have an alibi.'

'What would I do without you, dearest friend?'

'It is little enough that I do for you, my love,' Xenobe replied, squeezing her friend's hand.

Guards, eunuchs, slaves, messengers, were questioned for hour upon hour. Aletha was restrained, kept in a room that was closely guarded. Cassia was left to her own devices, although as she and Xenobe observed, they were closely watched, and extra guards were posted outside her door at night.

The questioning was over, and Cassia had relaxed, thanking God for her safe delivery, when someone remembered Ben Ali.

Ben Ali, one of the eunuchs who had been on guard during the night of the celebrations, had gone down with fever and was being nursed in the slaves' hospital. Hamid could not conclude the investigations until he had been interrogated.

Cassia heard this with a sinking heart. As surely as if she had heard her death sentence, she knew that Ben Ali was the guard who had been bribed by Vincent.

'You think so?' Xenobe was scornful. 'What evidence have you? You are being illogical, Cassia.'

'Vincent said that if he could bribe a guard, then others could do the same. How reliable will this Ben Ali be?'

'Is he likely to admit that he has been bribed? Think of his punishment for allowing a man – and a Christian at that – into the harem! He would be hacked to death at once. No, Ben Ali would have to be a fool and an imbecile to confess.'

Cassia said that Xenobe was right, but still she could not throw off the feeling of impending doom.

No one ever knew if Ben Ali would have lied or not, for he did not recover consciousness. The Kislar Agah's servants, sent to guard him until his recovery from the fever reported every word of his fevered ramblings to their master.

Although he did not mention the name of Vincent Sauvage, Ben Ali spoke incoherently of an Englishman who had paid him a huge sum to be allowed into the harem on the night of the Sultan's celebrations. When Ben Ali's room was searched, the money was found hidden behind a loosened tile in the wall. The sick guard was carried out from the slaves' hospital, his hands and feet tied, and he was then cast over the palace wall into the strait beyond.

Seconds later, the Palace guard descended upon Cassia who was sitting in her bedroom having her hair dressed for the evening by her slave while Xenobe read to her from a book on the history of Byzantium.

There was no time for farewells. Cassia was dragged away, speechless with terror, while Xenobe jumped to her feet screaming over and over, *'No! No! No!'*

Cassia was dragged to a balcony overlooking the Bosphorus and there she saw a group of deaf mutes standing waiting with thongs and a sack.

It was then that she began screaming hysterically, lashing out with her feet and trying to free her arms from the grip of the implacable eunuchs. It was hopeless. Two of them held open the sack while the others savagely bundled her into it, careless of bruising her flesh or damaging her limbs. The sacking was dusty, fragments of the dust filled her throat and nostrils. Coughing, she struggled for breath. Someone aimed a cruel blow at her head, but she moved just in time and the blow struck her shoulder. A huge black hand pressed down on the top of her head, and her knees buckled. The neck of the sack was pulled together, tied securely and knotted with the thong, and then four of the deaf mutes dragged the sack to the balcony's edge and heaved it over into the Bosphorus.

The horror of that blind, plunging descent into the sea surpassed all the terrors and the cruelties that had gone before. Down, down, she went, screaming Vincent's name, her body rigid with terror, into the icy water.

The sack hit the waves with a loud smacking sound, then disappeared beneath the surface of the water for long moments. Cassia struggled vainly and desperately to try and free herself. The current caught the dark bundle, twisting it along, dipping, raising it. Cassia's struggles grew more frantic as the cold wet sacking began to cling to her skin.

'Vincent, Vincent,' she moaned, linking her fingers together and jabbing upwards at the neck of the sack. Again and again, she pushed, but the thong was too tightly knotted to give way.

She was tiring now, her head spinning, and she felt sick and faint from lack of air. The sack bobbed along, buoyed by the current that kept her head above water for some time. Her eyes were smarting unbearably, tears flooding down her face. Her arms aching agonizingly, she was forced to rest them. Chills swept through her, and she shuddered uncontrollably, goose flesh prickling on her skin. She sneezed, then sneezed again; glittering silver stars exploded in her head. A cold that was like the coldness of death was seeping through her, rising steadily up her body until she felt as if she were encased in ice. The powerful current thrust at the sack yet again, as if playing with it, bobbing it about on the water's surface, then twisting it round and round like a toy.

Terrified, helpless, she ceased to struggle, her limbs were leaden, her head was pounding from shock and shortage of air. She knew now that she was going to die. Consciousness left her; everything went black. The sack continued to bob and dip on the water, like a child's plaything, abandoned.

CHAPTER TWENTY-ONE

Leo, fourth Earl of Marchington, had hired the pleasure boat to get a closer view of the Grand Seraglio for his next painting. He had come to Constantinople to sketch, after being told that no other city in the world could equal old Byzantium. Having found this to be true, he had so far made some two dozen sketches, bases for paintings he would do when he returned to London the following year.

It was dusk, and he should have told his boatman to row back to the shore, but he was intrigued by the evening lighting over the palace. Violet and silver, palest tangerine and pewter grey framed the Grand Turk's home, while the surrounding seas were now black as pitch. His boat was the only one still on the water.

He knew of the appalling history of cruelty and barbaric punishments associated with the Grand Seraglio, but he had never expected to see one of these punishments being carried out. When he saw a sack being tipped over the palace balcony, and sinking down into the Bosphorus, he stared at it with stunned amazement. For a few seconds he remained transfixed, unable to believe what he had seen, while the sack bobbed to the surface of the water, disappeared, then bobbed up again. By the time Lord Marchington's craft had reached the spot, the sack had vanished for a second time. Marchington scanned the water anxiously for sight of the sinister bundle. Could it really contain a human being, or was it perhaps some dead or unwanted animal? His skin tingled uncomfortably, then just as he was beginning to think he might have imagined the bundle in the sea, it came to the surface again.

'There!' he cried to his boatman, who steered the boat round quickly towards the sack so that his master could get hold of it. Marchington leaned forward, arms outstretched, every muscle tensed, but just as he thought he had the thong in his grasp, the current swept the bundle away again. Uttering an expletive, he watched the movement of the sack while the boatman rowed furiously after it. Again they came level and again Marchington had almost caught it when it bobbed away.

By now he was determined that he would retrieve the bundle even if it were the last act of his life. Gritting his jaw, beads of sweat standing out on his brow, he tried yet again to catch at the dark, lumpy shape in the water. This time he held it for some moments before the current bore it away.

Once more he reached out over the side of the boat, huge muscles straining, and managed to grab the thong in his hands. Exultant, he began to pull at it, heaving with all his strength, while the blood pounded in his head. And then the current cupped the little boat, merrily twisting it round, and his prey rolled away once more, far out of reach.

Cursing, Marchington knelt in the bottom of the boat, and tore off his jacket and boots before poising himself to dive into the cold and murky waters in pursuit. He was an excellent swimmer, for he was both extremely strong and very skilled. His father had once nearly drowned at sea and had vowed that his son would never have a similar experience. Lord Marchington slipped through the dark waters like a merboy, searching, looking all round him. Then he saw the sack, reached out, grabbed the thong and despite its weight and the freezing cold, hung on to it for dear life until the boat came alongside. Even with the help of his two servants it was a struggle to hoist the burden aboard, for the waterlogged bundle was a deadweight. Had it not been for Marchington's colossal strength they would not have succeeded at all. Tossing back his wet hair, he reached for a blanket to throw round his shoulders before he knelt to examine their find.

Tim Bert had untied the thong, and pulled back the soaked sacking. The first thing that met their eyes was the head of a girl, deathly white, her eyes were closed and her hair clung in wet strands to her head.

'After all that, she is dead, m'lord,' Tim Bert said, looking up at his master.

'It's a woman?' Interest stirred in him. A concubine from the Grand Seraglio?

'Aye, m'lord, and she were a beauty too, by t'looks on her. See, m'lord.' Tim Bert pulled away more of the sacking to reveal Cassia's shapely shoulders, barely concealed by wet blue silk.

At that moment, the boat lurched and Cassia's head tilted to one side. Her stomach convulsed and she vomited.

'M'lord, she's alive!' Tim Bert cried.

'I can see that, man!' Marchington hastily divested Cassia of the wet sack, but even he was not prepared for the sight that met his eyes. The thin blue silk showed more than it concealed, and it clung to Cassia's breasts and hips showing them to voluptuous advantage. Her shapeliness stirred him more than he cared to admit and a wave of sensuality swept over him. A helpless and shapely beauty, one who had almost fallen out of heaven at his feet . . . He had never been a man to waste an opportunity.

Flinging the sacking over the side of the boat, Marchington covered the rescued girl with two blankets and then he ordered the boatman to row them back to the island with all speed.

Tim Bert was looking about him nervously. 'It were a good thing 'twere dusk and 'tis now dark, for if they saw us do what we done, they'd be arter us with their knives!'

His employer did not reply, although he knew that Bert was right. Had they been seen, they would have been pursued and cut to ribbons. The Turks were vengeful and merciless where wrongdoers were concerned, and it was dangerous to tamper with their laws. He gave Cassia his full attention as they rowed to his island home. Turning her on to her stomach, he pressed her back to empty her lungs of water, and having done this, he surveyed her. She was wet, bedraggled, and bone-white, her skin almost luminous in the dusk, but she was lovely too. Who was she? Some victim of her Sultan's whim? Probably a sister of or a daughter of some Circassian peasant, sold into the harem for gold. Condemned to a life of servitude, and then this vile manner of death thrust upon her for some misdemeanour. He was delighted that he had been here to save her – for otherwise she would surely have been dead by now. If she recovered consciousness soon, he would try to converse with her and find out who she was and where she came from. As the boat headed in towards the island, he tried to think of ways in which he could tackle the language problem that would surely arise between them. He knew only a little Turkish.

The boat drew into the shore of the lush island where Lord Marchington's holiday home stood. Palm trees and exotic flowers surrounded the white stucco building that was clearly English in style. It had been built some years previously by an English duke who had wanted to die in a more temperate climate than that of his homeland. The house had stood empty, until Leo Marchington had rented it.

The jolting of the boat against the little jetty failed to arouse Cassia. She was still shocked and unconscious, inert beneath the blankets. She did not see the tropical night, the feathery palms waving above her head, nor hear the screech of nocturnal birds. Marchington scooped her up into his strong arms as if she were no more than an infant and carried her up the sands towards the beach path which led to the house. He looked down at her once or twice as he walked. Her face gleamed whitely in the dusk. He was gripped by a feeling of possession. She was so very helpless – he could in all truth do anything he liked with her now. Her beauty had deeply affected him. His artist's eye had seen and appreciated the ivory skin, the voluptuous curves. Hitherto, he had cared patiently for sick animals, dogs and wounded birds, horses, but never before for a sick human being and a woman at that. He told himself that this was the reason for the girl's profound effect on him.

Tim Bert hammered at the door of the house and after a few moments it was opened by a tiny hunchbacked butler wearing shabby livery. He looked taken aback for a moment at the sight which greeted him, then bowed to his master and stepped back into the hall. Firing orders at the servants who hovered in the hallway, Marchington soon had a warm clean bed ready.

As he placed Cassia in the bed, between the clean sheets, he caught a glimpse of Earlton his butler. The man was peering round the door, mouth agape.

'Begone, damn you!' roared his lordship. 'Fetch tepid water, not hot, not cold, and more sheets and a warming pan. And be quick about it, man!'

Marchington removed the blankets from the inert body. His breath caught in his throat at the sight of her ivory curves. He had never seen such rounded, silky breasts, and her stomach was like velvet . . . He reached out a hand to stroke her breasts, her belly. He caressed the shaven triangle that excited him strangely, and then began to explore between her thighs, feeling an answering sensation between his own.

Earlton burst in with the water and with fresh sheets over his arm. Marchington immediately threw the covers over Cassia. Glaring furiously at his butler, he asked him where the other servants were.

'In the kitchens listening to Tim Bert's tale, m'lord,' Earlton replied, eyeing the girl in the bed as he spoke.

'I want no gossip, do you hear? We want this kept secret – if word gets to the Sultan, he'll be down here with his Janissaries like lightning, and they love to cut off people's heads, and hack off their hands and feet. Do you understand?' Marchington stood over his butler, his grey eyes cold as crystal.

Earlton had paled. 'Yes,' he said. 'I'll pass on your orders, m'lord. At once, m'lord.'

Alone again, his lordship turned to his patient. He touched her forehead and found it unnaturally hot, so he pulled back the sheets and began to bathe her body with the tepid water. A shudder coursed through her; she moaned, but did not waken. When she was bathed, and dried with warmed towels, Leo thought of persuading her to sip some wine, but she was still motionless, and he did not want to run the risk of choking her. She was too precious, this nereid whom he had rescued

304

from the sea. As she lay tucked in the great bed, a fire roaring in the hearth. Leo thought back to the rescue and realized that he was a little tired despite his customary vigour. His muscles ached, and he would dearly have loved to sleep, but he was not going to leave until the girl was well enough to speak to him.

He stood by the fire, rubbing his hands together to warm himself, occasionally glancing back towards the bed to see if his patient stirred. She did not, but when he looked at her closely some time later, she appeared to be in a more natural sleep. He found it hard to tell what was natural for her and what was not. Was she so very white-skinned, or was it the shock of her ordeal? He found that he was impatient to see the colour of her eyes – would they be brown or grey, green or blue? Her hair, which he had rubbed with warm towels, was beginning to dry and he could see that its colour was auburn. Fluffy tendrils were spreading out over the pillow and framing her pale face like a halo.

That day he had gone in search of a legend to paint, and he had found instead a sea nymph. Already in his mind he was visualizing the way he would paint her when she was well, standing on the shores of the island, her russet hair streaming free, her beautiful ivory body naked, a great white convoluted shell in her hands. Venus, a Venus to rival Botticelli's. Fresh excitement rose in him, mingling with the sensuous feeling she aroused in his body. Suddenly, he could not wait to paint her, to have her healthy again, so that he could sketch her in charcoals, watercolours, every possible medium, every possible pose. Now he realized why he had always painted scenery and buildings before – there had been no woman to inspire him. But now he had saved Venus from the Bosphorus and she was his own. His possession.

All that night he kept watch, sitting by the hearth in a huge armchair, muscular legs swathed in rugs. Occasionally he woke and went over to the bed to see that she was still sleeping soundly, and then he would return to throw a log on the fire before settling himself in the chair again.

He dreamed of the rescue, a wild, vivid dream which made him sweat and cry out. He was drowning, he could not save himself or the girl, down, down into the black, freezing waters he plunged, shouting a silent shout which no one heard, for it was muffled by the waters. He woke with a start, hearing a cry. The girl was crying out in her sleep and this had been transposed into his dreams. She was flinging wide her arms and tossing her head from left to right. Instantly, he was across the room and talking to her.

'You are safe now – relax, rest as much as you like. No one can harm you. I will look after you. I will see that you get well. Sleep, sleep, my dear, and you will get well.'

She seemed to respond to his words, and he gently replaced her arms under the covers. Only when he had sat down again by the fire did he chide himself for imagining his words had soothed her, fevered as she was. He had completely forgotten that she would not be able to understand English.

The next day the Earl was as attentive as before to his invalid. Ignoring Earlton's scowls, and after ensuring that Tim Bert had recovered from the previous night's ordeal, he settled down to watch over his patient. She was still in a coma, her eyes were closed, her face so translucent that he imagined he could see the bones and veins beneath her skin. His nereid, his Venus, all his, and his alone! This new feeling of possession filled him with an exultant joy. He could not recall having experienced it ever before. It had sprung from the manner in which he had met the girl – her near death, the rescue attempt that had diverted the path of fate and had brought her into his keeping. Destiny had meant them to be brought together, he knew that now.

As he stood looking down at her, he vowed that he would keep her with him for the rest of his life. She would be his concubine and his slave, just as she had been the Sultan's; she would be well versed in the arts of tempting and intriguing men; she would be accustomed to servitude, to submission. This fact roused him most of all: she had been the Sultan's. The toy and sexual plaything of one of the most powerful men on earth. Now she would be his bondswoman to exalt or degrade as he pleased. He imagined her standing naked before him – that glowing Titian hair contrasting with the velvet white body. He saw her spreading her legs and waiting for his pleasure, her eyes pleading . . .

Earlton interrupted his reverie. 'M'lord, Tim Bert wants to know if you'll be using the boat again today, or if he should put it away. He suggested it was hidden, in case anyone should see it as they pass and recall having seen it by the palace last eve.'

Leo frowned. 'I do not think such extreme caution is necessary,' he growled. 'If anyone had seen us, we would be dead by now, I assure you. The Turks waste no time with reprisals. And no, I shall not be needing the boat again for the moment.'

Earlton bowed out, scowling. His master had changed since finding the concubine – if concubine she was, and Tim Bert thought it more than likely. His lordship was not a man to mince his words, but he was usually reasonably civil to his servants. He had chosen them especially to accompany him on his trip to Turkey – men he trusted, and who had served him faithfully. Earlton had always felt proud of that trust, but now his master snapped at him, and drooled over the girl like a lecherous schoolboy. It was not right. He did not like it at all.

Two days passed and Marchington still nursed his patient. Cassia was feverish for four days, and then, during the night, her fever broke. The Earl was exultant. Those four days when she had been entirely at his mercy, helpless, comatose, had evoked the most mixed feelings in him. He delighted in having a helpless creature in his possession, bathing her, combing her hair, changing her sheets and making nightgowns for her out of linen, tied, sarong-like, beneath her arms. But he was impatient to speak to her, to see her eyes, to discover what colour they were, if they were large and limpid, or small and sparkling, to hear what she would say to him, if they could converse at all. He had gone so far as to send Tim Bert out to the markets to find a trustworthy Turk from whom he could learn more of that language in preparation for the concubine's recovery.

The Turk arrived, a bowing, beaming man who rubbed his hands together constantly, as if polishing them. His name, he said, was Abdul Ali Mahmoud, but the Earl called him Ali, for it was simpler. While his patient was sleeping, Marchington took Turkish lessons with Ali, who could also speak fluent English, for he had been a sailor for many years, travelling all over the globe until ill-health caused him to give up his roving life and settle for growing vegetables. He had met Tim Bert in the markets, and they had talked together many times.

Marchington said nothing to Ali of the patient's origins. Although he was paying the man generously, and had demanded total secrecy, he intended playing safe. Ali seemed affable and good-humoured. He was a patient tutor, and Marchington soon found he had a grasp of the language.

'You natural born clever at Turkish,' Ali grinned, rubbing his hands round and round together. 'Not easy for Englishman speak my tongue. Rare. So you twice over clever, yes?'

The Earl arched one silver-grey brow. 'That is kind of you to say so, but I would prefer tuition to praise, if you do not mind.'

'Yes, yes, oh yes,' Ali grinned. 'I tui – tui – teach you well, oh yes, yes, yes!'

His lordship found this obsequiousness irritating, but he had no intention of annoying his mentor. He wanted to learn Turkish, and like all the accomplishments on which he had set his heart, he had vowed to succeed. When his slave awoke, he would astonish her by speaking to her in the language of the harem. It would set her mind at ease to hear a familiar tongue, and it would further strengthen the bond between them. For the bond must be strong, so strong that she would have no wish to sever it. He envisaged her grateful, suppliant. He wanted no shadow of discontent to mar her total subservience.

Ali made a place for himself in the household. He was

happy fetching and carrying for his lordship, and even the servants, hostile to any foreigner, softened towards him. It would have been impossible to dislike him for long for he was kindly and keen to please. Even Armand, the haughty French chef, was appeased when Ali told him of a place where he could buy the freshest, most tasty vegetables and fruit. As Ali made himself at home, Marchington decided that it would be far safer if the Turk did stay with him. He was useful, and quick to respond to orders. On the island, there would be no risk of his blabbing about Cassia to other Turks who might not be so circumspect.

On the evening of the fourth day after the rescue, Cassia opened her eyes as Lord Marchington's shadow fell across her bed. She saw, her vision blurred by what seemed to be a blinding light, a man with silver-grey hair bending over her. He had light grey eyes, and his brows were slightly darker grey than his hair. But what most startled her was the contrasting youth of the broad, strong-boned face. Incongruous with the silvered hair, his skin was lightly tanned, his teeth square and even. He was smiling at her, his eyes alight. He looked marvellously happy.

Dazed, and still only half awake, Cassia stammered, 'Am I d-dead? Are you God?' At which the man laughed aloud and sat down beside her on the bed.

'You are awake – and after all that, you speak English. This is incredible. Absolutely incredible.' He laughed again, taking her little hands between his own vast palms and looking down at her fondly.

'Who – who are you? What has happened?' She remembered suddenly what had gone before, and the colour drained from her face. 'I – was – was–' Her voice broke, a sob catching in her throat.

'You have been through a terrible ordeal. Do not speak of it now. Later, when you are strong, we can talk all you wish. For now, you must eat and put back some of the weight you have lost in the last four days.'

'Four days? I – have – been – ill for four days?'

'Indeed you have, and it is not surprising considering

what you have suffered. But you are safe here, and we are looking after you. So there is nothing to worry about at all.'

Ali appeared at that moment, laden with the supper tray for his master. Seeing Cassia awake, he grinned broadly. 'Allah the Most Merciful, the Most Powerful, be praised for He has seen fit to heal the sickness of the white lady!' Setting down the tray, he put his hands together and bowed twice with quick bobbing movements, his eyes cast heavenwards. Then he came to the bedside, and smiled at them both. 'Ah happy you now be, great, much happiness. Allah smile down on you, white lady.'

'Thank you, Ali,' said the Earl, his tone one of curt dismissal, and when the Turk had gone, he turned again to Cassia. 'You will eat now. You may have chicken soup, home-made, with vegetables, or some beefsteak. And of course you must have milk. I tried more than once to get you to drink while you were unconscious, but I had little success. I was wary of your choking.'

'You nursed me? Is there no woman here?' Cassia felt the heat flooding her cheeks. This man – an Englishman – had somehow found her, where, she could not imagine, and he had been looking after her in his own home for four days – it seemed difficult to comprehend. Her head ached, and she wished she could assimilate better what he had said.

'This is a completely male household, which is why I have been looking after you.' Marchington smiled genially, piling a plate with meat for her, and filling a goblet with milk.

'Where – how did you find me? I don't seem to remember much. A sack, I was being pushed into a sack –' she shuddered, feeling ill at the memory – 'and then, and then –'

'Please, my dear girl, you will only make yourself ill again if you persist in resurrecting such horrors. Now, eat some of this meat, and drink a little milk.' Leo seated himself on the bed beside her, and held out the platter of succulent beef. Cassia looked at it and her mouth watered. She swallowed. How parched her throat felt. She did feel ravenous, but could she swallow all the meat, or indeed any of it?

'I – I will try a little milk,' she said, and Leo held the

goblet to her lips as she drank. Having tasted the fresh, sweet milk, her throat relaxed and she drank it all, then another goblet full, after which she lay back sleepily on the pillows. 'I will have some more later. Oh, I feel so tired now. Th-Thank you – Mr – Mr?'

'Marchington. Leo Marchington,' he replied, removing the tray and settling the bedcovers around her, his huge hands surprisingly gentle. 'Sleep now. There will be no disturbances to waken you. I will leave one lamp alight, in case you wake, and Ali will be within hearing if you want me. Just call.'

'Thank you, sir,' Cassia whispered, her eyes closing as she dropped immediately into a deep sleep.

Walking in the gardens with Sigismund and Basil, his two favourite hounds, the Earl smiled to himself. So his slave could speak English, perfect ladylike English. Well, it had certainly surprised him, for he had expected anything but that. When she was well again, they would be able to talk freely on every matter, without Ali having to act as interpreter. Marchington increased his pace, striding along the sward, the two hounds leaping and barking around him joyously. He too felt like running and shouting with joy. In his house, in the very bedroom near to his, the nereid lay sleeping, his very own beautiful, auburn-haired sea goddess, who would also be his concubine. And her eyes – after four days of waiting, he had seen her eyes open at last. They were blue, a delicate hydrangea-blue, the prettiest colour he had ever seen. His artist's hands ached to begin painting her. But he must wait, of course. When she was up and about, strong again, smiling and happy, he would paint her in a flowing white robe of Grecian design, her hair loose, those glorious eyes looking straight at him.

'Come, Sigismund, Basil!' he commanded the dogs, who were already tiring at keeping up with their indefatigable master. How was he going to survive the next few weeks until she was strong again? It would take all his self-control.

CHAPTER TWENTY-TWO

'Tell me, how is it that you speak such excellent English?'
Lord Marchington asked Cassia as he propped up the pillows behind her so that she could eat her breakfast.

'It is really quite simple, sir. You see, I was born in London of a Cornish father and an Irish mother.'

'That explains it. I had imagined you to be Circassian, with that colouring, and I fully expected you to speak the Sultan's language. In fact, that is why I hired Ali, to teach me to speak Turkish in readiness for your recovery.'

'You have gone to a great deal of trouble on my behalf, sir. I am deeply grateful.'

'Trouble? No trouble, my dear. From the moment I realized what I had rescued, my heart went out to you. You have endured far more than any human being I know, and the least I can do is try to make you happy now.'

Pink coloured Cassia's cheeks. 'You are truly kind, and I do not know how I shall be able to thank you. When I am well again –'

'When you are well again, we shall speak of this, but for now shall we have our breakfast, and enjoy that. Would you like eggs, or porridge?'

'Eggs please, sir, and coffee – with plenty of milk.'

Cassia watched her saviour filling her plate with eggs and pouring coffee into her cup. Physically, he was a very striking man. Tall, extremely broad, muscular; the breadth of his shoulders gave him a bull-like quality. His young, unlined face was similarly powerful, but, framed by the hair had a look that, she thought guiltily, was almost sinister. In the few days since she had recovered consciousness, she had realized that she owed this man her life. Not only did he exude power, but he was capable of great bravery, risking his own life to save hers. He was her deliverer, taking her from the sea and certain death. She could not help but think of Vincent who had done exactly the opposite.

She was too weak to formulate her thoughts clearly, beyond feeling intense gratitude towards this stalwart man, but each day her energy was returning. She enjoyed their talks, and she loved the two devoted hounds who loped everywhere after their master. Ali too she found amusing, and he could not do enough for her. It was the other servant to whom she could not respond – Earlton was his name. She had never seen such an odd personage. He was tiny and hunchbacked, his face wizened, his eyes glittering beads. He had not been in her room often, only to bring in logs or to remove a tray, but he never failed to dart her a malevolent look. At the moment, she was not able to ascertain why the man should be so hostile towards her, but when she was better she fully intended to try to make friends with him. Discord of any kind was abhorrent to her.

Piece by piece, memory of her ordeal returned to her. She found it horrifying, and also a little unreal, as if it had happened to someone else, far removed from her. Had she really been a concubine in Hamid's Seraglio, had Kadine Mimosa and Aletha and Xenobe really existed, or could she possibly have imagined it all?

Her host told her not to fret over her past, and she tried to obey him, but it was not easy. How could she stop thinking of Vincent, who would now think her dead? When he returned to save her from the harem, he would hear of the drowning of Briar Rose, the Sultan's favourite, and he would never guess that she had escaped her terrible punishment. He would leave Constantinople, and return to the Pasha's sister, who wanted to marry him.

Cassia's heart began to beat painfully. Vincent. Her Vincent. He would marry this woman – this Muslim woman, what was her name? Cassia could not recall it. She felt so impotent, lying weak and ill in this bed. What could she do? She had no idea where he was, she could not even remember where the Pasha's sister lived. It was hopeless. She knew no one here, except her rescuer, and he had already impressed on her the need for her to remain in hiding. Of that she had little doubt. The Sultan and his Janissaries would swoop down on her at once if they knew she had escaped. She felt faint at the mere thought of being discovered by them. She would have to remain here on this island, hidden away, until she was herself again, and then – well, she would think about that later when her head stopped throbbing as it was inclined to do if she thought for too long.

Sigismund put his two front paws onto the bed at that point, begging for titbits, and Cassia smiled, giving him a buttered crust.

'He is not supposed to beg,' said his master, 'but I will forgive him, my dear, if it makes you happy. It is a pleasure to see you smiling.'

'He is a handsome dog, and so affectionate. I have never owned a pet of my own, but I would dearly love to.'

'Then he shall be yours. Treat him as if he were your own.'

'I can't do that!' Cassia protested.

Leo Marchington leaned towards her, his grey eyes clear. 'All that I have is yours. Treat this house as your home, these dogs as your pets, my servants as your servants.' His huge hand brushed across her slender one, making her skin tingle. Blushing, she thanked him, patting Sigismund on his silky head to hide her embarrassment.

Later, she asked Marchington where the island stood. 'A safe enough distance from the Grand Seraglio, I do assure you, my dear, have no fear of that. No one will find us here – even if they think to look. My servants are all sworn to secrecy, and as they have no desire to be chopped to pieces by the Janissaries, I am confident that our secret will be safe. It is not likely that someone tied in a sack and thrown into the sea will survive the experience. Obviously, Poseidon was keeping watch over you.'

His words so startled Cassia that she blanched, but the Earl had by that time gone to the window to look out, and did not see her reaction. She was heartily grateful. She had said nothing to him about Vincent, or her earlier experiences, for she was unsure as to how she could speak of the man she loved so deeply. She feared that she would weep, and become hysterical, and so she had said nothing.

She knew by now that he was an Earl, for she had heard the butler calling him m'lord. It meant little to her that he was one of the aristocracy. But she was interested in him as an artist, and loved to make him talk about his work. Sometimes a frisson of something akin to revulsion would make her wonder how this bull-like man with the huge hands could execute delicate works of art.

He sometimes called her Aphrodite, with a twinkle in his grey eyes, and she would laugh and say that Aphrodite had fared better in the sea than she, at which her host replied it must have been just as cold, wet and uncomfortable in a shell as in a sack.

Ali brought in a tray with tea; spiced wine, and fluffy honey cakes made by Armand's skilled hands. Cassia's appetite had now returned in full, and she ate the cakes with relish, but only sipped at the wine. Sigismund sat by the fire, watching her, ears cocked, tongue lolling out like a pink snake. She hid a smile, pretended to finish all the cakes and then as he was about to slink down on to the floor, she held up a cake for him. He bounded eagerly across the floor, swallowing the cake in one gulp. Basil did not beg, for he was more sedate, but he was not averse to titbits.

'He was ill-treated before I saved him,' the Earl explained to Cassia. 'He had been whipped, and kicked. I took him home, and tended him, and gradually he came to trust men again. But he is always somewhat reserved.'

'So I am not the first lame dog you have rescued?' Cassia twinkled.

Marchington laughed. 'Lame dog, you? Bedraggled nymph more like.'

'Come, Basil, for your cake,' Cassia summoned the hound, but he came to her reluctantly.

She liked to watch how the dogs vied for their master's caresses, tails whisking, tongues hanging out. She wondered if Lord Marchington were like Basil, or more like Sigismund . . . or like neither of them. Then she reproached herself. What did it matter to her? The Earl must be married, for he was past forty. Somewhere in his life there was bound to be a Lady Marchington, no doubt a society beauty possessing every possible virtue and talent. Fortunate creature, Cassia thought, to have married such a handsome, caring man, and to be able to live such a carefree, safe life with a blessedly normal, English husband.

Having thought this, she immediately dismissed her notions as being disloyal to Vincent. Such a great deal had taken place in the last two weeks that she was bemused, and in desperate need of peace and relaxation. She was free of that hated Seraglio, where, she now realized, she had lived in fear and apprehension, and her relief was so vibrant that she had room to feel little else.

The shock of nearly drowning had certainly affected her. She could not think of anything except being safe in this house. Safe, where neither eunuchs nor Kislar Agha could get to her. It was bliss.

She leaned back against the soft pillows. Glancing up at Marchington she caught a curious expression in his eyes which had vanished before she could decipher it.

'You are tired now, my dear. I will leave you to sleep. Sigismund will guard your door.'

'I – I would rather the door were left unguarded if you do not mind, my lord,' she replied, thinking of the omnipresent guards in the harem she had hated.

'I would like to feel that I could obey your desire, my dear, but as we are in a foreign country, it would be best to keep such a pretty young woman under guard. Especially when we think of how I found you.' He smiled disarmingly and she was forced to respond. No doubt he was right. She must trust his good judgement, for he would know what to do for the best.

When he had gone, she slipped easily into sleep, drifting on soft pillows through her dreams. She dreamed of a pirate ship sailing into clouds and angry waters, and evil-looking men, sabres in hand. Arms and heads rolled, and she heard the screams of the dying, the groans of the wounded. Then she was plunging into blackness, falling, falling. She could not breathe, she was suffocating. She was dying.

She woke with a cry, drenched with sweat. Ali was leaning over her, his face full of concern.

'White lady have bad dream, yes? Ali asleep in corridor but Ali hear and come quick. All right now, lady, yes, yes?'

'Oh yes, I was having a bad dream – a horrible dream. Thank you, Ali, thank you for coming in.'

'No trouble, lady. You call me you need me. I tell you story. Long ago, when I young, I sailor, travel all the world. That how I learn your language. In Liverpool, I meet lovely lady. Red hair like you, but much more –' he grinned, making a shape in the air with his hands. 'She say she marry me, but her brother not allow. Fight, quarrel with me. He warn me go or he kill me. Lady – name was Joan – run away with me. I hide her on ship, and she say she marry me. But she take sick – fever – and she die. Others of crew die too. Terrible, terrible.' He closed his eyes, shaking his head from side to side. 'I too take fever but I get well, though weak from then and not suit life at sea. I come home sad, sad man, without my Joan.'

Cassia's heart went out to him. 'You must be very lonely now, without your Joan, and unable to go to sea. I know how the sea gets into the blood. My ancestors were seafarers – Cornishmen and women.'

'I meet many Cornishmen on my ships. They born with sea legs, that is what they say. True?' He cocked his head, his dark eyes sparkling.

'True,' Cassia laughed; the nightmare receded. Ali was so kind, and she was grateful. She watched his blue-robed figure as he walked to the door, and there he turned, to remind her that he was just outside if she wanted him.

'Thank you, Ali.'

The next morning, Marchington woke her with ham and eggs, kidneys, toast and coffee.

'Do you like kidneys, my dear? If you do not, Sigismund will have them, for they are one of his special favourites.'

'I shall not deprive him of his favourite food. Ham and eggs will be marvellous. It is years since I had breakfast in bed and now I get it every morning. The last time was when I had measles as a child.'

'So you had measles? So did I. The physicians told my father that I would be damaged as a result – in my mind, that is – but as you see I am quite normal. Except of course when the moon is full, and then, ah, the change that comes over me – I sprout hair and growl like a lion!' he jested.

Cassia could not help but laugh. 'My father did that most days – in fact, he was normal only when the moon was full.'

Lord Marchington looked at her with renewed appreciation. 'What spirit you have, my dear. So recently recovered from your dreadful ordeal and already so light of heart.'

'You cannot know how happy I am just to be free of that harem, my lord. Its rules and regulations – oh it was intolerable. I was there for months, having to submit to people who cared for nothing except keeping the Sultan happy. Feelings mattered nothing to them at all, as long as Hamid was content.'

'Did you meet the Sultan? I have heard that it is possible to spend one's entire life in the harem and never so much as see him.'

'Yes, I saw him. In fact –' Cassia paused, unaware of how eagerly her host waited her reply. 'I – I was his favourite.' Having said that, she blushed furiously and wished it unsaid. She must remember that she was now back in the West and that what was normal in the harem was totally unacceptable elsewhere.

'You were his favourite – his wife?' Leo waited tensely for her answer, thinking of the Sultan bedding with his nereid, of the dark brown body moving over her ivory form. A spear of heat rose within him, heat, and desire for her. He was finding it increasingly difficult to quell his ardour in her presence, but he knew that it would be foolish to alarm her by making his feelings known while she was still an invalid. What he had been prepared to do when he thought she was Circassian had now to be rethought in the light of the discovery that she was English and had received a very respectable upbringing. The look in his eyes disturbed her and she prattled on nervously.

'I – I was a concubine, but not a Kadine – that is, a queen and wife. I had not borne the Sultan a son, you see, nor any child. I was in the harem months only – not years. It was an unbelievable place, I cannot begin to describe it. It was a prison, and yet a scented, luxuriously cushioned place. Many loved it of course. I do not think anyone detested it as I did, but then, being English, you can imagine how I felt. It was all so different – so unreal, like something out of a story.'

'I read something of the Sultans and their history before coming here. They are, as you say, different. A race apart. They have not adapted to the evolution of the times as we have. In the harem, it is still the Middle Ages.'

'Oh yes, that is it exactly,' cried Cassia. 'I felt transported backwards in time, hundreds of years backwards. I had no power, no freedom, not even the freedom to be myself. Everything must be alike, clothes, perfume, jewels, dancing, ritual.'

'That must have been soul-destroying,' the Earl said sympathetically. 'I wish that I could have rescued you earlier my dear.'

Cassia lowered her eyes, thinking of the man who had visited her in the harem and who would, by now, have rescued her and taken her away to safety had it not been for her punishment. She still had not spoken of him to her host.

'Am I wearying you with all this talking?' he asked.

'Oh no, no. I enjoy talking to you!' she returned swiftly.

'Talking is valuable sometimes. It helps to expunge unpleasant experiences.'

'You are quite right.'

'Would you like more coffee, my dear?'

'Please. Your cook is excellent, as you say. Where do you get your supplies?'

'From all over the place. The markets locally, and some we grow ourselves. Already Ali has cast an eye over the kitchen gardens and is choosing vegetables to grow there. I do not know how we managed without him. Armand is a brilliant chef, but he is useless with anything except the finished product. Tim Bert usually buys the fruit and vegetables outside. Also I brought large stocks of non-perishables with me.'

'You plan to stay here for some time – or have you come here for good?'

'I am here for a year in all, and we have been here already quite a time.'

'So you will eventually be returning to England?'

'Yes, to my home in Derbyshire, Malcott Hall. I go abroad frequently, to find material for the paintings that I shall execute when I return. I have annual exhibitions.'

'You are famous then? I used to draw a little when I was younger. Mostly nature sketches, trees and flowers and so on. Nothing elaborate.' How long ago that seemed, she thought. Like another century and another girl.

'It is true that I sell many of my works,' said the Earl modestly. 'I paint scenery and famous buildings of great beauty. I have been to Venice, to Rome and to Paris. Now I am here to paint, amongst other things, the Grand Seraglio.'

'I fear that I have come between you and your work, my lord!'

The Earl smiled, brushing her cheek with his fingers. 'Perhaps I have discovered something of far greater beauty to paint than the palace of the Sultans, my dear.'

She looked into his pale grey eyes, hardly daring to recognize what she saw there. His fingers lingered on her cheek, caressingly, they seemed to burn her skin. Part of her longed for the caress to continue, another part wished that he had not touched her at all.

He went on, as if nothing had happened. 'I have sketched

birds and hounds too, and sometimes flowers. When I was in Italy I had a marvellous time with the scenery. This year I was drawn to Turkey – to old Byzantium in fact. It is virtually unchanged you know, and that I find quite compelling. Just as the harem has not changed for centuries, neither has the city itself, nor the outlying areas. Mosques have been added of course, by various rulers, but nothing has altered the central structure.'

'I had a friend in the harem whose knowledge of history was amazing. She told me all about Constantinople's past. Poor Xenobe, she is still in the harem. She will think I am dead and she will grieve over me. But what can I do?'

'I would not let you do anything which would endanger your life, my dear. May I call you Cassia? Any message despatched would proclaim that you did not drown. The Grand Turk is a vengeful man. He has spies everywhere. I believe that his wives and concubines belong to him even after their deaths. They would search you out and this time you would not escape. Nor, I imagine, would I. Myself, my servants, even Ali, would be despatched mercilessly.'

'That would be dreadful. Yes, I had realized that I cannot send any message. I will not do anything stupid, do not worry.'

'I have complete faith in you,' the Earl smiled benignly, knowing as he did so that there was absolutely no possibility of any message getting past him.

But how do I find Vincent? Cassia asked silently. Where is he now? What is he doing?

Aloud, she said, 'You are very considerate, my lord. When I think of how you saved me from drowning I can scarcely believe my luck. The chances of anyone – let alone an Englishman – rescuing me must have been remote indeed.' She could not keep the gratitude from her voice. She owed him an enormous debt, and felt keenly the need to repay him.

'I only did what any man would have done. I acted without thinking, if the truth be known. When I dived into the sea, I had no idea that it would yield such a radiant young nereid. When I saw you, I could not believe my eyes. I still cannot.' Again he touched her cheek.

'I suppose it must have seemed astounding, but then the last months have all been like that for me. One after the other, things have happened, each more amazing. I – well, it all began in Morbilly Cove while I was out walking. I had been staying with my aunt, Julitta Morbilly, and I used to visit the cove regularly. It was a most attractive spot. When the pirate boat beached, and they scooped me up, I was utterly stunned – it was like a nightmare.' She twisted her hands together.

'They ill-treated you?' Lord Marchington's grey eyes had become frosted crystal.

'Indeed no – their Captain was not unkind. He immediately decided to sell me to the Sultan, however, and nothing I said or did could change his mind.'

Privately thinking that the Captain must have been out of his mind for wanting to part with this gorgeous creature, his lordship asked her what her captor had been like.

'He was tall – and black-haired. He had green eyes. He was of French lineage. One of his ancestors was a lovechild of Francis the First of France.'

'You found out a lot about him while he was taking you to the Grand Seraglio.' The Earl fought the jealousy which had him in its grip. A pirate captain possessing his concubine – if only temporarily – was unbearable to him. But combined with the jealousy was a feeling of extreme excitement at the vision of Cassia being bedded.

'We did talk, it is true. He was – civil to me.'

'I see.' His lordship bent to stroke Sigismund. 'And then he sold you to the Sultan?'

'Not immediately.'

'He kept you with him?'

The abruptness of this question made Cassia blush. But again she felt compelled to conceal the truth of her love for Vincent.

'My lord, you embarrass me. I cannot answer such questions. I still find it very difficult to come to terms with all that has happened to me in the last year. You must forgive me. The reason I remained with the French Captain was simply that he had to visit Algiers, and then when we set off for Constantinople, one of his great enemies, a man called Nathan Dash, attacked us. The crew of the Captain's ship – he himself – were slain. Dash himself took me to the Sultan.'

'I see.' Lord Marchington leaned back in the comfortable armchair that he had drawn up by Cassia's bed. His bulk completely filled it. She felt heartily thankful that he seemed to accept her explanations. To talk of Vincent, of her love for him and their relationship was not something which she could do with anyone: not even with Xenobe. It had been too confusing, too bitter-sweet. And now it was too painful.

Marchington insisted that she continue to remain in bed while he and Ali waited upon her. Earlton too played his part. The butler was surly and ungracious when he cared for her in his master's absence, but paid her every deference when his lordship was present. Cassia still strove to build up a polite relationship with Earlton, but her efforts were in vain. The hunchback would neither converse with her nor answer her questions about the house and the dogs. Cassia had to make do with Ali's sometimes banal chatter, but she found his geniality most welcome. He was always in a good mood.

Once on the mend, Cassia recovered quickly. She was eating well, nourishing, well-cooked food, and she drank plenty of milk and sometimes light wines. She was soon considering getting up, but Lord Marchington would not hear of it.

'After nearly drowning, my dear Cassia? I could not possibly allow it – what if you had a relapse? All that careful nursing gone to waste! We are here for some time, you know. The house and the gardens won't vanish. You will have plenty of time to see them later.'

'Now that I am stronger, naturally I feel curious about

my surroundings. It is so long since I was able to walk freely wherever I wished,' she sighed.

'You must be careful where you walk here, or there is a risk of your stepping into the sea.'

She smiled. 'After my ordeal, I do not think that I shall ever willingly go near the sea again.'

'You are an exceedingly brave woman, and I have every admiration for you.' Marchington smiled down at her, his eyes roaming from her face to her neck and then lower, where they remained for some moments. Aware of his scrutiny, she blushed. He was dressed for riding, in a smartly-cut black riding jacket and beige cloth breeches. There was a riding crop tucked in his belt, its handle carved with the Marchington crest, two gilded eagles on a blue background. Cassia asked him about the crest to hide her discomfiture at his praise.

'It signifies a search for attainment. Our motto is, To fly even higher. Sadly, few of my ancestors complied with this maxim. In fact, they were notable for sinking even lower.' He grinned, but Cassia could not help noticing that the frosted crystal look was in his eyes.

Had his ancestors been profligates then, and was he ashamed of them? That would not be startling – the aristocracy were notorious for such tendencies. What of him, though? His grey hair might be that of an older man, but he had fresh skin and such clear eyes. He could not be a heavy drinker, nor a womanizer; it would have revealed itself by now in his face. His skin would have coarsened, his eyes become bleary. If he were ashamed of his ancestors, would he not have risen above that shame, as his family motto implied?

She bade him enjoy his ride, and then he left her with a book to read. Looking down at it, she saw the title and tears filled her eyes. It was *A Journey to Paris*, her aunt's favourite book.

At last she was allowed to get up, but only for an hour at a time, and on condition that she did not leave the bedroom and overtire herself. She did not argue with her host, for he was solicitous and determined to see her well again. He told her of his mother who had risen too early from her sickbed, collapsed, and died of a chill.

'I would not wish the same to happen to you. My mother was a handsome woman, with blue eyes and long golden hair. She was one of the most famous beauties of her day – Eleanora Marchington, Countess of Bache in her own right. She was only twenty-one when she died. It was tragic. My father never got over it. I was a mere few months old at the time, and was then raised by nursemaids who did not have my full interests at heart.' He thought of Moll Bottomley, one of those nursemaids, who had introduced him at the age of four to the delights of the flesh. She had run her hands over his body, and taught him how to do the same to her. Even now he could remember how her face became pink and beaded with sweat as he touched her, and the strange squirming feeling that such activity aroused in him. There had been others after her, but he would never forget Moll.

'I, too, lost my mother when I was a baby. She did not die, though, she left me. She was Irish, an actress, and she loathed domesticity. My father was bitter about her desertion and as a result he was very strict with me. He does not like women, and he could never conceal it.'

'So you were raised in a household with a father who hated women, and who kept you caged like a bird? You could not have been happy. My own father was kindly, and he ensured that I was well educated. He attended to my health as well. Sporting pastimes played a large part in my rearing, and, apart from that one time I had the measles, I was never ill.'

'Nor was I, save for that. I suppose I have taken my good health for granted now that I think about it.' She had decided to say nothing of the fever through which Vincent had nursed her.

'And we must ensure that you retain your good health.

325

Plenty of rest and Armand's excellent cuisine, and you will be fitter than any of us.'

Cassia smiled, warmed as always by his kindness. He had no real reason to be so attentive, so considerate, and yet he was unstinting in his care of her.

'Ali will look after you while I am out. Call him if you want anything.' The Earl smiled. It was a stroke of good fortune that he had brought the Turk into the household, for Earlton did not like waiting on females, thinking it beneath him. That was what came of giving him too much importance in an all-male household for so many years.

When Marchington had gone, Cassia began to think of her lost lover. (How could she not?) And she thought of Xenobe too. Having time to spare now, she pictured them both in her mind's eye, sending out silent messages to them. I am safe and well, and alive, she told Xenobe. And, to Vincent, she said, I love you, and I always shall.

As her spirits returned in full, she thought even more about her lover. She wanted to see him again, to be held in his arms. Over and over again, she relived their night of love in the harem. And then pain would sweep over her, for however thoroughly Vincent investigated, he would learn only one thing: that she had been sentenced to death and that the punishment had been carried out.

What would he have felt when he learned this? Would he be heartbroken, inconsolable? Yes, she thought, but then he would recover, and marry his Muslim. She was sure that he would. He would no longer search for her. He would mourn, and then he would get married and have children . . . the thought of that caused her terrible anguish. Her lover in another woman's bed, legally united to her, giving her sons and daughters, while she, Cassia, was alone, believed dead. Wild plans of disguising herself as a boy and riding in search of him occurred to her, only to be discarded as impossibilities.

The days became dreary, and she sank into a lethargy from which Ali did his best to revive her.

'White lady sad again? Ali cheer. See –' and he picked

up some fruit from the bowl by her bed and began to juggle it with such skill that she had to applaud his expertise, and laugh at his beatific expression. 'Good to – see – Lady – with – jollity,' he said, leaning first forward and then backwards to keep his balance.

Having made Cassia laugh once, Ali determined to do so again. Snapping his fingers, he summoned Sigismund to his feet.

'Sigismund now die. *Die!*' he commanded. The dog immediately rolled over on its side and lay quite still.

'Did you teach him that, Ali?' Cassia asked, impressed.

'Well, I not tell lie. He know it. Master tell me he have tricks to learn when pup, so I remind him of it now. He not forget. Dog learn young, he never forget.'

Ali then commanded Sigismund to sit up and beg, and to hold out his paw. Watching, Cassia forgot her unhappiness for a time. Later, when Lord Marchington came in to see her, he commented on how well she looked.

'It is true that I feel much stronger,' she agreed.

'But there is still that shadow in your eyes. Can you not tell me what troubles you? If I knew, then perhaps I could solve it?' He smiled at her kindly, thinking how desirable she was – so very appealing that he yearned to take her in his arms and kiss her passionately, then lead her to the bed where they would do anything but sleep. For a few moments he almost put aside his resolve to wait for the appointed hour, letting passion rule him, lust gorge his body.

'I think there is no solution for what troubles me, if the truth be known, my lord. I shall have to continue as best I can, and keep my mind from it,' Cassia said.

He heard her as if from an immense distance, as passion seared him. With an effort he pulled himself back from the brink, keeping his voice steady.

'It is very bad, this secret trouble?'

She would have answered evasively, but at that moment the door swung open and Earlton came into the room with his usual surly scowl to deposit a tray of madeira and two glasses on the table by the hearth. Marchington went to the table and poured out madeira for them both. He handed Cassia her goblet and smiled down at her reassuringly. She took it, although wine was the last thing she felt like drinking. She would have much preferred creamy coffee or hot milk. Sipping, she hid her distaste.

Tentacles of gilded light were intruding through the leaded windows of the room, spearing certain areas. The gold thread in the brocade bedhangings glittered. Lord Marchington's silver-grey hair gleamed like a halo around his head. He smiled at her, but as the light was behind him she could barely see his face. His eyes looked dark, cavernous, while around his head his wavy hair shone and sparkled in the sunlight.

It was at that moment that the most terrible screeching sound filled the air. Cassia all but dropped her wine. The Earl grinned. 'Do not be alarmed, that is only Cromwell. He must have been disturbed by one of the servants cleaning.'

'Cromwell?' Cassia gasped. It sounded like someone or something being murdered.

'My owl. He found his way here one night, his wing damaged, and of course I put it in splints and looked after him until he recovered. He is quite himself now, but he will not leave. I have given him every opportunity, but he prefers the house. He goes on hunting forays of course, but always returns here. He is nocturnal, so he will not pester you in the daytime.'

'You mean he is allowed to fly where he pleases in the house?'

'Indeed. He flies out of the upper windows of the attic when he wishes to go hunting. For that reason, the windows and doors are always kept open. He is harmless of course unless you happen to be a mouse or a frog – and then he would eat you, but as you are neither, there is no cause for alarm.'

Somehow, her rescuer's words made her feel uneasy. She could not share his easy attitude to the cruelties of nature, although she did love all wild creatures, especially birds.

The thought of an owl eating tiny, helpless creatures filled her with revulsion and a strange sort of fear.

She finished the madeira. The Earl would have filled her goblet, but she shook her head. She knew what she was going to ask him, but somehow she had not yet gathered her courage. Also, she felt very tired again. It was the same sudden weariness that had swept over her in the earlier days of her illness.

His lordship smiled down at her benevolently. 'You look exhausted, my dear, how stupid of me to keep you talking when you obviously need to sleep.'

He went quietly out of the room and closed the door silently behind. She heard the murmur of voices outside in the corridor and then she sank into the most profound sleep.

She woke in a daze. Strong arms were imprisoning her; holding her fast. She could not get free, nor did she want to, for in her drugged stupor, she believed it was Vincent making love to her. She sighed, pliant in the muscular arms. The feel of warm naked flesh against her was ecstasy; a mouth was on hers, kissing deeply, a tongue exploring between her teeth. How strong he was and skilled, caressing her breasts so that an answering passion began and she wanted to cry out to him to take her. But he stroked her body more skilfully still, murmuring her name over and over, and words of love that she would have thought crude had she not been so roused by now and still only half-conscious.

The words went on, growing in roughness, words which no man had ever used with her before, their novelty giving the speaker a power that made her feel degraded and excited all at the same time. Lips fastened over her breasts, kissing, biting, making her writhe voluptuously. Her hands went round his broad, muscular back to pull him down closer to her. Breathing swiftly, she moved against him, her legs opening. She wanted him inside her – loving her – crushing her to him. She could not wait another second.

She cried out, 'Now, now, oh, love me now!' and then

suddenly she was alone in the bed. He had left. Chillness washed over her. Where had he gone? She tried to open her eyes, but she saw only a blurred room. No one was there. Could she have imagined it? But no, her body ached, her lips tingled. Putting her fingers to her mouth, she felt the blood still throbbing there. And then as her head cleared a little, she realized who had been in the bed with her. And her body had betrayed her, for she had responded with all the passion of which she was capable, welcoming him as if he were Vincent. Alarmed and miserable, she lay back to think of the Earl's powerful arms around her, his warm naked limbs crushing hers, his lips searching out her own, and with shame she recalled the rough words that he had used to rouse her.

Marchington returned to his own room and sank down into a chair. He was still shaking with passion. He did not know how he had found the control to leave her when what he most wanted was to spear her body repeatedly and then begin to use her all over again. He had sent the grinning Turk out with the dogs, so there had been no bar to his scheme, but now he regretted what he had done. She was to be saved for the appointed hour – and nothing must mar that decision. He cared too deeply for what he was doing to spoil it all by being premature. How he wanted her! Shudders coursed through him. He was still roused. It took every ounce of his iron will to prevent him from returning to her room to make her his. There was only one thing he could do now. He would go to the library and pore over the collection of books and drawings which he kept hidden there behind a mock panel. They had consoled him before, and they must do so again.

When Cassia woke from her drugged sleep, she remembered little. Had there been a weird dream, something that had stirred her desire? She could recall it vaguely, but as with most dreams, it receded with the daylight. She was besieged by a peculiar lethargy, every day now seemed like a mountain to be climbed unaided. She knew the cause, but had no access to the cure. Her earlier life seemed so far removed from her that she began to doubt it had ever existed. Hadn't she always been here on this island? Her host had made such a strong impression on her that she came to believe this was so, that her life with Vincent and the months in the harem had been a figment of her dreams and these must now be repressed. The only reality seemed to be Penwellyn, her Aunt Julitta, and memories of undertaking cosy household tasks in her aunt's home. If Marchington would let her cook or help in some way with the domestic routine of his house, she knew that she would feel more cheerful. She began to exercise secretly, walking up and down in her room, flexing her limbs to invigorate the muscles. Soon, the memory of her dream and the man making love to her had faded totally.

She waited until Marchington was out on a day's sketching trip, then she dressed in one of the voluminous gowns that, in the Turkish style, she had stitched from a sheet. It was marvellous to be out of her room at last, and she walked down the long shadowy corridor to the wide balustrade of the stairway. There were doors on each side of the corridor, but at this moment she was more interested in the kitchens. The hallway was wide, the floor tiled. Enormous portraits framed with massive gilt frames lined the walls and there was red and green stained glass in the windows on either side of the front door. She looked around impatiently for the entrance to the servants' quarters, and at last found it at the back of the hallway, a tiny door half hidden by tapestries.

The scent of roasting meat and bread baking greeted her as she opened the door. Sniffing rapturously, she went down a stone passage and through the heavy oaken door into the kitchens. A reassuring picture greeted her. The *chef de cuisine* was humming to himself, stirring a huge metal pot over the stove, while two kitchen boys were peeling vegetables and plucking hens.

Cassia coughed, to attract their attention, and at once the chef whirled round, his eyes bulging. Uttering a rapid stream of French, he flapped his arms and strode threateningly towards Cassia. She shrank back despite herself.

'Monsieur, forgive me for intruding upon you without warning, but I was eager to see the house, and I thought perhaps I might be allowed to assist you . . .' her voice trailed away, for Armand was staring at her as if she had grown another head.

'Mademoiselle will please leave. This is no place for my lord's guests. *Mon dieu*, what would milord say if he knew that I had allowed you in my kitchens? I would be spoken to as if I were a miscreant of the lowest order! Mam'selle will please go now, before I, Armand Villeneuve, am brought down in milord's favour.'

'I – I am sorry, Monsieur Villeneuve. Please forgive me,' Cassia stammered. She could still hear the chef's voice ranting on when she reached the upper part of the house. Feeling thoroughly dejected, she crept into bed and lay there staring at the bedhangings.

That evening, having returned from his day of sketching, Lord Marchington fixed his grey eyes sternly upon her.

'You must not annoy my servants, my dear Cassia. They are menials, with limited intelligence. Rules and regulations mean everything to them, and if one encroaches on forbidden territory, they are lost at sea so to speak. These rigid rules are made as much for their protection as for ours.'

'I – I am sorry – I only wanted to make myself useful. I have nothing to do here, and I wanted to try to repay you in some way,' Cassia blushed, angry at herself for feeling so ashamed of her harmless behaviour.

'I understand, but surely there is no necessity for you to do menial tasks? You are a lady, you were gently reared. Labouring over a hot stove is not exactly compatible with that upbringing, is it?'

'I have always enjoyed baking, and similar domestic tasks. I realize that you would not be accustomed to women of your class labouring in the kitchen, but I do assure you, I love such work.'

Lord Marchington linked his hands behind his back, his eyes narrowed. For a moment, she thought he was going to shout at her, but then he said:

'Have you been in my library? Have you seen my collection of books? Some are the previous occupant's choice, but mostly they are mine, books which I brought with me.'

'No, my lord, I did not go in the library. May I do so?' Cassia's face shone.

'Of course. And there are books in there to please the widest predilections. I have no objection to a lady studying.'

Dinner was served then, and it was delicious roast beef in a piquant sauce, with six different vegetables and iced pudding to follow. Not the stolid iced pudding Cassia had known in London and which settled in the stomach like lead. This pudding, thanks to Armand's culinary skill, was light and fluffy, melting in the mouth.

Lord Marchington sent for a bottle of port to end the meal, but Cassia did not like its strong, cloying taste. When he saw her trying to hide this, Marchington rang for Earlton and asked him to bring a decanter of a light French wine that Cassia found delightful.

While Sigismund snored in staccato tones by the fire, and Basil stretched out on his back, with all four legs in the air, Cassia and her host sipped their drinks and sank into a peaceful, domestic mood. Anyone looking into the room would have taken them for a contented, much-married couple sitting tranquilly together by the hearth before retiring to the same bed.

Only Cassia knew how she yearned for the Earl to be her lost lover; how she looked at her rescuer from time to time, seeing Vincent in his place with his glossy black hair and emerald eyes, that beloved wry smile on his face.

Oh Vincent, Vincent, where are you? What are you doing now? she sighed silently, but, like her half-remembered dream, the French Captain seemed a world away from her.

That night she had a dream. It was not the falling, drowning dream which she had from time to time, nor the one where her lover held her in his arms, but the dream where she and Vincent had seen one another from a distance. They were walking, running, towards one another, arms outstretched, and then just as she reached him, he faded from her sight and her arms closed on emptiness. She woke in tears, the night had never seemed darker or more terrifying. For once, she was glad of Ali's snores as he lay on guard outside her door.

She stayed awake for some time aching to have Vincent beside her. She imagined him holding her, caressing her and kissing her breasts, covering her body with his so that she curved up to meet his thrusts with joyful ecstasy. Facing cold reality, she felt desperately lonely and isolated. She longed to go in search of her lover, but she knew how wildly impractical any such scheme would be and that her only chance of survival in this foreign land was to stay hidden in the house.

CHAPTER TWENTY-THREE

In the Kiosk of Pearls, the Pasha's sister Jasmina lay on silk tasselled cushions sipping mint sherbet from a jewelled goblet. In the gardens just outside the Kiosk walked the man she had loved now for many months. He had been brought to her in a sorry condition by her slaves, her physicians had despaired of his life, but she had never lost hope. Not for one second. She had seen his beautiful face and the glossy black hair, the brilliant emerald eyes, the broad strong shoulders and slender waist, and she had wanted him. Widowed when young, she had returned to her brother's court where she had made a place for herself. Her brother, who adored her, had no wish for her to marry again and leave him. Muslim widows had far greater power and freedom than Muslim maidens and wives. The richer they were the more freedom they were able to claim. Jasmina had made her place secure by helping her brother's people with their problems. The poor and the unfortunate with their petty disputes and wrangles came to her and she never failed them. She was known in her brother's domain as The One with Much Heart.

Had she not set eyes on Vincent Sauvage, she would have remained content with her life, but once having seen him and desired him as her husband, she could not rest until they were married. He would have to become a Muslim before the ceremony, but she was quite sure that he would not baulk at that. He had seemed grateful for her careful nursing, and she had seen how his eyes admired her. Naturally he was weak after his great loss of blood but in time she was more than sure that his passion would equal hers.

It was not easy for her to be patient, but she had skilfully drawn the handsome Captain closer and closer into her mesh, assured of his eventual submission. Then, when she believed the time right, and had proposed to him, he told her that he was already affianced, that he loved a girl named Cassia Morbilly – an English girl abducted by his great enemy, Nathan Dash. He was, he told Jasmina, determined to recover his health so that he could find his love, and revenge himself on Dash.

Jasmina had been stunned. Employing all her consummate artistry, she had managed to sound sympathetic, sisterly. She offered to despatch her servants in search of the girl. She knew Dash well, she said, and feigned horror at having purchased items from such a dastardly villain.

'He sold you merchandise?' Vincent said, astonished.

'Jewels, gowns, materials, perfumes, and such,' she had replied, wringing her hands together and shaking her head from side to side as if in dismay. 'If I had only known what sort of man he was, I would never have granted him an audience.'

'Do not blame yourself,' Vincent replied reassuringly. 'How could you have known? Would you show me what merchandise he sold you?'

'Of course,' she smiled, ordering her women to bring some of the gowns and jewels for Vincent to see. He was lying in his bed propped up on soft pillows covered with delicate lawn, in a room lavishly furnished in sea-green and gold. In one corner a fountain sang, and lilies splayed their wax-white petals on the water's surface. The pacific beauty of the room dimmed as Vincent recognized two of the gowns and some of the jewels that he had last seen worn by Cassia. Memories crowded into his mind; sorrow washed over him.

Jasmina felt her heart constrict as she saw the expression on his face, and a furious, wild jealousy rose within her. Swallowing her dismay, she ordered two of her chief eunuchs to make enquiries as to the whereabouts of Nathan Dash. They were also to find out, very discreetly, where Cassia Morbilly was, and return at once with their news.

Days, weeks passed, and the men came back silent from each sortie. Then one day they heard a drunken sailor shouting in the streets, and recognized him as one of Dash's men. They brought him to the palace, sobered him up, and led him to Jasmina herself for questioning. He told her everything. Dash's lust for the English girl, his attack on *The Poseidon*, the wounding of Captain Sauvage, the abduction of the girl. Saying nothing about Vincent, Jasmina asked the sailor where the English girl was now. With Dash? 'No,' he replied. 'She tried to knife Dash, and in a fury he sold her to the Grand Turk. She is now in Constantinople, in the Grand Seraglio.'

Jasmina thanked her informant, paid him handsomely, then instructed her deaf mute to escort him to the rear gate of the palace and strangle him.

Thinking herself safe, Jasmina hurried to Vincent to tell him that his woman was now one of the royal concubines. He must forget her. No concubine ever came out of the Grand Seraglio alive. She was overjoyed at this happy solution, honestly believing that the man she had set her heart on would now see reason and marry her. She had also been saved the task of having the girl murdered.

Vincent fell silent when he heard the news. For a day he said very little; he seemed to have taken it badly – or so she thought. She refused to attach any significance to this for she always got what she wanted. Allah was all-powerful, all-generous. Had he not helped her to rid herself of the vile old husband whom she had loathed?

Vincent said nothing of his plans for rescuing Cassia. He knew himself to be still too weak to travel, and besides, he would have to devise a faultless plan. The Grand Seraglio was as staunchly guarded as a prison and the Turks were dangerous people when angered. While he concentrated on regaining his health, Vincent thought about Cassia. He knew how foolish he had been not to admit that he loved her while they were together. It had taken near death and her loss to show him on the one hand that life was meaningless without her, and on the other, that there was no excuse on earth for his career as a slave dealer. At last he devised a plan, chose his time carefully and while the palace slept he slipped away, heading along the coast for Constantinople and the Grand Seraglio.

Tears of rage filled Jasmina's eyes when she found his bed empty the next morning. He had deserted her – she would not forgive him. Even her brother failed to soften her fury. As soon as he had left her suite she despatched her deaf mutes to bring Vincent back.

The fight was a savage one. Vincent killed two of the deaf mutes and wounded another, but finally they overpowered him, for they were some half dozen and he only one. When he stood before Jasmina again, he was in chains, and she at her most entrancing. Vincent thought only of Cassia, waiting for his return, believing that he had betrayed her again. Through the mists of anger and grief he heard Jasmina promising that he would be freed from his chains if he swore that he would stay with her. Angrily, he refused.

From that moment onwards, he was closely guarded day and night and not until Jasmina's spies brought her the news of the drowning of the English girl did she relax. Allah had answered her prayers. It had only needed faith – and determination.

'It is best that you forget her,' she told Vincent, after giving him the news. 'Allah had a hand in this. He has decided that you and I shall be lovers, husband and wife until the end of our days. Oh, I can make you happy, you know that I can,' she had coaxed. 'My brother is old and has no sons. He will be happy to leave his lands to my husband when he dies. You and I shall reign here together.'

Vincent did not answer. Turning his head away, he gave her the only response possible – cold rebuffal.

She did not lose hope. Now that she knew Allah was on her side, she worked towards the day when she and Vincent would be married. He was a passionate man, she knew it, and one day when he had mourned his fill he would turn to her. She would be waiting to console him, to show him the meaning of true love. Meanwhile, she would engage his help in ruling her brother's lands and people; he would be taught all that she knew and more, and he would be present with her in her audience chamber when she received supplicants. That way, the people would become accustomed to seeing him and it would be no shock to them when he eventually replaced her brother.

Cassia still had not managed to befriend Earlton. The strange little butler refused to speak to her save when his master was present, and even then permitted himself only the tersest rejoinders. She could not think why he hated her. Perhaps he was a misogynist and treated all women with equal loathing. Had her father not been the same? Maybe he blamed his deformity on his mother, and ranked all women with her?

Putting aside her thoughts on Earlton, Cassia took full advantage of the permission she had been given to visit the library. Books grey with dust filled the library shelves from floor to ceiling, volumes of every size and content. She found a cookbook full of Cornish recipes and a wave of longing gripped her. What would her aunt be doing now? She dearly hoped that Julitta would have fully recovered and be finding pleasure in watching Satan's foal growing up. A copy of *A trumpet Blast Against the Monstrous Regiment of Women* by John Knox made her think of her father – without nostalgia.

She had found a history of the Dukes of Bourne, and was reading about the duke who had had this house built on the island, when her host entered the library. She thought that he looked especially handsome, his silver-grey hair neatly groomed, his eyes sparkling.

'My dear, it is a beautiful day and the gardens look so colourful. Some fresh air would benefit you, so I came to escort you outside if that would please you.'

Cassia stood up, delighted. 'That would be marvellous.' This was such a change from being told that she must stay in bed that she could not help but feel excited.

Marchington offered her his arm and led her out through the house. The scene which greeted her was one of brilliant colours, rambling, natural beauty and above were china-blue skies without a cloud in view. Breathing deeply, Cassia walked down the drive with her rescuer, looking from left to right at the shrubs and trees, flowers and stone statuettes placed at strategic intervals. Somebody had gone to a great deal of trouble to have the gardens laid out in the Italian style, but they had long been neglected and acquired a rioting attractiveness of their own, which Cassia far preferred to the clean-cut, severe lines now in vogue in England. She adored overgrown shrubs and hedges, masses of blooms, and winding pathways edged with scented shrubs. There was a secluded arbour overhung with fat pink roses; their perfume lingered alluringly in the air and made her homesick for England. She sat down on the little rustic seat.

The Earl sat down beside her, the bench creaking beneath his bulk. Then he casually took her arm.

'You like flowers?'

'I love them – how I have missed English gardens – the harem gardens were beautiful, but there is nothing as refreshing and lovely as roses, is there?'

She leaned across to sniff at one of the fat pink blooms, unaware of Lord Marchington's eyes sweeping covetously over her, across her breasts and down to her hips. She fancied that his arm gave a little movement where it touched hers, but when she turned round his face was as smiling and genial as ever.

'Now we should return to the house for some refreshment. I do not want to overtire you,' he beamed, drawing her to her feet, his huge hands clasping hers. For a second or two longer than necessary he held her hands, looking down into her eyes as if wishing to explore their depths, and then he led her back towards the house. He could see that she did not recall anything of their time in bed together, which was as he had expected, for the drug was powerful.

Earlton awaited them in the drawing room with a tray of seedcakes and a flask of wine.

Cassia sat in the window seat, half turned towards the leaded panes so that she could still see the gardens. The Earl handed her her wine, and she sipped it absently, still thinking of the roses. The wine had a slightly acrid taste, and she gritted her teeth. Another of those strong wines which her rescuer so loved. She looked across at him. He was pouring himself a second goblet. Shrugging, she continued to drink, trying to erase the acrid taste with the seedcakes.

They talked for a little longer, and then Cassia began to feel tired. She knew of old this sudden exhaustion that swept over her, and that it was useless to fight it. She attempted to hide her yawn but Leo Marchington's sharp eyes saw it; he immediately took her arm and insisted that she retire to her bed.

'My dear, I knew that I was taking a risk inviting you outside and now I fear that I have drained you of what little energy you have. It was foolish of me, and you must return to bed at once and sleep. If you should become ill again, I would blame myself entirely.'

Yawning again, Cassia leaned on his arm. She felt bemused, asleep on her feet, and frightened too that what her host said might be true. She was terrified of having a relapse and becoming helpless again.

She was stumbling by the time they reached the corridor outside her room, and she only half saw Ali watching them pass, his face full of concern. Then Marchington was lifting her as if she were a doll and tucking her into the soft clean bed and she was asleep in an instant.

It was dark when she woke and the house was silent. Then as she was trying to rouse herself from the remnants of sleep, she heard the eerie screeching of Lord Marchington's owl. It was a terrifying noise, and exactly like someone being tortured or murdered. She sat up, her head spinning. There was not even a candle alight in the room. She called Ali's name, her voice sounding quavery in her ears. He was beside her in an instant.

'White lady wake, hungry? Ali get food. Master out — gone ride. Ali care for lady.'

Cassia leaned back; the effort of sitting up had drained her. Why did she feel so feeble? Ali returned with slices of meat and hot chocolate, fruit in a bowl, and fresh cream syllabub. Cassia felt ravenous but her arms were so leaden that they ached when she lifted them. Ali helped her to eat, ministering to her as if she were a baby. He was gentle, and patient, and she was moved by his kindness.

Afterwards she felt tired again, and Ali said that he would guard her door as usual while she slept. He looked anxious, his eyes creased with lines. Sighing, she closed her eyes again, and fell back into deep slumber.

The Pasha's people soon became accustomed to seeing Vincent Sauvage with their Princess. He was, she told them, attracted to the Muslim religion and when he had learned its rules he would be accepted into their faith. She also made it known that she would one day marry the French Captain whom she loved and trusted implicitly. She did not mention this in front of Vincent, who continued to be morose, although he was moved by the plight of many of the supplicants who came before them, and could not repress his desire to help those in distress. It was necessary for the Princess or her interpreter to translate when the supplicants spoke only Turkish, but when they could speak French, as some could, Vincent would often see them alone. This way they were able to help more people than before.

Vincent enjoyed this part of his day. He was able to fill his thoughts with the problems of others, which was an excellent panacea for his own indissoluble problem, and made him feel that he was redressing some of the wrong he had done during his years as a pirate. He was also grateful for any opportunity to escape the Princess's attentions. He found that Cassia's memory did not dim with passing time but made any pretence of desiring Jasmina almost impossible.

Weeks passed, and his grief did not abate. He brooded incessantly on Cassia's terrible death – gloatingly reconstructed for him by Jasmina. Again and again he reproached himself for selfishness in seeking her out so rashly. If he had never visited the harem she might still be alive now.

He wondered painfully what her choice would have been – his idealistic Cassia. Death or royal slavery? One last, glorious night of love, or the possibility of a career as a Kadine, mother, perhaps, of the Sultan's heir? He thought he could guess what she would have said, and it made his pain more intense rather than less, for it brought her so sharply to mind. So hopeful, so vividly alive, so passionately loving. So dead. Tied in a sack like a drowned kitten and cast to the bottom of the sea. It was said that the sea bed was covered with the sacks of hundreds drowned at their Sultan's command, of concubines who had displeased in some way. They might have been faithless, or they might simply have bored their royal master. Some had even died because the Sultan wished to clear out the harem and start again.

Vincent, tormented by these thoughts, tried to occupy every minute of his waking life. He also tried to avoid the Princess as much as possible. But it was her palace, her home, her domain. To avoid her was like trying to avoid himself.

It was not that she was unpleasing visually, or in any way repulsive. He just did not want to be involved with anyone. Jasmina was insisting now that Vincent study the Muslim religion daily, in preparation for his acceptance into the faith. To keep her at bay he did so, welcoming the use of this time in which to plot his escape. The lack of freedom was beginning to crush him, but at least he was lulling the Princess into belief that he was adjusting peaceably to his new life. She was impressed by his work with the people, his diligent studies, and his tranquil outward air. She believed that Cassia's death had removed his desire to escape. How wrong she was. He still wanted revenge on Nathan Dash and he had now decided that he would go to America to start a new life. He had friends there, men whom he had met through his sea-faring existence, and who had gone to the Colonies to make their fortunes legally.

Imperceptibly, Jasmina began to relax the guard on him. She wanted above all for him to think of the palace as a home. She believed that he would respond to her with a greater warmth if every move were not being watched by hostile eyes.

She was right in one respect. Once the guard was relaxed, Vincent did respond with a greater warmth, but the warmth was directed to his immediate escape. At midnight one night he put round his waist the money belt that he had made in secret, and inside it he tucked the gold coins and small objects of value which were gifts from Jasmina. He then made his way stealthily along the corridors of the palace, climbed over one of the balconies and out onto the roof of the Kiosk of Pearls in the gardens. The filigree work of the Kiosk gave him hand and footholds, and he was soon making his way into the stables to saddle up one of the stallions. Minutes later, he was heading for the hills, the night air blissfully cool against his face, the newfound freedom exhilarating him beyond measure.

To be free, to be on horseback and alone, without the omnipresent eunuchs with their cold, menacing eyes was glorious. He had ridden for some five hours and the horse was tiring, when he saw, stretched out far beyond him, the sea, its colour pewtered-silver in the dawn light. Joy bubbled through him. The sea, his old love, and there waiting patiently for him. He had but to reach her, and she would be his again.

He had been travelling for eight hours when the deaf mutes caught up with him. They had ridden with such fury that two of their horses had dropped dead. They had scoured the villages through which they had passed, and they found Vincent asleep in the loft of an old derelict cottage, his stallion resting in a barn. The horse was winded, or he would have ridden on without pausing, but he could not risk trying to purchase another mount. He had deliberately avoided the villages. But his efforts had been fruitless. They had found him anyway. Two of them had been in the company which had brought him back from Constantinople, and they hated him. There was venom in their eyes when

344

they kicked him awake, but they dared not do him any serious damage for fear of the Princess's wrath.

He was taken back to the palace in chains. He had thought of fighting his way out but there were ten of them and he had known that even if he could kill two or three, he could not overpower ten. Raging with fury, he saw the palace loom into view, and such loathing filled him that he would have tried to fight his way out then, despite the odds, had he not been so heavily chained. His anger pulsed for some time, and eventually gave way to a dull rage. He would not give in. They might have captured him this time, but there would be another time and another – he would never cease trying to escape. He would die before he surrendered his soul.

The Princess was waiting for him in the audience chamber. Her face was twisted with rage. Her disappointment at his defection overruled her commonsense. She ordered Vincent to be flogged publicly. He stood before her in chains, his ankles manacled, his face stony. When she pronounced the method of his punishment, he did not move one muscle. He simply looked through her as if she were not there.

The flogging watched by the Pasha and his court was a rare event, for Vincent was the first free man to receive this ignominious punishment. His wrists were tied with thongs to a cross bar, from which he was suspended. He hung there for thirty minutes before Jasmina gave the executioner leave to begin. The whip sang through the air, striping Vincent's back with brilliant crimson weals, five, ten, fifteen, twenty, thirty lashes. Not by one flicker of pain did Vincent display the agony he was undergoing. It was Jasmina who weakened first. Jumping to her feet, she ordered the flogging to be stopped and Vincent released; and then, white-faced, she hurried to tend him herself. Only half-conscious, he turned his face away from her, gritting his teeth.

During the days that followed Vincent continued to refuse to speak to her. Nor would he meet her eyes. She did everything in her power to coerce him into talking, she even demeaned herself by apologizing, but still he would not unbend. He would not take any medicaments from her hands, nor would he allow her to bring him food. She felt like a pariah, as he had intended she should. If he felt like weakening, he had only to think of his ride to freedom and his vision of the silver seas in the distance before his recapture. This woman had deprived him of that, of his freedom and his chance for revenge on Nathan Dash. He detested her.

Jasmina was torn in two. She knew that she must have a double guard watching over him from now on, and yet he would loathe her even more if he saw eunuchs everywhere he went. She had badly misjudged events at a time when she wished to show him who was ruler here and that he could not escape her. She had forgotten that he was not one of her brother's peoples, that he was not a Muslim, nor raised as one, and that in his land men always had mastery over women. Repressing her misgivings, she ordered the guard to be extra vigilant by day and by night, and she then attempted to throw herself into the preparations for her brother's anniversary celebrations.

She found some pleasure in selecting new materials for the gowns that she planned to wear for the celebrations. The Pasha would have been ruler of Bada-Alhim for twenty years; there would be festivities throughout his domain. Jasmina had decided that she would give her brother a feast to remember, one filled with colour and incident, and of course beautiful young girls. After that his 'illness' would begin. It might end swiftly or be lingering depending on the quality and quantity of poisons she chose to administer. If he died now, there would be shock and chaos because there was no heir of his body. If he died later, when she had eventually won Vincent round and married him, there would be less upheaval, but more time for her brother to detect her plans.

Jasmina selected blue silk for one gown, diaphanous and starred with silver rosebuds, for another, rose satin beaded with gold and a deeper pink, and oyster brocade fringed with gold. Then she picked white muslin sprigged with blue flowers – a material which her supplier had said was all the rage in London. Vincent should like that; it would remind him of his English girl. Jasmina held up the sprigged muslin in front of her and looked in the mirror. She would have the muslin made up in a similar style to the court gowns that she had purchased from Nathan Dash and put away when she discovered who they had belonged to. Vincent would have been furious had she continued to wear them. It was a pity for they were sumptuous.

She chose new jewels, emeralds and rubies, diamonds and black pearls as large as her thumbnails. She bought new perfumes, patchouli, and musk, which was said to incense a man's passions, and she practised different methods of painting her face. The Pasha gave her a huge ruby on a gold chain. She had never seen such a splendid gem.

'It is known as the Barbarossa Ruby,' he told her as she fastened it round her neck and admired its florid colour between her pale coffee breasts. She and her brother were lying together on a daybed draped with silver tissue, drinking ambergris sherbet and eating *Rahat Lokum* flavoured with almonds. Jasmina had discarded her entari so that she could admire the ruby to better advantage, and it glowed like a second heart against her naked breasts. Aware of her brother's eyes upon her body, she half smiled. She knew he adored her, that he had been glad she was widowed and had come back to him. She had been eleven when he first made love to her, for his predilections were for young unformed girls but she had captured his affections and held on to them tightly, for that suited her. Secretly she thought him an old lecher and yet she was relieved he had never sired a son. It made it all the easier for her future husband.

Jasmina thought of her childhood. She and the Pasha were in fact only half brother and sister, for her father had had many women. He died when she was small, but she had hardly missed him, for her mother had doted on her. Then her mother had been poisoned. Jasmina had always thought it was because she was expecting a child who might have been a son to rival the future Pasha. The obvious suspect was his mother and the young Princess promised herself then and there that if she could find a shred of proof she would kill her. It had been a time of terrible fear and sorrow for Jasmina, but her brother had protected her throughout. He had declared his love for her, and later that love had been consummated. After that, he visited her bed every night for four years until her breasts began to bud.

She now looked up at him, wondering what he was thinking. He knew nothing of her skill with poisons, a skill that she had carefully developed after her mother's death, with thoughts of revenge in her mind. Her first victim was her half-brother's mother. Later, she had despatched her old husband. It would be a small thing to poison her brother too, for he was already far older than she. His hair was grizzled and thinning, his skin parched and embossed with lines, his eyes faded. An illness a few years ago had robbed him of much of his vigour and it had never returned.

'I have found some new girls for your anniversary feast, brother dear,' Jasmina said, caressing his beige, parched hand. 'Sweet nubile young creatures from one of the villages. They are eager to meet you and to show you their dances.'

The Pasha's eyes glowed. 'They are young? Very young?'

'But of course, dear brother. I would not waste time with girls who did not interest you. One is only ten, the slenderest sweetest creature with long black hair and skin like cream. You will adore her. But first of course I must train her for she is an uncouth creature of low stock and she has no idea how to address a prince.'

'Do not train her too well, sister, for I shall look forward to doing that . . .' The Pasha took his sister's hand and kissed it fervently, while Jasmina looked up at him shyly, beneath her painted lids, her lips curving into an angelic smile.

CHAPTER TWENTY-FOUR

Cassia felt weak and her mind foggy for some days after her stroll in the gardens with Lord Marchington. It could only be that she had over-taxed her strength, just as he had feared. He was wise, she now realized and she must listen to him in future.

He visited her morning and evening, bringing her gifts. Books to read, a scented pomander filled with attar of roses, red wine to replenish her blood, and this he always insisted she drank in his presence, for it was part of her treatment he said, smiling.

She was grateful and touched by his thoughtfulness, and now determined to heed his advice.

'No doubt this is a delayed reaction to your terrible experience,' he said, refilling her goblet with wine. 'The body is very astute. It knows what it needs and will demand it. It is vital that you rest now for as long as possible, or you will strain your delicate reserves even more.'

Cassia smiled up at him, 'You are so very knowledgeable about these things, my lord. I don't know how I would have got better without your care.'

'I have enjoyed looking after you, my dear. The pleasure of your presence is more than enough reward.' He leaned towards her, touching her throat lightly with his fingers. 'And would it not be easier if you called me Leo? You would not object?'

'Object? Why no, of course not – Leo,' Cassia said, her skin tingling where he had touched her. Absently, she raised her own hand to let her fingers brush the place where he had caressed her.

The Earl saw this gesture and smiled to himself. It would not be long now. As he had guessed, she was a creature who needed gentle courting, at a slow, relaxed pace. If he had forced himself upon her at once, he would have terrified

349

her; she would have been alienated, and that he did not want. His women must be willing, eager. It was not necessary that they loved him, but they must submit to his desires, for force repelled him. In truth, he had rarely met an unwilling female; from Moll onwards, all women had been eager. He had soon brought round the few who had not been to his way of thinking for there were methods of coercing even the most stubborn.

He would prefer not to use them with this exquisite creature who now looked up at him so trustingly from her pillows . . . but impatience was beginning to get the better of him. He found her presence unbearably exciting, for on the one hand he conversed with her like a civilized woman, on the other he longed to use her as the harem slave she really was. He knew that she would be skilled in all the deviations and perversions of love and that her body, like a fine lute, had been tuned to an extraordinarily high level of arousal. All women were whores at heart – none knew that better than he – but this one had been trained in the most sophisticated brothel in the world. What obsessed him now was the problem of making her his, body and soul. At last, reluctantly, he had conceded that in the Western world there was only one way a man could make a woman his property for life, and that was to marry her.

Once attuned to the notion that Cassia would become his wife, the Earl found the concept rather titillating. In the sinful darkness of their private life she would be a slut, the wanton, performing her whore's tricks for his secret pleasure. In public she would be Lady Marchington, his pure and untouchable girl-bride, who in time would become a celebrated society beauty, and a famous artist's model.

During the following week Cassia's strength slowly returned. Marchington spoke of her coming downstairs to dine with him, but told her sternly that she must obey his commands if he allowed her such activity.

'Of course I shall do as you say,' she replied. 'I have no wish to be ill again, and cause you so much inconvenience.'

He took her hand, squeezing the soft white flesh in his

own broad grip. How strong he was, his hands like iron, and yet he could paint such exquisite pictures. Not for the first time she marvelled at his dexterity.

'Inconvenience? Have I not told you more than once that your sweet presence is my great delight?' Raising her hand to his lips, he kissed it, once, then twice, while Cassia flushed a rosy pink and she lowered her eyelids to hide her discomfort. He did not release her hand, but caged it in his.

'I – but you came here to sketch and to paint, and you had not planned to be taking care of an invalid.'

'I have months yet in which to do my work. And at the moment I am carefully studying the subject of my future painting,' he gazed down at her intently, his eyes glittering, his hand fiercely gripping hers even more. Cassia flushed again.

'You – you truly want to paint – me?'

'Indeed. From the first instant that I saw you, I knew you would one day be my subject. I want to paint you in every pose, every guise, as Venus, a nereid, a siren, as yourself.' He could not keep the excitement from his voice.

'I see.' Cassia did not know whether she felt flattered or alarmed. It was true that she found it pleasing to so have impressed an artist, but on the other hand, she had not planned to stay with him indefinitely. If she returned to England with him she would go straight to Penwellyn, to join her aunt.

'But what will happen when you go back to London?' she now said, trying to keep her voice from trembling as she unsuccessfully attempted to free her hand.

'But you will be coming with me, my dear, what else? I cannot part with such a charming model can I? Had you imagined that I could leave you here, friendless and without money?' He now took both her hands in his, looking down at her with eyes which shone like silver coins when the light caught them. 'You will come with me to London of course, to my home, and there I will paint your portrait and make you famous. Your picture will be hung at my

351

next exhibition, and all of London will come to view you and marvel at your radiance.'

Cassia bit her lip. 'I – of course I want to show my gratitude for all that you have done for me, and it is not that I am not immensely grateful, because of course I am. I shall always, always, be in your debt, but if – if I go back to England I shall be going to live with my aunt. I miss her so, and I know that she will have missed me. I will want to stay with her – she needs me.' As soon as she had spoken, she regretted it, for the Earl dropped her hands and stood up, his face darkening.

'So you will leave me?' he said, his voice sounding strangled. 'My dear, you do not think that I offer this lightly, do you? I want you to be mine – forever, if you wish.'

Cassia hid her perturbation with difficulty. Whatever did he mean? Was he proposing marriage? How on earth could she answer without offence? But he was speaking again.

'You are taken by surprise – of course, I quite understand. You are a lady of sensitivity and now I have rushed you. I have no wish to hasten you into something so serious. I will give you time to see that it is the best solution. You are everything I have ever wanted in a woman,' he confessed. 'Your beauty and sweetness have won me entirely, and if you should decide against becoming mine you will make me the unhappiest man on this earth.'

Cassia felt hot with embarrassment. A sense of unreality washed over her. Had she really heard aright – he wanted to marry her? He wanted her to become Lady Marchington? Commonsense told her that this could not possibly be so. He hardly knew her. She did not love him. He was too old. If not marriage, then what? Housekeeper, mistress? In a turmoil of bewilderment, revulsion, and remorse at her ingratitude to one who had been so unstintingly generous, she replied:

'You – you have indeed startled me, sir. I – we hardly know one another, that is –'

'That is true,' he interjected firmly, 'but isn't marriage the most amiable way of getting to know one another? What could be more delightful than exploration within the confines of such a relationship?'

'Marriage, my lord . . . Leo . . . Oh heavens!' She wished she didn't feel so leaden, so confused. The suggestion was impossible, ridiculous . . . but, said a small voice, if Vincent has married his Muslim princess, what is left for you?

'So please, my dear Cassia, think about what I have said, and do not gainsay me or you will break my heart!' He looked at her steadily, his grey eyes so clear, yet so compelling. His gaze was almost mesmeric; she felt her resistance ebbing away . . . To extricate herself from the awkwardness of the moment, she said that she would think about it, and that she hoped he would be patient with her.

'I – I am hardly recovered from my illness and I shall need time to consider. Please grant me that.'

'Of course, my dear!' he said, taking her hands again and raining kisses upon them, holding himself back from closer intimacies only with an effort. He wanted to get into bed with her, to kiss her into a frenzy of passion, cover her white body with his and thrust himself inside her repeatedly. He wanted to confirm possession of his slave, to mark her out as his and his alone.

When he had gone, and Ali had brought in her coffee, she looked up at him, her eyes shadowed.

'White lady in great dilemma?' he said, acutely aware of her moods. 'Tell Ali.'

'I can't Ali – it would not be fair to – to someone. I shall just have to think about my dilemma and see what can be done about it. But, oh, it is very awkward.'

'Lady in trouble Ali always help. Tell Ali if need help and Ali do all he can. Ali think of his red-headed lady, lost to him, and he want help you because of her. Our secret, yes?'

Cassia smiled. 'You are indeed kind, Ali. Thank you. Yes, I will let you know if I need your help.'

The Earl had been so brave saving her life, so generous and attentive since he had brought her to his house. She had grown to like him but the mention of marriage had terrified her. What on earth was she to do? Leo Marchington's proposal had brought home her predicament to her with terrible force. She knew that she could not bear the thought of living with another man after loving Vincent, yet she was honest enough to admit that she was terrified of a lonely middle age, mourning a lover who had long since married another woman and given her children. Wild despair swept over her as she thought of the time that had elapsed since her rescue, time that could have been put to good use finding Vincent Sauvage. Time that she had spent in lethargic dullness, while she should have confessed her love to Lord Marchington and implored his help. Tears started to her eyes, remorse, hopelessness, and anger at her own stupidity flooded her heart.

She saw only too clearly where her feeble-mindedness had led her. She had encouraged Leo Marchington to think that his suit might prosper. She dreaded telling him that there was no hope for him. It was a dread born partly from her genuine sense of obligation, and partly from the fact that she had grown to fear the crystal coldness of his eyes and the frigid menace in his voice when he was displeased. An instinct told her that he would be a dangerous man to cross.

She thought about all this until her head ached, and then she slept during the afternoon, to wake with her mind still tormented. Remembering that she was dining with the Earl that evening, she tried to make her one hastily-assembled dress more feminine. Ali brought her thread and needles and she made a shoulder cape from the remnants of the white sheet that she had used for the sarong. Ali brought her a selection of Turkish-style slippers, backless and with toes that curved slightly upwards. She tried them on until she found a pair that was not too large. If she kept her feet hidden she would not feel too odd.

Ali admired her in the finished gown. 'Much nice lady. Like goddess of old days, all in white. Hmm,' he rubbed his hands together appreciatively.

'Thank you, Ali. I fear that I would not pass muster in a London drawing room, but at least my shoulders are now covered. I wish these slippers were not so loose – if one falls off, I will feel so silly!'

Ali at once lifted his hand, forefinger raised. 'Ali get paper to stuff toes. Simple.'

He returned with some paper which he screwed up and pushed down into the front of the slippers. It cramped Cassia's toes a little, but the slippers felt more secure.

That evening Armand prepared a very special dinner *à deux*, of roast chicken in honey and almond sauce, and Lord Marchington sent for a wine which he said he had been keeping for just such an occasion. He looked formidably smart in a cherry velvet suit, and his linen was, as always, starched and immaculate. Despite her misgivings, Cassia found that she was drawn to him. He emanated a strength and confidence, which, after all she had been through she found irresistible. She felt that no one would dare harm her while he was present. Suddenly the other life seemed infinitely far away – aeons ago – a distant, shadowy memory that had never really had any true meaning.

She had little appetite and the meal dragged on interminably. Despite her protests, the Earl kept refilling her glass.

At last bedtime saved her from further embarrassment. Her host escorted her up to her room, leaving her at the door as any gentleman would. It was as if he had never nursed her through her week of fever or seen her naked and helpless – as she knew he must. She was heartily thankful for it. He had never referred to those days except to remind her of how very ill she had been.

Bowing over her hand, then raising it to his lips, the Earl kissed her palm, and then the tip of each finger, his grey eyes inscrutable. Blushing, Cassia thanked him, and then turned into her room as hastily as she could without causing offence. Leaning against the door, she breathed a sigh of relief.

She woke with a start. How long had she slept? Was that a sound outside her door? 'Ali?' she called, but there was no reply. She slept again, deeply, helped by the wine her host had forced on her. When the door swung open, and the man approached her bed, she did not hear. He was naked beneath his black cloak, and he gently lifted the covers back off the bed to look down at the shapely white body lying there. His reaction was immediate, and savage. Gritting his teeth, he slipped into the bed and pulled Cassia into his arms, crushing her against him, his breath increasing in intensity so that it rasped in his throat. He should not be here – but how could he stop himself? She was so desirable. He needed her, wanted her desperately. How soft and heavy her breasts were. He nuzzled his face in them, then kissed her stomach and lower, his breathing harsh.

'Wh-who is that?' she gasped – 'Oh, O-o-h,' she sighed, as he kissed her thighs and moved between them, exploring with his tongue. In her drugged stupor, she could not resist, but this time it was clear to her who the man was. Marchington. This was no erotic dream to be pushed out of memory; this was *real*. 'Leo,' she whispered, and he curved his powerful arms round her so that she could not have escaped even had she wished. He was like iron, solid, hard, she could feel him pressing against her thighs. She knew what was going to happen, and her own passion was beginning. She sighed again, acquiescing to her fate, unable to stop herself or him, the drugs draining the last of her resistance. He moved over her, murmuring her name along with those words that she remembered from her erotic dream, and then she knew the truth. But she did not care; she could not help herself now.

Then, when she wanted it to happen more than anything, he let out a cry. She stared up at him, her vision blurring as he moved away and left the bed, tugging at the end of his cloak which had become lodged beneath her. 'No!' he cried again, as if in torment, and then he turned on his heel to leave her staring after him, thoroughly bemused. What had she done? Why had he gone like that? Disappointment encompassed her; she had felt safe in his strong arms, she had been so sure that it would happen, and now . . .

She stared bleakly into the dark. In some way she had disappointed him. She was not what he had been expecting.

356

Had her passionate response displeased him? Was that it? But she could deliberate no longer, for sleep was capturing her and she could not fight it. Down, down she sank into velvet blackness. When morning arrived, she remembered only fragments of the night before.

But two aspects of her experience were clearly imprinted on her unhappy mind. One was that Leo Marchington had visited her bed, and the other was that he had left her, while she cried out for fulfilment. The slow tears began to slide down her cheeks. Had her education in the harem, then, been all too effective? Was she now a wanton indeed, tuned to respond to any man who cared to arouse her? She wept bitterly in anguish and shame. She was defiled, dishonoured. She had responded without coercion to a man she did not love and he had turned away from her in disgust. As the storm of weeping subsided, she told herself that she would rather die at the hand of the Sultan's Janissaries, while looking for Vincent, than live in dishonour with the man who had rescued her.

But even had she laid plans to escape, she would not have been able to put them into practice.

She felt unlike herself all day. Not tired, but slow to respond and she yawned frequently. She felt sure that a breath of fresh air would help her, but when she expressed a wish to walk in the gardens, his lordship refused outright.

'If you are unwell, bed is the proper place for you,' he said, cupping her chin in one broad hand and looking deep into her eyes. In vain she searched for some sign of awareness in his gaze, but there was none. Instinct told her that she had best pretend that nothing had happened. With an effort, she forced herself to cajole.

'But I have spent so much time in bed, and I get so bored lying there. I did so enjoy that walk in the gardens with you –'

'Nonetheless, my dear, in your present condition, I feel I should not allow you to take any risks. If anything happened to you, I would never forgive myself. Now that I have found you, I cannot risk losing you.'

357

'But what could possibly happen to me in the gardens here? They are secluded and would you not be with me, anyway?' She would have been angry had she not felt so torpid.

'I was thinking of the climate, and your fragile constitution. Look what happened after that other walk . . .' he cocked his grey head on one side.

Cassia sighed, and decided to say no more. At the moment she did not have the strength to persist. Later, when she felt more hardy, she would insist, and more than that, she would lay plans to leave him.

She visited the library, almost on tiptoe, although she knew that Marchington had gone out riding. Hastily she selected some reading matter, ready for a quick retreat should he return, and then she examined the titles of some of the other volumes more slowly. What a feast of reading there was in here. History, geography, philosophy, cookery, household management, religion, the arts. She came to a shelf of books that did not yield when she tried to remove one of them. One had the intriguing title of *Indoor Pursuits for Confined Gentlewomen*, and she had thought there might be something in it to help her pass her time. But the book would not move, nor would the others on that shelf. Looking more closely, she realized that they were false books, not real ones. She imagined that the old Duke of Bourne who had built the house must have had them designed to fill a gap in his shelving.

She was about to step down from the wooden stairs which were provided to assist those wishing to reach the higher shelves, when she caught her heel in the uneven hem of her gown and almost fell. Clutching at the artificial books, she clung wildly for a few seconds to regain her balance.

There was a whirring noise, then a sequence of clicks, and the shelf of false books slid to one side, revealing a recess some two feet in width. She stared for a few moments, startled, then excitement gathered inside her. A secret compartment. How intriguing. She reached inside, into the darkness, feeling nothing at first and then one or two hard

358

objects that felt like books, and a sheaf of crackling papers. She drew them out.

What she saw made her feel nauseated. Had they belonged to the eccentric old Duke? If so, he must have been a fiend. Pictures of men and women in vile and perverted activities, sketches of women naked and with their legs wide, men with other men doing unnameable things that she had not even thought physically possible . . .

Her excitement was quashed by a sick feeling of disbelief. Hastily replacing the obscene drawings, she searched wildly for the method of closing the compartment. Her fingers ran over the façade of books, in vain. She could not find the device which would move them back across the recess.

Then she heard the clatter of a horse's hooves in the courtyard, and the shout of the grooms as they took Lord Marchington's horse. His booted feet rang on the cobbles round the side of the house as he came from the stables. Breathless with dread, Cassia continued her frenzied search for the closing device. She heard his footfalls at the front of the house, then him entering the hall. Earlton and his master exchanged a few words, and then the Earl began to walk down the hallway towards the library.

Panic was a pain within her; almost sobbing, she ran her hands once more over the books and then to her intense relief she heard the whirring noise, the sequence of clicks, and the books slid back into place. Gasping, she stepped down off the wooden ladder and when Marchington stepped into the library she was sitting at the leather-covered desk, reading *Mortimer's Book of Exotic Flora*.

'You enjoyed your ride,' she said, as lightly as she could manage, her voice sounding strained to her ears. She could not think of anything save the shocking pictures at which she had just been looking. Having seen them, her mind was filled with their images. Did he know they were there, or had they remained a secret since the old Duke's death? She would never mention what she had found, of course. That was quite unthinkable.

They had tea in the drawing-room, Cassia sitting in the

side window seat again, her attention outside on the gardens. The Earl told her about his ride, which had been invigorating but uneventful, and he then said that he planned to make a longer trip to sketch at Bursa.

'I have been yearning to go there for some weeks now. The tombs and mosques of earlier Sultans abound there, and it is, so I am told, the most fabulous of places.'

She must have looked anxious, for he said, 'Ali will look after you. He knows of my trip. And Earlton will attend to your wants. Armand has been instructed to make your favourite dishes – you have only to send your orders to him via Earlton. My dear, please treat my home as yours, which, if my hopes are satisfied, it will shortly become. When you are my wife, there will be no more of this surly nonsense from Earlton. He will accept you then – and if not I shall thrash him until he does.' For a few moments, Leo Marchington's grey eyes were cold and sparkling as frosted glass. Cassia could not think she had heard correctly – was he jesting?

'I had wondered at Earlton's hostility,' Cassia said, helping herself to an almond tartlet.

'He was left on a doorstep when an infant of only a few weeks old. Nuns raised him. They crammed his head with religion and hellfire, and I fear that it tilted his mind. He grew up loathing women, probably because of his mother's desertion and the nuns' rigid upbringing. When he was seven, he was placed in my father's household as a page. He has been with us ever since. There was only one woman he revered and that was my dear late mother. After her death, he became even grimmer. Naturally, he resents anyone whom he thinks aspires to fill her place. But once you are Lady Marchington I am sure that he will see sense. If not, I shall deal with him . . .' His lordship stirred his tea, his eyes now clear and tranquil once more.

'Poor man, he has suffered.'

'But do not forget that he is but a servant, a menial, and as such there is no necessity to waste your sympathies on him. He will survive without them.'

'All the same – to be left on a doorstep, unwanted, unloved.'

'You have a tender heart my dear, and that is just one of the many qualities that I admire about you.'

Cassia lowered her gaze, feeling the heat rush into her cheeks. At least when Marchington left on his trip, she would have some respite from this constant barrage on her sensibilities.

She decided that she would do a number of things while the Earl was away. She would get hold of some decent dress materials and make herself two gowns, one for day, one for evening. She would attempt again to make friends with Earlton; she would explore the house as thoroughly as she could without causing comment amongst the servants. And she would find some way to reach the outside world. More than that she dared not hope for.

She found that she was expected to preside over Marchington's departure. He was taking Tim Bert, and they were furnished with saddle bags containing food and requirements for the journey, as well as all the Earl's art materials. She waved goodbye to them, watching Marchington's powerful equestrian figure disappearing down the drive, and then she looked expectantly at the gardens. Almost as if he had read her mind, a huge, sour-faced man stepped out of the shadow of the house, arms folded across his thick chest, hooded eyes fixed on her. Nervously she stepped back and saw the man taking up his place at the front door, where he was to remain on guard until his master returned.

When she went to the rear door, and opened it, she saw the grooms and stable boys squatting on the cobbles playing dice and cards. They looked up at her, their rough brown faces cold. One got to his feet and walked towards her in a threatening pose, eyes narrowed.

She retreated into the house, shutting the door behind her, her breath catching in her throat. She was a prisoner.

CHAPTER TWENTY-FIVE

Although Vincent still felt some discomfort from the stripe marks on his back, he was determined that he would not neglect his duties, nor would he let Jasmina see that he suffered. He returned to his work with the petitioners as soon as he could move without being tortured by pain. His ribs and back still ached, but he was once more receiving people in Jasmina's audience chamber every morning. She, meanwhile, was coaching the dancers for her brother's anniversary feast. Because the names of the girls were totally unsuitable for the occasion, she had renamed them. Anemone was the one she was sure her brother would desire the most. The names of the others were now Poppy, Muskrose, Alinda and Lalla. They had been bathed and bathed again, their hair had been washed repeatedly. If they were slow to learn or reluctant to do as they were bidden, then Jasmina did not hesitate to slap them soundly. She got a great deal of pleasure out of hearing her palms ringing against their flesh, seeing the scarlet imprint of her hands appearing on their bodies, hearing the sobs as the girls cried for their mothers. They would not see their mothers again, for they had been bought, their prices high. Jasmina did not want any ill feeling amongst the people.

Anemone seemed sensible, and eager to be coached. She had a pointed face, almond-shaped brown eyes and black hair down to her ankles. Her hands and feet were minute, her bones tiny and her chest completely flat without being concave. She could not have weighed more than five stone. Knowing that this girl would bring her brother the most intense delight, Jasmina warmed to Anemone, and smacked her only infrequently.

This morning the girls were dancing together in their new festive costumes. Jasmina kept them closely guarded in a room apart from the main section of the palace. Not even Vincent knew of their existence. She knew that he, as a Westerner, would not tolerate the idea of these little girls being coached for her brother's bed, and she had no wish for the man she loved to scorn her even more.

Having watched the girls perform their dance three times, Jasmina commanded them to do so again. Their little arms and legs ached, but they were terrified of being smacked by the hard-handed Princess, so they obeyed, fighting back tears and yearning for their mothers' arms.

Vincent, with the help of an interpreter, was having excellent success with the petitioners. He had comforted an old woman whose land was being encroached upon by a determined farmer, and he had despatched Jasmina's men to speak to the farmer. He had decided which of two girls a certain man should marry, thus ending a family quarrel that had caused disruption in a village for several months. Vincent found it amazing that the people listened to him, but his authority as the Princess's representative was incredible.

It was now time for the midday meal and Vincent knew that the Princess would be waiting for him in her chamber. However there was still a long queue of people waiting to see him, and he was not prepared to keep them waiting. Even though his back was throbbing with pain, he continued to welcome the suppliants until well into the afternoon, when Jasmina and her guards appeared. The queue of suppliants immediately bowed, parting to let her through. Smiling regally, head high, sumptuous lemon silk robe swirling, Jasmina walked towards the dais where Vincent sat. She seated herself in the massive gilded throne which was reserved for her or her brother. Vincent had been given a smaller seat to the right of this.

'It is going well, Vincent?' Jasmina asked, clicking her fingers at her little black pages who seated themselves cross-legged at her feet.

'Very well, Your Highness. We have had no indissoluble

problems so far, and I seem to be making headway.' He did not look at her.

'You have had an easy day then. Some days are easy. Some are exceedingly hard.' Jasmina smiled, to remind him that she was superior here and that if he had found today's dealings straightforward it was because they had been so and not because of any startling acumen on his part.

Vincent said nothing. Two more petitioners were kneeling before them, awaiting his attention. He did not like to keep them on tenterhooks – it was unmannerly and also bad policy. Jasmina when she chose was quite capable of disappearing for hours at a time while the queue stood in the corridor, and the people grew grey-faced with exhaustion.

He had vowed that, for the rest of the time he must spend here (and that would not be long, for he was determined to escape) he would exercise as much power as Jasmina would allow him. He intended to ensure that no one was ever made to wait too long again.

By the end of that day he was exhausted, aching, and light-headed. The work was not what he would have been doing by choice, although he was discovering that he had a naturally compassionate nature, but he was being useful and that was a reward in itself. He would have felt almost contented had it not been for the prospect of the evening with Jasmina stretching out before him.

She wore a wine-coloured entari fringed with gold silk and the great Barbarossa ruby was suspended between her full breasts. Pearls were entwined in her glossy dark hair and a *ferronière* of pearls lay on her forehead. Rubies, diamonds and emeralds glowed on her fingers and gold slippers encased her feet. She wore a gold chain round one ankle and diamonds shone in her ears. The scent of patchouli billowed around her as she moved. She was beautiful, exotic and voluptuous. In the past he would have felt no hesitation in taking her into his arms, but he could not have done that now for any reward. She represented everything he had come to detest in a woman, and she was his gaoler.

Jasmina hid her fury at Vincent's continuing disinterest. To look her best, to have worked so hard to attract him, and then to be scorned, that was indeed bitter, but she would not lose heart. Allah was with her, she must remember that. Allah was behind her in all she did. She had showed Him that she loved His peoples, which was what He demanded of the faithful. Had she not become famed throughout the country for her charitable deeds? Last year the Sultan himself had sent her an emerald collar. She was known as the One With Much Heart now, and that title never failed to exhilarate her. Allah would see, Allah would be grateful. He would not forget her other needs.

When he was able to excuse himself to go to his own room with the eunuchs padding after him, Vincent undid his money belt and counted its contents. He had managed by careful contrivance to keep its existence a secret when he was captured in the cottage loft. There was a sizeable amount of money and jewellery there. Enough to pay for his travel across land, and for the ship to Algiers where he would begin his search for Nathan Dash. Once there, he would have access to his own money and he was sure that Captain Dash would be only too willing to help him bring Nathan to justice for his crimes. After that, he would take a ship for the Colonies and his new life.

Lying in bed, Vincent thought again of Algiers and the days he had spent there with Cassia. If only he had come to his senses in time and decided against taking her to Constantinople, they would have been together now, lovers, husband and wife. Regret was like acid inside him. He told himself bitterly that he would never come to terms with it if he lived to three times his age. He vowed then and there that he would put his mind to evading the eunuchs this very night and getting away once and for all. To stay here, fettered like a prisoner, was demeaning and soul-destroying while Nathan Dash continued his free, fiendish existence in the world, unpunished for what he had done to Cassia and to Vincent's men on *The Poseidon*.

Earlton slammed down the tray of cakes and coffee in front of Cassia as if daring her to remonstrate with him.

Colour flooded her face. 'I cannot imagine how I have offended you, but if I have, do please forgive me and let us be friends,' she pleaded.

The hunchback's eyes narrowed to slits and his mouth twitched at the corners before turning down into a sneer. Scorn flooding his face, he turned on his heel and stamped out.

Frustrated, Cassia sighed deeply. What was the matter with the man? Eunuchs were more responsive.

She was trying to come to terms with her confined existence. Ali had brought her materials to sew into gowns, and he had found her a pair of comfortable shoes. How he had managed the latter she did not know, but he seemed to be able to produce virtually anything she required, even at short notice. When she was not sewing, she read and explored the house. The views from the different windows were charming, and she loved them all. Some of the bedrooms were locked – and one of these she imagined would be her host's. She thought it a little odd that he should lock his door, but then that was his business. She had no desire to see his bedroom.

Many of the rooms were shabby, dusty and sadly neglected, but their past splendour was still in evidence. If this house had been in London one could have imagined the grand balls and parties, the *soirées* and the Yuletide festivities enjoyed here. What it needed was a large happy family to fill its echoing emptiness.

Poor empty, desolate house. How bleak it must feel without laughter and chatter ringing round its walls. She had always thought that empty houses were places of sadness. There had been one in Orchard Park, its windows and doors shuttered for months, and she always glanced at it as she passed, in the hope that someone would take down the shutters and begin to care for the house and make it a home. But no one had.

She did not go near the shelf of mock books again. She preferred to forget that incident entirely and to put the revolting drawings from her thoughts.

There was one thing she did notice. After a few days of the Earl's absence she began to feel much more energetic. By the time he was due to return, she felt like her usual self and she was standing at the door of the house, dressed in one of her new gowns, made simply from russet brocade in a style that had lent itself to hasty sewing. She knew that her skin was glowing, her eyes sparkling, and that she was very pleased to see him again, for she had promised herself that there would be an end to this stupid pretence. She would tell him that she needed to find Vincent Sauvage and he would help her. She was no longer afraid, weary or ill, and her shame was a private matter between her and Vincent.

Leo Marchington looked well too, and was suntanned. Tim Bert unpacked the saddlebags, carefully removing rolls of parchments and sketch blocks while Lord Marchington led Cassia into the house and ordered Earlton to bring them tea.

'Bursa was splendid! The beauty, the sheer breathtaking splendour – ah, if only you could have seen it!' He smiled down at her, then bent to kiss her. His mouth was warm and dry, and his lips lingered on hers. She had no idea that he was fighting down the desire to pull her into his arms and kiss her more passionately. He wanted to strip off that encompassing gown which she had sewn for herself, fondle her breasts and make violent love to her. But he had made his plans carefully and whatever happened he always adhered to them. There was no reason why they should fail – they never had before.

They had tea and talked about Bursa and the mosques and tombs there, their colours and forms and decorations. Cassia listened raptly, seeing them in her imagination, built by and for previous Sultans like Hamid himself.

Hamid . . . 'an icy chill scored her skin. How she had survived those months of incarceration in the Grand Seraglio she did not know – and yet, was she not now equally Lord Marchington's prisoner? She watched him talking, his silver-grey hair brushed back off his face, his skin a rich golden brown after his days of sketching in the open air. How clear and open were his grey eyes – how alive he seemed in his enthusiasm. She was bracing herself to carry out her resolve when he flung wide his muscular arms to describe one of the buildings to her, his open-necked white shirt immaculate, despite the dust they must have set up on their ride back. His throat was tanned, and the gold medallion at his neck glinted in the late sunlight peering in through the windows. A ray speared his head, turning his hair to platinum, making his strong, youthful face seem even more incongruous.

Cassia found the old fear return, mingled with reluctant attraction, and she could not help thinking of the oppressive presence of the guard at the front door of the house, of the hostile grooms at the rear of the building. Later, she told herself, later, when we can be more private, I shall tell him. He will be angry, but he will forgive me. Yet as she thought it, she cursed herself for not being honest at once. How much more sinister was a secret concealed over a period of time . . .

She decided that she would compromise; she would win her independence gradually, by asking him to escort her over the island. Then, she thought, then will be a good opportunity – when I have proved how strong I am.

'But I want only to ride with you,' Cassia protested, as the Earl repeated that she was not to be allowed to mount a horse. 'Give me an old, safe mount – I do not wish to race.'

'Alas, my dear, that is not possible. Gladly as I would like you to accompany me, we do not have a safe, old horse in the stable. There are only three horses there and all are spirited. Should you take a fall –' he shook his grey head from side to side.

'But I can ride well. I have had plenty of practice.'

Marchington cupped her chin in his massive hand. 'Next week perhaps, but not now, my dear.' And then he turned on his heel leaving her seething with fury.

When he returned, she was waiting for him, determined to argue the matter out once and for all.

'Leo – I want to go out and you are not going to stop me!' she began, but he looked at her through half closed eyes, and then said:

'Have some wine with me, my dear, and I will tell you something,' intriguing her so much that she followed him into the library and let him pour her out some madeira.

She sat with the wine in her hand, sipped at it once or twice, and waited for him to speak. As he did not seem in any hurry to begin, she drank the wine and replaced the goblet on the desk. Her head began to swim. Looking up, she saw two Leos standing before her, two giants watching carefully. From somewhere she heard Sigismund's whimper, and the answering bark of Basil, and then all sound faded from her ears.

The room was dark when she awoke. She was in her own bed – and she could not remember having got there. Terror pierced through her mind. What had happened? How had she got here?

'Ali. Ali!' she called, her voice shaking, but he did not come. She felt tears pricking behind her lids, and struggled to sit up but her head whirled when she did so and she had to lie down again. Hours seemed to drag by, her feeble cries were not answered, and then she heard footfalls coming down the corridor towards her. Tensing, she waited to see whose they were.

Marchington appeared at her bedside. He was wearing his cherry velvet jacket and breeches and spotless linen. He was also wearing an enveloping black cloak on which strange silvery symbols glittered. She made out a star and a trident and then the effort of concentrating made her close her eyes.

'Dear Cassia. You do not feel too ill?' He lifted up the cloak to sit himself beside her, leaning close, his face tender, to take her hands in his. His grasp seemed gentle and yet she could not pull her fingers free however hard she tried. 'I am so sorry that you had to have this relapse, but it was necessary you see. Sweet Cassia, you will forgive me when it is all over. We shall be so happy together, you will see. I have never had any doubts on that score, my beautiful nereid.'

Her mind tried to grasp the meaning of his words. Necessary? What did he mean by that? She tried to ask him, but the words jumbled in her head and came out as nonsense.

He gave a little soft laugh. 'Do not be frightened my sweet, there is nothing to worry about. Am I not looking after you? I am here to love you and care for you. You are going to be my wife.'

'Wife? Wife?' she said faintly. 'Vincent, oh Vincent is that you?'

The Earl's face lost its gentleness. Almost snarling, he gripped her hands fiercely so that she gave a cry of pain.

'Vincent? Who is this Vincent? Tell me. *Tell me!*'

'I – I – the Captain – he is dead – dead,' she gasped, tears flooding her eyes.

Marchington relaxed. 'Ah, that captain. So he did mean something to you after all. Well he is dead, as you say, and now you are mine. My very own. I am a possessive man, my dear. But I do take care of what I own. You will have seen that with the hounds and the owl. All helpless creatures are my interest, my great interest, but you most of all, Cassia, my dearest, will occupy my thoughts. When we are married, and in London, when you are famed for your beauty and your portrait hangs in every drawing-room in society, you will thank me. I cannot wait for your thanks, my darling.'

He leaned towards her, his fingers brushing against her breast, so that she squirmed away from him, but he laughed and repeated what he had done, this time more intimately. She lay there, her head spinning, unable to push him away.

He went then, and she was left alone. She slept, to be woken by the discordant, blood-chilling screech of the owl in the night. She imagined that it had caught some tiny powerless mouse and was devouring it. Marchington and the owl – they were alike. And she was the prey. The dark shadows of night pressed in upon her, sweat broke out on her forehead. She could see the shadows lumbering closer, enveloping her, dreadful fiendish faces looming out of the dark.

When she cried out, Ali came in at once. He looked down at her with concern.

'Where have you been?' she said plaintively.

'My master told me to take the dogs out. I was not over-long, lady. I sorry that you need me. I here now. Look after you.'

Was Ali all that he appeared to be? Should she tell him of her dilemma? She hesitated for only a few moments, then began to tell him of Lord Marchington's plans, of her fears that something was very wrong – that he was keeping her a prisoner against her will.

'Why am I so ill so suddenly, Ali? One minute I am strong and healthy, next minute I am weak and bemused.'

Ali listened, his mouth dropping open. 'You not happy marry master? He tell me you very happy it so and you not able wait for wedding. He say only your illness stop wedding, but once you better, wedding take place here on island. Not so? It not so?'

'Here – he – he said that!' Cassia gasped, horrified. 'But it just is not true!'

'Not true, lady? But he say –' Ali's mouth fell open as knowledge dawned.

'No – I have not agreed to marry him. I said I could not, that it was out of the question, but he will not listen to me!'

Ali sucked in his brown cheeks, dark eyes thoughtful. 'This fearful thing. In my land, men, women different, but in your country women never forced to marry. I know this well. I learn much when on ship. You sure not happy to marry master and become great white lady?' He peered at her searchingly.

'No! It would not make me happy. But – well, he did save my life and I owe him a lot. What shall I *do*?' she sighed.

'Ali think on this. Big surprise on him, he not prepared yet, but he think hard on matter. Help needed for lady, yes? I think of way to help.' Ali slapped his chest with one brown, gold-ringed hand and then he grinned reassuringly, before tip-toeing out of the room to take up his vigil on the pallet in the corridor.

She sank into a restless sleep, waking now and again with a jolt, and by morning her head was splitting. Earlton brought in her breakfast tray, and she must have looked surprised, for he actually spoke to her.

'M'lord sends the message that he is busy. He will see you later,' he said gruffly, his eyes averted, his mouth drawn down at the corners.

'Thank you,' she replied, sitting up on her pillows and looking at the tasty breakfast before her. Fluffy egg and golden toast thick with melting butter, strawberry preserve, steaming coffee and a jug of rich yellow cream. Yawning, she began to eat, pouring out her coffee and adding a liberal helping of the cream which she loved. It did not taste too offputting, but this Turkish coffee was always so bitter and she longed for the bland but rich coffee of England.

The effort of eating had tired her; so had her thoughts. She had a half-remembered recollection of Lord Marchington's visit of the previous night – or had she dreamed that too? Had he really sat on her bed, a cloaked figure, and caressed her breasts? Or more? Dimly she recalled a greater intimacy, his arms around her and – her befuddled brain must have imagined it. It was so hard to remember things these days, so difficult to separate dreams from reality.

She slept most of that day, sinking into a dreamless slumber. It was late afternoon when she woke, her neck aching from the sleeping position she had assumed. How deeply she must have slept, she had barely moved after closing her eyes. The house was silent, not even the bark of a dog. And no one had woken her for lunch.

Ali brought in her tea as soon as he heard her stirring. She smiled up at him, her vision hazy. She blinked, trying to focus.

'Lady pale. Lady all right? Sleep much long. Ali great worried when he look in at you and always sleeping.'

'I didn't sleep very well last night, I expect that was it,' she smiled. 'But I feel better now, only my head is a little fuzzy.'

'Tea make better. Nice strong tea, and look, rich cakes, golden. Mmm,' he licked his lips.

'Have one, Ali.'

'No, no, lady, you eat all for strength.'

She began to eat the delicious cakes, and sip the sweet tea. Ali watched her, smiling happily, and then he said:

'You decide marry master now?'

She stopped chewing. 'Oh, no, certainly not. What made you ask that?'

'It is just that women change mind often. I know.'

'No, I haven't changed my mind. Nor will I,' she added firmly. 'I find him attractive, it is true, but – I cannot marry him.'

'Tell master so. Tell him not marry. He understand, yes?'

'Yes, I shall tell him. Today, or rather, tonight. You are right – he will understand, Ali I was silly last night. Things always seem worse in the dark.'

Ali beamed, leaving her to finish her tea. She heard the dogs barking, and the sound of hooves on cobbles. Leo must have been out riding. She took some deep breaths, in readiness for what she must say to him. There could be no question of her marrying him. She would tell him so, firmly, and he would just have to accept it. But she would be gentle, for she owed him so much and she had no wish to anger him.

The Earl cantered up to the house smiling, while Sigismund and Basil bounded at his horse's heels. The temple was ready now. He had prepared it for the ceremony. The grime and decaying leaves had been swept out, the tiles cleaned, and he had tenderly polished the impressive mosaic of the god Poseidon, which dominated one wall of the temple. A suitable place for his marriage to the beautiful nereid who was to be his, a pagan temple dedicated to the God of the Sea, whom he worshipped. What better location? The idea had come to him when he had first found the temple. Branches and foliage had half screened it, but once he had cut them down, the temple was revealed in all its Doric simplicity. There were six white columns, a white roof, and the wall at the back which boasted a magnificent mosaic of the god Poseidon. The background was blue, green and white tiling; the god's head was picked out in black and green and gold; the waving black hair and the emerald eyes were so realistic that the face looked human.

The Earl had left in the temple the bundle of objects necessary for the ceremony, the green candles, the silver-gilt trident, the holy water that was not holy water at all but something far more repulsive, and on the tiled floor of the temple he had carefully drawn out the pentagon, the five-pointed star in which he and Cassia would stand while Poseidon, God of the Sea, joined them together. The ceremony would be long and intricate; and he had practised it repeatedly to ensure that he did not make any mistakes and cause any terrifying elemental spirits to appear during the ritual.

When they returned to London, there would be a proper ceremony, a public one for the sake of propriety. He could not risk a son and heir being born a bastard. As far as Cassia was concerned, the One who would attend them in the temple was a Christian priest. After the marriage was consummated, he would offer their union up to Poseidon, and they would both become His acolytes. Cassia would make the most beautiful handmaiden ... Marchington smiled again. He could barely wait. He would make her a robe of the whitest silk, and she would have flowers twined into a wreath for her head, and roses pinned at her breast . . . her feet bare, and overall a cloak which was an exact copy of the one he had always worn for his assignations with the Sea God.

Dismounting, he handed his horse to one of the grooms and strode up the stairs to Cassia's room. She was finishing her tea, her cheeks still flushed from sleep. How beautiful and sweet-faced she was, and how helpless. She could do nothing to gainsay him.

He bent over her hands, kissing them, and then he stroked her soft auburn hair.

'My nereid. Soon I shall begin to paint you.'

Cassia did not answer. She was gathering her courage. She let him stroke her hair and talk for a little while about how she would pose for the painting. Then he said: 'And by the time we return to England, I shall have at least one picture finished, ready to be exhibited. Are you not excited, beloved?'

She looked up at him. Dreading his anger, knowing she must take her courage in both hands.

'My lord – Leo – I must talk to you. I am so grateful – you know that. You saved my life and you have cared for me generously. But – well, I would like to return to England with you, but if I do, I shall be going back to my aunt's house. To Penwellyn, to live with Julitta, in Cornwall. I – she loved me, and I am very attached to her. I left her ill, terribly ill, and I must see how she is and stay with her to look after her. I – I am sorry,' she finished lamely.

Marchington's jaw muscles clenched. His grey eyes became icy, frozen, glacial wastes devoid of emotion, of feeling. His fingers on hers felt like pincers. She winced, but he did not relinquish his grip.

'My dear, I thought I made it plain to you. You are to become my wife. It is all arranged. I shall brook no refusal. It is decided. We are to marry tomorrow night.'

She stared up at him. 'T-tomorrow night? But – I don't understand! How can that be? The priest – the banns!'

'I have my own priest,' he said. 'He will be marrying us. There is no need for banns.'

'But my family – I am under age. You cannot marry me without my father's consent!' She clutched at straws, trying to think of ways to deter him, suddenly panic-stricken.

'I am the law here on this island,' the Earl said. 'I have said that we shall be marrying and it would be pointless to fight my decision, my darling. I saved your life, and your life is now mine to do with as I wish. There is really nothing more to be said.'

'I cannot marry you! It is impossible!' Cassia cried. 'Look, take me back to England and we can ask my father – please, if you must, do this properly – legally.' Tears threatened. She was filled with such a feeling of foreboding that she felt cold, chilled to the heart. Lord Marchington's eyes were boring through her; she felt like a moth on a pin. Disbelief and realization that he was serious warred within her.

That was to be the last clear recollection she had for some time. The Earl stood up, smiling, relaxed, helped himself to tea, and poured her a second cup. She drank, her mind throbbing, her hands trembling. Terror was rising inside her. What on earth was she going to do? Oh Vincent, Vincent where are you? she thought, her mind straining to send out a message to him.

She felt drowsy by the time the tea was finished, and she vaguely saw her host bending over her, smiling, to take away her cup.

'Sleep my nereid, in preparation. When you wake, you will be my bride. Sleep, my beloved.'

She wanted to scream, to cry out, but sleep was clasping her mind. She disappeared into the dark vortex.

Ali was listening at the door, eyes peering through the crack where the door stood ajar. He saw Lord Marchington open the top of the ring on one of his fingers, the ring bearing the Marchington family crest, and tip its contents into Cassia's tea. Unaware, she had drunk, and now she slept.

The magnitude of the situation impressed itself upon Ali.

He was fond of the white lady. She was so warm of heart and face. She did not want to marry this English Lord – even if that meant becoming a lady of great power in her country. If she did not want to marry him, then she must have a very good reason. Ali also knew that at such short notice there could be no legal marriage on the island. He had lived in England; he knew of the marriage laws for had he not wished to marry a Liverpool girl himself? And the drug which milord had put into the lady's tea – what was that?

It was not right that she should be drugged and helpless. It was a frightening thing, a terrible thing, Ali thought. She slept now, and he could not help her to escape – even if he could have stolen horses for them and got them off the island. That was too great an undertaking for him. But could he not get help himself alone? He toyed with that idea, unable to decide because it would mean he had to leave the lady unguarded. But if he did not act she would be forced into the marriage she did not want.

Ali curled on his pallet and pretended to be asleep as Lord Marchington strode past him away down the corridor. He pondered for some time on what to do. Who could he get to help this poor lady? His mind roved over various possibilities. His cousin who lived in Yamin? But no, he was old and half-blind. Milord had some fierce men in his house. There would be a fight, much bloodshed, if Ali brought anyone back to save the poor lady. He would need to bring someone of great strength and authority in the country . . . but who?

The enormity of the problem weighed on him. He doubted his abilities to succeed – and yet he had to try while that poor sweet lady, who had hurt no one, was being drugged so that she could not resist. He thought of his own dear English girl and how he had delayed marrying her, frightened of her brother's anger. He had procrastinated then, and he had lost her. If he had married her and taken her away earlier, they would not have been on the ship which had been decimated by the fever. It was this last thought

377

that stirred him finally. He could not bear another tragedy on his conscience.

He crept into her room and looked down at her. She was very pale. There were smudges of shadow beneath her eyes. Poor innocent lady with red hair. He would help her, oh yes he would. He must, for no one else cared.

He waited until his lordship was having dinner in the room below, then he crept downstairs and out of the back of the house. Making no sound, he reached the camouflage of the trees and walked down the beach to the water's edge to look for a boat. He knew there was one there somewhere, for Tim Bert had talked of it – and that was how he himself had come to the island. But he was unsure of its mooring place. He searched for some time, breathing impatiently through his teeth. And then he saw the little cove where the boat lay, and he sighed with relief. Pushing the boat down to the water's edge, he climbed in and took up the oars, before steering the craft out to sea. He was an old hand at rowing, for his life at sea had taught him the skills of navigating almost every variety of boat. It was good to be back on the water, to be the master of his own little world again. Grinning, he rowed vigorously, while the island receded behind him. In the darkness ahead, he could make out the lights of the mainland, and the fishing village there. He had friends in the village, and he could borrow a horse and cart from one of them. He had given them many favours in the past.

He knew now where he was heading. Perhaps he had known it all along, but only now had his thoughts clarified. There was a woman who would help Cassia. She was famous throughout the land for her kindness. She was called the One With Much Heart, and the people spoke of her in reverent tones. He had known about her for some time, for there were few villages without problems, few who had not begged the Princess Jasmina for aid. She always gave it generously. Men, women, children, she helped them all, but she was particularly benevolent towards those of her own sex. If he could get to her brother's palace in Bada-

378

Alhim–before dawn broke, then he was certain that she would send her men to save the poor white lady.

The Princess had helped his old cousin. She had given him a pension and ensured that this home was not taken from him when he could no longer work because of his failing sight. She had helped one of the vegetable growers when his crops were ruined – that was the first time Ali learned of her charitable deeds and tender heart. His only worry was that Cassia might be harmed in some way before he could get back to her with the Princess's men. But if he made all speed, and let nothing slow him down, not hunger or weariness, he hoped to reach the palace before dawn.

Sending up a silent prayer to Allah the All-Powerful, the All-Merciful, Ali rowed the little boat to the jetty by the fishing village, laid down his oars and leapt out on to the shore.

CHAPTER TWENTY-SIX

Anemone had finished her dance and was looking expectantly at the Princess. But praise did not come, for Jasmina was out of sorts that morning. She had slept badly, and her dreams had been unnerving. Now she felt disgruntled and could not stop yawning. Knowing that she looked pallid and lacking in vitality, she had decided to keep out of Vincent's way for the time being. He would be happy anyway with the petitioners; he cared for the poor devils better than she ever could.

Seeing that the Princess was not going to make any comment on her performance, Anemone withdrew to the side of the room, allowing the other girls to assemble for their display with hands joined and faces thrown back. They looked like a row of flowers in their multicoloured silk entaris, their necks encased in jewelled collars, rings glittering on their tiny fingers. The musicians struck up the first notes of the dance, and the girls began to sway like irises gently nudged by the breeze.

Ali had borrowed a good horse from Imini Naballah, a farmer whose home stood a few miles outside the fishing village opposite the island. Imini was impressed to hear of Ali's journey, slapping him on the back and calling him a crusader. Imini grinned, showing his gapped teeth, now stained a mustard colour after chewing the tobacco that Ali had brought him back from one of his sea voyages.

'You choose right to go to the Princess, Ali my friend, she has an overflowing heart. When she hears of the poor prisoner on the island, she will send her men here straightaway. She has done these things before to help others. Remember Mustapha? She gave him money and seeds for his land, and she sent men to help him plant before the rains came.'

'It was partly Mustapha that made me think of the Prin-

cess, Imini. But I must go now, there's not much time.
Thank you for the horse. I will leave it with your cousin in
Olik-al-Dul, as you ask, and give him your message.'

'My cousin will give you a fresh horse. You should leave
your tired horse with him. He will give you food, too, and
here is some refreshment for your journey –' Imini held out
a parcel of bread and goat's cheese to his old friend. 'Allah
go with you on your journey and grant you all you desire,
Ali.'

'And may Allah give you much good crops for your kindness to me and watch over you and your sons, Imini.'

The night seemed blacker after his short rest in the farm-
house, but he did not hesitate. Leaping on to the back of
the big horse which Imini had given him, Ali set off towards
the Princess's palace.

Clouds sailed across the sliver of moon that barely illu-
mined the night, and Ali concentrated hard on the rutted
track ahead, leaning closely over the horse, trying not to
look to left or right. He thought of brigands and devils and
savage spirits leaping out of the shadows to ambush him,
and his blood froze. He must put such terrors aside and
think of the poor lady on the island. What would be happening to her now? Allah watch over her and keep her safe
until he got back with help.

'Allah, be with me,' Ali prayed. 'Watch over the poor
lady, keep her from harm, protect her. If you will do this
for me, your faithful servant, then ask of me anything in
return and I shall obey.'

Black humps appeared on his left, mountains whose peaks
would be a hazy purple in daylight. Bunches of trees
appeared at regular intervals; he hunched down and urged
the horse on to a faster pace when he saw them, for brigands
might be hiding behind them.

Birds squawked as the horse disturbed them; strange
nocturnal creatures screeched and babbled to one another.
All around him he felt danger pulsing, like a living thing;
the very air seemed to throb with it. Sweat trickled down
his face. His back and knees ached. His hands were raw

from gripping the reins. The horse was snorting and breathing gustily. He feared that it was tiring. He could not wait for Olik-al-Dul, and the house of Imini's cousin.

The cousin was enraged at being woken up in the night, and when he looked out of his window and saw Imini's horse and the stranger holding its reins he let out a shout.

The front door opened and Imini's cousin bustled out with his sons ranked behind him. Hastily Ali explained what he was about, showing them the scribbled note from Imini. The change in the cousin was remarkable.

'I dare not stop,' Ali explained, 'but if you would be so kind as to pack me some food, I much grateful. Must get to Her Highness Princess Jasmina soon. Soon,' he repeated.

Imini's cousin rattled out orders to his family who packed up cheese, bread, a slab of cold meat, a flask of goat's milk, and then Ali was on his way, on a fresh horse.

He felt happier now, passing Ben-al-Dim an hour later and then other smaller, scattered villages. He munched the meat and cheese in a dell, letting the horse graze for a time and drink its fill from a stream. He was making good time, for dawn was not yet close. He would have loved to lie down on the soft bed of grass and sleep, but he could not risk that. When the horse seemed refreshed, he climbed on its back and turned it along the rutted track towards the palace.

The sky was peach and gold and lemon when Ali first glimpsed the Pasha's palace. Bulbous ivory turrets adorned with filigree made mysterious and beautiful silhouettes against the dawn sky. Ali sighed, for his back throbbed with pain and his palms were raw. He would never be able to sit down again, he decided, and he pitied the horse, whose steaming flanks were hot against his thighs. Thank God he could see their destination only a few miles ahead. He pulled up the horse and they rested for some minutes before setting off again until they reached the drive leading up to the palace.

They passed people heading in the same direction. Old men, women who stumbled as they walked, children in rags. One or two prosperous looking men who kept themselves apart from the main throng of tattered petitioners, their noses high. Ali grinned, passing all those who were on foot, some who were on horseback and even one or two in wooden carts. He heard an angry shout behind him, but he did not look round.

Eunuchs dressed in shalwar, with massive nodding turbans on their heads stood at the palace gates. More were inside, lining the path to ensure that no one stole or tampered with the royal property. Ali cantered past the men and reached the end of the queue, then he let the palace grooms take his horse. Bread and hot coffee were being distributed by slaves, who handed round the refreshments with unsmiling faces. Ali, delighted to be on foot again, sipped at the thick sweet coffee and swallowed the bread in gulps.

Time passed as the people before him were taken one by one into the audience chamber. One of the petitioners came out grinning, and saying, 'Why did I not think of it myself? Allah is here in this place today – Thanks be to Allah!' at which those who had heard his words chorused after him, 'Thanks be to Allah!'

Someone behind him shuffled their feet and sighed. 'Last time I came I waited here three days, but that was before the Princess chose a husband. He helps her now, and so there is less waiting for us.'

'A husband?' Ali said. 'I had not heard that.'

'Where do you come from?' the man asked.

Ali named his village.

'Well that is a long way; perhaps news hasn't reached there yet, but we all know. She chose her own husband. That is allowed for a widow, as you know, and he is to become a Muslim, so all is well.'

Interest gripped Ali. 'She chose a husband who is not Muslim? How could that be?'

'He is French. A sea captain. He has been with her now for some time to learn our ways. His justice is as the sword wielded by Allah Himself.'

Ali quirked his thick brows, his spirits raised. If that were the case then there should be no problems for him.

It was midday by the time his turn came. The eunuchs led him into the audience chamber, flanking him on either side, their black faces saturnine. Ali gasped when he saw the brilliant chamber hung with tissue of gold, its floor tiled in gleaming yellow, white, and sea-green tiles, and the massive gold throne on the dais, with the smaller chair beside it. In the smaller chair sat a man with jet-black hair and shrewd green eyes. As Ali flung himself down before the man, who must be the Princess's future husband, he was gripped by a feeling that all would be well now. The man instructed his interpreter to speak to Ali, but Ali began to explain that he could speak English and French if His Highness would bear with him. The black-haired man smiled at the title and spoke to Ali in English. Ali grinned, peering up from his prone position on the floor. The man gestured to him to get up and come closer, which Ali did, his heart beating noisily.

After one or two false starts, from nerves, and awe at his surroundings, Ali gabbled out the story of the helpless girl on Poseidon's Island some thirty to forty miles hence.

'I know of the island. How did the girl come there? Is she Turkish?' Vincent said.

'Oh no, Highness, she English. Beautiful lady, red hair, blue eyes, ah so fair. English Lord own island, he want make her bride. He give her drug to quiet her. She say no bride, but he put something in her wine. I Ali saw this with my own eyes.' Ali pointed to his eyes, his forefinger jabbing through the air twice.

'*English?*' Vincent rasped. 'This girl is *English?* But how did she come there?'

'Lord, English Lord, rescue her. She put in sack to drown by –' Ali paused, making the mental connection between the Sultan and the Princess. Royal people knew one another. The Princess and her brother were under the jurisdiction of the Grand Turk . . . He paused, his face colouring; he fidgeted with the thongs which fastened his robe.

'Go on, go on!' Vincent ordered, his voice faint, his heart pounding. 'She was put in a sack and – ?'

'It meant she drown but she not drown. English Lord save her.' He lowered his voice.

'Where – where did this happen?' Vincent interjected, leaning forward, hands gripping the arms of his chair so that his knuckles gleamed whitely.

'I – do not know I should say – but she in danger. Great danger, Highness!' Ali wrung his hands together. 'Tonight she marry English Lord! He make her his yet she not want it. She wish return to aunt in England. I hear this. I listen . . .'

'Her aunt in England? What is this girl's name? Tell me, tell me!' Vincent commanded but he already knew. By some miracle, a miracle he did not deserve, she was still alive.

'Cassià, Highness, Cassia Morbilly.' Ali said, wondering why the Princess's future husband was now standing up, his face taut.

'It is her!' Vincent said, beneath his breath, scarcely able to believe what he had heard. Somehow his Cassia had been saved – and she had been taken to Poseidon's Island by this English Lord – whoever he was. Vincent knew of the island for he had studied the Pasha's maps, ostensibly to learn more about his future wife's domain but in reality to devise the speediest escape route when he finally managed to elude Jasmina's guard. The name had caught his eye immediately – Poseidon, the name of his lost ship. What was he to do now? He looked about him. How peaceful everything looked, the eunuchs and slaves standing at their posts, faces relaxed. He thought of the change that would come over them if he tried to escape now. How in God's name was he going to get to his beloved?

'Ali – come with me,' he said. The puzzled Turk followed him out of the audience chamber and to his suite. For once Vincent left the petitioners waiting. Alone in his room, with a eunuch outside his door, Vincent questioned Ali more closely, intent upon learning all that he could tell him about the island. When he had finished, he wracked his brains to think of a way to get to Cassia without Jasmina finding out. He thought of her favourite horse, the Arab stallion she had named Cadi, which meant Judge, and which she had sometimes let him ride. Cadi knew him now, and would let him mount. Once on the horse, he would out-distance everyone else because Cadi was the fastest stallion in the Pasha's domain – some said in the entire country. The Pasha had given his sister the horse as a gift the previous year. She was a superb horsewoman, and rode like a female centaur.

But how to get away from the palace?

'Ali, do you like hunting?'

'I not hunt ever, Highness,' Ali said, even more puzzled now. Why had he been brought to the French Captain's suite like this?

'Well, you are going to hunt now.' Rapping out orders, Vincent sent one of his slaves to the stables to have Cadi saddled. Then, assuming a nonchalant air, he strolled through the palace with Ali. When one of Jasmina's ministers saw them and asked Vincent why he was speaking with the Turk, he told the minister that this was one of his sailors – a man who had once been on his ship, and that he had invited him to stay at the palace with him for a few days.

When they were out of earshot of the minister, Ali grinned up at Vincent.

'How you know, Highness? How you know I once sailor?'

Vincent looked down at him, not really hearing, his mind intent on his scheme. Had the man once been a sailor?

They walked through the gardens, Vincent pointing out various sights as if showing Ali round. The rose arbour, the Kiosk of Pearls, the banks of golden rod and acacia, all received Ali's intent interest, but the Turk was growing impatient. Finally, thinking of Cassia, he said:

'You will help lady on island, Highness? You *will* help?'

'Yes,' Vincent hissed, smiling as if he had not a care in the world. 'Say no more of that. Just follow me.'

'Yes Highness,' Ali whispered back, smiling the same benign smile.

'Abooka –' Vincent summoned the eunuch who was watching them. 'Tell your mistress that I am going hunting with this man who was once on my ship. He will stay here with me for a few days, and soon another of my friends will be arriving, another of my crew. Ask Her Highness if a room can be prepared for these two friends of mine. I will see her myself later today.'

Abooka bowed, his black face serious. Ali looked up at Vincent. 'What friend? Stay here, Highness? I not know what you mean?'

'Trust me, Ali. It is not easy for me to leave here – we must get out without rousing suspicion.'

Ali nodded, but he only half understood. Was this handsome Frenchman a prisoner? He behaved as if he were. Yet he seemed to have authority here. How strange it was.

Vincent was finding it hard to hide his impatience and his fears for Cassia. He wanted to be away, on Cadi, heading for the island at full speed, but to behave in such a fashion would be disastrous. He would be captured immediately and brought back to Jasmina in chains yet again. It was humiliating and infuriating, but he must be cautious and play this game to the utmost.

When they reached the stables, Vincent showed Ali the black stallion and told him a little about Cadi. Ali listened, grinning and nodding, playing the game as he had been instructed. Anyone listening would indeed have thought they had once been shipmates for they then talked of ships and battles, the sea and its virtues.

'Fetch a horse for my friend,' Vincent commanded one of the slaves, and this was done. He mounted Cadi, while Ali clambered on another stallion whose name was Ullah, while behind them the eunuchs who were watching Vincent climbed into their saddles.

They rode away at a gentle canter, heading for the hills where Vincent had been allowed to hunt before. He was rigid behind his casual pose, dreading that messengers would come after them, that Jasmina might send for him and that he would be taken back. But they cantered on, the eunuchs behind them, until the palace was out of sight and the landscape became wild. Suddenly Vincent sat up in the saddle, pointing excitedly, crying that he had seen a movement in the thicket ahead of them. One of the eunuchs bounded towards the thicket, his spear ready to frighten the animal so that it would leap out and Vincent could chase it. All eyes were on the thicket; the eunuchs loved the thrill of the chase.

Ascertaining that they were not looking his way, Vincent hissed instructions to Ali, then he crept up behind the nearest eunuch. The two guards were disarmed before they could recover from their surprise; Ali kept them in place with one of their own scimitars held threateningly in his hand, while with another scimitar, Vincent attacked the guard who had been beating the thicket. The man fought fiercely, but he was no match for the Frenchman. Steel clashed, spat sparks, Sauvage driving the man back towards a boulder until he stumbled and Vincent's blade sliced deep into his throat. Ali let out a cheer. Taken off guard, he did not see one of the captives reach into his crimson sash for a small but deadly dagger. But Vincent saw, shouted a warning. Ali leaped aside just in time, thrusting out one foot as he did so, bringing the guard smashing down on to his face. Vincent snatched his knife and stabbed the guard who had been about to bring a rock down on Ali's head, while Ali picked up the rock and brought it down against the skull of the prone eunuch.

Not until Vincent and Ali had ridden for many miles did they pause to rest, letting the horses graze and drink at a stream. Ali looked at the Captain with reverent eyes, highly impressed by his behaviour. He still did not understand it all of course. Why did the Captain have to sneak out of the palace like a felon when he could have snapped his fingers and sent two dozen guards to save the white lady? It was perplexing, but Ali knew that one did not question the ways of the great ones.

CHAPTER TWENTY-SEVEN

Cassia woke with a jolt of terror as she felt the bedclothes being pulled off her and arms lifting her up off the bed. It was dark, and she had slept her drugged sleep all that day.

She tried to analyse what was happening, and who was carrying her, but whoever it was had a masked face. Their arms were strong and she was borne along like a baby, out of her room, into the corridors and down the stairway. The house was black and silent, and the man in whose arms she lay had not said one word from the time he had picked her up.

'Leo?' she said, her tongue feeling thick and heavy, her lids wooden. 'Leo is – that – you?'

Her answer was an eerie chuckle that made chills run along her spine. She tried to lift one hand to tear off the mask but her arms and legs felt too heavy to move. It was as if she were paralysed.

Outside, the night air veiled her face, clearing her brain a little. She was lifted up into a saddle, while the man climbed up behind her. The horse began to move, and she swayed against her escort, head spinning. Past dark trees and bushes, across a sward, and then they were approaching what looked like a tiny temple, its columns glowing whitely in the gloom.

She blinked twice, trying to clear her vision. Yes it was a miniature temple.

The man reined in the horse and lifted her down. She slumped and would have fallen had he not lifted her into his arms and carried her inside the temple to place her on a bench there. Then he turned from her and she heard him moving about. Light flared. She looked up, dazzled by the glare, to see him lighting candles on what looked like an altar. Green candles . . . a shiver ran over her skin. A silver-gilt, three-pronged fork of some kind, stood by them. Whatever for? The candles could be explained away, despite their odd colour, but a trident? She tried to mumble what she had seen, but the man laughed, turning to her, and she saw Leo's grey eyes lit by a fanatical gleam.

'There is nothing wrong, my darling. Our marriage ceremony is going smoothly. I have only to do one or two more things and we shall be ready. You will not regret this, my beloved. When you are my bride, and we are one, you will know the meaning of true happiness.'

'No – no,' she gasped, trying to sit up, but he pushed her down on to the bench and then she felt his hard fingers tearing at her shift. She tried to stop him, crying out, sobbing, but he did not stop until she was completely naked. He was going to rape her here, now, and she could not stop him. She closed her eyes, faint with terror.

But to her surprise and relief nothing happened. Instead, he produced a white robe and a wreath of roses for her hair, and proceeded to dress her in these. The robe was of soft material, and a black cord tied it crossways over her breasts in the Grecian style. Once he had dressed her in the strange robe, the Earl lit more candles until the air was filled with the scent of candle grease and smoke. Cassia coughed, stifled. There was another smell in the air and this was growing stronger. It was the most unpleasant scent she had ever known . . . both repulsive and terrifying.

'Vincent, Vincent,' she moaned, and at this Marchington turned on her, his eyes flaming like crystals in the candlelight.

'He is dead, remember? Your Captain is dead. You are mine now. My bride, my beautiful bride and concubine. Soon, He will be here and we shall be lawfully united. He will marry us, my Master, the Great One . . .' the Earl threw back his great head and laughed.

'Wh-who?' Cassia stammered, crouching on the bench, as far away from Marchington as she could.

'Poseidon, my beloved. My Master. Son of Saturn and Rhea, brother of Jupiter and Pluto – had you not heard of Him? Well He will be here very soon. Can you not smell that smell? That means He will be here any minute. When He sees you, He will want you for Himself – but He is fair, my Master. He will only take you if I give him permission – and I might, I just might, for He has been good to me . . .'

Cassia gave a cry of horror, shrinking back. The tiled wall felt icy against her back. She turned round to see if there were a niche where she could hide, or a gap through which she could escape. She saw instead emerald eyes and waving black hair – and it was as if Vincent himself were there for just a few comforting moments before she realized that she was staring at a mosaic. She sobbed, wrapping her arms round her waist, shivering. The Earl was kneeling before the altar, mumbling strange words in Latin, repeating them like an incantation. Now his arms were upthrust towards the silver-gilt trident and he fell silent. He seemed to be waiting.

Cassia was shaking, her teeth chattering. The man was mad - crazed. He thought he could summon Poseidon. He really believed that he could summon one of the mythical gods. She knew that it was impossible, but her skin crawled and the nauseating smell seemed to grow stronger. The smell of decay and putrefaction . . . A sighing noise filled the temple, and there was a rushing of wind. Then Marchington said:

'She is here, Master, she is here, my bride!' and he turned to drag Cassia, screaming and struggling, towards the altar. The smell was sickening now, choking her, and her eyes stung. The Earl pulled her across the floor and thrust her, face down, before the gleaming trident. He held her wrists together behind her back so that she could not move. The pain was intense. She felt the blood ebbing away from her head.

Laughter bubbled in the air. Maniacal, raucous. It terrified her. She thought it was Marchington's but when she looked at his face it was rapt, his mouth closed. She strained to look up, seeing the smoke from the candles beginning to clear and a face appear through the haze. Prickles of fear seared her skin. The face was glaring down at her evilly –

a devil's face with slanting acid-yellow eyes, and wild, shaggy hair . . . She screamed, her heart jolting and pounding unevenly.

'God save me,' she whispered. The Earl whirled towards her, his eyes staring, his mouth twisted.

'Do not say that name here – hold your tongue, do you want to send Him away?' He came closer, his hand raised.

She waited for the blow but it did not come. The smell of decay became stronger, she gagged and tensed herself against the fumes. Leo returned to the altar and the face above it, babbling reverently, genuflecting, his black cloak with its pattern of cabbalistic symbols swinging wide. To her dismay she saw that he was naked beneath it.

When he turned to her, to introduce her to the wild-haired creature, she saw the acid-yellow eyes look down at her appreciatively, the mouth curving into a leer. Terror twisted inside her, catching at her heart so that it beat madly until she could barely catch her breath. The maniacal laughter began again, filling the confines of the little temple, and the face shimmered, moved, began to descend towards her. Screaming, she tried to get up to run away, but Marchington gripped her hands and twisted them behind her back until she felt faint from the pain. Then he forced her down onto the tiled floor, and straddled her, grinning.

'No!' she screamed, beating her fists against his chest, but he seemed undeterred. As the wild laughter increased, Marchington flung back his cloak and began to push her robe up round her hips, his fingers hard against her thighs, searching intimately . . . Her face flaming, she hooked her fingers to try and gouge at his eyes, but he leaned back so that she could not reach them.

She was beginning to tire. The past weeks in bed had weakened her muscles although the effects of the drug were wearing off. When the leering face hovered over them, she realized that it was not suspended magically in the air but belonged to a man whose lower body was cloaked in black. He – It – was watching them intently. She continued to struggle, to try and kick out but Marchington was weighting down her legs with his own.

'My bride, my slave,' she heard him rasp, 'Why this foolish struggle – you know that you are fated to be mine . . . Poseidon, make her willing!' he turned round to look at the yellow-eyed god entreatingly. Her own heart deafening in her ears, Cassia saw the god approach them, scaly hands outstretched to restrain her . . .

'No – no – get away! *Get away!*' she screamed terrified, retching as the rough, scaly hands dragged on her flesh.

Then suddenly the scaly hands withdrew, and the Earl loosened his grip on her. They had turned to the temple door – they were listening, watching.

She heard running feet, shouts, Ali's voice, and then – no, she could not have heard right. Excitement scintillated inside her. Joy, delight followed on one another. That voice! The footsteps approached, a tall figure was framed in the temple doorway, took in the scene in one swift glance and strode towards her.

'*Vincent!*' she cried joyously, while the Earl let out a bellow of fury and leaped to his feet. Reaching out, he grasped one of the massive candlesticks on the altar and held it out threateningly towards Sauvage.

Vincent scooped her up into his arms, thrusting aside the wild-haired creature as he did so. The acid-yellow eyes tilted, the mask slipped, and the cloaked figure stumbled and fell. On the floor at their feet she saw Earlton, cringing and babbling for mercy. Poseidon!

Marchington let out another roar, bidding Sauvage to fight him like a man.

'If you wish it. Outside, a duel,' Vincent said curtly, carrying Cassia out on to the grass and giving her into Ali's keeping.

Biting her lip, her hands clamped together, Cassia watched the two men take up duelling stances. She had no idea if Lord Marchington were a skilled swordsman – he might well be. Quaking with fear for her lover, who had appeared like a miracle to save her, Cassia prayed as she had never prayed before.

Ali was praying too to Allah, his hands gripped together so fiercely that his palms were scored with crimson.

The clash of steel filled the night air. The Earl looked confident. He began almost jauntily, wielding his sword with consummate artistry. Cassia's heart plummeted. If he won – if he killed Sauvage! She gave a little moan of terror, but Ali glanced at her reassuringly.

'Highness win. He great man, not lose, you see.'

She was too involved in watching the duel to ask Ali why he had called Vincent 'Highness'. The two men thrust and parried, stepping nimbly aside, avoiding thrusts that would have speared more heavy-footed duellers. Time passed, and Cassia knew that Vincent must be tiring. Sweat gleamed on his face. Marchington darted at him, and she saw to her horror a slit of scarlet appear on Vincent's forearm. Flinging her hands over her eyes she did not look for some seconds, then her eyes were drawn back inexorably to the scene.

The Earl of Marchington was lying on his back, Vincent's sword at his throat, and he was murmuring, 'No – do not kill me!'

Then Cassia saw the little cloaked figure creeping up behind Vincent.

'Vincent, look out!' she screamed. Vincent whirled to strike down Earlton with one blow, the butler rolled over and over on the ground, the dagger in his hand flying across the grass. Leaping to his feet, Marchington leapt for the fallen dagger. Cassia screamed another warning. Vincent turned to see his opponent attacking with the blade. There was a struggle, the dagger glanced off Vincent's forearm, but he shot out a leg, twisting it between the Earl's knees and brought him down with a crash.

Marchington landed on his face, his arm buckling beneath him. In his hand was the dagger meant for Vincent. It was now plunged deeply into the Englishman's stomach.

Barely breathing, Cassia watched the Earl trying to get

up. His lips were moving soundlessly. For a few moments he struggled, then he collapsed and lay still.

'Vincent!' she ran across to her lover, flinging herself into his arms, anxious about his wound. Was it deep? But it was a graze only, and she soon tore a strip of linen from her robe and began to bandage it. 'Darling, darling, how did Ali find you? How did you get here? It's like a miracle!' she said as she wound the linen round his arm and knotted it tightly.

'Perhaps it was, *doucette*, perhaps it was,' he grinned, drawing a hand across his forehead. Then he bent to kiss her, over and over again, while Ali watched them, his face almost split in two by a grin. Now he knew why the Captain had come here himself, and in such great haste.

'We must head for Greece as fast as we can ride,' Vincent told her. 'I imagine that there will be quite a crowd after us by now.'

'A crowd? Why?' she wanted to know, but he told her that they had no time to talk. He would explain to her later.

'Will you come with us, Ali?' he asked the grinning Turk. But Ali shook his head. 'I stay here. Go back to vegetables. Friends all here. I happy.'

'Then we must thank you,' Vincent said, and Cassia put her arms round Ali and kissed his cheek, thanking him for saving her. None of them looked towards the two men lying some way away under the trees. They headed back together for the boat and made for the mainland, and there they said their goodbyes again to Ali, waving as they set off on Cadi and Ullah, towards Greece.

They did not stop until they had put a good distance between themselves and the island, and then they rested in a grove within the sound of the sea. There they talked, and Vincent explained how Ali had found him. Cassia listened in astonishment.

'You – you did not marry your Princess?' she whispered, recalling how Ali had used the title of Highness when he spoke of Vincent.

'Marry her?' Vincent threw back his head and laughed

out loud. 'I would sooner have married a cobra! *Doucette*, I was in mourning for you – and I would have stayed that way. Nothing was going to make me forget my Cassia. Nothing. Not even the wiles of Jasmina. I told her that I loved you and that I always would. I never gave her reason to believe that I would change my mind. If she thought otherwise, then it was wishful thinking. How could I ever forget you? Have we not been a part of one another for as long as time has existed, two halves which can only be truly happy when joined together? Is that not true?' He caged her in his arms, kissing her forehead and lips.

Cassia felt a pang of real guilt as she remembered how certain she had been that he would forget her, and how her faithless body had betrayed her with Leo Marchington. As soon as possible, she promised herself, she would tell him about all that. She would confess her guilt and shame, and it would make their love stronger. That was the strangest and most wonderful effect of all their troubles. She knew without a shadow of doubt that she could trust him with her very soul. If before he had been her dream lover, now he was brother, father, friend and lover rolled into one.

'*Chérie?*'

She broke her reverie with a start. He was looking at her quizzically, puzzled by her silence.

'Oh yes,' Cassia sighed, 'promise me that we will never be parted again.'

'I promise. But first we must get well away from Turkey, and with all speed. When Jasmina discovers that I have escaped her, she will be furious. I would not like her deaf mutes to catch up with us – they might not harm me, but you . . .' He kissed her again. 'I think Jasmina would like you dead more than anyone else in the world.'

'You did not love her at all, not even a little?'

'Not even a little, *doucette*. I felt nothing but gratitude to her for her care when I was wounded. I have been planning my escape for some time. How could I rest while Nathan Dash went unpunished?'

Cassia shuddered at the mention of Dash's name. 'Do

not remind me of him, darling. That serpent! How I suffered because of him and his vile ways – the things he wanted me to do with him!' She clung to Vincent, cradling her head against his chest. The sound of the sea came to them, and seabirds wheeling in the sky, calling out to one another.

'There is so much I have to make up to you for – all of that was my fault entirely. All of it. But for me, you would have been happy in Cornwall with your aunt. You would have found some adoring husband and settled down to have a family.'

'And is it too late for that now?' Cassia dimpled up at him, her eyes twinkling. 'They won't have a Cornish father, my children, but what is wrong with a French papa?'

Vincent laughed out loud. 'So you would have me for your husband after all this? Oh my love, I shall make you so happy. Even when I so stupidly tried to deny our love, what were my futile denials when compared to the power of destiny?'

'Ah darling, when I think back to those days I feel that I knew nothing about love and life, even though I was so confident. Now you are not just my own love, you are my dearest friend. I would never have understood that before. So in a way we were both right. I to love, you to doubt.' She traced the line of his throat with little, nibbling kisses.

'It would be marvellous to lie here and make love beneath these palms, with the moon shining down on us,' he said gently, 'but we shall have all our lifetime ahead of us to do just that *doucette*. We have a long, hard ride ahead of us, we should go.'

He knew that he would not feel easy until they were well out of Turkey, far beyond the reach of Jasmina – and the Sultan. They would take the escape route that he had so carefully planned, and, if Cadi and Ullah kept up their present good pace they would soon be in Greece. Kissing Cassia once more, he helped her on to Ullah's back and then they set off as fast as the horses would gallop.

Vincent had enough money to get them back to the Barbary Coast, for his belt was filled with coins, jewels and gold. Once in Algiers, he could procure his own money and they would be able to bring Nathan Dash to justice. He knew that Cassia would want to say goodbye to her aunt, and then they would leave for their new life in America. Vincent grinned as they rode, glancing towards Cassia. She smiled back, exultant to be on horseback once again riding freely with the wind in her hair and the starlight in her eyes. They had all their future ahead of them now. The glorious future that they had believed lost to death and separation – Lovers for all time, riding together towards their kismet.